THREE FATES

ANDREW GREY   MARY CALMES
AMY LANE

Dreamspinner Press

Published by
Dreamspinner Press
5032 Capital Circle SW
Ste 2, PMB# 279
Tallahassee, FL 32305-7886
USA
http://www.dreamspinnerpress.com/

Cover Art by Christine Griffin
alizarin_griffin@yahoo.com
http://christinegriffin.artworkfolio.com/

ISBN: 978-1-61372-623-5

Printed in the United States of America
First Edition
July 2012

eBook edition available
eBook ISBN: 978-1-61372-624-2

I'm sure Leif and Hacon aren't the only ones who've ever discovered the tapestry of their lives had a wrinkle or two. This one's for Mate, who discovered that I was woven into his and wasn't going to get untangled any time soon.

Also to Josh, here's hoping the Fates are kind. You deserve it.

And it really was all Grey's idea.

Fates Delivers a Prince

Andrew Grey

CHAPTER ONE

THEY were as old as time, three ageless sisters of neither beauty nor ugliness; they just were. Created by the gods at the beginning of the world, they existed at the center of the Earth, far away from the life-forms they controlled. These three women, these sisters, were the Fates. They existed in their own portion of the world, controlling it and yet completely separate from it. In their cave, for lack of a better way to describe it, for they knew neither day nor night, these sisters did their work, never tiring and always vigilant.

It was one sister's job to call the names, one watched the wheels and called the reading, and the final recorded the fate in the book of time.

"Sisters," the oldest one said. She was older only because she had been created a millisecond before the others. "It's time to switch." The others nodded, and without missing a beat, they shifted position with grace and speed, as they'd done once a century ever since the first thinking being appeared on the planet.

They called each other "sister," their actual names long unused. To say them they would subject themselves to the randomness of the wheels they alone controlled. Those very wheels lined the walls of their cave, floor to ceiling, spinning constantly unless a name was called.

"Urnst Hunblotter!" the middle sister called in a level voice.

Then, and only then, would the wheels stop just long enough to be read before whirling again. Each wheel had thousands of possibilities, and not every wheel stopped for every name. Some were lucky and the wheel of disease continued spinning; others weren't. Sometimes the wheel of wisdom hit the jackpot, and other times it never slowed. There were times when the longevity wheel read days, and sometimes decades. And it was the sisters' job to keep the wheels running, the fortunes spinning, and record the fate of each for the gods, because once a fate was recorded, it was written for all time.

"Mario Vitelli." The name sounded in the cave, and the wheels stopped for a split second before starting again. "Do you ever tire of this, sister?" she asked before calling another name.

"No, sister," the eldest answered before reading and calling what the wheels had said so the youngest could write it down. "This is our fate, and you know what happens when you rail against us."

The others nodded, and another name was called. They very rarely spoke of anything other than the wheels. Some might say they were cursed, others that they were blessed, but to them, they just were.

"Cheyenne Dobson." The name sounded through the cave, and all three sisters stared at the wheels, unmoving. Every once in a while the wheels spun something the sisters had never seen before, and they would stop and stare before recording the fate, which would start the wheels spinning once again. This happened rarely, but every so often something or someone captured their attention. That attention could be for good or bad, the life long or short, but it always guaranteed one thing: a very interesting ride.

CHEYENNE sat in his room with the door closed and tried his best to ignore the persistent itch on his arm. Over the years he'd gotten quite used to it, and if he concentrated and kept busy, he could wait it out, usually. He hadn't wanted to come along with his parents on this trip, but when his father, who also happened to be his alpha, asked him to do something, it might be phrased as a question, but in actuality it was an order. So here he was, staying with his family in a baroque nightmare of a house outside Munich, in Bavaria. After wandering over to the window, Cheyenne gazed at Danube River Valley and the mountains beyond. The country was beautiful, but the mountains weren't those of home. He hadn't been gone all that long, but he already missed his Rocky Mountains and the pack lands where he and his wolf could run.

Cheyenne sighed as he moved away from the window and settled on the side of his bed, looking around the huge bedroom. Everything in this place was massive, from the entrance hall and living room to his bedroom. He swore his parents' room was large enough to play basketball in.

He heard a soft knock on the door and realized that he'd been rubbing his arm. He stopped his hands and forced his arms back to his sides. "Come in," he said, his eyes nearly watering with the need to scratch *everywhere*. Sometimes the urge was so overpowering he could hardly stand it. The door opened, and Cheyenne saw his father enter.

"Your mother and I are attending a diplomatic reception this evening, and I'd like you and your brothers to attend as well," his father said as he strode over to where Cheyenne was sitting. He was a huge man, nearly six and a half feet tall, and strong both physically and in personality—every inch the alpha, and he wore it well. Cheyenne's brothers took after their father in almost every way, which had always made Cheyenne feel like a bit of an outcast.

"What is it, Chay?" his father asked as his expression softened.

"Nothing," he lied as tears threatened to come to his eyes. Then, when he couldn't take it any longer, he lightly rubbed his side. The relief was almost palpable as the itching finally subsided. "I'd really prefer not to go." He knew he'd do something to embarrass his family; that was the one thing he seemed to be good at. "I'll stay here and read."

His father's expression softened further, and he sat on the bed next to him. "I'd really like you to come. You spend way too much time alone, and you need to meet people and make contacts and friends. You can't do that if you stay here and never go out." His father placed a hand on his shoulder. "I know you feel self-conscious, but you have no need to be. I have never been ashamed of you in my life."

Chay lifted his gaze from his shoes and looked his father in the eye. "Please, Dad. Remember that reception we were at with the British ambassador last year? The itching got so bad, half the people on the room saw me scratching my back on the potted palm."

To Chay's surprise, his father smiled. "No one would have noticed if you hadn't knocked the dang thing over and into the ambassador's wife." His father began to laugh, and Chay looked at the floor once again until he felt his father's amazingly soft fingers under his chin. "For the record, that was the highlight of the most boring party I've attended in a decade. So, no, I'm not now nor have I ever been embarrassed by you. I know you have a skin condition that itches terribly all the time, and if there was something I could do to make it go away, I would. I've heard there's a doctor over here who can possibly help you, and I've got people trying to contact him."

Cheyenne shook his head. "No more witch doctors, Dad, please. The last one damned near turned me green."

"He did not," his father protested and then shook his head. "Look, if we can get in touch with him, will you at least consider it?"

Chay sighed. "Okay." His father tried his best to do whatever he could for him. "I'll consider it."

His father patted his knee a couple of times and then stood up. "You don't have to go to the party tonight. Your mother and I will understand, but I wish you'd reconsider."

His father left the room, and Chay lay back on his bed, looking up at the elaborate plasterwork in the ceiling. His father had made a career in the foreign service and seemed to have a gift for mastering diplomacy. Chay always figured he was so good at it because of his quick mind backed by the power that lay just below the surface. His father's wolf was the most powerful Chay or anyone in their family had ever encountered, and he exuded an authority that even humans seemed to feel. That sense of power helped back up his reasoning skills and extreme sense of honor.

Chay knew his father would be disappointed if he didn't go, but he simply wasn't sure how he could face all those people. He hated feeling that way, but it was better than hurting his father. Besides, something truly embarrassing or stupid always happened when he was around. This time he was determined to spare himself and his family the humiliation.

With that settled firmly in his mind, Chay settled back on the bed after grabbing the book he'd been reading. He sat on the thick bedding and began to read. The warm afternoon breeze wafted in through the open windows, and more than once Chay inhaled the scent of the river, the old trees, and the clean, fresh air.

When his father had purchased the estate, he had made sure they were well away from the scent of the city. Chay knew his father had done that largely for him, because the one thing that they'd found out over the years was that the fresher the air, the easier it was on Chay. That was one of the few things that made any difference. Breathing the sweetness of flowers from the garden on the air had a calming effect on Chay, and he soon closed his eyes, the book falling open on his chest.

Chay reached for his book again, figuring he must have dozed off for a few seconds, but he couldn't seem to find it. When he opened his eyes, he saw a woman standing at the foot of the bed. He tried to move, but he seemed frozen in place. "Who are you?" he asked, but the form didn't speak. It simply turned toward the far wall, or where the wall had once been. In its place was a view into a ballroom with people milling about, some dancing. The figure pointed toward the scene, and Chay watched for a few seconds. Then both she and the scene vanished.

He woke with a start, gasping for air. The book that had rested on his chest thumped to the floor. Chay gasped and looked all around him, but the room looked the same as it always had. "Weird dream," he said to himself as he got out of bed. He bent down to pick up his book and then placed it on the table next to his lamp and alarm clock. It looked as though he'd been asleep for an hour. Walking toward the door, he stopped when he saw a tuxedo hanging on a portable valet next to it. Wondering where that had come from, he once again looked around the room. No one seemed to have come in, yet here was everything he'd need for the evening.

"You're not at all pushy, are you, Dad?" he said out loud. He reached out and felt the fabric. It was soft, almost buttery in the way it felt on his skin. Figuring it wouldn't hurt to try the things on since his dad had gone to all that trouble, Chay lifted the hanger and carried the clothes to the bathroom, where he hung them on the back of the door. Peeling off his clothes, Chay avoided looking at himself in the mirror. He knew what he'd see, anyway: light-red blotches in all the places that itched. The human doctors he'd seen had said it was some sort of eczema, but they couldn't place it, and neither could anyone else. At least his face and hands were clear for the time being, but that wasn't always the case.

Chay washed up and then rummaged in his kit, finding a small tube of lotion that sometimes helped keep the itching at bay for a while. He put some on the worst spots and then began to remove the clothes from the hanger. Beneath the jacket and shirt, he found a pair of boxers that seemed to be made of the same material. "Dad sure thought of everything this time," he murmured to the white tiles lining the walls. After pushing off his underwear, Chay pulled on the new pair. The fabric was like nothing he'd ever felt before. He reached for the white shirt and pulled it on. He couldn't help flexing his arms and back, it felt so good. The pants came next, and then Chay tied his bow tie. He'd expected a black one—that was his father's style—but the one on the hanger was a deep red, and Chay wondered if this was his mother's doing. He straightened the jacket and then shrugged into it. Every part of the tuxedo felt as though it had been made especially for him, and when he walked back into his bedroom, he spied socks and a pair of highly polished shoes waiting for him on the valet. He put them on before finally allowing himself a look in the full-length cheval mirror.

He immediately hurried back to the bathroom to retrieve a comb, and then stood in front of the mirror again. For the first time Chay could ever remember, his hair actually did what he wanted it to, and he had to admit, he looked as good as he figured was possible. Maybe he could go to the reception for his father after all. After stepping back from the mirror, Chay walked to his bedroom door and pulled it open before leaving his room and heading down the hallway to the main staircase. He could hear the voices of his parents and brothers in the hallway, talking as they got ready to leave. Feeling a bit like Cinderella, or in this case Cinderfella, he took his first steps down the stairs.

"Chay," his father said as he approached the bottom of the stairs, "I didn't think you…." His father stopped as Chay saw his mother, in her emerald floor-length gown, nudge his father in the ribs. "I didn't think you were going to join us."

"So, Scratchy, you decided to come," his youngest brother, Alex, chided with a smile, and Chay's oldest brother, Reese, smacked him on the back of the head. "Hey," Alex groused, rubbing the spot. Chay stepped back in case the growling began. It wasn't likely, since Reese was most like their father when it came to his wolf, but Alex's compact body held a wolf few would mess with.

"Both of you," his mother said in her melodic voice that could stop a runaway train with barely a whisper. Turning back to Chay, she said, "I'm glad you decided to come," with a beatific smile that could light up any room. "You look very handsome," she continued before taking Chay's father's hand and letting him lead her out of the house. The three sons followed dutifully, with Chay bring up the rear.

There was a definite pecking order in the family, just like there was in any pack, and Chay had known for a very long time that he was at the bottom of theirs. Not that it really mattered to him—he'd long ago accepted his place and he was content in it—but as they stepped into the limousine, Chay was surprised to see that the single space next to his father had been left free. That was usually Reese's place, and he guarded it almost jealously. Chay looked at both his brothers and saw Reese nod to him before Chay sat down next to his father.

"What's going on?" Chay asked, but his father ignored the question as the driver closed the door, and then his father signaled the driver.

"This evening will most likely be the usual diplomatic reception. There will be a receiving line, of course, and your mother and I will lead you through and make introductions. You all know the proper way to behave."

"Unless Scratchy decides to get it on with one of the plants again," Alex teased, and thankfully his father ignored it and continued.

"There will then be cocktails with appetizers, and then dinner followed by dancing," his father explained. "I want all of you to keep your wolves under control." He looked pointedly at Alex. "There will be no going after the host's daughter—I don't care how good she smells." He glared at Alex, who straightened right up. "While this isn't an official state function, there will be a lot of informal business conducted, and I don't want to have to worry about any of you. This evening is important, and if you pay attention and act graciously, there will be many important people worth meeting." All three of them nodded, and their father smiled as the limousine bumped slightly and then pulled onto a long, smooth drive. When the car stopped, they waited until the door opened, and then Chay's father got out of the car before extending his hand to help his wife. Reese and Alex exited next, and Chay brought up the rear, as usual.

They all walked as a small group along a covered portico toward the front door, where they were greeted and Chay's father showed his invitation. From there, they simply followed the others. Everyone was announced, just like in the movies: "Sir Jackson and Lady Dobson, Misters Reese, Alexander, and Cheyenne Dobson." Chay usually forgot that his father had been knighted at some point years ago.

They then made their way down the receiving line, where they were introduced to the host and hostess. Chay always hated this part because often his hands weren't presentable, and he'd had people seem afraid to touch him as they passed through. With that over, they found themselves in a grand reception room with waiters carrying trays of drinks and canapés. Chay took a glass and a bite from a passing tray, watching as his brothers took a drink each and proceeded to snag something to eat from every tray that passed their way. Their metabolisms were so fast they ate great amounts, and Chay usually did the same, but he was a bit too nervous to eat, so he ate the tidbit and sipped from his glass, observing and listening as more people were announced.

"Cheyenne, dear," his mother said as she approached him, probably on her way to "powder her nose," and lightly touched his shoulder. "Mingle and talk to people. They won't bite, I promise," she said with a wink before gliding away.

"His Royal Highness Prince Arthur Keuerningen of Paragonia and Lady Lizette Stanton."

The announcement made Chay turn his head to see what an actual prince looked like. He'd met more titled people than he could count or remember, but not a prince. A man in an elegant tuxedo with actual ribbons and medals pinned to his chest entered the room, and people around bowed slightly. Chay did the same, but not for the reason everyone else did. All the air had suddenly flown out of his lungs, and his heart rate had skyrocketed. Chay felt his wolf try to leap forward, and he pushed him back down as everyone in the room straightened up once again.

As the prince and the woman with him passed Chay, he couldn't help taking a small step closer and slowly inhaling. The richest, most intoxicatingly heady scent he'd ever come across went up through his nose and right to his brain before plummeting south. Chay had to turn slightly and shift things so they wouldn't be noticeable to everyone in the room. His wolf, in the meantime, was sitting up and ready to charge full force. He'd heard his mating call, and it took all Chay's strength to keep him under control.

The prince began to move away, and Chay chanced one more inhale, but the scent he longed for was gone, and instead he got a noseful of the most cloying perfume on Earth. Chay's eyes watered and he began to cough. Belatedly, he realized he didn't have a tissue or a handkerchief, so he tried to make his way through the milling crowd toward the restrooms. But he could barely see, and just when he thought he'd made it out of the room, he bumped into someone and began to tumble to the floor.

"Ich habe Sie," a rich voice said, and once Chay managed to breathe again, the scent he recognized and wished he could smell until the day he died filled his nose. The urge to cough abated quickly, and Chay got back to his feet, blinking away the tears from his eyes.

"Please excuse me," he gasped as the prince moved away from him. His wolf bounced inside him, trying to propel Chay closer. He wanted that touch back, at the very least. Hell, his wolf wanted the prince laid out for him to take on the floor right damned now. "I didn't mean to bump you," Chay stammered with the last of his breath as he stared into the bluest eyes he'd ever seen. The blue was nearly impossible for Chay to describe, as if the western sky had met the bluest ocean and somehow they'd mixed to form this man's eyes.

"It was my fault for not watching where I was going. I'm Arthur," he said, holding out his hand.

"Cheyenne, but my friends call me Chay," he said a bit breathlessly as he took the offered hand. His wolf wanted him to lick it to see if the prince tasted as good as he smelled, but Chay had to keep his head and remember where he was. "It's a pleasure to meet you," he added, letting go of Arthur's hand, already missing the softness and warmth of his skin.

"It's nice to meet you too," Arthur replied, and now that the pleasantries were out of the way, Chay simply stared at him, wondering what in hell he was supposed to say. "Are you here alone?"

Thank God he asked a question. "No. I'm here with my father, Jackson Dobson... Your Highness." He almost forgot to add the last part and realized he had forgotten it earlier.

"Yes, you're one of his sons. Please skip the 'Your Highness' bit, though. Everybody calls me that day and night, and it gets annoying after a while."

Chay smiled and nodded, and was wondering what he should say next when the cloying scent from before began to surround him, and Chay tried to stop himself from breathing it in.

"Arthur, I'm ready," the woman said, and then she seemed to notice Chay. "Hello," she greeted him pleasantly but with no warmth.

"Lizette, this is Chay Dobson," the prince said, and Chay shook her hand, trying not to breathe in her perfume as the way Arthur said his name made his chest quake. "We sort of bumped into each other."

"What do you do, Mr. Dobson?" she asked properly.

"I'm studying to be a veterinarian," he answered. The animal-healing part came quite naturally to him. "I have just a few years to go and then I'll take care of large animals like horses and cattle."

"How interesting," she said, turning to Arthur. Chay thought she was about to say something, but Arthur interrupted her.

"I'll be along in a minute," Arthur told her, and she reluctantly released her hold on his arm before heading back toward the reception. "Thank goodness," Arthur said as soon as she was out of earshot. "I keep telling her that ridiculously expensive perfume she wears gives me a headache." Arthur took a deep breath of fresh air and smiled.

"It's pretty awful stuff," Chay agreed, and thankfully both she and her scent were gone.

"I've known Lizette since we were children, and she's been my date to things like this for the last few years," Arthur said as he slowly walked toward one of the side rooms. Chay followed because he wasn't about to let Arthur get away from him, at least not if he could help it. "She'd love nothing more than to be a princess." Arthur rolled his eyes as they entered what looked like a lavishly appointed library with books in cases that ran from the floor all the way to the fourteen-foot ceilings. Chay was in awe, and he openly gaped at all the books. "It's quite impressive, isn't it?" Arthur asked, and Chay nodded slowly before pulling out of his daydream.

"It is," Chay said as he shifted his attention back to Arthur, leaning a little closer.

"Did you just smell me?" Arthur asked, and Chay lowered his gaze to his shoes.

"Sorry," Chay said, expecting to hear Arthur walk away from him at any moment. Instead, the scent that captivated him became stronger.

"Why would you do that?" Arthur asked in a whisper.

"Because you smell so very good," Chay said, lifting his gaze to meet Arthur's eyes. He'd be damned if he was going to lie, and if this was as close as he ever got to Arthur again, he was going to have as many sensory memories to treasure as he possibly could. Chay closed his eyes and inhaled deeply, nearly losing control of his wolf as he inadvertently let his guard down. A soft growl formed in his throat, but he managed to swallow most of it.

"Jesus, I must smell really good for you to make a sound like that," Arthur said with a bit of a chuckle. "Are you always this forward with everyone you meet?"

Chay stepped back, a bit mortified. "I'm sorry," he answered, shaking his head. "I'm never forward at all with anyone. I don't know what...." Chay swallowed hard. "Shouldn't we return for dinner? They'll start without you."

Arthur smiled a wide, beautifully perfect smile that made Chay want to run his tongue over Arthur's lips and teeth to see what they tasted like. "That's the one nice thing about being a prince—dinner will never start without me." Arthur began to chuckle deeply. "Come on, let's give them a break."

"Are you always this free with the people you meet?" Chay asked as they reached the door.

"Heavens, no," Arthur answered, and his expression changed as he seemed to realize all the things he'd said. "I haven't felt as comfortable with anyone as I have with you in a very long time."

"I suppose people see you as the prince first, just like they see me as my father's youngest son before they see *me*. I know it isn't the same thing, but I can sort of understand how you feel. I mean...." God, he needed to shut up, because he was rambling, and Arthur was going to think he was some sort of idiot.

"Yes," Arthur said as they left the room and walked back toward the gathering. "So I spend most of my time with people who understand," Arthur explained before leaning close, giving Chay another whiff of heaven. "But the thing is, they're all about as exciting as dirt."

Chay began to giggle, and after a few seconds Arthur did the same.

By the time they reached the reception room, they had both gotten themselves under control, and Arthur's date attached herself to his arm as soon as he entered the room. Chay backed away as soon as Arthur's sweet muskiness was replaced by her cloying, almost alcoholic, floral scent. Arthur and his date made their way across the room as people moved out of the way. They joined their host and hostess as the dining room doors were opened.

Chay smelled his parents and brothers as they approached from behind him. As usual, he followed behind the others and took his place at the massive table. Once everyone was seated, Chay looked down the table and watched as Arthur and Lizette were served, followed by the host and hostess. Then the dinner service began for all the other guests, and the room burst into conversation as glasses were filled and people began to eat.

"Was that the prince you were talking with?" Alex asked from next to him, and Chay nodded, trying to keep a smile off his face as he peeked down the table. Then his good humor faded, and Chay concentrated on his plate. "What did he say to you?"

"We just talked. He was really nice," Chay said, peeking down the table once more as a realization slammed into him. Setting down his fork, Chay looked at his mother and father, wondering just how he could get out of here as the walls seemed to close in on him. But there was nowhere for him to go without making a fool of himself and his family, so he closed his eyes and took deep breaths, willing the rising panic away.

Opening his eyes slowly, Chay then carefully ate a few more bites of his course and then waited as the plate and utensils were taken and the next course brought.

Dinner finally drew to a close, and everyone moved to a grand ballroom, where a small orchestra was set up. The orchestra began to play and couples began to dance. Of course, Arthur and Lizette shared the first dance as Chay stood off in one of the corners. He hadn't felt a single itch all evening, and right then it was like all the scratches he hadn't been feeling caught up to him all at once. As the dance ended, Chay found his parents and told them he was leaving.

"Are you sure?" his mother asked, and Chay peered out onto the dance floor as Arthur and Lizette moved beautifully together. His wolf was set to howl and pounce, and his arms felt like they were going to fall off, he wanted to scratch them so badly.

"Yes," he answered, already turning away. He couldn't bear to watch Arthur with her any longer or he'd do something his family could never explain away. He saw his father talking softly into his phone, and then he gestured toward the door, and Chay walked out quickly.

Outside, the fresh air smelled wonderful, and his mind began to clear as the limousine pulled up. Chay got inside and the car moved away from the estate and out onto the road. He moved from seat to seat, unable to sit still as he rubbed both arms with his hands. As soon as the car pulled to a stop and the door opened, Chay jumped out and rushed into the house and up to his bedroom. He stripped out of the fine clothes and left them on his bed, then pulled on an old pair of sweatpants and a T-shirt. He then hurried through the house and out into the back gardens.

Chay began to run. As he approached the edge of the gardens, he stopped, intending to pull off his clothes, but he was already shifting before he could stop himself. He'd already done this so many times he didn't think about or even feel it anymore, even as his bones reconfigured and hair sprouted everywhere. In a matter of seconds, he was snared in the clothes he'd been wearing. He slithered out of them, leaving them at the edge of the grass before lifting his head, howling the forlorn cry he'd been holding in ever since dinner. One howl led to another, but there was no answer, and none was expected. Then Chay began to run again.

He'd explored these woods a few times before, but this time there was no plan, no curiosity, only the need to move. Chay took off, sprinting faster first down one path and then another, over and under fallen trees. He didn't care where he ran as long as he kept moving. He crossed a small stream and stopped to lap at the water before continuing his run, then eventually stopped when he could run no more, his hindquarters collapsing onto the ground. Lifting his head to the sky, he cried out again before dragging himself off the path and into a small indentation near a fallen log. There he closed his eyes and simply breathed through his exhaustion. He tried to go to sleep, but his body felt as though he were covered in a million fleas all biting him at the same time.

"At least something is normal," his human half thought. Many of his kind totally became their wolf, but Chay had always retained much of his consciousness when he was in wolf form. That was a family trait he had inherited. The longer he remained as a wolf, though, the less prominent that consciousness became. Chay's human consciousness forced his wolf not to go after the itching, or he would scratch himself bald trying to make it stop. Chay could already feel the urge beginning to grow. After forcing himself to stand, he followed the scents of his family and loped back toward the house.

Approaching the lawn, Chay scented and approached, smelling his father in wolf form sitting right next to his clothes. Chay walked right up to him and rolled onto his back, expecting to be chastised. But his father bumped him playfully with his head, and Chay rolled back onto his feet before shifting to human form. He immediately collapsed onto the grass from total exhaustion.

"Get dressed, Chay, and tell me what's wrong," his father told him, and he looked up and saw his father standing over him, holding out his clothes.

Chay pulled on the sweats and T-shirt, barely able to move.

"What happened, Chay? I thought you were having a good time. Reese and Alex told me you spoke with the prince."

"I did," Chay said, sitting up on the grass and pulling his knees to his chest. "That's the problem. He's a prince and I'm... I'm... Scratchy." Chay clamped his eyes closed. "He's human and he's my mate, Dad." Chay heard his father gasp and then nothing more.

CHAPTER TWO

CHAY spent much of the next two days in his room, talking to no one if he could help it. He knew he had a mate, but that person was so far out of his league—and a human, no less—that there was no way he could ever get close to him. If Prince Arthur had been a wolf like him, he would have felt the mating pull just like Chay had, and maybe Chay would have had a chance, but there was no way now. Each night, he'd slipped out of the house and spent time running, because the only way he could keep his wolf under any sort of control was to run him out. That the exercise exhausted him as well was just an added bonus.

Chay was nearly asleep, having just come in from another nocturnal run, when he heard a knock on his door. He unburied his head from the covers and sniffed the air lightly. "Come in, Dad," he called.

"Chay," his father began even before he'd even closed the door, "you can't keep acting like this. I know you think Prince Arthur is your mate, but are you really sure? You only spoke with him for a few minutes, and hiding yourself away from everyone isn't good for you." His father sat in the chair in the corner, and Chay slowly sat up.

"When you met Mom, when did you know she was your mate?" Chay asked.

"As soon as I laid eyes on her," his father said, and Chay smiled slightly when he saw the wistful look on his father's face. Chay had seen him rip apart another wolf who'd challenged his leadership, but talking about his mother still made the powerful man look like a lovesick teenager. "But, Chay—"

"What?" Chay asked snappily, and he received an answering growl from his father. Chay pushed back the covers, got out of the bed, and walked naked to where his father sat tracking him with his eyes, just as Chay was doing to him. "You think that because my mate is a man rather than a woman, that it's different? That I feel the pull and the loss less than you did just because your mate happened to be a woman?" Chay had never challenged his father before in his life. He'd never even tested the boundaries, not really. "How arrogant of you, Dad." Chay sneered.

"That's enough," his father said with a soft growl, and Chay could see his father's eyes beginning to shift.

"Why, because it's not what you want? I'm gay—I've always been gay. You've known that ever since I was a teenager and you could smell my arousal around other men. Did you ever realize that I never smelled that way around girls at all?" Chay moved closer, and when his father stood up, Chay's wolf couldn't be contained any longer, and he shifted.

Chay saw a massive black wolf towering over him where his human father had once stood. The wolf blinked and opened his massive jaws, baring sharp white teeth. Chay stood his ground, snarling back. The black wolf prowled closer, but Chay stayed where he was, his eyes locked on his father. A massive paw took a swipe at him, but Chay dodged it. His father obviously didn't think Chay was a threat, because he wasn't moving very fast, and as the paw passed, Chay clamped down on it hard with his teeth and tasted blood. Another swipe caught Chay on the side of the head, this one backed with much more force, and he slid along the floor before his body thumped hard against the wall. His hind legs hurt, and he watched as his massively powerful father loomed over him. Chay bared his neck and closed his eyes, hoping his father would simply put him out of his misery. Instead, he felt nothing, and Chay waited before slowly opening his canine eyes. A world of black and white greeted him, and Chay saw his father's wolf sitting near him, remarkably at ease.

Chay closed his eyes once again and shifted back to human, remaining on the floor. He watched as his father's wolf began to shimmer, and then in little more than the time it took him to blink, his father stood in front of him. Like most wolves, Chay had to strip out of his clothes before shifting or he'd have to squirm out of them before he could move. His father, on the other hand, could shift without stripping, and when he shifted back, he'd still be in the same clothes as though he had never shifted. That was another manifestation of his father's power. Reese could do the same thing, but neither Alex nor Chay could.

His father stepped back, and Chay slowly stood up. "Are we done?" Chay asked as he crawled back into bed. The last thing he was going to do was apologize. His father had beaten him the way Chay had known he would, but Chay had also stood up for himself in some way, and that made his wolf feel less beaten and rejected. Without saying anything else, Chay shut his eyes and listened as his father walked across the room, then closed the door as he left.

Chay closed his eyes, but his thoughts refused to settle. His mind turned to Arthur, just as they had in every spare moment he'd had over the past few days, and as soon as they did, his wolf begged for freedom. The memories of how Arthur looked, the way he smelled, and his deep, rich laugh were enough to make Chay's eyes shift and his canines start to lower. "I know you want him. I do too, but we can't have him," Chay told his wolf. "So we better get used to doing without him."

Maybe he should just go home to the main pack, lick his wounds, and try to forget. After all, his parents were scheduled to return in a week or so anyway. Going home would give him a chance to think things through—because not only was he heartbroken, he'd actually challenged his father. First, though, he needed to sleep for a few hours. Maybe then he'd be able to think more clearly. Chay closed his eyes, and he could feel his wolf prance and prowl for a while before finally settling down as well.

He woke to the sounds of the house as his brothers moved outside his door. Thankfully, they were leaving him alone. As he looked around, he realized he was dreaming again as he saw the same woman in white standing at the foot of his bed. Just like before, he couldn't move, even though he tried. This time, though, she pointed toward his door, and it opened by itself, but instead of the hallway, Chay found himself looking out the front door of the house. He moved through the opening, and suddenly he was zipping along the street on a motorcycle behind a figure in black leather, leaning from side to side, weaving through traffic, the wind in his hair. Chay smiled and then laughed as the scene around him dimmed.

Chay blinked and sat up, trying desperately to get enough air into his lungs as he held his head in his hands to ease the dizziness. Once his head stopped spinning, he got out of bed and padded to the bathroom for a shower. His wolf loved the water as much as he did, so Chay stayed in the shower a lot longer than was necessary before drying himself, putting on lotion for a respite from the itching, shaving, and then getting dressed. At least he felt somewhat better as he descended the stairs, intent on finding something to eat. He heard his father and brothers discussing something in his father's office, but like the good little wolf he was, he paid no attention and continued on toward the kitchen.

He pulled open the refrigerator and began pulling out the fixings for sandwiches, which for him meant sliced meat of every imaginable kind. After opening the containers, he rolled a few pieces and popped them into his mouth before making a thickly stacked sandwich.

"Hey, Scratchy, how's it going?" Alex said jovially as he joined him, and immediately snagged his plate and sandwich before settling on a stool down the way. "You can make yourself another one," he said before taking a huge bite.

"You're an ass, Alex," Chay said before getting up to reach for the bread. He quickly made another sandwich and put it on a plate. As he got ready to leave, he waited until Alex had taken a huge bite and then reached over and smacked the back of Alex's head the way Reese always did, before hurrying out of the room. Chay heard Alex sputter and cough as he nearly choked, and he used the delay to his best advantage, joining his mother in the morning room.

"You're up," his mother said as he approached, and he set his plate on the table before kissing her cheek and taking a seat across from her. "Your father told me what happened last night. You know I love him dearly, but sometimes he can be a stubborn mule." She knew his father could hear every word she said. In a house full of werewolves, there tended to be very few secrets. "He's always hoped that you would meet your mate and she would be perfect for you and you'd settle down to have a houseful of pups."

"But I'm gay," Chay said before taking a bite of his sandwich. He knew his mother understood better than anyone else.

"Yes, but that didn't stop him from hoping. We don't get to choose our soul mates, you know that, and I think your father hoped you'd find yours in the shape of the perfect woman for you." She lifted her teacup to her lips and sipped before setting the cup silently back in its saucer. "He wants you to be happy, as I do."

"I know," Chay answered.

"If you were meant to be together, then fate will find a way," his mother said as she took his hand and lightly squeezed it.

"And if we're not...," Chay said as he caught her eye, and he noticed that his mother didn't have an answer for that. He was saved from descending into another bout of self-pity when Reese stepped into the room.

"There's someone here to see you, Chay. He's waiting in the entrance hall," Reese explained, and Chay said good-bye to his mother and walked toward Reese. "Stay away from Alex," Reese warned with a wink and a slight smile, and Chay nodded.

As he approached the hall, he knew exactly who was waiting for him. He could smell the heavenly scent of his mate getting stronger and stronger, and his wolf was ready to bound down the rest of the hallway. By the time he reached the hall, Chay's vision had shifted and his canines were already descending. He had to stop just outside and will himself to remain in control. Deep breaths and calming thoughts to his wolf had his eyes and teeth shifting back to normal, even if his dick remained painfully hard. He sniffed again, his mate's scent filling his nose, along with the distinctive scent of leather.

"I have a score to settle with you, Scratchy," he heard Alex call from the top of the stairs as he stepped into the hall. Chay's throat went dry as he saw Arthur standing near the front door, dressed in black riding leathers and holding a bright-red motorcycle helmet.

Chay heard Alex on the stairs. "Not now, Alex," Chay said but knew his brother wouldn't listen; he rarely did. Chay braced himself and closed his eyes, ready for whatever tackle his brother had in mind, but it never came. Instead, he heard a thud, and when he opened his eyes, Alex was on the floor with Arthur holding him down by the throat. "It's okay, Arthur. That's my brother Alex," Chay said, a bit surprised that his brother hadn't shifted. Chay could sense his barely controlled anger ready to burst out.

"Don't even think about it," Arthur said, and Chay could see his eyes were locked with Alex's. "I'll take you down before you can move a single muscle." They stared at each other for a few seconds, and then Alex did something Chay had only seen him do to Reese and his father—Alex bared his neck to Arthur, a human. Arthur let go and backed away, watching every move Alex made.

"I'm sorry, Arthur, he was being a little overly playful," Chay said, trying to defuse the situation as Alex stood up. Chay turned to his brother. "Do you remember Prince Arthur from the party?" Chay said, and Alex nodded, lowering his eyes.

Arthur barely acknowledged Alex before turning toward Chay, his face losing its tension. "I came to see you. I was wondering if you might like to go for a ride with me." Arthur smiled at him, paying no attention as Alex left the hall.

"I'd like that," Chay said, his wolf doing leaps of joy even as he looked down at his clothes. "I need to find something to wear. I'll just be a minute."

Chay headed up to his room with his wolf fighting him the entire way. In his bedroom, Chay pulled open the closet and tried to find something he wouldn't look ridiculous in on the motorcycle. "I hope jeans are good enough," he mumbled as he moved to his chest of drawers. Next to the chest stood the portable valet with a leather jacket and pants hanging on it. Chay looked around, wondering where those had come from. He knew damned well that neither his mother nor his father had bought them for him. The room was empty, and he turned his attention back to the clothes. Lifting the jacket, Chay found it was soft, but still firm enough for protection, and the pants were equally fine. Realizing he was leaving Arthur waiting, Chay stripped off his clothes and pulled on the gear. Once he was dressed, he saw a pair of leather boots he hadn't seen before. Everything fit perfectly, and the boots slid on his feet, hugging them like they'd been custom made. "How can this be?" Chay asked as he took a few tentative steps and then hurried out of the room and down the stairs.

Arthur was waiting for him in the foyer, and Chay saw his eyes widen as he came down the stairs. He couldn't have suppressed his smile if he tried. "So you ride often?" Arthur asked, and Chay shook his head.

"I've never ridden a motorcycle before," he confessed, feeling a little foolish.

"Well, come on," Arthur said, leading him outside to where a gorgeous red BMW cruiser awaited. Arthur opened a hatch on the back and handed Chay a helmet that matched Arthur's. "Put that on. I hope it fits. I had to sort of guess at the size."

Chay placed the helmet on his head. "You got this just for me?"

Arthur helped him fasten it properly. "Of course I did," Arthur said, as though he got helmets for people every day. He threw his leg over the bike and showed Chay where to sit behind him. "Just put your arms around my waist."

Chay didn't have to be told twice. He climbed on the bike and settled in behind Arthur, wrapping his arms around his waist, and he was in total heaven. All he could smell was Arthur, and his wolf rumbled softly in his chest. The engine of the motorcycle started, coming to life beneath him, and his wolf rumbled louder. Chay hoped Arthur wouldn't notice it over the sound of the engine. "Hang on," Arthur said as they took off down the driveway before turning onto the road that ran in front of the estate. Chay hung on and moved with Arthur's body. Being this close was problematic, especially since he was throbbing in his pants and there wasn't a damn thing he could do about it.

Arthur accelerated, and they whipped down the street, picking up speed as they flew down a long, straight roadway. This was just like his dream, especially as they approached busier roads and Arthur wove the bike through traffic. Chay felt so free, both he and his wolf wanted to howl, and before he knew it, he was. Turning his head toward the sky, he let loose a cry of joy like he'd never done before. He wanted to hold Arthur in his arms forever and never let him go.

"I take it you're happy," Arthur commented as they got closer to town and stopped at a traffic signal.

"God, yes!" Chay responded honestly, grinning like an idiot inside the helmet. "Where are we going?"

"It's a surprise," Arthur called as the traffic began to move and they took off once again. They rode near the center of town, the spires of the churches and city hall towering above them. Chay thought that maybe Arthur was taking him to the square, but he kept going. Not that Chay wanted the ride to end. He could sit right here behind Arthur until the end of the world, he was so happy.

The city density began to thin, and Arthur turned again and again. Chay began to wonder where Arthur was taking him, but he felt a momentary touch of Arthur's hand on his, and they rode on.

Arthur turned into a driveway and rode along a manicured drive before pulling up to some sort of castle. He parked the bike near the main entrance and turned off the engine. The sound of the motor reverberated in Chay's sensitive ears for a few seconds before slowly fading away.

"Do you like it?"

Chay didn't know what to say as he tugged off the helmet.

"It was built as a castle at the end of the Hundred Years War and was never used for much other than posturing."

"You mean it's a real castle?" Chay's gaze traveled up one of the towers on the corner of the building.

"It was. Now it's home when I'm in Munich." Arthur smiled as Chay gaped while looking all around. His parents had a lot of money, so he'd seen big houses, mansions, and estates, but he'd never met anyone up close who lived in an actual castle. "Would you like to come inside?" Arthur asked, and Chay nodded. To his surprise, Arthur took his hand and led him through the massive front door.

The hall wasn't particularly large, but the walls were covered with lances, swords, daggers, and even a gigantic sickle. "Are all these real?" Chay asked, trying not to reach out and touch.

"Almost everything in the castle is real. There are very few reproductions, and the ones we have are only because the real items are simply too fragile to actually use." Arthur pulled the huge sickle off the wall and handed it to Chay. The weapon was incredibly heavy. "That was used by my ancestors to behead some of my other ancestors. These swords were used by kings."

"Can you ever be king?" Chay asked, handing back the weapon, and Arthur hung it back in its place.

"No. There is no kingdom anymore. It's part of Germany now. I inherited the title of prince, but it's just a title, although all this and two other castles go with it. When I'm not in residence, this is open for tourists." Arthur took Chay's jacket before slipping off his own and then setting them on one of the chairs. Taking his hand again, Arthur led him through the impressive air-conditioned rooms. "This is what I wanted to show you." Arthur opened the door with a flourish, and Chay stepped into the library. It was two stories tall, with bookcases going all the way up to the ceiling.

"Arthur," Chay marveled as he craned his head. "This is...."

"Yeah. These are the printed books. The manuscripts require special care and are stored separately. I actually have a librarian whose full-time job is to take care of the collection. Go on, you can open the cases, just be sure to put any book you take out back in its place." Arthur was grinning as Chay hurried up the stairs and walked all around the second floor. He couldn't help peering down at Arthur and saw him looking back at him, following his every move with a happy gleam in his eyes. Chay made an entire circuit before joining Arthur back on the main floor.

"How many books are there?"

"Nearly twenty thousand, all told. They go back as far as the twelfth century," Arthur explained as he took his hand again. "There's another reason I brought you here." Arthur slowly led him out of the room, and Chay reluctantly followed. He could spend the rest of his life with Arthur in that one room. "Why did your brother call you Scratchy?" Arthur asked, and Chay stopped walking, tugging his hand away.

Slowly, Chay rolled up his sleeve. "I have a skin condition that sometimes makes me itch all over. No one can figure out what causes it. So there are times when the itching becomes uncontrollable. Alex is the only one who calls me that. It's sort of his nickname for me." Chay rolled his sleeve down and, for the first time, realized he hadn't felt so much as an inkling of an itch all day, and even when he thought about it, he didn't now.

"Do you have a nickname for him?"

"Yeah," Chay said. "Dumbass." Chay giggled, and Arthur began to laugh.

"It fits," Arthur said as he continued laughing.

Chay stepped closer. "How did you take him down today? You shouldn't have been able to do that." Chay looked into Arthur's eyes for some sign that he might have missed even as he continued inhaling his scent, which had changed and was now tinged with excitement and... arousal.

"Why?" Arthur pressed, and Chay stepped back without answering. He'd never had to tell anyone about who and what he was because all the people in his life already knew. Here he was with his mate and he somehow had to tell him that he was part wolf—something that most humans didn't think was real. Chay lowered his eyes and took another step back, not sure how to proceed. The words were on the tip of his tongue, but he kept thinking it was too soon. If Arthur found out about him, he might run away, and that would break Chay's heart. Or worse, it could put everyone he loved in danger. Chay had heard stories about people who'd been told and then gone on to hunt their friends down. Wolves who had been killed by their human mates who had rejected their wolf partners. He couldn't do that to himself or his family. Not yet. At the very least, he had to talk to his father.

"I was just curious. Alex is really strong," Chay fudged and tried to make it look convincing. He wasn't sure Arthur bought his explanation, but at least he didn't press him.

"This is what I wanted to show you," Arthur said and opened another door that led down a long hallway. "The rooms I'm going to show you aren't on the public tour. These are private, and usually only immediate family members get to see them."

Chay moved down the darkened hall. From the look of the place, he sort of expected to see torches in holders on the stone walls. The air felt comfortably dry, but he wouldn't have been surprised to hear the sound of dripping water. The room had a very earthy, connected feel about it, and his wolf felt immediately at home. Large, richly dark full-length portraits hung on both sides of the hallway, each person dressed to the nines, some in royal regalia, others in simple but elegant clothing. Each person's personality seemed to ripple from the canvas. The paintings portrayed power and compassion, all with dignity and grace, in varying painting styles that spanned centuries.

"These are my ancestors, going back almost eight hundred years. These aren't the portraits you'll see in museums—those are the public portraits. These you see here are the private portraits, the ones each male ancestor of mine had painted to show the real them." Arthur stopped in front of a particular portrait. "This one was painted by the famous German artist Albrecht Dürer. But the artists aren't important;

it's what the painting represents that really matters." Arthur motioned toward the next portrait, and Chay's mouth dropped open.

"Arthur," Chay whispered almost under his breath. "Was he a king?"

"Yes. From all accounts, he was a good leader who helped rebuild the kingdom and his people after the Hundred Years War."

"But…." Chay stared. What he was looking at seemed too good to be true.

"This is what I wanted you to see." Arthur touched his shoulder, and Chay turned away from the portrait. "I know what you are and what's inside you." Arthur turned back to the portrait. "This is Friedrich, and he specifically wanted his portrait done this way."

The man was tall and as regal a man as Chay had ever seen, wearing full royal regalia. Standing beside him was an equally impressive massive black wolf. "Legend has it that Friedrich nearly worked the artist to death when he sat for this portrait because he expected to artist to paint his human form during the day and his wolf at night."

"You're human," Chay said, sniffing once again just to be sure.

"Yes, I'm human. In my family, the ability to shift sometimes skips a generation. Not all of my ancestors could shift, either. But many of them could, and many used that strength to make themselves more effective rulers."

"Then how did you know about me?"

"Just because I can't shift doesn't mean I haven't inherited some impressive abilities. For example, I heal remarkably fast, I have amazingly sharp hearing, and I'm as agile and quick as any wolf. That's how I was able to take down your brother." Arthur took his hands, and Chay felt his heart rate speed up, his wolf's tail metaphorically thumping excitedly on the floor. "I don't feel the pull that you do, but I have an awareness of something very different about you. There's something I feel for you that I've never felt with anyone else."

"I know," Chay said excitedly. "You're my mate." The words were out of his mouth before he could stop them, and he waited to see Arthur's reaction.

"I thought so. You get this blissful look every now and then. I recognized that expression from my parents. They were mates, and rarely have I seen two people happier in each other's company," Arthur told him, but he made no move to get closer, and Chay wondered what that meant. He wanted to pull him closer so he could feel him in his arms the way he had when they were riding together, but Arthur had to make the first move. Chay knew how he felt because every fiber of his being was drawn to Arthur, but what if Arthur didn't feel the same way? He didn't have a wolf, so he couldn't feel the mating call the way Chay did. "I've dreamed about finding someone like that of my own," Arthur added.

Chay took a tentative step forward, and Arthur stepped back. "Then what's stopping you?" Chay asked, holding his breath. His heart had skipped a beat when Arthur had explained that he understood what was happening, and it had raced when Arthur spoke of finding his mate.

Arthur hesitated for a moment longer and then stepped forward. "Nothing," Arthur answered tentatively, and Chay wondered what the hesitation meant, but Chay's wolf had no such reservations, and he bounded forward as Arthur leaned toward him.

Their kiss was explosive. The minute their lips touched, Chay knew this was perfection. Arthur encircled Chay's waist with his arms, tugging them close together. Chay wondered if he should take it easy, but his wolf would have none of it. After the first taste of his mate, Chay was all instinct.

Clutching Arthur tightly, he pressed him back against the stone wall. But before they reached it, Arthur turned them, and Chay felt the stone press along his back. His wolf rebelled for a split second but then surrendered to Arthur's touch and taste. Chay whimpered as Arthur deepened the kiss before moving Chay's arms away from his body and above his head.

Normally, Chay wouldn't let anyone see him without his clothes. He hated the way his skin looked, but Arthur was already pulling off his shirt before he could think about stopping him. The cool stone pressed to the skin of his back, and he humphed softly as a shiver went through him. "Just stay there a minute," Arthur said, and Chay didn't move as his mate stepped back, looking at him.

Chay's first instinct was to cover himself, but he resisted, lowering his arms instead. This was his mate, and everything he'd ever heard about mates had said that his mate would be his other half. He hoped that meant accepting his condition. "Sometimes they go—" Chay started to explain, but Arthur cut off the words with another kiss that stole his breath away.

Arthur stroked along Chay's side, his hands doing magical, tingly things to Chay's skin. Chay moaned from deep in his throat, knowing it would sound a bit like a growl. Arthur nipped at his lips, the kiss turning hard and almost bruising, exactly what Chay wanted. He felt his knees weaken as Arthur pressed against him. His leathers had become way too tight, and he groaned when he felt Arthur slide his hand down his belly.

The pressure on his cock eased as Arthur opened his pants and slid the zipper down. Chay clung to Arthur as his mate pushed his boxers out of the way and gripped his cock. "Is this what you want?" Arthur asked, tugging on him, and Chay nodded, unable to speak. "Have you ever done this before with anyone?"

Chay shook his head, and Arthur's eyes darkened as he firmly stroked Chay's length. Rolling his head to the side, Chay showed Arthur his neck, and he felt his mate nuzzle him in just the right place, tasting him with his tongue and lips and then sucking hard enough that Chay would have a mark for a little while. It wouldn't last very long, but that didn't matter to Chay. He'd wear Arthur's mark with pride, and then maybe he'd get another one.

"I want you to come for me," Arthur murmured into Chay's neck, and Chay thrust his hips forward while Arthur tightened his grip even further. Chay gasped for breath as his climax slammed into him. Lifting his head, both he and his wolf howled, the sound filling the chamber, echoing off the walls until Chay's legs collapsed and he slid down the wall.

Chay breathed deeply, covered in sweat, as he looked up at Arthur with a grin on his face. "Wow," he muttered, and Arthur grinned before helping him to his feet. Chay worked to put himself back together, then stopped as Arthur pulled him into a softer kiss. "What about you?" Chay asked, feeling a bit selfish that he hadn't thought about his mate.

"I'll be fine until I can get you someplace more comfortable," Arthur told him with a wink, and just like that, Chay was ready to go again.

"Is there more you wanted to show me?" Chay asked without shifting his gaze from Arthur's.

"Yes and no," Arthur said. "There's plenty I want to show you, but right now, I think my private quarters would be best." Arthur took his hand and led him back the way they'd come, then locked the door to the gallery behind them. Then Arthur led him through grand rooms toward the back of the castle, where he unlocked a nondescript door that led to a whole series of warmly furnished rooms. The furniture in these rooms was probably hundreds of years old, but all of it said comfort and luxury. "These rooms are only ever seen by me and my private guests," Arthur explained as he led Chay up a flight of stairs to a sitting room and then into a massive bedroom. Here was the first piece of modern furniture Chay had seen: a gargantuan, tall poster bed with what looked like a canopy and curtains.

"Bed curtains," Chay said with a chuckle.

"Don't laugh," Arthur teased. "This place is drafty, and when it gets cold, the curtains keep out the chill. I also have a personal staff, and they may come into the room while I'm sleeping, so if I want privacy, I can pull the curtains." Arthur moved closer, guiding Chay toward the bed with his body.

A throat clearing stopped them. Chay turned to see a man of about fifty, wearing a suit, standing near the door. "Excuse me, Your Highness, but Lady Stanton has arrived. I led her into your quarters, and she's waiting for you in your lounge," he said in German.

"Chay, this is Helmut," Arthur said in English. "He's the castle manager and acts as butler when I'm in residence. Nothing would happen around here without him."

"It's very nice to meet you," Chay said, extending his hand with a smile.

Helmut glanced at Arthur and then shook Chay's hand. "A pleasure," Helmut said and then stood back. "Excuse me, please," he added with a slight bow and then exited the room.

"I need to see what she wants," Arthur said with more than a little exasperation. "Lizette can be more than a little pushy, if you take my meaning." Holding his hand, Arthur led Chay back down the stairs. "She wants to be princess more than anything in the world, and she thinks she's got me on the hook."

"Are you on the hook?" Chay asked, and Arthur stopped in the doorway.

"I don't love her and I never will, not that way. She would very much like our relationship to be more, but it can't be." Arthur touched his cheek lightly. "Remember, I know what having a mate is like because of my parents, and I want that. You are my mate, I know it. I may not feel the pull the way you do, but there isn't a way for you to disguise the expression on your face when I'm near, or the way my touch excites you. I see it now, and I felt it the entire ride here." Arthur winked as Chay blushed what he knew was a deep red.

"Should I wait here?" Chay asked as he looked out through the wavy glass to the gardens beyond.

"If you like. You can also wander the gardens. I shouldn't be too long. I promise." Arthur took his hand and kissed it lightly.

"I'm not some blushing girl, you know," Chay said, and he saw Arthur grin.

"No, you're not," Arthur agreed before moving closer. "I think we established that a few minutes ago. But you are blushing." Arthur kissed him before he could protest. With a wink, he left the room, and Chay listened as his footsteps retreated.

Gazing around the room, Chay inhaled the scent of plants and earth with an overtone of sweetness from tropical blossoms. He allowed himself a smile as he breathed deeply. After walking over to the glass door, Chay opened it and stepped out into the garden. The land sloped away from the castle in terraces. Those closest to the building were formal, with swirling shrubs and topiaries. Chay walked through them and then on to gardens of lush flowering shrubs and trees. Closing his eyes, he inhaled deeply, wishing he could shift, because he knew his wolf would love nothing more than to run through these plants, the soft grass under his paws, and scent everywhere in the lush garden. Maybe he could ask Arthur if it would be okay after dark sometime.

He continued around the building toward the side of the castle where the plants became less trained, wilder and more free, but still cultivated and beautifully rich. Following the path, Chay found benches placed around a clearing with an arbor stretching around the edge. He sat down, listening to the birds and the warm breeze. He would love to let his wolf loose to frolic and play here. Every now and then, he sniffed the air, because each breath of wind seemed to blow in something new.

A familiar rich scent caught his attention, and Chay stood up and followed it back the way he'd come. He stopped at the edge of the thicker garden as he saw Arthur and Lady Stanton step into the formal garden. They were talking, he could see that, and if the breeze had shifted just a little, he probably could have heard what they were saying. Slowly, Chay moved forward, and he saw when Arthur realized he was there, because he moved away from her and walked toward Chay. Chay could see the annoyed look on her face, and as Arthur pulled him into his arms, the look turned to disgust. Then Arthur kissed him, and Chay didn't pay attention to anything except Arthur's mouth on his, his hands cupping his cheeks.

"Are you trying to tell me something? Or Lady Stanton?" Chay asked, and Arthur pinked slightly.

"Maybe a little of both," Arthur admitted. "I can't hide my feelings from you. You already know that. If I lied, you'd smell it immediately." Arthur smiled, and Chay peered over his shoulder. Lady Stanton looked at him with abject hatred in her eyes. "Is she looking like she's going to kill you?" Arthur whispered into his ear, and Chay nodded.

Arthur moved away and pasted a smile in place. Taking his hand, he led Chay to where she stood. She was wearing a light-colored dress that must have cost a small fortune. As soon as he got close, Chay smelled that same terrible perfume from the night before, and thankfully, Arthur guided him upwind. "Lady Stanton, it's nice to see you again," Chay said with a honeyed tone that would have made his mother proud.

"Lizette, you remember Cheyenne Dobson," Arthur pressed, and Chay saw a slight smile form around the edge of his mouth.

"Of course, it's nice to meet you again," she said coldly. "Arty, could I see you for just a minute before I go?" She extended her arm. "Please excuse us for just a minute." She led Arthur away, but Chay could tell he wasn't happy. Chay furrowed his brow, wondering how he knew that. He'd never really been able to read other people, but every nuance of Arthur's demeanor and body language was like an open book to him.

He could now hear them talking softly, and from the tone, he knew neither of them was particularly happy with the other, though he couldn't make out the words. That was, until Lady Stanton raised her voice, and then he understood every word. "You're casting me aside for him?" she asked in German, and Chay turned away so she wouldn't see him smile.

After walking back to the conservatory, Chay went inside and sat in one of the chairs. As much as he wanted to listen to what they were saying, he needed to give Arthur his privacy. His mother would be pleased about that, as well.

A few minutes later, Lady Stanton breezed through the door and stopped just long enough to glare at him before continuing through the rooms, the ribbons on her dress fluttering in a breeze of her own making. Arthur followed behind her, and this time, Chay could not read his expression at all. Chay stood uncomfortably. "Maybe I should go." He'd caused enough trouble for his mate and didn't want to upset him more.

"Please don't," Arthur said, striding up to him, slowing to a stop only when he was kissing Chay, who nearly toppled backward at the force of it. "Please come with me," Arthur said, taking him by the hand once again. "I'd like to take you back to the bedroom, and this time we won't be interrupted, I promise you," Arthur said, and Chay shivered with excitement. He expected Arthur to rush, but they walked calmly and slowly through the rooms as if in sort of an architectural foreplay. By the time they reached Arthur's rooms, Chay was ready to jump out of his skin. Arthur opened the door, and Chay stepped inside.

He heard the door close, and then Arthur propelled him toward the bed. The kiss quickly deepened as they tumbled on the bed in a tangle of arms and legs. Chay frantically tried to remove Arthur's clothes, and a few times he knew he heard the sound of fabric ripping, but he needed to see and taste his mate, and he needed it now. Chay's wolf wasn't going to accept any further delays. When Chay got tangled in his pants, he jumped off the bed and shucked them as fast as he could before going after Arthur's.

"Sorry," Chay said as he bounded back onto the bed. His wolf wasn't sorry in the least, and Chay ran his tongue over Arthur's chest, tasting his mate's skin for the first time. Arthur's kisses were eye-rollingly good, but the taste of his skin sent Chay's heart racing. He wanted to taste him everywhere. Lifting his head, he peered into Arthur's eyes.

"I know," Arthur told him, almost reading his mind. "Take your time."

Chay nodded and licked his way down Arthur's body, squirming down the bed until his mate's cock bobbed near his lips. Extending his tongue, Chay licked along the length. Arthur's flavor, rich and musky with a hint of sweetness, was stronger here, and he wanted more. After opening his mouth, Chay took in first the large head and then part of the shaft, careful not to take too much.

"That's it. Take it easy," Arthur encouraged, resting his hands on Chay's head.

Chay's wolf, however, had other ideas and wanted everything as quickly as he could get it. Chay bobbed his head, licking and sucking while he tasted his lover. His entire body thrummed with excitement and relief as he became more intimate with his mate. Arthur moaned and whimpered above him, and Chay redoubled his efforts, knowing he was causing his mate to make those sounds.

"Is this okay?" Chay paused to ask, and Arthur grinned, guiding Chay's lips to his. Their bodies came together, Chay resting on top of his mate. But not for long. Chay quickly found himself beneath Arthur, with those rich, indescribably blue eyes looking down into his. Chay whimpered as Arthur nibbled lightly at his neck, their cocks sliding along each other. He'd never felt anything like this. Arthur's body was strong and firm, his mate taking control.

"Arthur," Chay whimpered as he bucked up against him. He wanted more, and his wolf cried for more. Arthur seemed to know just how and where to touch him, because Chay felt shiver upon shiver run through him.

"I know. My touch drives you crazy, and your wolf is begging you to join. He knows I'm your mate, and he wants nothing more than to join with me and complete the mating. But we can't do that right now," Arthur told him. "We need to get to know one another. There's more to it than just making your wolf happy. You need to be happy, and you need to know that this isn't just a matter of predestined matehood."

"But, Arthur," Chay begged, his hips continually shifting and thrusting, which he didn't stop until he felt Arthur place his hand lightly at his side.

"I'm not saying we won't join and become mates, but you deserve to be *loved*, not just mated, and that takes time. I know what your mind is telling you to do, but my father explained to me how important mating is. You will only mate once, and it's for life," Arthur said as he stroked Chay's cheek. "I want you, us, to do it for the right reasons and with everything you deserve. So just relax and let me take care of you."

"Can I taste some more?" Chay asked, and Arthur chuckled, shifting until he was straddling him.

"Keep your hands at your sides," Arthur told him, and Chay obeyed happily as Arthur positioned his cock at his lips and then slowly pressed forward. Chay hummed as Arthur's cock slid along his tongue, moving back and forth slowly. Chay wanted more, but Arthur was determined to take his time. "Careful of the teeth," he warned, and Chay realized he was getting so excited that his canines were lengthening. He was also seeing Arthur in black and white, but he really didn't care.

Arthur reached behind him, and Chay felt his hand firmly grip his cock. Chay hummed around Arthur's length and sucked harder, bobbing his head. Arthur's unique taste, scent, and touch filled his senses, and he could barely decide what to do. So he gave in and let Arthur take charge. As soon as he did, Chay's pleasure multiplied.

Arthur rolled his hips lightly, his abs stretching and tightening. Chay wasn't sure how much more he could stand as Arthur began stroking him deliberately, twisting his hand as he moved it slowly along his shaft. Chay began whimpering as the excitement and pleasure got to him. He'd always hoped he'd find his mate, and being here with him was blowing his mind. Arthur was amazingly beautiful stretching over him, all lean muscle and power that transferred itself to Chay everywhere Arthur touched him.

"I'm not going to last," Arthur groaned, and Chay sucked harder. He desperately wanted to taste his mate in every way, and in seconds, he felt Arthur coming. Chay swallowed and relished the unique taste of his mate, at the same time trying to hold off his own climax.

Arthur slipped from his mouth, and Chay saw him shift onto the bed. Without warning, he was surrounded by the hottest heat he'd ever imagined, and Chay clamped his eyes closed, filling the room with a near glass-shattering howl as both he and his wolf relished their mate. His breath returned much more slowly this time, and Chay lay wrung out on the bedding. This time Chay felt Arthur lay next to him, his chest pressing to Chay's back, strong arms wrapped around his chest, pulling him close. "Sleep, sweetheart," Arthur told him, and Chay nodded slowly, his eyes already closing.

He didn't sleep for long, though. Chay heard movement in the room and cracked his eyes open to see Helmut carrying their clothes away just before closing the door. Rolling over, Chay smiled as Arthur dozed. With him asleep, Chay took the opportunity to study him.

"Are you watching me sleep?" Arthur groaned.

"Yes," Chay answered, breaking into a smile. "Can you blame me?" Chay whispered as he stroked Arthur's cheek. Chay heard the bedroom door open, and while most werewolves were comfortable with nudity, Chay wasn't, and his wolf certainly wasn't comfortable with anyone seeing his mate but him. Chay's wolf growled loudly, and he heard Helmut start. Then he heard rushed footsteps and the door closed.

"I hope you liked scaring Helmut," Arthur whispered, his eyes still closed.

"Yes, I did," Chay said seriously before breaking into peals of laughter as Arthur began tickling him.

CHAPTER THREE

A WEEK later Chay hurried to get dressed for the day. He was expected at Arthur's in little over an hour, and try as he might, he'd been unable to break Arthur's tight-lipped silence about what they were doing. All Arthur had said was to wear comfortable clothes. When he was ready to go, Chay checked himself in the mirror before leaving the room. He bounded down the stairs and then listened. He could hear his parents talking at the far end of the house, so he walked in that direction and found both of them sitting around the table in his mother's bright sitting room. "Morning," Chay called happily as he joined them, nodding to his father and kissing his mother's cheek before sitting down.

"Would you like some breakfast?" his mother asked with a smile and began making up a plate for him. "You've been especially cheerful lately. I take it things are going well with you and your mate?"

Chay heard his father growl softly, and he glanced at him, but his mother continued. She was one of the few people in the world who wasn't affected by his father's growliness. She simply reached across the table and patted the big man's hand like she would a petulant child.

"I think so, really well," Chay answered, still concerned about his father's lack of support. His family meant a great deal to him, especially his father, and it hurt that he didn't seem to understand how important this was to him.

"Where are you going today?" his mother asked before lifting her teacup to her lips.

"I don't know. Arthur said he has a surprise for me." Chay was so excited he couldn't keep the smile off his face even as his father growled again.

"He hasn't claimed you yet, has he?" his father asked, and Chay shook his head.

"Arthur is human, so he can't claim me. You know that. I have to claim him, and Arthur wouldn't let me." Chay paused when his mother set the plate in front of him. "He said that we needed to take our time,"

Chay explained with a smile, "and I think he's right. He said that I deserved a relationship based on love, not just matehood."

"Prince Arthur is part *were* even if he doesn't have a wolf, so he can claim you just like you can claim him," his father explained, and Chay saw him sniff. "But I still don't believe he's your mate," his father explained, and Chay sighed, putting the hunk of bacon he'd been eating back on his plate.

"Jackson," his mother snapped, and Chay jumped slightly. His mother never raised her voice. "You may be the all-powerful alpha werewolf, but even you don't get to decide who your son's mate is. Only the Fates do that." His mother glared across the table at his father.

Chay heard footsteps outside the room, and he scented Reese as he approached. Turning toward the door, Chay saw Reese step into the room, take one look at his mother and father, and back out once again with a startled look on his face. Chay's parents never argued; they discussed things.

"If Prince Arthur is your son's mate, then you need to set aside your prejudices and accept it." His mother's tone softened slightly. "Because if you don't, you're not the mate I've loved all these years."

Chay heard his father take a deep breath and then release it slowly. "You're right, dear," he said softly, and Chay turned his attention to his plate to give his parents a bit of privacy. In their world, with a house full of wolves who could hear almost anything that happened at any given time, privacy was being courteous and not looking, or simply ignoring what you heard. Secrets of any type were nearly impossible to keep except if they were discussed in Chay's father's office with the door closed. That was the one space in the house where no sound escaped at all. "I can't pretend to understand why Chay would have a male mate any more than I can understand why he'd want one and give up the chance at pups."

"Dad, I am who I am," Chay said after swallowing. "If I had been destined to be with a female mate, I probably would have walked away and never told her. I have no idea what I could possibly do with a female mate." His father's eyebrows rose, and he looked aghast. "I love women, but not in any intimate way. I could never live with a woman, which is probably why I have a male mate. I know this is hard for you to understand, but I don't want the same things you do. I'm not strong, like you, and I'm not a great leader. I'm quiet and I'd rather spend my time in a library than roughhousing with Alex and Reese," Chay explained. "I'm sorry I'm not what you want in a son, but I am who I am and I can't change it." His arms began to itch, and Chay rubbed them, realizing just how little he'd felt the need to scratch over the past few days. Chay stood up and moved away from the table, kissing his mother goodbye before hurrying from the room. He didn't want to see the disappointed look on his father's face.

As he walked down the hall, he could hear his father and mother talking, but he ignored what they were saying in his quest to get out of the house. After walking out through the front door, he got in the car he used when he was in Germany and began the drive across the city.

It took almost an hour, and Chay was nearly late when he turned into the drive to Arthur's castle. He parked out of the way and walked to the front door, which opened as he approached. Arthur stepped outside. "Are you ready to go?" he asked, and Chay nodded. "What happened?" Arthur asked as Chay was tugged into a nearly crushing hug.

Chay rested his head on Arthur's shoulder, the scent of his mate calming him almost instantly. "My dad," Chay answered. "He doesn't understand." That was the best he could do to describe it without going into all the details, and he really didn't want to rehash all that now.

"Maybe I should have your family here for dinner. It's probably best if we get to know each other. He's your dad, and he just wants what he thinks is best for you. He may not understand, so we need to help him," Arthur whispered, and Chay nodded against Arthur's shoulder before lightly licking his mate's skin. He needed to taste as well as smell him just to make sure that what he felt was real. "We should go, or I'm going to take you inside and we'll never leave, just like we did yesterday, and I really think you're going to enjoy what I have in mind."

Arthur released him from the hug before taking him by the hand and leading him around to the garage. Arthur pressed a button on his key ring and a door lifted, revealing a red Ferrari. Arthur grinned as he released Chay's hand. "Your chariot awaits," he said as he threw Chay the keys.

"You want me to drive?" Chay asked with a smile.

"Sure," Arthur said as he pulled open the passenger door, and Chay opened his door, then slid behind the wheel. The leather seat cupped his body. "The car has a lot of power, so for normal driving, you need to have a light touch on the accelerator. Just go slow at first and you'll get used to her."

Chay grinned and nodded, placing the key in the ignition and starting the powerful engine. Familiarizing himself with the gears, Chay slowly backed out of the garage, and Arthur lowered the garage doors with another press of the button on the key ring. Cautiously, Chay backed the car out to the main drive, then stopped, shifted gears, and they were off. The back wheels spun, and Chay let off the accelerator. "You weren't kidding," he said, and Arthur smiled back at him as they rode down the drive before turning toward town.

"Toward the south of town are the Oktoberfest grounds. That's where we're headed, so you can drive back the way we came until you reach the Autobahn. We'll take that around the city, and then I'll guide you from there. Once we're on the freeway, you can open her up and have fun."

They rode to the Autobahn and glided up the on-ramp. Chay got into the left lane and slowly increased his speed. He wanted to get used to going that fast, but it wasn't long before he was going what he suspected was almost 140 miles an hour. The car felt like it was barely moving, and Chay clutched the wheel harder than he had to, his pulse racing. He felt his canines begin to lower, so he slowed down in case his vision shifted as well. As the speed decreased, so did the excitement, and his teeth returned to normal. He was approaching their exit anyway, so he got off and slowed to a stop at the end of the ramp. Chay knew where the Oktoberfest grounds were, but he let Arthur guide him to a parking area that Arthur seemed to know. After they pulled in, they got out, and the valet took the keys and the car as Arthur guided Chay out and toward the grounds.

The temporary pavilions used for the festival were being constructed, and Arthur and Chay walked through the grounds toward a large statue at the far end. "There's a path that leads into the forest above the grounds," Arthur explained. They easily found the path that wound up into the hills. Chay followed Arthur, and once the trees surrounded them, Arthur took his hand as they walked the wide trail farther and farther up the hill. As they continued climbing, Chay could see the back of a huge female statue through the trees.

Eventually the trail split, and Arthur took the smaller of the two ways, veering off the main path and farther into the woods. "People rarely come this way," Arthur said as they continued walking. "But I love this path, with the thick trees and only the sound of the forest." They continued walking, the trees and undergrowth getting thicker. It was hard to believe they were on the edge of Munich, the terrain seemed so wild.

"This is really beautiful," Chay said as the path widened out into a small clearing. "I'm glad we came."

Arthur stopped walking, looking all around. "Is there anyone close?" Arthur asked, and Chay sniffed before shaking his head. For a fleeting second, he wondered if he'd been reading everything all wrong and if he was being lured here, but Arthur's demeanor showed nothing but openness and honesty, so he relaxed.

"I don't smell or hear anyone. Why?" Chay asked.

"Because I brought you here so I could meet your wolf," Arthur explained, and it took a minute for Chay to realize what Arthur was asking.

"You want me to shift?"

"Yeah. Your wolf is a part of you. I was going to ask at the castle, but I thought both you and he would like it here." Arthur took him into his arms. "You don't have to if you don't feel comfortable."

Chay wasn't quite sure how he felt about it, but his wolf loved the idea, so Chay removed his shirt before pulling off his shoes. He then slipped out of his pants, folded his clothes, and set them on a dry log at the edge of the clearing. Stepping back, he felt his canines lengthen, and his vision shifted to black and white. Then his bones repositioned, and he felt the momentary discomfort as his face shifted. Closing his eyes, he waited for the rest of the change to wash over him.

Opening his eyes, Chay saw in a world of shades of gray. Arthur looked very different, but he smelled even better than usual. Chay loped over to him and looked up at his mate, hoping he liked what he saw. "You're incredible," Arthur said before kneeling down. Chay felt his mate's hands stroke along his back, and he extended his front paws, stretching the muscles of his legs before doing the same with his back. He groaned deep in his wolf throat as Arthur rubbed harder, the itching that usually drove him nearly crazy in this form instantly abating under Arthur's touch. Chay lifted his head and licked along Arthur's neck. He'd been aching to taste his mate in this form, so much so that he kept licking until Arthur fell back on his butt in a fit of giggles.

Chay stood over Arthur, wagging his tail furiously as he continued licking and rubbing against him. "You're even more tactile like this," Arthur commented, and Chay stopped, cocking his head to one side as he stared at Arthur before snorting lightly through his nose. He hoped the "duh" came through loud and clear. "Okay, I get it," Arthur said, and Chay went back to licking and rubbing against his mate.

Arthur sat up, and Chay backed away, watching his mate as he sniffed the air for anyone approaching or any type of threat. As Arthur got to his feet, Chay explored the clearing, scenting around the edges. He had gotten about halfway across when he picked up the scent of other wolves. Chay stopped and sniffed again, before moving slowly. The scents weren't extremely fresh, but relatively recent. Chay followed the scent, finding others—a pack, and these weren't the scents of regular wolves. He was on the land of a foreign pack without permission. Chay had begun to walk back to Arthur when he smelled another wolf in the trees. After hurrying back to where Arthur waited, Chay stood rigidly, following the scent as it moved through the woods.

A large gray wolf emerged on the other side of the clearing, and Chay growled, ready to protect his mate. The wolf stopped, sat down, and looked up at Arthur.

"I'm glad you could make it," Arthur said, and Chay stopped growling, turning to Arthur as he wondered just what was going on. "Chay, this is my cousin Wilhelm. He's the alpha of the local pack."

The gray wolf nodded once and then turned and walked back into the woods. Chay stared after him, scenting the air every few minutes. Cousin or not, Chay was not going to leave his mate unprotected. After a few minutes, he scented someone returning. This time a rather barrel-chested man in jeans and a T-shirt stepped into the clearing.

"Arthur, why did you bring a strange wolf here?" Wilhelm asked, and Chay growled again at the man's tone.

"It's okay, Chay. He won't hurt either of us," Arthur told him, and then he turned toward the powerful wolf. "Stop being such an alpha. This is Chay Dobson, and I'm his mate." Arthur rolled his eyes. Chay kept shifting his vision from Arthur to the other wolf, not trusting him around his mate. Chay would die to protect Arthur; he had no illusions about that. He might be weaker, but the other wolf would have to go through him to get to Arthur.

"Why would you bring a strange wolf into our territory without permission?" Wilhelm asked a little harshly.

"Knock it off," Arthur snapped back, and Wilhelm actually took a step back. "You may be the alpha wolf, but I whipped your ass when we were kids, and I can do it again." Arthur wasn't backing down. Chay was finding that around him, Arthur was warm and kind, but he could also be very much the prince if he had to.

"The question is valid," Wilhelm said in a more civil tone, but Arthur didn't respond.

Chay had had enough and shifted back into human form so he could speak. "I just met Arthur a few days ago, and I believe Arthur brought me here because he knew it would be safe for me to show him my wolf form for the first time," Chay explained as he quickly began getting dressed.

"So do you think you can knock off the asshole routine and greet my mate?" Arthur said. "I've been around wolves all my life, but there are times when I will never understand a one of you. You can tell that Chay isn't nearly as strong as you."

"No, he's not," Wilhelm agreed, and Chay saw his expression soften as he approached. Chay dipped his head out of respect and bared his throat to the much stronger wolf. Then he extended his hand, and Wilhelm shook it. "Dobson. Why is the name familiar?"

"My father is Sir Jackson Dobson," Chay explained as he buttoned his shirt, and Wilhelm nodded his understanding. There were few wolves in either North America or Europe who didn't know of Chay's father. "I didn't intend to intrude on your pack lands. I realized what they were only a few moments before you appeared, and I was about to leave."

Wilhelm nodded. "I don't blame you. Arthur should have known better, and he should have informed me." Wilhelm glared at Arthur and then broke into a huge smile before tugging Arthur into a hug. "So, cousin, I always told you I thought you had a wolf mate waiting for you, but you never believed me." Now that the tension seemed to have gone, Wilhelm smiled more easily. "I will confess that I thought your mate would be a woman."

Chay had just about had enough. His father didn't believe that Chay was Arthur's mate and wanted him to find a woman, and now Arthur's cousin was saying the same thing to him. Chay felt a growl rise in his throat, but he swallowed it out of respect, though it wasn't easy.

"Relax, Chay," Wilhelm said. "I believe you, but you haven't officially mated yet or I'd have known right away." Wilhelm flashed Arthur a look Chay didn't understand, and Arthur returned it. He could tell there was a great deal of silent conversation going on between them. Chay had never been able to communicate telepathically with anyone, but he knew it was sometimes possible. His father could do it, but neither he nor his brothers could. Judging by the expressions on Arthur and Wilhelm's faces, though, they both could, and they were having a brief conversation that excluded him. If he hadn't known what to look for, he probably wouldn't have noticed it.

"We should get back, but I'm glad Chay got to meet you, even if you were a bit of an ass," Arthur quipped, and Wilhelm growled before turning to Chay.

"Don't let my cousin get the better of you. Sometimes he can be too princely for his own good," Wilhelm retorted. But beneath the teasing, Chay suspected there was a deep and lasting affection.

"Thank you, I'll remember that," Chay told Wilhelm, and then he followed Arthur as they left the clearing and headed back down the path. "You really should have informed him," Chay told Arthur. "I don't want to step on anyone's toes." And if as Arthur's mate he was going to spend time in the area, he wanted the goodwill of the local alpha.

"I probably should have," Arthur admitted, "but he gets too alpha sometimes." Arthur turned toward him, and Chay saw regret and wistfulness in his eyes. "If I had been born with a wolf, I would have been alpha. It goes along with the title, but since I wasn't, there was a fight among some of my other family members for the position. I backed Wilhelm to the hilt and supported him through his rise, even though by rights, the position should have gone to his brother. Wilhelm was the better man for the job, without a doubt, and he's a good alpha."

"He could have turned you," Chay offered, and Arthur nodded as they continued back down the path.

"He could have, but it wouldn't have been the same, and it probably wouldn't have been fair, either. My father was prince and he was also the alpha. It worked for him, but maybe it was a little selfish. Looking back, I can see where my father was a good alpha and a good prince, but he wasn't great at either. There were times when he let the pack suffer, not purposely, but because the demands on his time were too great. This way the pack gets Wilhelm's full attention and energy, and the estate and family holdings get mine."

Chay listened as Arthur talked, and the more he heard, the more he realized just how lucky he was and how special Arthur was. Without thinking, Chay moved closer, needing not just to hold Arthur's hand. "You would have made an amazing alpha," Chay said, and Arthur stopped walking, looking at him quizzically as they stood at the junction where the smaller path met the main one. "Putting the pack above your own desires is the mark of a superior alpha." Their gazes locked for a few seconds, and Chay thought Arthur was going to kiss him, but he heard voices coming toward them on the path and stepped back.

They continued down the path, holding hands when they were alone. Chay wanted to ask Arthur about what he and Wilhelm had said to each other, but he didn't. Instead, he hoped Arthur would tell him on his own. During the entire walk to the car, Arthur talked about a lot of things, but he never brought that up. Granted, Arthur and Wilhelm had known each other for years and they had a history. Arthur wasn't acting any differently, and Chay didn't detect or scent any deliberate deception in Arthur, so he decided he was probably being paranoid. He didn't know for sure that they had been communicating, he only suspected, and he could easily have been wrong. "Where are we going?" Chay asked as they approached the car.

"I was hoping you'd come back to the castle with me. We could have some dinner and then maybe dessert." From the way Arthur leered at him, Chay had no illusions regarding what dessert would entail, and he was all for it.

Arthur drove, and Chay hung on as his mate drove the Ferrari like he was on a racecourse. "Getting back in one piece would be fine," Chay quipped as Arthur barreled through a traffic signal. Arthur smiled over at him and let up on the speed, and they pulled into the castle drive without incident. Arthur drove the car into the garage and lowered the doors before guiding Chay into the castle through what Chay had learned was his private entrance. Helmut greeted them and informed them that dinner would be ready in less than an hour.

"Thank you. Chay and I will be in my sitting room," Arthur said, and then he led Chay through to his private rooms. Chay sat on a comfortable sofa with Arthur right next to him. Almost immediately, they began kissing, which Chay could tell was going to quickly progress to other things. And it probably would have if there hadn't been a knock on the door.

Arthur backed away and Chay sat up, trying not to look as though he'd just been kissed within an inch of his life.

"Come in," Arthur called. The door opened and a strange wolf entered the room. Chay was immediately on alert, but Arthur calmed him with a pat on the hand. "This is Gregor, Wilhelm's younger brother," Arthur explained, and Chay stood up and shook hands with the other wolf.

"I am sorry to interrupt," Gregor began, "but I need to speak with Arthur. It will only be a minute." Gregor wore a very earnest expression, and Arthur stood, as well.

"Will you excuse me?" Arthur asked, and of course Chay agreed and watched Arthur lead Gregor out through the solarium and into the garden. Alone in the room, Chay began to wander, and drawn by the scent of the tropical plants, he walked into the solarium to sit down and wait. He hadn't planned to eavesdrop on Arthur's conversation with his cousin, but as he sat on one of the benches, he could hear them a clear as day. The wind must have been just right, because Chay could see them wandering the garden, and at that distance he shouldn't have been able to hear them, but he could.

"Wilhelm sent me right over to talk to you," Gregor was saying in German. "It seems our brother Joseph has gotten wind of the fact that you have a male mate and therefore will not have children, and you know that your position within the family is dependent upon having an heir."

"I know," Arthur explained. "Your brother has been a pain in the ass since we were kids, and I figured he would pull something once he found out. There's nothing he can do to me except force me to name one of his brats as my heir." Arthur was shaking his head.

"That's what Wilhelm wanted me to speak to you about. He said Joseph plans to challenge you as head of the family, and there is precedent. Your branch of the family inherited the title because your great-great-uncle had only girls. Wilhelm and I could care less—you're a good leader and you're good for the family—but Joseph had always had it in his head that he should rightfully be the head of the family. He just wants to get his hands on the purse strings because he lives way beyond his means, but I believe he's going to try to use your inability to produce an heir as an excuse." Gregor was becoming animated, and Chay couldn't make out a lot of what he said afterward.

However, he clearly heard Arthur's response: "Then I'll have to have an heir. Tell Wilhelm that I fully intend to produce an heir, and that the two of you can have the pleasure of telling him. That should put him in a foul mood for days. Too bad I won't be around to see it."

Chay watched as they continued talking, but he couldn't make out any more of the conversation. Not that it really mattered. Chay felt as though he'd been punched in the gut, and his wolf threatened to howl right there. His heart hurt, and Chay stood up, then hurried back to the sitting room. He couldn't stay and pretend he hadn't heard what he had. He had to get out of there, fast. Walking through the castle, he navigated his way back toward the front door. On his way, he saw Helmut walking toward him. "I have to leave," Chay said as he dashed toward the front door.

"What shall I tell His Highness?" Helmut asked with concern, but for what, Chay couldn't tell.

Chay nearly ignored the question and continued walking toward the door, but he stopped just before leaving. "Tell His Highness that I wish him and Lady Stanton well, and the best of luck in producing an heir."

Chay hurried outside to the car. He was so close to tears that he couldn't bear to have anyone see him like this, much less Arthur. After sliding behind the wheel of the car, he started the engine and then headed down the drive. "Fuck!" he cried, clenching the steering wheel so tightly his fingers dug into his palms. And to make matters worse, every inch of his skin itched. He could barely think straight, but he needed a clear head, so he pushed everything aside but the task of making it back to his parents' estate.

It took a great deal of concentration, but Chay eventually pulled into the drive and in front of the house. After getting out of the car, he raced inside with every intention of going to his room, but as he reached the top of the stairs, his brother Alex hurried toward him. "How's the prince, Scratchy?"

"Don't be an ass, Alex," Chay retorted, and he continued walking toward his room, but Alex stepped in front of him.

"I knew it was just a matter of time before he dumped you," Alex said. "You should have known it too." The unspoken portion of that comment stung hard: *What would a prince want with Scratchy?*

Chay stopped walking. "What did I ever do to you?" he demanded, looking Alex in the eye. "We're brothers, but you treat me like crap," Chay added, stepping defiantly toward his brother. "You think it makes you a big wolf to pick on someone smaller than you? Then have at it." Chay wanted to rail at Arthur, but since he couldn't, Alex would do. Chay was prepared to get his ass whipped, figuring the physical pain would hurt less than the hole in his heart.

"Little shit," Alex growled, and Chay saw him lunge.

"That's enough!" their mother snapped, and Chay turned his head to see his mother coming down the hall. "You know I will have none of that in the house from either of you." It had been a long time since Chay had seen his mother this angry.

"Sorry," Chay mumbled as he walked past her, continuing on his way toward his room. He could clearly hear Alex getting an earful from their mother, and he knew that wouldn't win him any points with Alex in the long run. He'd only be angrier the next time they clashed over something. Chay had often tried to figure out what he'd done to Alex to make him act like such an ass to him, but he never could come up with anything specific. He'd always thought that it probably wasn't him that Alex resented, but Reese, and since there was no way Alex could take on Reese, Chay bore the brunt of it.

Closing his bedroom door behind him, Chay let go of his confusion about his brother as his thoughts returned to Arthur. His wolf still wanted to howl, and Chay thought about trying to go for a run out back, but it was too light outside and he couldn't take the chance of someone seeing him, so that would have to wait. Regardless, he stripped out of the clothes he was wearing and headed toward the bathroom, where he found a bottle of the lotion that relieved the itching most of the time. Right now what he wished was that he had enough that he could take a bath in it, because there didn't seem to be a single inch of him that didn't feel like it was covered in bugs. Chay began spreading the lotion on the areas that itched most. When he was done, he chanced a look in the mirror and gasped. Red patches covered most of his body.

"No wonder Arthur would rather be with someone who can give him an heir," Chay said out loud to his reflection. "Who'd want a lifetime of being with someone that looks like this?" He put the bottle away and pulled on some of the softest clothes he had before heading downstairs to the kitchen.

The house was unusually quiet. Chay could hear a few soft conversations coming from the far side of the house, but they were hushed enough that he couldn't really tell who was speaking. In the kitchen, he opened the refrigerator and peered inside for something to eat. "I can make you a steak if you like?" a female voice said from behind him. "Mrs. Kartoum has the day off, but I can help you," she added with a slight bow. "I'm Gretchen," she said with a smile.

"That would be very nice," Chay said. "I'm Chay, and thank you."

"Rare," she said as sort of a half question, and Chay nodded once. "I can bring it up to your room if you don't want to use the dining room."

"Could I eat it here?" Chay asked, pointing to the table near the kitchen window. He wasn't in the mood to eat with everyone else, but he knew his mother would pitch a fit if he ate in his bedroom.

Chay sat down and watched as Gretchen got the food together. He noticed that she cooked plenty of meat and didn't bother with things like vegetables or potatoes. Chay ate them, but he, like most wolves, preferred meat. When she was done, she brought a huge steak on a plate with a large mug of beer. Then she went to work making dinner for the rest of the family as Chay sat silently and ate. He wasn't in the mood for a family dinner, and he really didn't want to face his father right now. As he ate, he watched Gretchen work, and once he was finished, he put his dishes in the sink and thanked her before leaving and heading up the back stairs to his bedroom.

Chay sat in the chair near his lamp and tried to read, but his thoughts kept coming back to Arthur. He knew his wolf was grieving the loss of his mate, the same way he would if Arthur had died. He'd been rejected in favor of someone who could give Arthur children, and there was nothing Chay or his wolf could do about it. But that didn't make the situation hurt any less. Picking up the book he'd been reading, Chay tried to take his mind off Arthur and the fact that his arms and legs itched like hell. After opening the book, he read for a while but kept losing his place as he rubbed his arms and legs between turning the pages. This was the worst the itching had been in a long time, and it was about to drive him crazy. He knew he could scratch the skin off his body and it would be of little good. Giving up, he dropped the book on the floor and sat, wallowing in his heartache and misery.

A knock sounded at his door. "Chay?" his father said as he pushed open the door. Chay had scented him outside his door but had hoped his father would simply move on. "Why weren't you at dinner?"

"Didn't want to come down," Chay answered as he rubbed his arms. "I wasn't in the mood to explain to everyone that my mate rejected me because I can't have children and he needs an heir. Not that Scratchy Dobson could ever be good enough for someone like Arthur." Chay watched as his father shut the door. "You should be happy, Dad. Now you can have what you wanted. I'll spend the rest of my life without a mate, knowing who he is and even where he is, but I can't have him. Does that make you happy?" Chay stared at his feet rather than looking at the "I told you so" look on his father's face. "You didn't think Arthur was my mate, and you couldn't understand how I could have a male mate. Well, I don't, not anymore. So please just excuse me if I'm not up to eating fucking dinner with the rest of you." Chay stood up and walked into the bathroom, then closed himself in. He half expected his father to break down the door. Chay had disrespected him in a huge way, but nothing happened. He could tell his father was still outside the door, so he lowered the toilet seat and sat on it to wait.

His father did come in, but he didn't break the door down, and to Chay's surprise, he didn't yell. "Cheyenne."

Chay looked up from where he'd been examining the pattern in the black-and-white floor tiles.

"I am never happy when you or any of my pups have been hurt. And if I hadn't been a stubborn fool, I would have realized that you aren't a child anymore and that you're perfectly capable of knowing and understanding when you've met your mate. I should have believed you. Your mate isn't someone that you or I get to choose. The one person in this world that's perfect for us is chosen by the Fates, and we're at their mercy. We have to live with their greater wisdom. I should know that, and I should have been supportive."

"Thanks, Dad," Chay said with a sigh and then stood up. Before he could think twice about it, he'd thrown himself into his father's arms. He knew his father couldn't make it right or tell him it would be all right.

"I know you're grown, but sometimes I still see you as a little pup, and you're not," his father said into his ear.

"I may be, but sometimes I still need my dad," Chay replied, and he felt the grip around him tighten just a little bit. "Sorry I took my hurt out on you."

"I'm big; I can take it," his father said. "I was wondering, after dark, how about you and I take a run together, just the two of us?" Now it was Chay's turn to tighten his grip on his father.

CHAPTER FOUR

CHAY'S phone rang again, as it had three or four times a day for the past week, and Chay silenced it without answering. He knew it was Arthur, just like the previous two dozen calls had been. Chay had decided days ago that the only way he could function was to make a clean break. He really wasn't interested in whatever excuse Arthur was going to give him. Besides, in two days, he was going home. Classes were going to start again next month, and while he'd planned to stay a few more weeks, he was looking forward to being home. The ringing stopped, and Chay put his phone on the bedside table before heading out to the backyard for his nightly run.

At the edge of the lawn, Chay stripped and shifted before taking off at his wolf's top speed. Once he was away from the house, Chay lifted to eyes to the moon and howled again and again. He knew his family could hear him, but he didn't care. This was the only way his wolf could grieve the loss his mate. After hours of running, howling, and scratching to beat the band, Chay returned to the edge of the grass, leaves and small sticks hung up in his coat. He was bleeding in places because of the scratching, but Chay couldn't get up enough energy to really give a damn. After shifting back to human, he put on his clothes and went inside. Sometimes he noticed that one of his parents would just happen to be coming down the stairs to get a snack as he came in, but tonight he knew he was the only one up. The others were asleep, and Chay went straight to his bathroom, where he showered and put on the last of the lotion he had before climbing into bed. He fell asleep almost immediately, barely able to move in his exhaustion.

When he opened his eyes, he was surprised to see the woman in white standing at the foot of his bed. This time he could move. "Cheyenne, you can't run from your destiny." She actually said something. "You're not asleep, not this time. I've visited you before, but this time I wanted to see you in person."

"Who are you?" Chay asked, but she didn't answer and merely waved at one of Chay's walls. It vanished, revealing a scene. He was back home, and Chay was walking through the yard of the family ranch toward the house. When he went inside, Chay expected to see his family and other pack members the way he always did, but the house was empty except for him. There weren't even any signs of other people—no pictures, just emptiness. Then the scene shifted, and Chay saw one of the rooms at Arthur's castle. As he watched, Arthur walked in, carrying a baby, and he looked happy as he swung what could only be a little boy in his arms. He could hear Arthur's happiness and laughter as they twirled and played in the huge room. "See? He's happy without me," Chay said, and the scene darkened to nothing. The space remained black for a long time, and then his wall returned.

"You can't change your fate. Either embrace it or it will embrace you," she said as she began to fade.

"Wait," Chay called, and she stopped, hanging in the room like a shimmery specter. "Please tell me what I should do."

"Only you can decide that," she explained. "My time is short. Make your decision and follow your heart." With those parting words, she faded to the point that Chay could no longer see her.

Chay blinked a few times and actually had to make certain he hadn't been dreaming, but he really wasn't quite sure. When he looked around the room, everything looked the same. The walls were all there and nothing had been moved. Lying back down, Chay stared at the ceiling, trying to make sense of what he'd been shown. The woman appeared in his dreams when it looked like he was going to veer away from his destiny. The first time, he wasn't going to go to the party where he met Arthur and realized he was his mate. The next time she'd come to his dreams, he was getting ready to go home because he thought he couldn't have Arthur. She was obviously trying to nudge him toward Arthur, but what she'd shown him this time had made no sense—at least, parts of it made no sense. She'd obviously been showing him that if he left, he'd end up alone, like that was a huge revelation.

The thing he couldn't figure out was why, if she wanted him and Arthur together, she'd shown him how happy Arthur was with his son, a son that Chay obviously couldn't give him, and then the blankness. Was that someone dying? Chay had no clue, and his head was beginning to hurt. She had told him to follow his heart—that was one of the few things he'd understood clearly, and his heart ached for

Arthur and his wolf grieved for him. It was painfully obvious, but that also didn't change the fact that Arthur wanted and needed an heir.

Chay was so confused he could hardly think. Closing his eyes, he tried to let it all go and get some sleep. He'd been running most nights with his father, and he needed to rest. His mother would tell him he was using sleep to escape, and he probably was, but it was the only thing that seemed to numb his broken heart.

Chay must have fallen asleep, because he dreamed, gorgeous happy dreams of a life with Arthur. Parties, outings in the country, picnics together, the two of them riding horses back on the ranch, even a trip to the swimming hole, just the two of them—and they did a lot of things in that water, but swimming was not one of them, at least in his dreams. The last thing Chay saw before waking up was he and Arthur playing together with their son.

He started awake, blinking, looking all around. He expected to see the woman again—this had been just the type of dream she appeared in—but there was no sign of her, and disappointment set in. He wished all those things he'd seen were true, including a son that was his and Arthur's. Although Chay definitely drew the line at getting pregnant, the thought was amusing for a few seconds until the last of the dream's happiness faded and reality settled on him with a thud. It was time to leave. He'd made his decision, and Arthur had quite obviously made his, as well—Chay had heard him say so. Letting himself get caught up in whatever was happening with these dreams and this woman was not helping him. Pushing back the covers, he got out of bed. After pulling on sweats and a T-shirt, Chay then stripped the bedding and began setting his clothes on the bed. It was time for him to go home.

The bed was nearly covered in small, carefully arranged stacks of clothes by the time Chay pulled out the tuxedo he'd worn the evening he'd first met Arthur. Running his hand over the soft fabric, Chay set the clothes on the bed, and the jacket slipped off. As Chay carefully put it back on the bed, he noticed the label inside. *Made and woven especially for you by Clotho.* Grunting softly, he set the coat on the bed and continued the packing process.

When he pulled the leather pants and jacket out to lay them on the bed, he glanced at the labels as well. *Made especially for Cheyenne*

Dobson by Clotho, the label read. Chay wondered what was going on and who this Clotho was. He'd asked his father and mother, and they'd told him that neither of them had purchased the tuxedo. They both thought Chay had bought it for himself. After hurrying to the closet, Chay lifted the pair of black boots. Just inside the top was a small label: *Clotho, boots worthy of the gods.*

Chay set down the boots and was about to start up his computer to look up this Clotho person when he heard a soft knock on his door. Sniffing, he recognized his mother as she opened his door. "What are you doing, Cheyenne?" she asked as she closed the door and looked around the room.

"I'm going home," he answered without hesitation.

His mother clicked her tongue the way she had when they were pups and she was disappointed with them.

"I need to get away from this place," he explained, and she clicked her tongue again before moving aside some of his clothes to sit on the edge of the bed.

"You're running away," she stated.

"I'm going home," he corrected, and he began getting out the last of his clothes before pulling his luggage out of the closet.

"No, you're hurt and you're running," she stated with conviction. "I know you're in pain, but that's no reason to be cowardly." That hurt, and Chay stopped dead still. "You've told me and your father that Arthur is your mate. You even stood up to your father because you felt so strongly about it. Now, because of what—some notion you haven't even talked over with him—you're ready to run away?" His mother's scathing tone cut through his heartache like a sharp knife. "Some mate you turned out to be. Your father and I brought you up better than that. We didn't spoil you and give you everything in life. You and your brothers worked on the ranch and earned your own way." She stood up and glared at him. Chay had never seen this particular expression on his mother's face. He'd seen anger, and there had been times when she'd punished him, but now his mother looked… betrayed. "Sometimes you have to fight for your mate. Your father fought for me tooth and nail, and I loved him for it more than you'll ever know." She gracefully walked toward the bedroom door. "So if you're willing to walk away from your mate and live a half life because you willingly left the one person in the world who is meant for you, then you aren't the person I thought you were." His mother opened the door and silently left the room, then closed the door behind her.

To say Chay was stunned was an understatement. He stared at the door for a long while. He wanted to argue with her and began compiling arguments in his mind, but they all fell apart in light of the scathing truth his mother had presented.

Chay grabbed a pair of shoes and jammed his feet into them before hurrying out of his room and down the stairs. He passed Alex and Reese as they came up the stairs, but didn't pause as he hurried by. They called to him, and Chay lifted his hand to acknowledge that he'd heard them, but kept on going. He burst outside and ran to the car he used, starting the engine before taking off down the drive. He arrived at the castle quickly, but the main drive gates were closed, so he went around the corner to the private drive Arthur had shown him a few times, and parked outside the garage Arthur used.

Nervously, he stood outside the private entrance and knocked, but no one answered. Looking around, he saw what looked like tourists wandering the grounds, and he remembered Arthur had told him that the castle was usually open for tours. After hurrying around to the side, he followed the line of people going in the tour entrance door, where velvet ropes guided him toward a table where tickets were being sold. When it was his turn, the woman asked if she could help him. "I don't want to buy a ticket, but I'd like to speak to Prince Arthur, please."

"I'm sorry, but the prince rarely makes appearances during tours," she told him politely and looked to the middle-aged couple behind him.

"Could I please speak to Helmut?" Chay asked, making it clear that he wasn't going to get out of line, and she relented, talking quietly into a radio.

"Please step out of line, and he'll be up in a minute," she explained, and Chay moved away as she went back to selling tickets.

Chay stood at the roped-off base of the stairs, looking around the hall as he waited, remembering being here with Arthur.

"Can I help you?" Helmut asked as he approached, his expression bland until he recognized Chay. Then his mouth curled slightly. Chay knew he deserved that.

"I need to find Arthur," Chay explained earnestly. "I wouldn't ask if it wasn't important," Chay added in a whisper, hoping it communicated his desperation.

"He left the castle a few days ago, and he didn't inform me where he was going or when he would be returning," Helmut answered stonily before turning back the way he'd come.

Chay thought of making a dash for it. He knew his way around well enough to find Arthur's private rooms, but they were probably locked, and short of breaking the door down, he wasn't going to get in. What good would it do, anyway, if Arthur wasn't here? Helmut wasn't happy to see him, that was obvious, but he hadn't lied, either. Chay would have been able to smell it.

Leaving the castle, Chay hurried back to his car, turning around in the drive before heading away. He wasn't sure where else to find Arthur, but he did know someone who'd know where he was, so Chay headed for Munich and parked near the Oktoberfest grounds, then ran toward the statue and along the path he'd taken earlier with Arthur. At the fork, he took the smaller trail that led through the woods to the clearing. Chay thought about shifting but instead walked the perimeter until he found a small path near the place where Wilhelm had entered the clearing when he'd been here last. Chay had no idea where it led, but all he was hoping was to leave his scent everywhere, and maybe he could get the attention of one of the pack members. He touched trees and made sure his scent was on the wind. Chay did everything but mark his trail; his wolf wanted him to, but he knew it wouldn't be welcome.

After making the rounds a few times, Chay sat on a log to wait. It didn't take long until he heard and then scented Wilhelm's approach. "You're the last person I expected to see, pup," Wilhelm said as he stepped from the trees.

Chay stood up. "I'm trying to find Arthur, and they said he wasn't at the castle any longer," Chay said without preamble. "You were the only person I knew who might know where he is, and I didn't know how to get in touch with you, so I came here." Earnest honesty was Chay's only hope.

"I haven't seen him in a few days, so I can honestly say I don't know where he is," Wilhelm told him, and Chay stepped back as the huge man stalked toward him. "But if I did, I doubt I'd tell you. I know he's your mate, but after the way you treated him, you're lucky I don't rip you apart right now," Wilhelm growled deeply

"He's the one who wants to have a kid with some woman," Chay said desperately, fear surging inside him, his voice rising.

"Did he say that to you?" Wilhelm asked, his eyes blazing, and Chay shook his head. "I didn't think so. You overheard part of a conversation he had with my brother and put the rest together." Wilhelm shook his head, and Chay felt as low as the decaying leaves under his shoes. "I don't know where he is and I don't know if you deserve to find him or not, but for your wolf's sake, I hope you do."

Chay nodded as respectfully as he could and watched as Wilhelm walked back into the woods, his scent dissipating rapidly. Sitting down on a log, Chay tried to think where he could look next. Then he remembered the phone in his pocket and pulled it out. He probably should have tried calling first, but he had been hoping to explain things to Arthur in person. After punching in the number, Chay waited for the call to connect. It went to voice mail, and Chay hung up without leaving a message. Shoving the phone back into his pocket, Chat stood up and began walking back down the trail. As he walked through the woods, he got the feeling he was being watched, and a few times, he caught the slight scent of a wolf. "I'm leaving, Wilhelm," Chay said out loud as he continued down the trail without slowing his pace.

When Chay reached the main hiking path, he picked up his pace, running down the hill back to his car, not that he had any idea where he was rushing off to. He had no idea where else to look, so once he was in the car and started the engine, he drove home, knowing his only chance was for Arthur to forgive him for acting like a baby and contact him.

There was a limousine in the driveway when he reached the estate, so Chay drove around to the back, parked the car, and went in through what had been the servants' entrance when the house was first built. Being extra quiet so he wouldn't disturb whomever his father was meeting with, Chay took the back stairs and went to his room. Nothing had changed. His clothes were still laid out on his bed, but it seemed like a stupid gesture now that all he wanted was to find Arthur and tell him that he was sorry. His mother was right, he had been running, and in the process, he'd pushed Arthur away. Now he might not get him back.

Chay sat in his chair, his arms and legs itching like crazy. The only time he hadn't itched was when he was with Arthur. Nothing bothered him then. Maybe they could have worked out the whole pup thing and managed somehow to provide Arthur with an heir. Even his wolf didn't reject the idea outright—probably because he was pining so badly for his mate that he'd agree to anything to get Arthur back. But a thought crept into the back of his mind that allowing his mate to be happy was more important than anything he wanted. If Arthur would be happy with someone who could give him an heir, then he'd somehow live with his heartache knowing Arthur was happy.

A pounding on his door made him jump, and Alex barreled into the room, opening the door so hard it banged on its hinges. "Dad asked me to come get you. He's got someone he wants us all to meet."

Chay nodded as he stood up. "Tell him I'll be right down." Chay was already clutching some clothes from the bed, and stripped off his T-shirt as Alex reached the door.

A sharp intake of air made him turn around, and he saw Alex staring at him. "Is it always like that?" Alex asked.

Chay looked at his chest, which was covered in red marks that started itching as soon as he looked at them. "Yes. Though sometimes it's worse," Chay explained as he pulled on a cotton shirt and fastened the buttons quickly to hide his skin.

Alex didn't say anything more, just closed the door quietly as he left. Chay shucked his sweatpants and pulled on nice slacks. Then he hurried into the bathroom. He shaved quickly and combed his hair before tugging on dress socks and shoes. After making sure he was presentable, Chay left his room and walked toward the stairs. At the top, out of sight, he sniffed and knew his father was entertaining another wolf. Whoever it was wasn't familiar, and Chay descended the stairs, following the voices to the room his father used to entertain guests.

When he entered, everyone stood, and Chay wondered why. "This is my son Cheyenne," his father said in his booming voice. "Cheyenne, this is my counterpart in Europe, Hans-Holman Behrenbaum."

Chay bared his throat to show respect before shaking the man's hand. "Pleased to meet you," Chay said in German.

"It seems you've caused a bit of a stir," Alpha Behrenbaum began as he sat back down. Chay's father motioned Chay to a chair with one of his brothers on either side. "It seems you showed up on pack land without an invitation and have stirred up a hornet's nest with some very powerful families in the area."

"Prince Arthur took me to the pack lands, and as soon as I realized what they were, I asked to leave," Chay explained.

"We understand that, but you showed up there again today, uninvited and unescorted. We cannot have that. The alpha of the local pack was not happy about the intrusion. He made his feelings clear, and I agree that we cannot have non-pack wolves showing up on pack land without permission." Alpha Behrenbaum gave Chay a good dose of German sternness. "I have been further informed that you overheard certain conversations that were considered confidential, ones you should either have ignored or moved out of earshot from, but didn't. Instead, you took it upon yourself to act on that information in a way that disrespects our way of life and the institution at the very heart of who we are—lifelong matehood between souls."

Chay swallowed hard and nodded. He had nothing to say in his defense, and he didn't try.

"The most sacred bond that exists in our world is the soul-deep bond between mates. By turning your back on your mate, you have relegated your wolf to wither and eventually die. Your human side will survive, but you will spend the rest of your life wondering if things could have been different," Alpha Behrenbaum told him sternly. "Lone wolves are dangerous, and therefore you will not be welcome in any pack anywhere." Chay looked at his father, who nodded with equal sternness.

"It's what she showed me this morning," Chay said. "A woman came to me and showed me that I would be alone. But she also showed me Prince Arthur playing with his heir. He was happy, so if the price for him being happy is for me to be alone, then that's the price I'm willing to pay. Arthur is my mate, but if I can't give him what he wants and needs, then that's what I'm willing to do."

Chay saw the two alphas share a glance of confusion. "What woman, Cheyenne?" his father asked.

"I've had these dreams. The first was the night of the reception. She came to me in my sleep and showed me images from the reception, and when I woke up, I found the tuxedo I wore in my room. I thought it was from you and I didn't want to disappoint you, so I put it on and went." The words spilled out quickly. "That was where I met Prince Arthur, but I thought there was no way I was good enough for him, so I had planned to go home, and she came to me again. This time she showed me what I'd be missing, and I found the leather pants, jacket, and riding boots. That was when Prince Arthur came to the house to take me to his castle. Both those times she came in my dreams, but today she was in my room and she spoke to me. That's why I went to the castle and to pack land. I was trying to find Arthur, but I couldn't."

"Did the woman have a name?" Alpha Behrenbaum asked.

"She never said, but the clothes all had the same name in the label: Clotho. I don't know who that is, though," Chay explained. "Today she showed me what I told you earlier." Chay stood up. "Excuse me, but I have packing to finish. I'm going home." Chay nodded to Alpha Behrenbaum. "Please tell those I have wronged that I did not wish to offend and that I won't darken their doorstep again." Chay walked toward the door. "I am sorry for any trouble I caused you, as well. It was unintentional." Chay's back ached, he itched so badly. He was tempted to try scratching it on the doorframe, but he wasn't going to embarrass anyone. He simply had to get out of the room.

"That isn't good enough," his father said, and Chay stopped, standing stock-still. "Alpha Behrenbaum can deliver your message to Alpha Wilhelm and his family if he chooses. But he is not your messenger, and he cannot and will not deliver a message to the person you've wronged most. Only you can do that."

Chay stared at his father, hoping he'd enlighten him on how to do that. "I've tried to find Arthur all afternoon, and no one I've spoken with knows where he is. And I suspect that if they did, they wouldn't tell me anyway." Chay placed his hand on the door. He understood what he'd done, but he wasn't sure how to make it right, and everyone here was full of recriminations but short on suggestions. The itching was getting worse, and he had to get out of there before his head exploded. After pulling open the door, he stepped out and ran into someone.

Arms wrapped around him and Chay inhaled, the sweet scent he remembered and had longed for filling his nose. "Arthur," Chay mumbled softly into his shirt as he clutched his mate as tightly as he could. "I'm sorry," he said, even though he knew his voice was muffled by Arthur's shirt. "I should have talked to you instead of running off."

"Yes, you should have," Arthur told him. "Because if you had, you would have learned that when I said I would get an heir, I meant with you. We can find a surrogate. I didn't mean that I was going to marry Lizette." Arthur loosened his hold, and Chay stepped away, letting Arthur step into the room.

"I see he finally found you," Alpha Behrenbaum said to Arthur with a slight smile, and Chay knew he'd been played—not that he really cared, if it meant getting Arthur back. "How long were you out there?"

"I was just about to knock when Chay opened the door. I got your message that you were here," Arthur said, and Chay realized he wasn't being played as much as taught a lesson. It seemed both of the alphas had a few tricks up their sleeves. "What are you up to, Uncle?" Arthur asked. "Wilhelm told me Chay had been trying to find me."

"I think the two of you need some time to talk," Chay's father said before turning to Alpha Behrenbaum. "Could I interest you in a drink and perhaps dinner?" The two powerful wolves didn't seem to be paying them any attention for the moment, and Chay used the opportunity to take Arthur's hand and lead him out and up the stairs to his room. Chay closed the door and leaned against it, staring at Arthur, finding it hard to believe he was here.

"I missed you," Chay began. "I should have talked to you instead of leaving like that, and I shouldn't have listened in on your conversation. I need to learn to trust that the Fates knew what they were doing when they destined us as mates."

"I heard what you said," Arthur told him. "I know why you did what you did and that you were willing to make yourself unhappy because you thought that would make me happy."

"I thought you'd just arrived," Chay said, and Arthur smirked. "You lied? How? They would have smelled you."

Arthur rolled his eyes. "Do you think after being the only human in a family of wolves that I don't know ways to disguise my scent and move without making a sound? If I wanted to get away with anything as a kid, those were necessary skills." Arthur stepped closer. "You're shaking."

Chay nodded. "I've wanted to rip my skin off all day long. I went to the castle, and Helmut said you'd left. I tried the clearing and talked to your cousin, but he didn't know where you were either. The more I looked, the worse the itching got." Chay closed his eyes, and Arthur held him close, his hands lightly stroking along his back. Chay couldn't help the sigh that escaped as he felt the first relief from hours of relentless itching.

"I take it that feels good," Arthur said, and Chay nodded against his chest before angling his face to Arthur's for a kiss, which he got, in spades. Arthur took him with a hard, demanding kiss that took Chay's breath away. "There are some things we need to get straight," Arthur told him once their lips parted. "We're mates. That means no more leaving, even if you think it's for my own good."

Chay nodded. "And no having children without me." Chay's wolf definitely liked that idea.

"Agreed, sort of. I do need an heir eventually, but we can look into artificial insemination. There are mateless women in Wilhelm's pack who might be willing to help." Arthur kissed him again, and Chay felt them move toward the bed. "I had no intention of ever marrying or having children with Lizette. You're my mate, and whatever we do, we do together. That includes deciding how and when we have children. Agreed?" Arthur asked, and Chay answered with a lunge that propelled both of them onto the bed. "I'll take that as a yes," Arthur chuckled as they bounced on the mattress.

"Yes," Chay answered happily, raining kisses onto Arthur's lips. "I missed you so much," Chay confessed. "I went running every night so I could keep my wolf worn out, but he still mourned the loss."

"I know," Arthur said, and Chay stilled as their eyes locked. "I heard you calling. I couldn't stay away, so I drove over here a few times, and I heard you crying at night. It nearly broke my heart, and I wish I'd simply found you and shaken the truth out of you, but I figured you needed some time to come around on your own. Who would have known you would be so damned... stubborn."

"Stupid?" Chay offered with a self-deprecating smile.

"That too," Arthur said as he shifted them on the bed, and Chay now peered up into Arthur's blue eyes. "But I think we were both guilty of that. I should have been honest with you about my concerns instead of keeping them from you and trying to deal with it on my own." Arthur moved in for another kiss as Chay felt Arthur opening the buttons of his shirt. Chay placed his hands on Arthur's to still them. The kissing stopped as Arthur appeared confused.

"My skin is really bad," Chay said as a lump of fear formed in his throat.

"Do you itch now?" Arthur asked, and Chay thought for a second, taking a quick inventory, shaking his head. "But it did just a while ago?"

"Yes," Chay answered, and Arthur grinned and resumed removing Chay's shirt. When the fabric parted and fell away, Arthur smiled as he looked down at his chest.

"Looks perfect to me," Arthur declared before bending forward and licking a nipple, to Chay's delight. "You always looked perfect," Arthur added, and Chay arched his back as Arthur licked along his skin. "I'm going to mark you," Arthur explained as he licked up to Chay's shoulder. "I intend to make you mine and love you forever. If you have any objection, then say so now."

Chay's wolf leapt forward, nearly threatening him with revolt if he objected, not that Chay had any intention of rejecting his mate now or ever again. Shaking his head, Chay eventually managed to speak. "No... I mean, yes... I mean... do it!" Chay pulled Arthur into another kiss so he wouldn't babble on and used that to tell Arthur exactly how he felt. As their kisses deepened, Chay began to lose control of his wolf, the passion and excitement taking their toll on his control. He tried removing Arthur's shirt nicely, he really did, but the sound of fabric tearing filled the room, and then Arthur's chest pressed to his. Chay sighed at the touch and began working on Arthur's pants.

"Hold on," Arthur said as he jumped off the bed. "I like these pants." Arthur stripped them off as Chay stripped too, and clothes flew through the air before crumpling on the floor. Arthur stalked back onto the bed and tackled Chay down onto the mattress.

"Fuck me, Arthur," Chay pleaded. "Make me yours forever."

"You need to claim me, remember?" Arthur told him breathlessly, and Chay reached for the nightstand to retrieve some lube.

"I will," Chay promised. There was no way he was going to put off claiming his mate. His wolf had had too much disappointment and was not going to be held back again. "Now, take me!" Chay growled, and Arthur slicked his fingers. Chay lifted his legs, and Arthur's fingers plunged into him. Chay growled as first pain and then intense pleasure barreled through him. "Arthur!"

"I need to take my time," he explained. "This is your first time. I know your wolf is howling, but I won't hurt you," Arthur explained, and Chay keened when Arthur touched a spot inside him that sent electric shocks through his body. "You need to be quiet, we're in your parents' home," Arthur said, and Chay cried out again.

"Fuck it, and fuck me," Chay bayed, and he felt Arthur's fingers slide from his body. He immediately missed them even as Arthur lifted Chay's feet to his shoulders. He felt empty right up to the second Arthur began pressing inside him. Chay gasped as his wolf growled. Arthur stopped moving, and Chay breathed through the excitement and pleasure until Arthur pressed deeper. "Arthur," Chay moaned and tried to scoot closer. He needed his mate, and his instincts screamed at him to finally make his mate his forever. Arthur surged forward, burying himself deep as the breath sailed from Chay's lungs. "Yes," Chay moaned breathlessly. Arthur stilled, leaning over him and slowly lowering his head until their lips met. "Mark me as yours," Chay mumbled.

Arthur withdrew slightly and then snapped his hips forward. Chay gasped at the sensation. "I already have. You can feel in your heart that I'm yours. Your wolf knows it and your body knows it." Arthur lifted one of Chay's arms, showing it to him. "See. The redness is gone."

Chay looked at what Arthur was showing him. His arm was smooth and clear. No rash or red marks. Chay wanted to see if the rest of his body was the same way, but Arthur snapped his hips again and the thought flew from his head. That would keep.

Arthur deepened his strokes, driving into Chay's body. Chay had an overwhelming urge to mark his mate. After lifting his head, he tugged Arthur to him. He pressed Arthur's head to one side and felt his canines lower as his eyes shifted. Chay bit down on Arthur's shoulder and felt the bond with his mate form as a warmth and calm that he'd never felt before flooded through his body. Holding tight, Chay felt Arthur thrust deep and hard as he screamed his release. Chay retracted his canines, adding his own howl to Arthur's cry as he keened out to the gods and Fates that he was well and truly mated, coming with flashes of light and bursts of amazing clarity. In those few seconds, he flashed back to the vision the woman in white had shown him, but this time as Arthur played with his son, Chay heard their laughter and saw himself walk into the room, joining his mate and their son as they played together. She'd shown him how lonely he'd be without Arthur and how happy he'd be with him.

"Are you okay?" Arthur asked him breathlessly, and Chay opened his eyes to Arthur's concerned expression. "You zoned out for a while."

Chay nodded on the pillow. "I know, but I understand now. I know who Clotho is." Chay tugged Arthur to him, licking the shoulder he'd bitten.

"I don't understand," Arthur said, and Chay explained what had happened.

"Every time I did something that might take me away from you, she intervened and pushed me toward you. I think she's a goddess."

Soft laughter filled the room, and they both jumped as a woman dressed all in white appeared at the foot of the bed. Arthur stared and moved closer to Chay, who looked back and smiled.

"Thank you for everything," Chay said.

"You're welcome, Cheyenne," she said softly. "Be happy," she said to both of them. "As usual, the wheels were right," she explained enigmatically, and Chay wondered what she meant, but she was already starting to fade.

"I'll think of you whenever I wear the clothes," Chay said, and she stopped, her image shimmering but no longer fading.

"Think of him; love each other," she said, indicating Arthur, "and you'll make me very happy." With those last words, she faded from sight.

"Do you know who that was?" Arthur asked.

"Clotho," Chay answered.

"Yes," Arthur agreed with a kiss. "She's one of the Fates." Arthur kissed him hard, wrapping Chay in his arms. "She said to love each other and we'll make her happy," Arthur reminded him as he pressed him into the mattress. "I think we should get started with that," Arthur said with a mischievous grin and wriggled his hips against Chay's. "I love you, Cheyenne, forever and ever."

"I love you too, more than I can express," Chay said before kissing the grin off Arthur's face. And far away, deep in the cave, as the wheels spun, names were called, and their fates written down, Clotho smiled.

ANDREW GREY grew up in western Michigan with a father who loved to tell stories and a mother who loved to read them. Since then he has lived throughout the country and traveled throughout the world. He has a master's degree from the University of Wisconsin-Milwaukee and works in information systems for a large corporation. Andrew's hobbies include collecting antiques, gardening, and leaving his dirty dishes anywhere but in the sink (particularly when writing). He considers himself blessed with an accepting family, fantastic friends, and the world's most supportive and loving partner. Andrew currently lives in beautiful historic Carlisle, Pennsylvania.

Visit Andrew's website at http://www.andrewgreybooks.com and blog at http://andrewgreybooks.livejournal.com/.

E-mail him at andrewgrey@comcast.net.

JUMP

MARY CALMES

PROLOGUE

HIS smile was wicked, his canines noticeable. Clotho, the spinner, oldest of the three, the one who wove the threads of each life together, did not like the looks of him. Why was he there? No one ever came to see them unannounced; it simply wasn't done.

"You? Who are you?"

"Hermes," he answered as he stalked closer.

But she knew Hermes, didn't she? And this man was sleeker, darker. Weren't the messenger god's eyes blue? Not flashing onyx?

She called, then, for her sister Lachesis. Surely the measurer—the one who counted and checked the threads—would know what to do.

"Yes?" the beauty Lachesis asked as she strolled into the comfortable, richly decorated chamber. The entire temple was lavishly furnished, adorned with all manner of treasure. Thus did all the gods of Olympus seek to find favor with the Fates for their beloved mortals. Gifts were always appreciated.

"Look there." Clotho pointed at the bronze-skinned, raven-haired man. "Is that Hermes?"

"Something like that." Lachesis tilted her head thoughtfully. "I heard his name just the other day, and it was… close."

"Call Atropos. I want her to see."

He grinned at both Fates, and Lachesis felt a shiver run down her back. Surely a god would not frighten and entice her at the same….

"You've come to kill us." Clotho's eyes got huge.

"Not kill," he assured her, and she saw it then; he was a predator. "Unless you force me."

"What have you done to Hermes?" Lachesis asked, the fear sinking into her.

He made a sound in the back of his throat. "I am he, haven't you heard?"

"What's going on?" Atropos asked as she sailed into the room, the most ravishing of the three, her russet hair falling in silken curls almost to the floor. The sheer, gauzy toga she wore collected around her feet like a cloud.

"He came in past the temple guards," Clotho informed her newly arrived sister—the cutter—the ender of life, the one with the shears. "But he's not one of us, Atropos. He's an outsider. He's not a god."

She narrowed her eyes, taking his measure. "No, he's a god. A very powerful one and more… like us. How?"

The sinister look returned. "I decide the fate of souls as well, just like you."

But he wasn't one of them, one of the Moirai, and yet Atropos could find no deceit in his words. He spoke the truth; he dealt in fate, but how…?

"Atropos?" Both her sisters called her.

They needed her to figure it out. All of them had the sight, but Atropos—who had to know when exactly to end a life before it touched too many, became more than it should, or crossed over into immortality—was the one the oracles revered.

"But who…?"

She inhaled, and the aroma of sandalwood and cinnamon, juniper and cedar, reached her. "You smell divine."

"And I taste like honey," he said, his dark, hooded eyes having their desired effect as he spoke. Atropos felt her skin heat.

"Who are you?" she whispered.

"Hermes," he answered softly for the second time and walked toward the enormous loom that sat by the window, noting the many spools and the singular, wickedly sharp shears. He had never seen another pair exactly like them and that made sense, really.

"You're not," Lachesis challenged, finding her voice and her courage, advancing on him. She was angry. Never was she supposed to feel threatened in her holy temple. Zeus himself protected them.

"I wasn't at the beginning." His predatory gaze fell on her. "But I am baptized anew. And as the people worship, then is it made real. Yes?"

Atropos agreed. "That is so. You are a god and a Fate. Speak your true lineage."

"I am Hermanubis, and I have come simply for a favor."

"Tell me."

"I seek a thread newly cut."

A soul newly ended. He was looking for someone. But that made no sense. Why? Why did he need a favor? He was powerful. He... unless.... "The one you seek, the one you desire, is not yours, but ours."

"Yes."

All three Fates looked at him with interest. Surprisingly, it was Clotho, the worker, the weaver, who was able to find her voice.

"Anubis, from the mountain, you have no power here."

"But I do," he informed her, and this time parted his lips so she could clearly see the sharp teeth of the jackal. "Your own people allowed me here; your gods gave me entrance."

"What have you done to Hermes?" Lachesis nearly shouted at him.

He licked his lips and they knew.

Atropos paled. "Such big teeth you have."

Again it was Clotho who took a breath, calming her nerves, and then spoke. "Tell me of the one you seek. Man or woman?"

His eyes met hers. "*He* was born in the city of the warrior goddess but found a home by my river, with my brother."

Everything changed in that instant because the request was no longer a selfish one.

Brother.

"You don't seek this man for yourself?"

He shook his head, just a little. "I'm a lover of women, can't you tell?"

Lachesis was going to go up in flames if he didn't stop looking at them like that. "I... you... who?"

Clotho rolled her eyes. "Your brother, you say?"

He didn't respond, instead pointing to a row of stacked spools. "The boy's life was freshly ended. It would be one of those."

"Boy, you said. So I did not cut because the thread began to fray, because it was time?"

"No," he snapped, and from his tone, the way his voice rose for a second, they all understood why the thread of life had been cut.

Atropos furrowed her brow. "Was it quick, what was inflicted on him?"

"No, lady. My brother Horus, he had enemies, and his man was alone when they found him."

She took a breath. "When did it happen?"

"He was lost to my brother on the night of the hunter's moon."

"Which was two days ago." Lachesis bit her lip. "How goes your brother?"

"He was inconsolable."

"Was?"

There was no answer to the question, and Clotho saw the pain on the god's face for only a fleeting moment—all he would allow.

"I know the one." Atropos cleared her throat. "I cut as fast as I could."

"Yours was the only mercy."

"Tell us what you would have us do."

"Give it to me," he said, holding out his hand. "His thread, and I will leave this place."

There were stunned. A small thread could be thousands of lifetimes. Each soul had so many, and they were supposed to oversee and safeguard every incarnation. A reel of string was never to be parted with; it simply wasn't done. It was all stored and then used over again each eon.

"You cannot be serious."

The heat and glint in the inky depths of his eyes vanished in a heartbeat. "I am. I ask only for the one and will never again darken your door should you do me this service."

"But… but who will weave it? There are none who can spin the thread of life but us."

"I know another."

"Who?"

"I need the thread," he demanded instead of answering, his low tone suggestive of warning.

Atropos crossed the room to where the spools she had recently cut sat. "Tell me the man's name."

"Cassius."

"Something more."

"He had the sight."

"A seer?"

"An oracle, yes."

Lachesis looked at him. "You cannot bind a mortal and a god together. One always frays and breaks."

"Horus has already forfeited his immortality."

They were stunned; the only sound in the room was the warm breeze blowing through it.

"That is unheard of," Atropos finally said around the lump in her throat. There was no greater gift, no greater sacrifice for a god to make. "Truly?"

"Truly," he said, his voice hoarse and gravelly. "I placed him in his tomb myself." The look on his face, the pain there, was fleeting.

"His decision was regrettable."

"No. The men who killed his love, and in turn him—" He clipped his words, and the ice in them was evident. "Their actions were regretful."

"They were treated to your displeasure."

"They were treated to my wrath," he whispered.

Atropos could not help but feel a shiver of dread. Anubis unleashed in fury and pain was far too terrifying to contemplate.

No one spoke, and only the flower-scented air softly ruffling curtains, touching skin, playing with thread, created any sense of normalcy.

"If you bring your brother's thread," Clotho began, taking a breath. "I will spin it with that of Cassius when next it is the mortal's time on Earth."

He stared at her a moment before glowering. "I must be certain, and Isis is very good at piecing things together. She will do it."

Atropos understood. "There is no doubt that she has the power to do so, but we have the practice. In this instance, we are best. Bring the thread. We will weave it."

"And what is your price for this?"

"Your protection," she implored. "Already there are changes. You are here when you should not be able to be. Keep us well within our temple."

He thought about it a minute because his word was his bond. Once he agreed, it was done.

"What do you say?"

Isis had said she would try, but she was not certain she could do it. Doing something out of obsession and fear was different from doing it out of compassion for another. What she had done for Osiris.... Failure had never been an option. It was not *her* soul bereft of love if she failed. She said she would do her best for Horus, but Anubis needed a guarantee. It was his way.

"I agree. I will give you my brother's thread and you will weave it with that of Cassius."

"Even woven together," Clotho said almost sadly, "they will still need a connection to make the thread become one, for it to become a true joining. Thread can be woven close. That is fate, but union is not."

"You're saying that some repeat a thousand lifetimes finding each other, knowing each other, but never truly bond?"

"Yes."

He shook his head. "Had you seen them, you would understand. I never saw Horus rise to the true height of his divinity until he loved and was loved in return."

Atropos studied him, and even though he had at first threatened them, she still felt a pang of concern. Surprising man, to make her feel so much.

"When will you bring the thread?"

He turned his hand palm up, and she saw the spool there. The thread was jet black, and when he passed it to her, the smell of sandalwood rose from it.

"When it is Cassius's time again, we shall call you." Lachesis sighed, softening toward him in spite of herself. His eyes, his voice, were mesmerizing.

"No need to call. I will arrive. I'll know."

"You are so sure?"

"You will bind both threads together, my brother's and that of Cassius. I will know."

Atropos saw his melancholy then, finally, and just like her sisters, her heart went out to him.

"You miss him, your brother."

His bottomless black eyes told her everything.

"You should have just asked instead of threatening. We are the same after all, you and us."

"No," he said as he turned to leave. "You weave and measure and cut. My part is after the severing. I see the truth and weigh the life and pass judgment."

All eyes followed him.

"Honor your side of the bargain as I honor mine lest I return when I'm hungry."

They didn't bother wondering what change his interference would bring. Better to simply do as he bade them and be graced with his divine protection.

CHAPTER ONE

I WAS in my office after eight, finally finishing up for the night, all fires put out for the day, when my assistant, Snow Drake, walked in and locked the door behind her.

"Oh God, what," I groaned.

She made a cutting motion across her neck at the same moment she turned off the lights. I had to sit there with only the light of my laptop and wait. Someone knocked on the door. Whoever it was tried to peer through the frosted glass pane that stretched the length of the door on one side and then rapped on it.

"Who are we hiding from?" I whispered to Snow.

"Reece," she whispered back.

I rolled my eyes, which she couldn't see in the dark, and went back to finishing up the e-mail I had been working on before she came in.

Long minutes later, Snow turned the lights back on, but only after she peeked out the door to see if Reece was gone.

"You know," I said as she dropped papers she carried with her into my inbox. "If you don't want to see him again, maybe you should just tell him."

"I did, but now he wants to talk," she said, like there was nothing in the world as revolting as the idea of doing that. "I don't want to talk to him. We fucked, case closed."

"You're such a romantic," I said, standing up, still looking at my laptop screen.

"It was boring as hell," she grunted, stepping in beside me, the scent of whatever perfume she'd put on that morning still clinging to her. "He was all 'tell me it feels good, baby, tell me you want it.'" She made a gagging noise in the back of her throat before rolling her eyes. "God, what a tool."

"You didn't laugh in the middle of sex again, did you?"

"Uh, yeah, I did." She made a face, nodding at the same time. "How could I not?"

I groaned. "That's just mean."

"Needy men give me hives."

I stopped listening to her then, distracted by a text message on my phone. I was apparently late for drinks with friends, my friend Stuart reminding me that I had promised. Must have been a moment of weakness, because normally after a whole day of working and experiencing my visions, I just wanted to go home and be by myself in the quiet. Not that I was some solitary loner, but I needed my downtime to decompress more than most.

"That guy Lucas came by earlier to see you," Snow mused on. "But you were swamped with meetings today, so I explained to him he had no chance of seeing you."

I grunted, turning back to my laptop to finish up my last batch of e-mails. I had to forward closed contracts to the processing department so they could send out statements for final billing. New contracts went to records, my billable hours and expense reports to accounting, and a spreadsheet of clients I had met with and would not be taking on went to my boss, Director of Client Services Rosalie Chun. After four years of working together, she didn't question me anymore. If I said I couldn't help a certain person, she sent them a letter of rejection. And I felt bad, but the truth, for me, was not just a feeling. I *knew*.

If I took you on as a client, I could, and would, find your love for you. From computer matching to speed dating to long romantic weekend getaways, I would move you from interest to lust to love. They were a gift, my visions, and I was using it, I felt, for good. My boss was thrilled with me; I was her number one counselor, cupid, matchmaker... whatever anyone wanted to call me. The real title was relationship coordinator, and I was, without a doubt, the best one at Nostalgia.

At our company, the emphasis was on a sort of sweet yesteryear approach to a relationship. It was romance first, and then love. If you jumped the gun and slept with the person you were supposed to be simply seeing, you were dropped from the program, and you didn't get your deposit back. It was why the first five dates were chaperoned; we really wanted people to feel the difference between dating and Nostalgia dating. Our competitors, other matchmaking services, made fun of us, but our Chicago-based company that had started five years ago was still going strong. We were always hiring new coordinators to keep up with the influx of clients, and just this month, we had added three more to our staff. Not that I would get to know the rookies, not at first. They all migrated toward Kyle Jennings, not me. They all wanted to learn from him, talk to him, hang out with him, and bask in the glow of his reflected beauty.

And I understood. I did. If I was new and I had the choice of sitting in the office with the short, thin, bald guy with rimless glasses and a bow tie who wore a fedora when he went out, or the tall, square-jawed, athletic, golden sun god, I would pick Kyle too. The man was all long, sinewy muscles and sleek, sun-kissed hair and skin, with a grin that could melt you through the floor. New clients always picked him. The new coordinators always wanted to shadow him. Everybody *had* to have him, and I understood why. If he looked and sounded like that, then he must have been the top producer at the company. He was perfect; it had to be him. Except… it wasn't him. It was me.

And what was funny was that the people who got assigned to shadowing me, the ones who didn't raise their hands quickly enough to get Kyle instead, those people usually ended up wanting to remain with me after the first day. Even if the model crooked his finger at them, even if Kyle offered to take them out with him as well, they politely but firmly turned him down. Being under *my* wing, it turned out, was good too.

While Kyle spent the first day talking about his favorite thing—himself—I talked about what our newest employees needed to know and what they could accomplish with us. I explained what they could make and where they could be in two years with the right contacts, loyalty, and dedication. In short, I told them how I could help make their dreams come true. They wanted to excel, they wanted to make money, and they wanted to gain experience, build their reputation and their client list. Everyone had seen the reality shows; they knew where the big money was. If you got enough of a buzz going, secured an influential customer base, became the go-to person for the rich and powerful—and you were discreet—the sky was the limit. Everyone dreamed of having their own show on a channel like Bravo, and it was obtainable if you cared and were willing to work hard. The right clientele was the key, and the first benchmark was success. You had to be able to point at a well-made match, and then several, and have people gush about you. I had an endless stream—from multimillionaires to CEOs to nice people who were just too damn busy to date.

The thing was, though, that looking at me, no one saw I was, in fact, the love god. They missed me because I was quiet and shy, and the bow tie was the kiss of death. No one ever took a second look at me unless they had to.

The fact that I was ignored didn't bother me in the least. I preferred it that way. I had a small circle of friends, the few serious-minded people who wanted to learn from me and follow in my footsteps, and my really annoying assistant.

"… and you know whenever I see that guy Ted from asset management, he always asks about you. He wants to know if you're still seeing Ben Coffman and makes me promise to tell him the second you guys break up."

I came back into a conversation Snow was still carrying on even though I had checked out for awhile. The woman never stopped talking.

"Did you hear me?"

It was impossible not to hear her. "You know very well that Ben and I broke up months ago," I reminded her, turning my head to look into her eyes. I was five nine to her five eight, so towering over her and glaring her into quiet submission had never been an option. "But that's none of anyone else's business but mine here, is it?"

She sucked in her breath, which she did whenever I suddenly stared at her. It was cute and so was she. "What?"

I chuckled. "Ted Crowley can kiss my ass."

"I'm sure he'd love to," she said cheerfully. "A lot of men would."

It was nice that she thought so.

"What?" She was suddenly scowling.

As I stared at Snow and she gazed back at me, I wondered how an ex-stripper had come to be the one I depended on for everything.

"Why're you looking at me like that?"

"I can't look at you?" I asked.

"You can do whatever you want," she assured me, trembling just a bit.

Snow Drake did not look like the kind of woman who would be working in an office; she looked as if she belonged in Hollywood, all fragile beauty and big Bambi eyes. Her skin reminded me of those Greek statues in museums—alabaster perfection—and her eyes were a warm chocolate brown with long, thick lashes. Short-cropped platinum blonde curls framed her face. She looked like a 1940s silver-screen siren come to life, complete with full, pouty lips and an hourglass figure. The woman stopped traffic.

She got offers constantly, legitimate photographers stopping her on the street, asking her to let them photograph her. They usually got scowls in return for their flattery because all she wanted to do was sit at her desk outside my office. I said often that her life's ambition couldn't be to remain my assistant forever. I wanted her to follow her dreams. She always came back with the same snarky retort: What did I know about her dreams? To her, security, safety, and routine were the most important things of all. Her loyalty to me was absolute because I gave her life order, and she, in turn, took care of me.

She had been working days as a walking courier and nights as a stripper when she had delivered a package to an office down the hall from mine. She saw me walk by and, for whatever reason, followed me. In my reception area were several people with clipboards, filling out applications, waiting to see me about an assistant position. In our interview, she informed me that I could put her in any position I wanted.

I scowled.

She waggled her eyebrows at me.

I explained that she couldn't dress like a whore in my office.

She asked me what I wanted her to wear to bed.

"I'm gay," I said.

"We'll see," she volleyed.

I rolled my eyes and she flashed me dimples. She then proceeded to tell me that if I hired her, she'd take me to a really good Mexican place.

"How good?"

She gently jabbed me in the side with her elbow.

"Why do you dye your hair white blonde?"

"Platinum blonde," she corrected.

"Why?"

She tilted her head. "Why do you wear a bow tie?"

"I like it."

She shrugged. "Same."

The flirting was funny, but underneath there was a desperation that worried me. She was on the brink, staring down into the abyss. Stripping wasn't enough, and she wasn't getting by on her second job either. She needed one career, not three or four jobs. She did not want to exchange stripping for escorting, but the money she knew she could make was getting harder and harder to turn down. She slept around anyway; why not make some cash doing it? We had a frank conversation, and for whatever reason, she felt safe to dump it all on me.

Of course I had seen it, as I did everything, the moment she looked into my eyes. I saw what the transformation would look like on her. It had made me shiver.

She really liked that.

Of course, when I told her she was hired, she leaned out into the hall and informed all the others that the job was hers.

"Get up outta here, bitches; I'm the new decoration in the man's office."

God. When I had looked into her future, I had missed that her personality was so loud. She was an itty-bitty kitten with a huge attack-dog personality. The woman was impossible not to both love and want to throw out a window. Just the constant barrage of conversation was exhausting.

But I was the first person who had believed in her enough to take a chance with my time and money. Since my faith had never wavered and after two years, going on three, I was still in her life—the one and only constant she could point to—she guarded me and our relationship with fanatic devotion. I teased her often with the promise that even if a bus hit me, she would still have a job at Devlin Hammond. Everybody wanted her.

"Super," she simpered. "I just want to work for you."

I understood finally. I equaled home for her. It was fine with me.

"What did you ever even see in Ben?" she asked suddenly.

I had been dating Ben Coffman for a year before I got up the nerve to tell him my secret. And of course the moment the words were out, I *saw* him running out the door before he actually did it. Lesson learned. I had spoken to my mother that night, called her in Taos where she lived with my artist stepfather. They were both on the phone with me, and it was nice.

"Screw him," my stepfather, Jeddah Prince, said.

"Jed, you're supposed to be all Zen," I teased him.

"Well, what the hell, Cass." He was annoyed for me; I could hear it clear as day. "You finally decide to trust someone, and he turns out to not be worth the effort? I'm pissed!"

"Me too," my mother chimed in. "But, honey, what did I tell you?"

"That my guy will be someone that my gift chooses," I said, trying not to roll my eyes.

"Don't placate me, Cassidy Jane," she warned. "Your gift will pick someone, and he'll know you're special, know that you're a prize and what your heart is worth. I would have never made it without you. You, your father, and now Jed are the blessings of my life. Wait for yours, angel, he's coming."

She always said the same thing.

"But in the meantime, put a lid on it."

Jed thought that was funny. His laughter was warm over the phone.

It had always been my mother's hard and fast rule. Never, ever, trust anyone with the truth about the gift.

Ben Coffman had returned a week later, having calmed down from thinking I was crazy. He'd decided that maybe I had just been testing him, for whatever reason. It was the only logical conclusion he could come to. The thing that kept going through my mind was *thank God I never gave him keys*. Locks were a pain in the ass to get changed.

I said it was me, not him; he was too good for me, so I had come up with a wild story to push him away. He deserved better, blah blah blah, and we parted on good terms, or at least he thought so, and I turned the deadbolt behind him when he left. No more Ben.

"Cass?"

I looked up at Snow. "Sorry, my mind drifted."

"Yeah, I got that," she said sarcastically. "So? Why Ben?"

It took me a second. "I thought he was nice."

She made a sound in the back of her throat. "He wasn't even hot."

"There's more to a man than just looks."

She grunted. "If you say so, but have you noticed that you only go for the ugly ones."

"Ugly?"

"Yeah, I don't get it."

"There's more to life than being pretty."

"Is there?"

"People used to say that's all you were," I reminded her.

"Yep," she agreed, "used to."

"You're such a snob."

"And?"

I grunted at her and was going to close my laptop when her hand on my wrist stopped me. Our eyes met.

"All joking aside, I want you to find somebody nice. You deserve it."

"Yes, dear, so now tomorrow—"

"Cassidy," she said softly, stepping in close to me, tipping her head back just a bit to hold my gaze. "I'm serious. I don't want you to be alone with cats."

I chuckled. "I like cats."

"I like them too," she said with a snort, "but I want you to have some human companionship."

"Fine."

"And he needs to be at least decent looking, okay? Pretty goes a long way."

"But I'm not pretty. How is not-pretty supposed to trap pretty?"

She hit me hard on the bicep. It hurt.

"Shit, Snow," I whined. The woman was stronger than she looked.

"You're gorgeous. Cut the crap!"

I was nowhere near there. "Whatever you say."

She lunged at me, wrapped her arms around my neck, and pressed her face down into my shoulder. "I swear you're beautiful, Cass, and for the record, no one would ever guess that under the boring-ass clothes you wear, this body is rock hard."

I chuckled, which made her face soften.

"I adore you."

"Me too. You know that," I said, hugging her tight.

There was a soft knock from the direction of the door, and when Snow and I looked up, we found my friend Lucas there.

"Yes," Snow groused as we parted, our hug over, "may I help you?"

He pointed at me. "Your boss. I came back to see him. I was here earlier, remember?"

"I don't," she lied. "No."

The woman was such a snot.

Lucas pointed at her now, addressing me. "Is she for real?"

Snow's face got all squinty and dark. "Do you have an appointment?"

"It's okay," I soothed my assistant. "Go home, Snowy."

She moved around my desk, and Lucas Tate walked into my office. As they passed each other, Snow caught my eye. "What the fuck?" she mouthed the words at me.

I dismissed her with a wave. "I'll see you in the morning."

"Yes, you will," she replied, her voice full of forced cheerfulness.

I was smiling as I went to my coat rack and pulled on my topcoat, only then turning to look at my friend. "Yessir, what can I do for you?"

He walked forward, then stopped at my desk, his hands in the pockets of his leather jacket. "I wanted you to get a drink with me so I can say sorry."

I stared at him. "What'd you do?"

"I fucked Ben. I called you Sunday morning to tell you that I bumped into him at a party on Saturday night. Is this ringing any bells?"

"Was I awake?"

"You were talking to me."

"Yeah, that doesn't mean anything," I said, trying to recall the conversation to any degree.

"So, what then?"

"Now you lost me."

"Jesus, Cass, are you pissed or not?"

"Oh." I chuckled. "Not."

"Not?" He was surprised.

"Yeah, I'm not mad."

"Are you sure?"

"Yeah, I don't care." I yawned, seeing flashes of what Lucas would be doing in the next few hours. It was like the teasers they let you see on the porn sites. I wanted to remind him to take a box of condoms with him.

"Swear?"

"Yeah," I sighed. I really wasn't upset. Lucas wasn't a good enough friend for my exes to be off limits, and Ben didn't respect me enough not to go to bed with my friends. It was disappointing, but that was all.

His sigh was loud, like he'd been holding his breath. "So where are you going?"

"Having drinks with Stuart and company over at Borderland."

"Lemme go with you."

"No."

"Why not?"

"Why not? You hate Stuart, and he doesn't care much for you, either."

"That's because I fucked his boyfriend."

I grunted. "I guess I should be thankful you waited until I was broken up with mine before you seduced him."

"That's not—"

"Yeah, it is," I said. "You're a home wrecker. You should have a T-shirt made."

"C'mon, I wanna make up."

"We can't make up because I'm not mad," I assured him, waving him toward the door. "C'mon, let's go."

"Just ditch Stuart and come out with me."

"No."

"But I came all the way over here."

"Your office is a block away."

"You're actually really pissed at me, aren't you."

I groaned loudly, shoved him out my office door, followed him, and turned back to lock it.

"Cassidy?"

I studied him—his face, his defeated posture, the sad eyes. "I swear to God, not mad."

"I am sorry. I had no idea you actually loved him." He looked really uncomfortable.

Love had never been on the table with me and Ben. And now, looking at Lucas, noting as I always did how pretty he was, I realized taking him along to Borderland had obvious benefits. If Lucas was there, that meant I would have to talk that much less. He and Stuart swiping at each other with claws and snark was always fun to see. "Fine, come with me, but you better play nice with Stuart."

"Me? What about him? He's the one who's still holding a grudge. That boyfriend was like ten of them ago."

I started laughing.

"I might fuck every guy in sight, but he dates them. How is that better?"

"Do you even remember the guy's name?"

"Uhm… Joe, I think. Some kind of Italian last name."

Casual sex was so completely lost on me. There had to be at least the potential for greatness before I climbed into bed with anyone.

He smirked at me, and I groaned. He was an ass, but for whatever reason, I seemed to draw them like flies. I was a jerk magnet.

The elevator we got on was packed with people going home or headed to happy hour at the bar in the base of our building. Lucas was explaining to me about all the phone calls he got Sunday morning.

"Everyone was pissed at me about leaving the club with Ben."

"Because they know you broke the bro code," I said as we got off the crowded car.

"I thought the bro code was only for straight guys."

"Nope, gay too."

"Well, I got told off by a lot of people, girls *and* guys, who were worried about you, thinking I fucked you over. You have more friends than you think."

I scoffed at him, and his grin widened before it suddenly fell away as something, or someone, caught his eye. Glancing around, I understood. His gaze had fallen on Andy Gregor, and Lucas Tate was the picture of awestruck.

I gave him a gentle shove forward with my shoulder to get him moving.

"Cassidy," Andy said breathlessly when he saw me, moving fast to step in front of me. "How are you? I've been meaning to get up to your office to invite you to lunch, but—"

"Andy." I cut him off before turning to look at Lucas. "This is my buddy Lucas Tate. Lucas this is Andrew Gregor, one of our accounting managers here at Devlin Hammond."

"Oh," Lucas said, offering the younger man his hand.

Andy looked up slowly at the man through his long gold lashes. "Lucas Tate, as in Tate Pharmaceuticals?"

Lucas nodded and locked his eyes on Andy's pale pink lips, then let himself be swallowed in Andy's big blue eyes. Andy was like a hot cherub, all sleek and sexy and wide-eyed innocence. The urge to debauch the angel was a heated desire many men succumbed to. I myself had felt the allure but had not been invited into his bed. Not hot enough. He was, I understood, Kyle's regular booty call. Although I was guessing from the amount of eye-fucking going on, if Kyle was planning to hit Andy up for sex that evening, he was going to be disappointed. It looked like Lucas Tate would be next on Andy's menu.

Neither of them noticed when I walked away.

CHAPTER TWO

WHEN he walked by, his gorgeous pale-jade eyes had locked on mine for only a second. But that was enough. The vision hit my brain like a sledgehammer, vivid and violent. There was absolutely nothing I could do but get up and go to him. So against every instinct of self-preservation I had, I crossed the room. Normally I would never have done it. Even when I saw things as clear as day, I usually let events play out and didn't interfere. It wasn't my place. Who was I to change someone's destiny? I was nobody, I was nothing, and besides, it was supposed to be a secret.

My mother had drilled it into me when I was a child. I was never, ever, to tell anyone what I could truly see. Never reveal my gift…

Angela Jane, now Angela Prince since she had married my stepfather, always called me her miracle. She waited at home that afternoon, skipping the night classes she was taking to get her master's degree in education, to tell my father she was pregnant. Earlier that day she had confirmed it with her doctor and now had champagne waiting for my father and sparkling cider for her. She had been assured that being a mother wasn't in the cards for her, so the fact that she *was* going to be one had filled her with blinding joy the entire day. She shivered with anticipation when the phone rang a little after four, and then she was informed that my father had been involved in an accident. Death was instantaneous, they informed her. He would not have suffered.

"I thought I was going to die," she recounted when I was old enough to understand. "And then I wanted to."

At the funeral, my father's mother brought her a plate of food. My mom didn't want it.

"But Angie," my grandmother soothed. "Honey, you have to take care of yourself for the baby. You're going to be a mom."

And that was the day, the day she buried my father, that my mother went to church and thanked God for me. I was her miracle.

When I was five, I made her take her umbrella when we left the house. There was hail on the way home. She nodded at me as we took refuge at the bodega down the street from our graystone. That had been a lucky guess, hadn't it?

Soon after that I suggested we needed to get a new spare tire. A week later on the way home from the school play, we got a flat. She winked at me as she unscrewed the bolts with the lug wrench. From then on it was one thing after another, things that could be explained away—coincidences, serendipity—until I was ten and a half and threw a fit of biblical proportions to keep my mother off a plane.

She was going to a teaching conference in Houston. I explained that the plane was broken.

"Baby, I have to go."

"If you go, you'll die!" I screamed. I had been unpacking her suitcase for the last hour, getting more and more agitated.

When she turned to look at me and actually saw the tears, my hands balled into fists and the way I was shaking, she got on the phone and called the airline. For a fee, they let her change her departure date, and she grabbed me and hugged me and promised me everything would be fine. But I didn't need the reassurance; I already knew it would be. On our way to the airport the following day, she got a call from one of her colleagues, whose irritation from the day before—my mother was, after all, arriving late—had changed to relief and happiness. The plane my mother was originally to be on was in pieces strewn across several miles of empty fields in Ohio. My mother pulled over, trying not to hyperventilate. She gripped the steering wheel and turned to me.

"Mom?"

"Baby, what did you see?"

I bit my bottom lip.

"Please, love."

"I saw you crying because you wouldn't see me anymore," I let her know without mentioning the blood. There had been a lot.

We sat on the side of the road in the rain in our 1979 Toyota Corolla wagon. It had a snowplow piece on the front of it and had been my father's car. I lost track of how long I listened to the drops on the roof and the windows.

"Okay," she said finally. "Tell me everything."

So I did.

It was like looking at pieces of a movie. When I stared into another person's eyes, I could see what would happen in a few hours or a day or a week, if an individual stayed on their present path. So I saw my mother packing, then I saw her as she would be hours later, screaming as the plane went down, and then another jump ahead to her bleeding out amid the wreckage. I couldn't see a month away, or a year, and honestly I was glad. What I got was enough.

It came in handy now, especially at my job.

I could meet a woman and see a man beside her, and then he would sort of *change*, morph from wearing jeans and a T-shirt to a suit and tie, and possibly be offering her flowers. So I knew that they would progress to a certain place if she said yes to coffee or lunch. But beyond that, I was blind. So maybe he turned into a psychopath, or maybe she did. I couldn't say. But I could say for certain if there was or was not going to be a connection. It was easy for me to say that yes, sparks would fly, since I had, in fact, seen it.

The visions were clear as day, but I needed help controlling them. That day, my mother and I had the first of many talks as we sat there in the car, in the rain. After a bit, she pulled the car back onto the road and took me to my grandparents' house. We would talk more when she got back, she swore it. As I stood next to my grandmother and waved goodbye, I felt such a sense of relief knowing we would finally make a plan when she got home. It felt good to finally share my gift.

My mother thought about me the entire time she was gone, and when she was home and sitting with me on my bed, she said that I needed to keep my ability a secret, except in cases of emergency. Small things like losing your keys or forgetting to turn out lights, life's tiny challenges, those were up to the individual to navigate. Where she drew the line was at getting hit by a cross-town bus. I could warn people, and try to get them to listen to me, if, and only if, they were going to die.

It was good to hear, because before that I went around telling everyone everything. I warned cashiers, teachers, janitors, librarians, friends, their parents—I was wearing myself out telling my math tutor that she shouldn't ride down Madison Street to get home or she'd get a flat tire. It was exhausting to endlessly warn people, even worse because everyone thought I was nuts. I had a reputation for being a weirdo and a freak.

It was nice when I got to go from elementary to middle school, and we moved, which meant I got to change districts too. I got a fresh start, and with my mother's new dictate in mind, I finally started to feel normal. I didn't have to carry the weight of the world anymore; my visions were simply blips of scenes I saw in my head. I practiced ignoring them. Fortunately, the life and death visions occurred infrequently. I could only imagine if I was the poor kid who had to endure horrifying revelations on a daily basis. They would have had to lock me up in a rubber room. As it was, the ones that made my spine tingle, my jaw clench, and my stomach flip over were few and far between....

The one I had just seen was a doozy. It made me retch and gag.

"Jesus, Cass," my friend Stuart griped from across the table. "That was disgusting."

He was lucky I had not decorated the entire table with the beer and wings we had been eating. It was the only thing the noisy sports bar had to offer.

"What's wrong with you?" he continued.

But I didn't have time to answer; I had to go interfere instead, honor my cardinal rule about getting involved only when it was a question of life or death. I could not let them torture him. I would not. So I was up and across the room, moving fast to cut the man off.

I raised my voice. "Excuse me!"

He was walking in a crowd of men, the guy I needed to warn, all of them in suits and heavy trench coats. I was stopped and grabbed, slammed hard into the wall beside the door that led out front to the sidewalk, and held tight.

"Who the fuck are you?" one of my interrogators snarled.

I looked behind him to my quarry, to the beautiful man with the jet-black hair, dark skin, and pale green eyes. "May I talk to you, please?"

He scowled at me, and one of the many guys with him frisked me and pulled my wallet out from the inside breast pocket of my suit jacket. He verified who I was, Cassidy Jane, and that I lived in Hyde Park and had a gym membership. It was funny that of all the things in my wallet, that was the only card besides my driver's license that the bodyguard looked at.

"Give him back his wallet. Let him go."

I was instantly released and my bright red leather wallet was offered back to me. As I took it and replaced it in my pocket, the man I was trying to save stepped in front of me. I had to tip my head back to meet his gorgeous eyes. He had at least six inches on my own five foot nine.

"Do you know me, Mr. Jane?"

I shook my head.

"What do you want?"

"I need you to keep an open mind."

His perfectly shaped glossy black brows furrowed.

"Listen, I know you're going to some meeting tonight with some guy who wears diamond studs in his ears."

The look of irritation I was getting changed to an all-out glare.

"But he's dangerous, okay, the guy with the earrings, and he's gonna shoot—" I leaned around him to look at all the men who were with him, found the man, and pointed. "—him first, and then the men with earring guy are really going to hurt you before...." I swallowed hard.

"Before what?" he asked, studying me.

"Before they kill you. So if you just please skip the meeting, that'd be good."

He crossed his arms and kept looking at me.

I forced myself to breathe. "Please don't go, okay?"

There was a long silence as he studied me. I wasn't sure if I should say something else or just keep quiet. I figured he was trying to decide if I was crazy.

"Who do you work for?"

"I work at Devlin Hammond," I replied. "I'm a relationship coordinator."

"A what?"

"Like a matchmaker," I offered.

He was processing.

"I find people their true loves."

"You're a matchmaker," he reiterated.

"Yes."

"That makes no sense."

"What doesn't? Being a matchmaker? You got something against true love?"

"You are so odd."

I was odd? I wasn't the guy going to a meeting where people wanted to kill me.

"Who are you?" he demanded.

"We just covered this."

More scowling.

"Can I go?" I asked.

"How do you know me?"

"Again, I don't."

"Where did you come from?"

I pointed back over my shoulder. "Over there."

He was trying to work things out in his head, but even as I stood there, I saw scenes changing around him.

"What are you looking at?"

The problem was, the death was still going to occur, although the torture was no longer in the picture. "Jesus, who are you?" I said under my breath. "Why do they want to kill you so bad?"

"Who?"

"Earring guy." I was exasperated. "Are you even listening?"

"I know you, don't I?"

"No," I said, reaching out to touch the lapel of his cashmere trench. It was soft and felt nice under my fingertips.

"Are you drunk?"

I jolted and dropped my hand, because what the hell was that about? I never touched anyone without being invited, without knowing absolutely a 110 percent that they wanted me to. I wasn't forward, I didn't flirt, and first moves were not in my repertoire. And I most certainly did not go around touching perfect strangers. I took a step back.

He stepped forward and took hold of my bicep.

"I need to go," I said.

"No." He cleared his throat. "You need to come eat with me so we can talk."

My head snapped up, and I was swallowed in pale spring green all over again. "I have to get back to my friends."

"If they were really your friends, they would have either come to check on you or not let you come over here into a group of strange men all by yourself."

"They would if they thought I was picking you up."

"And that's you, is it?" He arched one eyebrow knowingly. "You're a player?"

I wasn't and even a stranger could see it.

"But if those people over there gave a crap about you, they would have come to your defense when my guys grabbed you."

That was true. Was no one keeping an eye on me at all? Where was my wingman?

"You're not going to ask why I have men with me?"

"I know why," I sighed. "People want to kill you."

He studied me.

"Are you in the mafia?" I asked.

"That's where your brain goes? To the mob?"

I shrugged.

He shook his head. "I'm Raza Bashandi."

"It's a pleasure." I exhaled.

Tightening his grip on my bicep, he tugged me after him out the front door to the sidewalk. Once we were there, he whirled me around to face him.

"I want to talk to you."

"Okay." I smiled at him.

We were back to his uncertainty. "Why aren't you scared of me?"

But he himself was nothing to be afraid of; it was *his* life that concerned me. "I don't see anything," I said before I thought about it.

"See anything?" he repeated.

Crap. I twisted my arm free and took a couple of steps back. "You know, I really should go home and—"

"No," he ordered, reaching for my arm again, only to have me maneuver almost beyond his reach.

He caught my fingers and I was too surprised to pull away, instead allowing myself to be drawn close again. His hand was warm and strong. I liked holding it.

"Who are you?" he asked softly, staring down into my eyes.

"Is, uhm…." I licked my lips nervously. "Bashandi… is that Egyptian?"

"Yes."

"People call you Raz for short?"

"No one calls me Raz."

"Oh."

His eyes were locked on mine. "You may, though."

My blush was uncontrollable and embarrassing, and I felt my face get hot as I bit my bottom lip.

The slight curl of his lip I got in return melted me to the sidewalk. The man was stunning when he was growling at me, but with a trace of warmth… God, he was breathtaking.

I whimpered in the back of my throat.

"Get in the car," he growled.

I… car? "What?"

He spun me around, shoved me forward, and there was a Lincoln Town Car, the kind with the tinted black windows I saw all over the city when I was walking. A man held open the door.

"Please, get in."

I did as I was asked, because even though normally I never did anything even remotely spontaneous, it felt right. Being close to the man made everything in me that was usually flying around and restless feel still and calm. He had a solid, quiet strength that I craved. I wanted to wrap myself around him and absorb the peace right into me.

"Cassidy."

I turned to look at him.

"I hope you won't be offended if I discuss some quick business in Arabic."

"Absolutely not," I assured him. *"Baa'ref Arabee Showayya."*

He did a slow pan to me and I waggled my eyebrows.

I had amused him, and I saw the effect of it in his eyes. They glittered. "You speak a little Arabic."

I lifted my thumb and forefinger to demonstrate how small it was. "I'm a matchmaker. What if the person I'm trying to find love for is interested in someone who doesn't speak English?"

"Good point."

I waved dismissively. "But I won't be able to follow anything long and convoluted, so you're safe."

"Am I?"

"For right this second, yeah."

He sighed before returning his attention to the men with him.

We drove out by the Kennedy Expressway, west to New West Loop. The restaurant we stopped in front of was one of the new up-and-coming places I hadn't been to yet. The area used to be a little rundown but lately had become a sort of foodie heaven with young hotshot chefs opening trendy dining spots with exciting menus. The line to get into The Fisherman's Daughter went around the corner, but as soon as we got out of the car, the hostess at the outside stand yelled a greeting to Raza.

In minutes we were inside, standing by the door as a man crossed the small, noisy dining room to us. He hugged Raza when he reached him and then led him and the rest of us through the maze of tables to the stairs that led to the second floor.

It was quiet and dimly lit in the private dining area, and there were fewer tables spread farther apart. Raza took my coat and passed it off to one of the waitstaff before directing me to follow after our host. He led us to a long table, and I was seated between Raza and the bodyguard I had seen in my vision.

I enjoyed listening to everyone talk and laugh, watching them pour the Ouzo that was already on the table, and seeing Raza speak to the man I was informed was the chef. The restaurant featured sort of Greek fusion food. I had no idea what to expect but was promised something remarkable.

"Cassidy." The chef said, offering his hand for me to take. "Milo."

I smiled at him and shook his hand. "It's a pleasure to meet you."

"I like your hat." He tipped his head behind me to the coat rack where I'd placed my small gray wool fedora.

"Gotta have a hat when you're bald." I commented, noting his own shaved-to-the-scalp head. "Am I right?"

"You are right." He chuckled, rubbing the top of his head. "I need to shave mine. The stubble drives me crazy."

"Me too," I agreed. "Letting it grow out drives me nuts. You should shave it in the shower. That's what I do. Every two days like clockwork."

"In the shower is a good idea."

"See, I'm a helper."

"Yes, you are. Drink?"

I thanked him but passed the glass sideways to Raza as soon as Milo turned to walk back to the kitchen.

"Not your favorite?" he asked, turning to look at me.

"No."

"How about some wine instead?"

"That'd be good."

He lifted his hand, and minutes later, there was a glass of rich red wine that didn't have the bite at the end that I hated for me.

"Thank you."

"Of course," he said.

Other people wandered over to the table. He greeted everyone, and I sat there beside him, drinking glass after glass as the food came: dolmades, moussaka, paidakia, and brizoles. There were potatoes and a horiatiki salad and flatbread. It smelled amazing and tasted even better. The only thing that diverted me from the food at all was Raza. When I leaned close to him, I got just a trace of some spicy, musky cologne. His suit jacket stretched across his wide shoulders, and I could not help but notice the heat from his thigh as it rested against mine. I had the terrible urge to lean into him.

"Are you all right?" he asked.

I nodded, taking a deep breath, realizing from how shiny everything looked and how good I felt that I had maybe drunk a little too much wine.

"I'm sorry we can't really talk here, but I wanted to treat you for saving my life."

I hiccupped. "You don't really think I saved your life."

"Of course I do."

I was blushing again. "No, you think I'm nuts."

"No." He was adamant. "I think you had a premonition that you were very brave to own up to having and then come tell me about. It took a lot of balls to confront me."

"Who was that man?"

"Which?"

"The one who wanted to hurt you?"

"It's just business."

I shivered, remembering. "It wasn't business."

His hand was on my thigh suddenly, and it felt so good, so possessive, that I shivered. The man was very demonstrative, and I craved it like a drug.

"You like to be petted," he said hoarsely.

"If you do it," I replied honestly, alarmed at my own boldness.

One of his eyebrows lifted. "How about I take you home with me and I'll do that."

I studied his eyes.

"What are you trying to see?"

"Nothing, for once," I sighed, wadding up my napkin and putting it on the table beside my plate. I was trying to see us, him and me, anywhere but in the restaurant together, but nothing came. "I should go."

"Pardon?"

I pushed back from the table. "I have to be at work early tomorrow morning. I've had a wonderful evening. Thank you for taking pity on me and feeding me."

He just stared at me as I stood up, pushed my chair back in, and walked away from the noisy, boisterous table. I was at the coat rack and had just put my hat on when he stepped in beside me.

"I say I want to take you home with me, and you think that's what? Charity?"

I flicked my gaze to his deep celadon eyes. "What else could it be... guy like you?"

"Guy like me?"

I groaned because he was being ridiculous. "Really? You need your ego stroked?"

"No, I don't," he retorted, grabbing my chin, forcing my eyes back to meet his. "What is this? You come off so confident, but you're not?"

I lifted my face from his hand and took a step back. "I know exactly who I am."

"I don't think you do."

I pulled on my topcoat, and headed for the stairs. Milo met me in the middle, stopping my progress.

"You are not staying for dessert?"

"No," I said, trying to move by him.

He stepped in front of me again. "But I have baklava."

"I can see that, and I love baklava."

"So, see, you need to stay."

I sighed because this man just breathed out sincerity. "I can't, but everything was amazing. Thank you so much."

He frowned at me.

I gave him a grin, or tried to, and again went to step around him. He wasn't having it and barred my path.

"Stay."

"I really can't. I have to work in the morning."

"It's not even ten yet."

"Milo—"

"You know," he interrupted. "You are the first man he has brought here."

I nodded, not sure what else to do. Thank him for telling me?

"I always tell him, 'Bash, bring someone special,' but he never does."

"Bash?"

"His last name, yes?"

Shortened, I understood. "You've been friends a long time."

"Yes." He gestured with his elbows, a little lift to indicate everything around him since he was carrying a tray of baklava. "All this... without family money, his money, his patronage, would not be. No one wanted to give me a loan to open my dream. My parents, aunts, uncles, we had some but not enough. Bash, he made it work for me."

"I'm glad he did."

"Me too." He chuckled.

"You have a good face, you know that?" I said, feeling like I could.

"Thank you, so do you." He tipped his head up the stairs. "Come back. Really, he brings his boys with him but never a date. He has shared a part of himself; don't throw it in his face."

"No, I didn't mean it like that."

"How do you mean it?"

Raza Bashandi could have anyone. Why would he want me, even just to sleep with? And I didn't do casual anything, so what was the point of being just another notch in the man's bedpost?

"Bash, he is the kind of man who appreciates quality in all things."

People, too, apparently, if Milo was any indication.

"He would not have looked at you twice if he did not see something he liked."

"I saved his life. That's the only reason I'm here. Your food is his thank-you to me."

He tipped his head, made a face. "There would seem to be more to it than that, don't you think?"

"No. He's just doing something nice for me since, technically, I did something nice for him."

"You should think more of yourself."

"Where's the modesty in that?"

"Perhaps modesty has no place here."

"The alternative simply isn't me."

"I think Bash probably sees more in you than you see in yourself."

"Could be," I agreed.

"Come back upstairs with me."

"I really do need to go home," I sighed. I understood the situation for what it really was. It was my insecurity and nothing else. All my life I'd been reminded that beautiful people sought out beautiful people. You couldn't mix gods and mortals; someone always ended up bursting into flames. The second a drop of my interest was maybe, possibly, being returned, I ran. And that was why I couldn't see anything when I looked at Raza, why I had no visions, because I was already making decisions that would separate us, not bring us together.

"The food was truly amazing."

"Thank you," Milo said softly enough that I knew he meant it.

"Take care," I said as I patted the man's shoulder and turned to go down the stairs.

Outside on the sidewalk, I called the only other person in the world besides my mother who loved me unconditionally and would listen to me vent.

"Cass?"

"Hey Wy," I sighed as I began trudging down the street toward the El station.

"It's about fuckin' time you called."

"The phone works both ways, you know."

"Yeah, but with the fourteen hours' time difference, I never know when to—"

I called him on it. "Bullshit. You've been in Hong Kong a year. You know when to call. I saw you in July, for chrissakes."

"Shit."

I had made the trip to see him, and it had been amazing—my first visit to a foreign country with the added bonus of it feeling like home because my best friend was there. "It's fine. We're both busy."

"I'll be better. Work just got stupid."

"That's because you're building skyscrapers in foreign countries. I mean, how cool is that?"

"I'd rather talk about you. What's up?"

"Nothing."

"You called to say nothing?"

I grunted as I climbed the stairs toward the El.

"Oh hey, I did send you a care package, okay?"

"For what?"

"For fuckin' October, idiot."

I sighed. "Thank you."

"It's okay, I know how you get."

Everyone who knew me understood about me and October. I just hated it.

"I wish I was there to pry you out of your graystone."

"Historic Chicago graystone. Get it right."

"It's an apartment in a shitty old building. Give it a rest."

I was waiting in the cold for the train and could not keep the sigh from rising up out of me.

"Please don't make me beg. Just fuckin' talk to me."

Ever since college, since I was eighteen, he had been the one, after my mother, I could dump all over. For whatever reason, he liked me.

"It's because you're worth the effort, dickhead," he said, like he always did, like he knew what was going on in my head.

We were so different. He was Prada and I was Dockers. He was steel and glass, and I was wooden floors and vegetable gardens. We were night and day different, and we fit like tomato soup and grilled cheese. We shouldn't have gone together, but we did. Whenever I was with him, I didn't feel like I was a step behind or uncool or like the nerd I was.

"I miss you," I said.

"I miss you too, asshole," he grumbled, irritated because I wasn't spilling. "Now, what the fuck?"

"I met this guy."

Snort of laughter. "Tell me you did not make the *Ben Mistake* and tell him you were a card-carrying sister of Delphi."

"Ohmygod, I'm gonna kill you!"

"What?"

"That's what we're calling it now? The *Ben Mistake*?"

"Well, yeah."

"Card-carrying what of what?"

"Just drop it."

"God, you're such an ass."

"You didn't, though, did you?"

"Didn't what?"

"Spill the beans about being able to look someone in the eye and see their immediate future? You didn't, right?"

"You sound like you're wincing."

"Yeah, well, I am, but just a little."

On the El, traveling toward home, I explained about Raza Bashandi.

"He sounds hot. What was the problem?"

"He wanted to take me home with him."

"And this was bad… why?"

"Because it's too fast, and I'm not the kind of guy who—"

"But you saved him?"

"Yeah."

"So… he could be special."

"No."

"Don't say 'no' like you know, 'cause you don't. You saved his life. He could be the one."

"You don't actually believe in fate."

"The fuck I don't. Even before I met you, I kind of felt like it could happen, the whole everything happens for a reason thing—but now… c'mon."

"Come on, what?"

"You are actually fate at work in the flesh."

"Wyatt, I—"

"Cass, you saved my life."

I had no argument for that.

"You locked me in my room the night of Tanya Becket's party, and when you got home and let me out, I punched you in the face."

"Yeah, I remember."

"And do you recall the fire? The gas explosion in her house off campus—is that ringing any bells?"

"Wyatt—"

"Do you remember how you went over there and tried to get people out of the house but no one listened to you?"

"Wyatt, you—"

"You ran around like a fuckin' idiot trying to get people out of that house!"

"Wyatt—"

"You did! Everyone told me. They said you made a spectacle of yourself, had the biggest fuckin' meltdown ever."

"Yes!" I barked, charging off the train at my stop. "I remember!"

"And you got stuffed into a dumpster at the house, and by the time you climbed out, the house was on fire?"

It had been horrible.

"Only the people that came to help you out of the trash weren't in the house when the kitchen blew up."

"Yeah, I know."

"Five people died that night."

I remembered. There had been no way for me to warm up for weeks. I had shivered for a month straight.

"But you saved a ton of them by making a complete ass of yourself. And when you finally dragged yourself home, I hit you."

"I know all—"

"But you saved my life because I was hot for Tanya Becket, and I would have been in the kitchen with her when she died."

I shivered hard.

"But you saved me even though I wouldn't listen. You acted."

"Yeah, but—"

"There's no 'yeah, but.' You are fate in the flesh. How do you not get that?"

"I just don't know if—"

"This guy with the exotic-ass name, you need to jump on that. You saved him and he wants to see you? Are you waiting for a sign from God or something? An alien ship over your apartment building making like the light with Paul on the road? What the fuck, Jane? Grow a pair and go get laid."

"You're such an ass!" I yelled in the middle of the stairs leading down from the platform.

"What are you going to do about it?"

And that was the real question on so many levels.

Chapter Three

I STOPPED, turned around, walked back, thought about it, froze, and did an about-face at least ten times before I finally made it back to the restaurant a little after ten. It made no sense—I had to work the next morning—but I had to see him so I would know if he had been hurt at all by my leaving. If he wasn't there, I would take that as a sign. If he was still at the restaurant, missing me, maybe he did actually like me.

The whole thing was absurd, but I just couldn't bring myself to not try. The whole trip back, I had felt like I couldn't breathe. I was gasping and anxious, barely thinking, panicked, almost. The idea of not going back was impossible, but returning after I left—that seemed insane. He would think I was much too high maintenance to bother with. I would, if the roles were reversed.

"It's like this," Wyatt said when I called him again once I was back on the train. "You'll be disappointed if it's not instalove 'cause you're a big romantic sap, but you'll be frightened if it *is* instalove 'cause that's too fast. There's just no pleasing you."

"If I go back—"

"Wait, aren't you already on your way?"

"Yeah, but—"

"Oh, this is a recap."

"No, ass, I'm thinking out loud."

"Why?"

"Because I have to figure what to do once I get there."

"What do you want to do?"

"I want to talk to him."

"So do that."

"He's going to think I'm crazy."

"No, he's just gonna think you're dramatic. And you are."

"Why do I even talk to you?"

"Because we've got a little history, you and I," he chuckled.

In my head I could see him laughing, the big bald bear of a man I simply adored.

"You really are on your way back there, right? You're not fucking with me?"

"No."

"Okay, just checking."

"Shit."

"Atta boy."

"I'll call you later."

"You know, you can just say screw this and come live with me, coward. You can watch my life instead of living your own, and follow along with the bouncing ball. My kids will love having a spinster uncle."

"You don't have any kids."

"Not yet," he agreed cheerfully.

"There's not even a woman in your life right now."

"No, there are too many in my life right now. That's the problem. I gotta pick one."

"You know, I think spinsters are only women," I educated him.

"What are unmarried men called?"

"Bachelors?"

"At sixty?"

"You—"

"If I'm still single at sixty then I was probably gay all along right?"

"Get off the phone," I grunted.

He was laughing when he hung up.

And now I was back at the restaurant, feeling like an idiot when I walked in. The smells were even better than I remembered, the place was packed, and the noise level was just deafening. I walked toward the back and started up the stairs.

"Cassidy."

I looked up, and Raza was coming down, descending slowly toward me, pulling on his cashmere trench coat as he did.

"You left."

I cleared my throat. "I did."

"But now you're back."

I nodded.

"I saw you," he said as he reached me, and I watched the muscles in his jaw cord. "I was looking out for you, hoping."

My knees went weak. It took quite a man to admit to wanting.

"Close your eyes," he ordered.

"What?" I was on the stairs and the angle was steep.

"I won't let you fall."

"Swear?"

"Cross my heart."

I closed my eyes.

"Good boy."

The tremble was involuntary.

"It's bullshit that you get to know everything I thought while you were gone, and I have to guess unless you tell me."

He was right. It wasn't fair that I could simply know and he had to ask and wonder. The playing field needed to be level because—

"Oh God," I moaned.

"You just actually heard me, didn't you?"

And I had. He believed every word of it. He had no doubt that I could see everything I said I could.

"Just because you're pretty isn't enough for me to alter my course for the evening."

My eyes snapped open.

"No!" he barked, slapping a hand down over them so I couldn't see him. "You don't get to look. You need to take a leap of faith. You have to decide on me alone, on my words, on what you know already. There's no checking."

The sultry sound of his voice and the warm breath on my ear made me shiver.

"Cassidy."

Easy to fall into the rumbling sound, how deep and low and—

"Cassidy Jane."

"I...."

"Look at me."

Even with my eyes wide open, all I could see was the pale green of his.

"So, why did you come back?"

"I wanted to talk to you," I confessed, all pretense gone as I swallowed down my heart. "It didn't seem right, leaving."

"No, it didn't," he agreed, placing his hand on my throat.

"Where were you going?" I asked, loving the feel of his thumb tracing over my jaw.

"To your house."

I couldn't contain my catch of breath. "You don't know where I live."

"I took a picture of your driver's license with my phone."

"You did not."

"Of course I did."

I bit my bottom lip and saw the laugh lines in the corner of his eyes crinkled. God, he was gorgeous.

"I'm glad you came back," he said softly, his hand on my cheek.

"Are you?"

"Yes," he said. Now he was staring at my mouth.

I leaned into his hand, then, because the way he was standing one step above me, so tense, so ready to grab me, was really nice. I could see it in his face. He wanted me right there with him.

"Cassidy," he whispered hoarsely.

I closed my eyes as he took my face in both hands, easing me forward until I was against his chest, my cheek pressed there, listening to the beating of his heart. He was warm, and his arms, wrapped around me, were strong. I slipped my hands under his jacket, and as I hugged him, I heard his deep, contented sigh.

"Come home with me."

"Okay."

He squeezed me tight, kissed my ear—which made me shiver—and then let me go. I found his scrutiny unnerving and confessed to it after a moment.

"I just feel like...."

"What?"

"Like I know you."

"Know me?"

He nodded. "Yeah, I feel very comfortable."

"Is that a good thing?"

"Of course it's a good thing."

I sighed as he pulled his cell from the breast pocket of his suit jacket and gave some sharp commands in Arabic.

"Bring the car around the front," I translated.

"Oh, see." He arched an eyebrow for me. "Your Arabic is probably enough to get by."

"I'll take your word for it."

He led me to the car then, and what was nice was his hand in mine. He held on through the restaurant, so anyone looking could see we were together, and then kept on outside as we waited together.

"You fit so well under my chin," he said, pulling me close.

I had to be so careful. I could fall hard for this man very easily—hook, line, and sinker.

The bodyguards came out of the restaurant and joined us on the curb as the car rolled up beside us. Once inside, seated next to Raza on the black leather seat, I turned to look at him. The others got in, one beside the driver and two across from us in the back. I took off my hat and leaned closer, pressing into his side, letting my head bump down onto his shoulder.

He said nothing, but he lifted his arm, put it around me, and drew me in tight. My sigh was loud, and as I closed my eyes, I heard chuckling.

I realized I had dozed off when I became aware that I was lying down, my head on a very hard, muscular thigh. The heat of his body soaked through his dress slacks, warming the right side of my face. My hat was gone, and I vaguely wondered where it was.

A gust of icy air swirled in as someone opened the car door, and I sat up, bleary and half-awake, turning to look at both Raza and the guy I earlier in the night had seen shot in my vision.

"Cassidy."

I looked at Raza and found him staring. "What?"

"I just had to make a quick stop here on our way home to drop one of my men off."

"Okay," I said, rubbing my eyes, turning to smile at the bigger man. "I'm so glad you listened to me. Some people don't. They don't believe me. They think I'm nuts."

"One must always trust the oracle, isn't that so?"

"You'd think people would learn, right?"

"You would think. But I'm safe because of you. Thank you."

"You're so welcome," I yawned, half-asleep and not really with it. I had no idea why I was so tired all of a sudden.

"Come here," Raza grunted, reaching out an arm, gesturing for me to move.

I slid back close, wrapping my arms around his waist, lifting my face to press my nose against the side of his neck. "You smell good."

"Yeah, so do you," he grumbled, and I felt a hand on the back of my head as I closed my eyes.

"Let's get this car moving, Dev."

"Yes, boss."

And then I was out again, held tight, warm, and safe. I was so thankful.

"CASSIDY."

I moaned.

"Nice noise," he said softly, and I felt lips over the shell of my ear. "Jesus, where the fuck did you come from?"

His warm breath made me shiver, and I sat up slowly, blinking several times as I realized we had stopped in front of a large two-story house. There were several steps leading up to the front door.

"Is this your house?"

"It's where I live for now."

"Oh? Where do you—"

"I'll tell you later."

"Okay. Did you do your errand?"

"I did."

I must have slept through it.

"Come inside."

I nodded but I didn't move.

"What do you want?"

I leaned forward, and when I did, he met me fast. "Thank you for having the balls to come talk to me," he said, taking hold of my chin, sliding his thumb across my bottom lip.

"C'mon, you're not that hot."

He chuckled, the sound deep and resonant, and my body heated with his closeness, the way he was holding me, keeping me still and displaying his strength without having to hurt me. The man was much stronger than I, but he was exerting a lot of control to be gentle.

"Do you trust me?"

I whimpered in the back of my throat.

"Do you?"

He was laughing as I scrambled into his lap, my hands on the hard chest and washboard stomach I could feel even through the dress shirt he was wearing.

"I'll take that as a yes."

"I'm never... I don't...." What to say when, to him, I was acting like a slut?

"Yes, I know," he said, hands on the sides of my neck, then sliding up to my face before he lowered me for a kiss. "I know. You're a good boy."

His lips pressed to mine and I opened for him, the feeling so strange, the flutter and anticipation of something brand new coupled with a familiarity that made no sense. It was electric—his tongue stroking over mine, pushing, tangling—but also, somehow, remembered.

"Oh fuck," he gasped, breaking the kiss, pulling back to look up at me.

"What's wrong?"

"Nothing's wrong. That's the problem," he sighed.

I tried to move, but his hands were tight on my thighs suddenly, holding me still.

"Do you… should I go?"

He furrowed those beautiful, thick brows of his. "You're not going anywhere but into my house."

It was a good answer, and when I bent toward him again, he lifted for the kiss.

I let my lips melt over his, surprising myself with how voracious I was, how rough. I bit and sucked and rubbed my tongue along his and moaned, deep and husky, into his mouth when he put me on my back and pinned me under him.

"No," he growled, untangling himself after another kiss, pushing off me before he scrambled out of the car.

Where was he…? I was grabbed by the hand and yanked out after him.

"I am not fucking you in the back of my car," he informed me, straightening my coat and clothes and shoving my hat down on my head.

I could not stop sighing. "You found my hat."

He rolled his eyes and I laughed.

"You have gorgeous eyes, you know that?"

They were just blue, nothing special. Not pale jade like his.

"And you look good all ravished."

His lips were just as swollen as I was certain mine were, but his gorgeous dark bronze coloring didn't show the flush I was sure I wore.

"I'm not ravished yet," I teased.

"Playing with fire," he muttered under his breath, taking my hand and tugging me after him.

I could get used to the man holding my hand all the time.

"This is gonna make everything so complicated."

He didn't sound happy. In fact, he sounded annoyed, but his irritation was belied by the way he was holding on. His fingers laced into mine, and I wondered if he held hands with all his one-night stands.

He opened the front door without a key, didn't bother closing it, and as we neared the stairs, a man was coming down them. A really beautiful one, much prettier than I would ever be, and just that fast, I was self-conscious.

He had a boy toy and he had still brought me home? What was he doing, slumming?

"Who—"

"I don't fuck him, I take care of him. You understand?"

I did, actually, because I had taken care of Snow.

"He's an annoying pain in the ass."

Yeah, I had one of those too.

He shook my hand like he was trying to loosen me up. "Let whatever you were thinking go."

So I did.

"I didn't hear the car in the drive—" the young man began.

"Get the door, Jamie," Raza barked as we passed him.

"Shall I make you some din—"

"Had it. Make dessert," he called back, never breaking stride.

"Do I get to meet—"

"Cassidy," Raza said. We reached the landing and he took a right. "Yes."

"Really?" Jamie gasped.

Raza stopped so abruptly I nearly tripped, but I recovered my balance as he sharply exhaled and then turned his head so he could see over the railing and look down at the other man.

Jamie stood on the next to the bottom step of the enormous grand staircase we had just climbed. I doubted I had ever seen a more adorable face. His eyes were huge round pools of turquoise blue sky, the color I had always wished mine were. He had high cheekbones, an apple-shaped face, long feathery lashes, and thick brown wavy hair pulled back from his face and spilled down to the middle of his back.

The pale pink lips completed the picture of absolute, striking, ethereal beauty. Easily the prettiest man I had even seen in my life.

"Yes, really."

I heard Jamie catch his breath. "You... I get to meet him?"

Exasperated exhale before Raza squeezed my hand. "Cassidy Jane, this is Jamie Kidd."

The smile Jamie gave me lit up his whole face as he waved. "Hi. I'm so happy to meet you."

"Nice to meet you," I replied, pleased but unsure why it was such a big deal.

He looked over at Raza. "I'll bake a cake."

"Don't make cake!" he snapped.

"I'm making it!" Jamie yelled back.

Raza growled and huffed out a breath like Jamie was the most annoying man on the planet, and tugged me after him as he started walking again.

"And you're holding his hand," Jamie whimpered, and I could hear the tears in his voice.

"Close the front door!" Raza barked again.

"Oh my God, oh my God, oh my God," Jamie chanted, and I would have said something, but I was nearly yanked off my feet and pulled sideways into a room.

Raza shoved me forward, slammed the door behind him, and flipped on the lights.

The room was gorgeous and opulent, from the polished wooden floors to the intricate Persian rugs, the dark cherrywood four-poster bed, and the lavishly carved armoire. It was clearly a man's room, but warm and inviting as well.

"It's beautiful," I breathed.

"Now it is," he said, his hands on me, pushing the coat from my shoulders, my suit jacket following before he started fiddling with my tie.

I leaned in because I couldn't help it; I needed to kiss him.

He parted his lips for me, and I tasted him as he stripped off my tie and went to work on the buttons of my dress shirt.

"You're complicating my life," he said between kisses, tipping my head back, knocking my hat off before he sucked and kissed and nibbled down my throat.

"Sorry," I panted, yanking and pulling at his clothes, wanting them off.

"Supposed to be leaving," he muttered, lost in his own thoughts. "Already have everything planned and now… shit."

I had the man good and aggravated, and I really liked it. The best part was that he could not stop kissing me.

"Not ready—" He paused for a moment to suck on my bottom lip. "—to tell my boss and everybody else that I'm gay, but they'll have to know who you are or… crap."

It sounded serious, the inner dialogue he was having.

"Fuck," he swore, and his voice was hoarse and low as he shoved me down onto the bed. I hadn't realized that at the same time I was being kissed and disrobed, he had been moving me across the room.

I looked up at him as he toed off his lace-ups and started on his cufflinks.

Dropping my own shoes next to his, I stood up and took off my shirt, tossing it away before starting on my belt.

"No," he moaned, falling to his knees, brushing my hands away, his own taking up the task of unbuckling it, unbuttoning the top of my pants, and working the zipper down over the front of my briefs. "I wanna do that."

I buried my hands in his thick, coarse hair, loving the feel of it, watching it run through my fingers as my pants puddled around my ankles. He careful peeled me out of my briefs, and when my cock sprang free, he moaned like he was in pain.

I was already leaking; it could not be helped. Just looking down at him, watching his lips part to take me in, almost made me come.

"You shouldn't," I said without any conviction in my voice whatsoever.

"I know you don't sleep around," he whispered. "And I'm good. Just let me."

I never got into bed with anyone without a condom, so the concern was not about me making him sick. He was right; I was careful.

The sensation of his tongue licking over the end of my cock made me jolt forward, and he gave me a wicked smile before sliding his lips down my shaft.

I fisted my hands tight in his hair when he took me deep, sucking and stroking, one of his hands on my ass, the other fondling my balls. He made the suction so good, so strong, and just the graze of his teeth made me tremble.

"Fuck my mouth."

I hesitated, but his hand on my ass, pressing me forward, shattered my control. I slowly began rocking my hips, watching my cock drag between those now dark, swollen lips—thrust in, pull back—pushing harder each time, feeling him swallow around me, the muscles in his throat contracting with each new plunge.

"I haven't… six months… gotta stop… stop…."

He shoved me back, and I tumbled down onto the bed, my feet caught in my pants.

I was stripped fast and a pillow was shoved under my hips before he was gone, moving to his nightstand for the lube and a condom.

It was very satisfying to see how fast he got what he needed and returned, the packet held tight between his teeth as he flipped open the cap of the small bottle and poured a short stream into his palm.

"Give me the condom," I chuckled.

"That's not hot," he assured me, speaking between clenched teeth.

"It is if I put it on you." I waggled my eyebrows.

He dropped it on my stomach and I really tried not to laugh.

"See, not hot."

But when I stroked my hand over the length of him before sliding the lubed condom on, the shudder let me know that heat had been restored.

I lifted my legs, and he leaned forward so I could settle them on his shoulders.

"I didn't ask," he said softly.

"Go ahead."

He bent over me so my socked feet slid down his back as his hot, wet mouth swallowed my now-seeping cock. When he slid the first slick finger inside of me at the same time, I bucked up into him.

"I want you to stay here with me."

"Are you gonna fuck me?"

"Oh yes."

"Then I'm staying."

He added two more fingers after that, skipping the second altogether. While normally that would have pinched or even jolted me out of my arousal, because of how he was taking care of me—the attention, the time—I just shivered as I flushed cold for a second before the heat rose on my skin.

"Raza," I breathed his name.

"God, that sounds hot when you say it," he rasped. He rubbed his fingers over my prostate, and he returned to sucking my dick, gently but relentlessly.

"Stop!" I yelled, trying to squirm off his fingers but unable to pull away from the delicious, persistent pleasure. "I want you buried in me when I come. Please."

He rose then, and I realized that the laughing, playful person I had started out with was gone. I had a very predatory man looking at me now with hooded, languid eyes and a grin of pure evil.

There was no doubt about it: he wanted me, and that knowledge was scorching. To see only desire, no judgment, was a brand new experience for me.

"Take what you want," I demanded.

He lifted up, and then grabbed hold of my ass. I arched up as he slowly spread my cheeks, feeling so decadent, knowing he was watching, enjoying what he was looking at.

He pressed against my entrance, and my cry was pleading and desperate.

I thought he would inch his way in. All my previous lovers had done it the same exact way: push gently, ask if I was okay, and then ease in a little more.

Raza sheathed himself in me in one powerful plunge that made me gasp. The lube that had been pushed inside of me and the slick condom allowed a slide that I had not been prepared for. He breached muscles that had given just a little after the stroking of his fingers but were still tight enough that the push brought an almost suffocating pain.

"Fuck, you're so tight," he groaned, pulling out partway, lifting my hips, changing the angle of his descent and dragging over my prostate on the next thrust.

Everything went white for a minute, the pleasure so acute that, at first, my body processed it as pain again before the heat gave way to rolling, sizzling pleasure.

Dear God, I had no idea it could be like that. I had spent my whole life afraid of being pounded into. I had thought it would hurt, and it did, but only for a moment. I had never thought the discomfort would give way to a deep throb of aching, devouring want.

I moaned his name.

"Fuck, you feel so good."

Words had never meant anything before. Never.

"You're so tight and hot... I'm gonna come. Grab your dick, baby. Get yourself off."

I was so full, so ravaged, so completely and utterly claimed. The feel of him sinking inside of me, so deep, so hard, had me trembling. "This is gonna make me come," I whimpered.

He changed his angle and pistoned his hips rapidly as his head dropped back and he gripped me tight with his hands. I would carry his marks on my skin for days.

"Cass," he rasped.

He swelled inside of me, pulsing as he came, his cock so thick that it was hard for him to keep moving, everything was so tight.

I spurted cum over his gorgeous, dark skin, seeing him marked making me cry out my desire. My whole body shuddered. My muscles clenched around him involuntarily, holding him tight, and I was powerless to stay silent.

"I wanna stay here with you," I said. Tears welled in my eyes, spilled, and rolled down my temples to my ears.

"Oh fuck, yeah." The sound rumbled low in his chest, and he stayed where he was, sheathed inside of me, and wrapped his arms around me. "You're not gonna leave me. I hope you're not all that attached to your job."

It didn't even matter what that meant.

CHAPTER FOUR

"SO TELL me how it works," he said, running his stubble-covered chin along my jaw, making his way to my ear.

I shivered because the man could not stop touching me, and I flat-out loved it.

"You're not talking." He chuckled and then sucked my ear lobe into his mouth, making me buck up against him.

I could barely think, let alone form sentences.

"Are you psychic?" He rubbed circles on my flat stomach with his hand as he spoke, the attention sending a roll of desire through me.

I didn't have the carved, rippling muscles Raza had: no six-pack, no chiseled pectorals, roped biceps and triceps, or gorgeous laterals. The man could make money just letting people take pictures of his beautiful, hard body and warm, sleek skin. I was not in his league, but at least what I had was tight and toned. He seemed appreciative, and I was in heaven.

"Cass?"

"Not psychic," I managed to get out, my breath choppy, my voice a husky rasp. "I can't find stuff or people. I just see what's in front of me once I look into your eyes."

"But you saw me get hurt," he said, pressing wet kisses down the side of my neck to my shoulder and then trailing his mouth down my collar bone to my chest.

"I saw you get more than hurt." I gasped as his lips closed over my right nipple and he bit down gently.

"You like that," he growled.

I arched up off the bed, pressing my skin to his, wanting more contact, wanting him to take me, ready.

He was staring into my eyes. "God, you're beautiful, I just want you wrapped around me all the time."

"That can *so* be arranged."

He took a deep breath. "I want you to look at me now."

"I am looking at you," I panted.

"No," he growled. "Look and see that I'm not sick with anything, and then I'm gonna go get the piece of paper out of my desk."

Never in my life had I gone without a condom. It seemed like too much too fast. "I—"

"Where is your clean bill of health?" he asked softly.

I carried a copy of my latest test results on my phone. "Why?"

"Because I want to fill you up and watch it drip out."

Fuck.

I threw my arm across my eyes because feeling him pressed against me and looking at him at the same time was too much. "It's on my-my… my…."

"Phone?"

He had actually melted my brain. "Yeah, the talking thing."

His chuckle filtered through me slowly, touched my skin, seeped through muscle and bone, and joined the blood rushing through my veins.

"So… condom?"

"Yes."

"Yes?"

"I mean no, I don't need one."

"Good. Move the arm."

Why the idea was so hot, I had no idea. Normally, I didn't even like to be messy, but the way he was looking at me, the dominance, the glittering eyes, the way his hands were possessive as he clutched me—I wanted to belong to him. I was crazed about the idea of him coming inside of me. It seemed necessary.

He kissed me before lifting off me, only to roll me to my side and plaster himself to my back. I heard the snap of the bottle cap even as he slid his right arm under my head and turned me into his kiss.

He slipped his talented tongue into my mouth and tangled it with mine. I felt a lube-slicked finger slide into my already quivering hole. The man was annihilating me, and as I lifted my left leg over his hip, I felt his cock nudge at my entrance.

"Let me in."

The mushroom-shaped head was wide, and even though I had never considered myself someone who cared about length or girth before, I knew I was spoiled for life at this point. He sank into me, and never had I been so stretched, so full, my channel rippling around him as he began slowly undulating within me.

"Your tight little ass can take all of me," he groaned deeply, pressing his hand to my abdomen, feeling my muscles bunch.

"Do I feel good?" I fished, head wedged beside his, my lips on his cheek. I pushed down with each of his slow, rocking thrusts, and our hips swiveled together in a sensual rhythm.

"Oh yeah," his voice cracked. He gripped my hard, leaking cock with his left hand and pressed his right to my forehead, holding me tight. "Your body fits mine so fuckin' perfect. You need to stay here, stay with me."

"Staying," I promised as he tilted up, catching my gland, pegging it. "Fuck!"

Slow was over. He rose fast, showing me the power in his body when he lifted me along with him into his lap. His back against the headboard with me straddling his hips, he snarled out his demand that I ride him.

My cock caught between our abdomens, now slicked with sweat, and I lifted up and levered back down, pushing deep, impaling myself over and over.

"I'm gonna come," I yelled, and he grabbed my face, startling me.

I was made to stare right into his eyes, not moving, not looking away, as I ground myself down onto him, my hips snapping forward even as the orgasm began its roll up my spine.

"Eyes on me," he said, taking hold of my cock, stroking me from balls to head with his right hand as his left slid around the back of my neck. "Don't look away."

"No," I whimpered. My balls tightened and I came in his fist, my muscles clenching all at once.

"Fuck, Cassidy, you're gonna kill me."

As I felt the hot liquid coat my inner walls, I shuddered with my own aftershocks. I clutched at his shoulders, needing to anchor myself, hold onto the connection.

He yanked me forward, and I parted my lips for his kiss. My mouth was ravished, mauled, and I returned all his passion, every drop of desire.

I could fall in love so easily. One more step and I would be at the edge of the cliff. The one after that would send me tumbling down into the abyss.

"God," he said, breaking the kiss, his lips hovering over mine, our breath hot and humid. "I don't think I can let you go, don't think I'm supposed to. Do you feel it?"

I felt him buried to the balls in my ass, my muscles trying to hold him there.

"Your heart, Cass, not just your skin," he directed. "I want to keep you, but what do you want?"

My body oversensitized, my heart wide open and raw, every defense down because of my obliterating orgasm, and he wanted answers from me? Wanted me to think?

"Cass."

I was not prepared to be witty or smart or even remotely clever. "Keep me," I said, because real and honest were all that was left.

He kissed me and wrapped his arms around me and held me tight to his chest.

I could have died right there, happy.

HE DECIDED to grill me in the shower because the man was a sadist. I was shampooing his thick black hair, massaging his scalp, and I was almost sure from the look of bliss on the man's face that he was going to have another orgasm.

"Feels good, does it?" I teased.

He whimpered loudly, and I cracked a grin I was sure was not cool in the least. There was no mystery, no guessing game, and usually there was for me. I made people wonder how I felt; it kept the ball in my court. But with Raza, I was there, an open book, and all he had to do was look at me and know I was head over heels, smitten.

As I watched him rinse his hair, simply looking at him got me excited again. I was a walking hard-on all of a sudden, and when I shoved him back against the wall of the shower and went to my knees, my name came out of his mouth as a litany. I had no gag reflex and so took him down the back of my throat without even choking on the length.

"Cassidy!" he roared, breath heaving, which made me feel like a god.

I sucked and laved, tugged and licked, and he fucked my mouth as I swallowed around him. There wasn't much when he came, but I drank it and then stood and let the shower wash him clean.

One arm braced on the stall, eyes closed, panting, he told me he was exhausted.

"Oh yeah? I wore you out?"

Then he grabbed me and lifted me into his arms, and I wrapped my legs around his waist as I hooked my hands behind his head. He was staring so intently.

"What?"

"I just—your eyes are the clearest blue I've ever seen, and I feel like I know them."

"How do you mean?"

"Haven't you ever heard people talk about meeting someone for the first time but feeling an instant kinship? Like old friends?"

I had heard about that but never experienced it until this man came into my life. "I feel it now."

He nodded. "Yeah, me too."

"That's good, right?" I asked, leaning in to trace his bottom lip with the top of my tongue.

He grunted out an agreement as he opened for me, one hand on my ass, the other on the back of my neck, making sure I didn't pull away. I kissed him and felt a tremor run through his big, strong frame. Apparently the man liked me just a little bit. I felt the same.

After we both toweled off and got back into his big, warm bed, snuggled down under the covers, he tried to ask me about my visions again. I gave him the abridged version.

"So," he said and yawned, tightening an arm around me to get me to wiggle closer. "After you look someone in the eye, it's like a flash of images and then gone."

"Exactly."

He yawned again, rubbing his eyes, and I enjoyed watching him struggle to stay awake. "Is it great or do you hate it?"

"A little of both, but my mother has always maintained that it was a gift, so I believed her."

"You're close, you and your mom?"

"We are. She's all I have."

"No," he said, matter of fact, both arms wrapped around me, the bear hug so needed and appreciated. His hugs were as good as his kisses, and I wanted more of both. "You have me too."

But that was too fast. Wasn't it? "Do I?"

"Yes," he said simply, and that was better than any other words he could have said. Just the facts. I had him. End of story.

"You're trying to kill me."

"No," he corrected. "You're gonna live… with me."

The man was much too good to be true.

CHAPTER FIVE

"PARDON me?" I asked the next morning over chocolate cake.

True to his word, Jamie baked the night before, and because we, Raza and I, had never reappeared, he sliced it up for breakfast the following morning. We each also got a large glass of milk, coffee, eggs, and bacon.

"This is so good," I gushed even with my mouth full.

Jamie wiped my mouth with a napkin. "Oh, I'm so keeping you."

"*I'm* keeping him," Raza grumbled, pushing my glasses back on my nose and staring at me. He could not keep his hands off me. He liked my head most of all, could not stop rubbing it before he put a hat on me, something that looked like what the sherpas wore in Nepal.

I could only imagine what I looked like, sitting there at seven in the morning in a pair of Raza's pajama bottoms, his dress shirt from the night before, my socks, and now a hat.

"I look like an orphan," I complained over coffee.

"You look amazing," he said, leaning in for a kiss.

Addicted.

After just one night, I was utterly addicted to the man and craved him like I had not wanted anyone else in my whole life. He felt right. It was inexplicable, completely without logic or basis in anything but lust, except… it wasn't just that. And no one would believe me, of course, but it was the truth. I looked at him and saw him asleep in an armchair, feet up as I flipped channels, saw him yelling at me, brows furrowed, furious that he couldn't make me grasp whatever it was he was telling me, and then saw him leaning his head on his fist, staring at me with love-soaked eyes. He wasn't perfect. I could already tell he was jaded when he talked about people, sarcastic instead of gentle, and grouchy and snarly in the morning. But God, the man had a soft spot for me. He was absolutely ready to turn himself inside out if I asked.

I would never ask.

And it was stupid that I would even care, but the fact that my being bald didn't faze him at all was just another reason to soak him up.

It was one of the things I normally thought about. All the romantic heroes had hair. Not one was bald, and I was, and it would come up...

"Why don't you try and grow your hair out instead of shaving it?"

"Have you ever thought about getting hair plugs?"

"You should put on a hat...."

But Raza—the only reason he shoved a hat on me was because it was cold and he explained that I lost heat through the top of my head. Hence the ugly hat with the fluffy balls at the end of the ties hanging off the sides. It had apparently been a gift from Jamie.

The man liked everything about me, even my boney little feet and my restless hands and the way my eyes were too big for my face. He complimented my upturned nose and my cheekbones and what he said were very expressive brows. But most of all, he liked my mouth and kissing me. So, lulled into a sense of loving languor, I was jolted when he said we had the worst timing ever.

"I'm sorry, what did you say?"

"I said," he sighed, reaching for my hand, "where were you two years ago when I decided to start this bullshit?"

"You lost me."

He took my hand in both of his, and Jamie came around the kitchen island to stand next to him.

"You missed the mark when you thought I was in the mob."

"I don't—"

"I'm on the other side."

"Please start speaking in full sentences."

He slid his wallet over to me, and I opened it and saw the badge.

I flicked my gaze up to his. "You're a policeman?"

"Look closer," he cautioned. "I'm a Fed."

Federal Bureau of Investigation. "So you're doing what?"

"Busting the bad guys, obviously."

I fiddled with the badge.

"Ask me something."

"This house," I said, meeting his gaze. "It's not yours, you said."

"It's been mine for the past two years while I've been living undercover, and I have to say that stepping back down into a house I can actually pay for will be hard." He grunted. "But this is paid for by the agency. We rented it for the duration of the operation to make me look like a player."

I nodded. "It's not just you undercover, right?"

"Nope. There's Dean you met last night, who you saved along with me."

"Did I blow your cover?"

"You saved my life."

"But with your undercover sting operation stuff."

He smiled at me as he shook his head.

"What?"

"Undercover sting operation?"

"That's not what it's called?"

"Come here," he said and chuckled, and when I leaned forward, he kissed me. "You taste like chocolate."

"I wonder why." I made my eyes big. "But really, I didn't screw things up?"

"No. Actually, the word from what we've been able to tell is that I've got a mole in Abel Reyes's operation now. Someone tipped me off. They just don't know who."

"But everyone saw me talking to you. Your guys grabbed me."

"Yeah, but all those guys with me are on the job. There are five of us altogether, so none of them said anything. People are scrambling inside Reyes's organization trying to figure out who said what. And that's good. That keeps everyone guessing, and when guys are afraid for their lives, they tend to want to turn state's evidence."

I was relieved. "I'm glad. I mean, I couldn't have done anything different, even if it would have messed up your operation. I had to keep you safe."

His eyes were really the most beautiful shade of spring green, and how warmly I was being gazed at made my stomach flip over.

"So who do the bad guys think you are?"

"They think I'm the guy who should have taken over from Kabo Bara."

"Go back, you lost me."

He released a deep breath. "Okay, Kabo Bara ran drugs here in Chicago up until two years ago, when Abel Reyes expanded his operation from Miami and, in the process, murdered Bara and all the guys under him."

"Oh, I remember reading about that," I said. "They found all those men killed in that warehouse in Chinatown."

"Yep, that's right. So Reyes is here, taking over, but then I come out of hiding as Hamad Aburi, and explain that I was Bara's number two man."

"And because you were here undercover already, anyone that Reyes checked with would vouch for you."

"Exactly." He shrugged. "I already had contacts, people knew me, and so I just stayed in place, stepping up into the role that Bara had."

"I bet Reyes was pissed."

"Yes, he was, and he's been trying for the past few years to get me out of Chicago one way or another, but he can't take over something that doesn't exist anywhere but on paper."

"Lost again."

"Well, we've dismantled Bara's entire operation here in Chicago, and it's been replaced with a computer trail, a money trail, and corporations and people that aren't real. The only people in Kabo Bara's old organization are me and my team—so, five guys—but as far as it looks from the outside, I have hundreds of people that work for me."

"So if Reyes checks, he sees and hears about millions, but there's actually nothing."

"Yes."

"And for the last two years, you've been cementing this relationship with Reyes as a rival but as a guy that he has to do business with."

"Right. He thought he would just take over Bara's business, but I was there so he couldn't."

"So you've basically put all Bara's old people in jail."

"Yes."

"That's amazing."

"We're pretty happy with it, yes. But now we want Reyes."

"And you've been at this for two years? Living this double life for that long?"

"Yes."

"And before that?"

"Still here. I've lived in Chicago my whole life, born and raised."

"But not undercover?"

"No. I was never out where people would see me or know me, just another guy in law enforcement, important to only a small group of friends and family."

"How do you have a life now?"

"I don't. I have no one except Jamie."

I turned to look at the beautiful young man beside him. "Are you his partner?"

"No." He shook his head. "I'm just something that followed him home."

I saw it then, the pinch of pain in the corner of his mouth, a haunted shadow in his big eyes. "Tell me."

Jamie bit his bottom lip. "It's a stupid story. You know the one. Mom threw me out when her boyfriend hit on me, so I was homeless and too young to do anything legal."

I waited, my eyes locked with his.

"So I did what I could, fell in with some scary people, and ended up traded around and a little druggish along the way."

But as I looked at him, all I saw was good. There was nothing bad anywhere near him. He was so bright and shiny and new.

"My here-and-now was looking a little grim, but then one day my knight here tells the guy who owned me, Kabo as it turned out, that he wants me."

I reached for Jamie automatically, and his hand came so fast to grab mine.

"Well, what am I, stupid? Does the sky have to down fall on me to get me to realize when my knight in shining armor is standing there in front of me?"

Right there… in front of me….

The mirth in his face was suddenly back, all happy bunny. "I had to follow, you know?"

I did. I was certain that Raza Bashandi had people trailing after him all the time.

"And once I got here and realized that I was gonna be his brother and not his lover, once I was clean inside and out, once I figured out what the hell I wanted to do… well, then I started looking out for a you."

"Because you were sure I'd be here."

"Of course."

"And that I would like cake for breakfast."

"Exactly."

"I do, you know. I love chocolate cake for breakfast."

"What took you so long?"

"I've never been punctual," I assured him. "But I promise to be better."

"Just stick."

"Like gum on the bottom of your shoe. You try and get away, but it stretches with you."

"Yes." His eyes got big as he nodded.

"You can pull other stuff apart."

"But not gum. It even has residue, so it's never really gone."

"Precisely."

"Can you two knock it off?" Raza interrupted. "You guys are, what, twins separated at birth? That's really annoying."

I turned my eyes on him and he growled at me. I was so crazy about him.

"And it wasn't that easy," he reminded Jamie. "You've worked really hard to get clean and get off the drugs and the alcohol and start your new life. Making up all that school was brutal, getting into college was even harder. Now you have to stay with it, and when we move—"

"Move?" I asked.

"Yeah," he sighed, hand on my cheek, dragging his thumb across my plump bottom lip, swollen because he'd been sucking on it all morning. "When you're this deep undercover, you don't get to stay in the same city when you're done."

"Where are you going?" I asked, heart in my throat.

"To Phoenix."

I took a quick breath. "When are you leaving?"

"Next week. This op goes down tomorrow night."

"Oh," was all I said, concentrating on breathing since it was hard all of a sudden. Of course he was too good to be true, that only made sense.

"So how'd you like to come with me?"

"Pardon me?" I inquired for the second time that morning.

He took my hand in his, tight, not letting me slide it from his grip. "I think I found you right now because you're supposed to come with me."

I just stared at him.

"It was fate."

"I don't believe in fate."

His grin made his eyes glow. "How can you not? What you do is, by definition, fate."

"No, I change fate. That's why I don't believe in it."

"But that is it," he insisted.

"Does anybody else's brain hurt?" Jamie asked.

"Listen, I was never going to get hurt last night because it was always my *fate* that you would be there to save me."

"But I saw—"

"You saw me beaten and killed first."

Jamie gasped, and Raza reached out and grabbed him, pulling him tight to his side.

"But then you saw me just killed."

It was worse now, because I knew what he felt like under my hands: his warm skin, the way he wrapped his arms around my bent knees when he hammered into me, and the slow drugging kisses I got lost in. The idea that I could have missed him was—

"And now you see what?"

All I saw was the virile man in front of me.

"You know you saved me. You *know* you did. You interfered, and isn't that interruption the very definition of fate?"

"No. Fate is like a line from the beginning of something to the end that doesn't—"

"But fate is everything, so how is it not you, saving me?"

My brain was spinning.

Raza passed Jamie his napkin so he could blow his nose. The thought of losing Raza obviously had the younger man very shaken.

"So you're, what, psychic?" Jamie sniffled.

"Not exactly."

"But you saved him?" he pressed.

"Yes, I did."

"How do you do it?"

"I look into people's eyes."

"Awesome." He was so excited. "So what happens? Do you get like a flash like Phoebe did in *Charmed*, or more like Cordelia in *Angel*?"

"You're watching way too many reruns."

"Yeah, but am I right?"

"He sees pictures in his head," Raza clarified for him. "Like a video."

"Oh, how cool."

It wasn't, exactly, but that was okay. What was amazing was sharing this part of me with not only one other person, but two. I trusted them to accept me and not judge, and they were perfect. They thought it was a gift, thought I was one… it felt like how a family would be.

"C'mon, how do I look?"

My attention flipped back to Jamie.

"Tell me what you see."

"You look fantastic."

"Are you sure?"

"Yes."

"No tears?"

"No tears."

"Okay, then it stands to reason that Bash will be okay."

Bash again, the same name Milo had used for his friend. Apparently, I was the only one who called him Raza, or even Raz. That was nice.

"Cassidy?"

"What?"

"That follows, right? I mean, if you look at me and see me happy… then he's fine."

Jamie was right; it had just been so long since I had been around people who were connected that I had forgotten you could measure one person's happiness with that of another.

"He's gonna be okay," Jamie sighed, turning to kiss Raza's cheek before leaning away from him, close to me, to kiss my cheek next. "And I have you to thank."

"No, I—"

"It was you," Raza said hoarsely. "Now just come with me."

"Where?"

"To Phoenix. Follow along."

"To Phoenix? Just like that?"

"Yes."

"You don't think that's too fast?"

"I don't care. The thought of flying out of here without you feels wrong. Just thinking about it makes me sick. I can't be thinking about you while I have a job to do. I'll get hurt."

Oh God, no.

"I'm supposed to keep you."

"It's too fast."

"Not if it's meant to be."

"That's ridiculous."

"You have to reach for what you want."

I did, he was right. But what if I was wrong? What if he was?

He leaned forward. "Say you'll come."

My gaze flicked to Jamie, who was looking at me with big pleading anime eyes. "He never asks anyone for anything, you know."

"Will you go away?" Raza groused at his ward before looking back at me. "And I know what you're thinking."

"What am I thinking?"

"You're thinking that I've been lying about who I am for two years, and so maybe that duplicity comes easy for me. You're thinking I could lie to you just as deftly."

It was frightening how well the man knew me after a day.

I watched the muscles in his jaw tighten. "I don't lie. I do my job. I'm living in a situation right now that to save lives, it's necessary for me to play a role. I live in this house, answer to a name that's not mine. I—"

"Hamad Aburi," I said.

"Yes."

"I like Raza better."

"I would hope so, since that's the one you'll be using."

I sighed deeply. "You're like a tornado."

His eyes were warm as he looked at me. "I've been told that before."

"Are you for real?"

"Yes, I am."

"How can you trust me? You just met me. I could be a mole for Reyes."

"Nope."

"How do you know? Did you have me checked out?"

He shook his head.

"Why not? I could have pretended to tell you something bad to get you to trust me, and then lulled you into—"

"Are you kidding? You left and then you came back. I was on my way to track you down."

"But you can't just trust strangers," I pointed out. "I mean, I'm glad you trusted me, but what if the next person tried to kill you or—"

He took my face in his hands. "Baby, I don't trust anybody, ever. All my instincts—that I never second-guess—said to grab you and not let go. So I'm not gonna do that. This is happening, and you're not getting away."

I could barely breathe as I took hold of his wrists.

"Always remember that you came back."

"And you remember that you were going to get me."

"Yes," he agreed and tilted my head up for a kiss.

The blatant ownership in every kiss was overwhelming. I felt so empowered—even though I was still wearing a really ugly hat.

"Awww, you guys are so adorable."

Raza growled and I started laughing. We parted and he turned to Jamie.

"What?"

"Do you have nothing else to do?" Raza grumbled.

"No, not really."

"So," I said as Raza let me go, "when you move, Milo will miss his friend."

"And I'll miss him and eating his food, but like I said, you can't be undercover like this and stick around. Tomorrow night's bust will put Abel Reyes behind bars for the rest of his life."

"So you're just going to disappear?"

"Yes."

"What's your cover story?"

"That I was busted too."

"So you're not going down in a hail of bullets or anything."

"No." He chuckled. "Only if I was retiring or being relocated permanently or something."

"Like into witness protection."

"It's not called that for law enforcement, but yeah, generally."

"Okay." It was a lot to take in.

"Cass?"

I cleared my throat because it had to be said. "You don't even really know—"

"I do know you," he said, easing me forward, taking hold of my hand, using his leverage, his superior strength, to move me. "You're it, my one shot. I usually hate October—all of autumn, but this month most of all. I don't even know why."

There was no way… he could not feel exactly as I did. It wasn't possible.

"I mean, the closer I get to the end of the month… I'm like a zombie. It's like I'm dead."

I normally described it as feeling empty, as though something had been taken from me but I had no idea what.

"Even when I was a kid, even though there was Halloween and all the candy—it's like I'm terrified all month. Like something happened that I can't remember."

"Maybe—"

"No, there's nothing. It's just me, just my gut."

"Your family, maybe?"

He shook his head. "My parents are both alive and well and living in Florence, where they retired eight years ago. My sister lives in Houston with her husband and her three kids. I have no mysterious family tragedy looming somewhere in the back of my subconscious. It's just me. Whatever this is, is all me."

I was scared, because, Jesus, I felt the exact same way. Every October filled me with dread. I had such a feeling of loss, and my dreams were worse.

"I have bad dreams too," he went on, and I felt my skin running with goose bumps. "Like I'm looking for something and I just can't find it."

He was reading my mind, and it was thrilling and terrifying at the same time.

"But now, I dunno," he said softly, his eyes meeting mine.

"What don't you know?"

He put a hand on my face, his fingers slipping over my jaw as he lifted my chin and bent toward me. "Since I brought you home, I don't feel it anymore."

His lips were right there, a breath from mine, but if I wanted the kiss I would have to take it.

"I think I was supposed to be there in that crappy bar that I've never been in before. I think you had to be there, meeting friends you never meet out because you need to go home, after a whole day of seeing the things you do, and rest."

"You think I need a—"

"Sanctuary, yeah," he said, smoothing a finger over my right eyebrow. "I think it's supposed to be me. I think I'm supposed to protect you, keep an eye on you."

Eye.

Keeping an eye on me.

Why did the idea of him just looking at me feel like it would be enough to keep me from harm? That was crazy. But everything about him and me, mostly him, was nuts. How could a man like this want me? And what was it about the man's eyes that just made me feel utterly safe?

The celadon eyes fringed with thick, black lashes, set deep beneath his glossy jet brows, almost looked as though they were lined. He reminded me of—

"Cass?"

"You're so regal looking."

"Oh yeah?" he baited. "I look like a king, do I?"

Like a king… or something.

"I feel—" he began, but he stopped himself, shook his head like whatever it was, was stupid, and kissed me instead. He pushed my head back, shoved his tongue down my throat, and got his hands under my shirt to my skin. I threw my arms around his neck and held tight.

With a heavy sigh full of whimpering happiness, I sighed against Raza's mouth as a frustrated groan came out of him. It was hard to pull free, but our lips parted, and we both turned to sweet Jamie. He was staring at us with dreamy-eyed wonder, chin on his folded hands, and he almost whined.

"God, you two are so beautiful together. I think I'm gonna go into diabetic shock from how sweet you are."

I chuckled and turned to look at Raza. His expression was not what I expected. He was not amused. But Jamie wasn't looking at him yet, and I wanted to save him from the glare.

"I have to get to work," I informed them both.

Jamie was sad; Raza was annoyed.

When I excused myself and returned to his bedroom, I was not surprised to hear him behind me minutes later.

"You can take a shower here," he said as I got dressed.

"And change into what?" I teased, turning to look at him over my shoulder.

His scowl was dark.

I faced him. "What's wrong?"

He was thinking, trying to put whatever it was into words.

"Tell me."

"I don't like other people seeing us."

I was lost. "I have no idea what you're talking about right now."

"I want privacy with you," he said. "I have this strange compulsion to—"

"Protect me."

His eyes met mine. "Yes."

It was just so strange. I was not a mind reader, but I could swear....

"THAT you can read his mind?" Snow offered helpfully.

I looked up at her and realized my mind had been drifting back to that morning. It was now after lunch, and I was trying to figure out what in the world I was going to do about the decision I needed to make. But today, Wednesday, was just as good as any other to decide my fate.

Certainly it was absurd to even consider, and yet....

"Please tell me what the hell's the matter with you, because you're so out of it today, I just wanna smack you."

I looked up into my assistant's big brown eyes. "Do you believe in fate?"

She flopped down into the chair in front of my desk. "This is going to be one of those long, convoluted discussions, isn't it."

"No, just tell me," I said, leaning forward to study her. "Do you or do you not believe in fate?"

"Of course I believe in fate."

"You do?" I was surprised.

"What kind of idiot doesn't believe in fate?"

"Well, me for one."

She tilted her head. "But that's stupid. Fate is arriving two seconds later at the traffic signal so you miss the guy who ran the yellow and plowed into the car in front of you. Fate is how your college roommate becomes your best friend ever. Fate is reaching for the same cup of coffee at Starbucks because the barista called out the name of the drink and not the person. That's fate. How can you not believe in that?"

"Those are just random acts, coincidences."

"But for some, that's fate. If the universe is indeed so orderly, I mean, if there are circles of life where one thing eats something else that eats something else—"

"Where are you going with—"

"Just—" She lifted her hand to shut me up. "If my heart, mine, can save some man's life I've never even met because I died, but he's got eight kids and needs to live. If those things can happen, how do you believe in random occurrences?"

"But then—"

"Cassidy, I—"

"Shhh," I hushed Kyle. He had just walked into my office. The door was open, as always, and he had sailed right in. "So, you're saying," I continued with Snow, "that you believe in predestination?"

"Of course."

"But where's the human element of choice, then?"

"You have a choice," she assured me, pushing her cropped curls behind her ears. "But there's not an infinite number of possibilities. There's going to be an A plan and a B plan."

"Cass—"

"Wait," Snow interrupted Kyle, never breaking eye contact with me.

"How can it be fate if there are two choices?" I asked.

"Because there has to be the hero's way or the coward's way, right? That just stands to reason."

"But that makes no—"

"Cassidy, I really—"

"Zip it," Snow growled at Kyle, her eyes still not leaving me. "Of course it does. Why do most big decisions come down to a safe way or scary way, a leap of faith way or the—"

"I have a whole room full of people here who—"

"—path of leaf resistance way."

"Least," I corrected. "Not 'leaf'."

"Least?"

"Yeah."

She thought a second. "That actually does make more sense."

"So, you're saying that I could either stay here and be safe or take a chance and jump."

"Yes, that's what I'm saying."

"But what if it doesn't work out? What if he ends up not wanting me or not loving me?"

"How is that possible if we're talking about a—"

"I must insist that you two—"

"—fated union?" she plowed on over Kyle. "If you're meant to be together, then what you're feeling, no matter how new, is the real deal. You can't go through life second-guessing yourself."

"No," I sighed, "I can't."

She clapped her hands together fast. "Oh, I helped, right?"

"Yes, you did."

Stopping suddenly, she leaned forward. "The *he* in question, who is that? Who are we talking about?"

"Raza Bashandi."

"Oooh, that's a pretty name. Is the man who owns it pretty too?"

"Yes," I assured her, "very."

"Like pretty by my standards or yours?"

I groaned. "Both—yours."

"Oh yum. And all the fate stuff, what are we deciding?"

"Whether or not I should move to Phoenix with him."

She caught her breath.

"And you," I said quickly. "I wouldn't go without you."

"Cassidy, for chrissakes!"

I turned toward the sound of the yell and saw that Kyle Jennings was red-faced and glaring. There were ten people with him, all looking uncomfortable.

"I am touring with the new counselors, and I was told to bring them in here to meet the top counselor in our—"

"Not anymore." I took a breath, standing up. "I'm going to Phoenix."

"You're what?" he asked.

"Really?" Snow was checking.

I turned to look at my assistant. "You could take my job here, you know."

"Oh fuck you," she yelled, standing up. "I wouldn't take your job on a bet. I hate these people that can't find their fuckin' soul mates for themselves. Jesus Christ, grow a spine and date."

I was stunned.

"What?"

"Grow a spine and date?"

"Yeah, I know, it's messy, you're gonna get hurt, but you dive in and find the one."

"So you stay here because—"

"Of you! I stay because you stay. If you're going, I'm going." She said it like I should, of course, have known that.

There was so much exasperation and attitude just dripping off of her, I couldn't help but smile. "You're so mad."

"Because you should know better!" she yelled. "The question should never pop into your head. Is Snow going with me? It's a given."

"I don't want you to waste your—"

"Cassidy Jane, I want to be your assistant until I die!"

It was morbid but cute, and so very heartfelt. I sighed deeply.

She huffed out a breath. "So, Phoenix?"

"Yes."

"Okay. To do what?"

"I don't know yet."

She nodded. "Fine. When are we going?"

"Next week."

She grunted. "All righty, then." She fluttered her eyelashes at me. "I'll type up our resignation letters, you can sign yours, and I'll hand deliver them both."

I came around my desk fast, pushing around Kyle to reach her. "Snow," I said, my hands on her upper arms, looking into her eyes. "Are you sure?"

"Don't you want me?"

Her face, her eyes, the sudden tremble that shot through her, told me everything I already knew, had known since we'd first locked eyes. It was me she trusted—just me. I was the only place she could look to and know for certain was safe. And I felt the exact same way about Raza Bashandi.

God.

"Cass?"

"Of course I want you, but you can't spend your whole life just taking care of me. You have to follow your own dreams and—"

"Why are you still talking? Please, enough already." She groaned melodramatically before she pivoted around with a fluidity only dancers have, shooed people out of her way, and strutted out of my office on her three-inch heels.

"My God, that woman is beautiful," one of the men said.

"Pardon me?" Kyle was instantly indignant as he turned on the newbie counselor. "That woman is an important member of this firm and not to be treated, or even looked at, with anything but the utmost respect."

I had to check to make sure I was actually looking at Kyle Jennings. *Gobsmacked.* Who knew the man even had that in him? He was really mad, and I was really impressed. I reached out and put a hand on his shoulder to get his attention.

"What?" He was irritated.

I wasn't even sure what to say.

"Before you go and jump ship, asshole, you need to talk to Rosalie with me."

"I... what?"

He was scowling. "For all you know, Phoenix might be a fantastic place to open a new office. Did you even think about that?"

No, I hadn't. The thought had never even crossed my mind.

"I mean, four years might actually mean something to her right?"

It might.

"It's not always all or nothing, you know."

Which was true as well.

"And maybe since you've been, like, the best counselor ever, she might actually think that it's a good idea."

I could not stop staring at him.

"Come on," he said, grabbing my bicep and tugging me forward.

Sometimes people really surprised me.

"Get out of the way," he grumbled at the crowd of counselors.

"This is amazing of you," I said as I walked down the hall beside him toward Rosalie's office.

"Yeah, well, I win either way."

I turned to look at his profile. "How so?"

"You leave, I'm number one here. You relocate, same deal."

"So then why?"

"An office in Phoenix might be nice to take over if I ever get sick of Chicago."

"What makes you think I'd let you take over my office?"

"There's the spirit!" He smirked.

God, you thought you knew a person.

CHAPTER SIX

"SEE," I said to Snow, pointing. "I told you."

"What?" she asked, looking up at me from digging around in her purse for lip balm. We had finished up our day and she had driven me home as she did upon occasion. Standing out in front of my graystone, it was a real treat to watch Raza coming down the sidewalk toward me. Our timing had been perfect.

I had no idea why Raza Bashandi was coming to see me before his meeting with Abel Reyes, but I wasn't about to complain. "I told you he was pretty."

"Who? Where—oh, is that him?"

"Yeah, that's him," I sighed, watching the big, strong, beautiful man with the scowl on his face hurry to reach me. He took my breath away.

"Oh, well done, Cass," she whispered as he reached us. "I think I swallowed my tongue."

"Hi," Raza said, his voice a low rumble, putting his hands on my face. "How are you?"

No doubt about it, I was madly in love with the man who bent and kissed my nose.

"How was your day?" he asked, kissing my right eye, then my left, then my cheek, and finally my lips. "Did you miss me?"

"Yes... and yes."

"Yes to...," he drew it out even though I knew from the heat filling his eyes he was following right along.

"You know."

"I want to hear it."

I cleared my throat. "Phoenix. Yes to Phoenix."

"And?"

"Yes to you, Raza Bashandi."

"Good boy," he said in a rush, grabbing me and wrapping me up in his big, strong arms.

I hugged him back as hard as I could.

"It's fast."

"Scary fast," I agreed.

"But real is real."

And that was true too. "I love you."

"Oh baby, me too," he groaned. "I love you back."

I let the last bit of uncertainty go, and I was suddenly standing on solid ground. "You need to go so you can get back home to me."

He let me go and stepped back, but he put his hands right back on my cheeks. "Listen, I won't see you tonight because I can't go back to my—"

"Come to my apartment," I begged. "Bring Jamie. I have room. Please."

He squinted at me. "Are you sure?"

"Yeah, I mean, it'll be safe, right? Nobody knows about me."

Nodding, he looked up and finally saw Snow. "Hi there."

"Hi," she whimpered.

I introduced them, the man of my dreams to the girl I was bringing along on the adventure with us. He held her hand in both of his, and she gazed at him like he was the second coming or something while tears welled up in her eyes.

"This is good," he said when he turned and took hold of the back of my neck. "Now Jamie has someone to play with."

"Who's Jamie?" she asked.

"His Snow," I clarified.

"Oh." Her face broke into a new smile. "I can't wait to meet her."

"Him," I corrected.

"Oh, thank God," she exhaled loudly. "I was worried. I have to be the only diva in the room."

Raza chuckled. "Only diva?"

"Jamie can be a little bit diva if he wants," she informed him.

"Good," he said before looking back at me. "Because he already is. I'll send Jamie to your place. He packed us both up this morning after you left."

"What about the rest of your things?"

"Most of my stuff was in storage, but it's on its way to Phoenix now. It'll be waiting when we get there."

"We" was nice to hear.

He ran the back of his knuckles up the column of my throat and then tipped my chin up. "Wait up for me, okay?"

"Of course."

"Okay," he whispered and then bent and kissed me.

It was not the sweet, gentle "I'll see you later" kiss, it was the "let me check your tonsils" kiss meant to make my knees weak. I was lucky I stayed standing.

"I love you," he said under his breath. "And I know that's damn scary fast, but I feel like you used to be mine or something—I dunno. It's like we're married. I could just grunt parts of words and you'd understand."

"I know." I smiled up at him. "I feel good today, like something lifted."

"Yes, exactly," he rushed on. "That's it."

"I want to figure it out."

"I don't think it's to figure, I think it just is. But you can dissect me in Phoenix, okay? You can start tonight."

"Promise?"

"I promise," he said. "Look and see."

I stared at him, into his eyes, and saw him walking, talking, and breathing. Saw him with me... later.

"Am I good?"

"Yes."

"Okay," he said and kissed me again, just as hotly, just as possessively as he did the first time. A car came as though on cue, and he got in and was gone.

"Why were you looking at him?" Snow asked. "What were you supposed to be seeing?"

I looked at my dear, sweet Snow. "I need to tell you something."

SHE was not sweet. She was a harpy from hell after she heard my confession, and it only escalated when Jamie got to my apartment three hours later. Snow had followed me home to yell at me some more.

"You didn't tell her?" Jamie asked. "I thought you guys were friends?"

"*He knows?*" She sputtered and fumed some more.

I wanted to go get something to eat because I was starving, but Jamie looked so sad. I wanted to talk to him and find out what... was... bothering....

He and Snow were talking, standing together, him with his low-rise vintage jeans hiked down even further, and her with her shirt up. They were comparing tattoos. He was laughing, charmed by her. He wasn't sad at all.

"Look at me," I said sharply.

Jamie was giggling. "Wait a minute, I—"

"No, that's his serious voice," Snow enlightened him, turning to me. "Ohmygod, what's with your face?"

Jamie's head snapped toward me.

It was the eyes; I always had to look into them, just for a moment, for the vision to kick in. Seeing a back, a hand, even the top of a head would not do it. There had to be a locked gaze, if only for a second.

"Oh God." Jamie trembled.

I saw the anguish then. Snow was holding onto him tight, and her eyes were flooded with tears as she looked up at... me.

"No no no no," I chanted, hands out in front of me. Something had changed, some piece had been altered. I had looked at the man I loved before he left and everything was fine, he was well, but now.... While I knew events were fluid, I had never been treated to so fast a reality shift. But neither had I ever known the level of danger Raza dealt with.

"Cass?" Snow was worried about me.

"Fuck no. I don't jump alone. That was so not the deal."

"What is he—"

"Into the relationship," Snow translated. "Cassidy's not jumping alone. Where the hell is Raza?"

"I'll call him," Jamie placated, pulling his cell phone out of his back pocket, hitting a button, pressing it to his ear.

I held my breath.

We all waited.

He lifted it away. "No answer."

"What's wrong?" Snow asked, her face scrunched up with worry for me.

"Raza's in trouble," I said quickly before turning back to Jamie. "Does he have a GPS on his phone?"

Jamie's smile was brilliant. "Yes, he does."

Yes, he did.

Best. Invention. Ever.

YES, it should have been scary. We were going to God knows where to face God knows who, and even with a broad definition of cavalry, we weren't it. We looked odd. I was in Dockers and a fisherman sweater, and Snow was in the sneakers, yoga pants, and hoodie she had changed into after work while headed to the gym. Jamie, in his jeans, too tight T-shirt, and motorcycle boots looked like he was on his way to a rave. We didn't look like we could save anyone. None of that mattered. All that mattered was getting to Raza and making sure that none of us was crying because he was gone.

I would not lose what I had just found.

What went through my head was what he had said about fate and me. Could just my knowing something save him?

The GPS on Jamie's phone, following Raza's, took us to an art gallery down off North Milwaukee Avenue, and it was so far off from where I thought a shady drug meeting would be taking place that I was sure for a second it was wrong. Someone else must have taken his phone.

"Do you guys hear that?" Jamie asked me as we stood in front of the locked glass doors.

"Hear what?"

"I've been dialing his phone," Jamie answered me, distracted, "over and over. I think...."

The Closed sign, a beautifully made piece in multicolored stained glass, sat squarely in the front window. The gallery itself, The Eye of Horus, specializing in Egyptian art, looked deserted.

"Wait. Do I hear techno?" Snow asked.

"Yeah." Jamie nodded, really concentrating for a moment before he began walking toward the side of the building.

One we stopped, all of us listened together, and then Jamie turned sharply and bolted. Seconds later, he had Raza's iPhone in hand.

"Okay." I took a breath. "So this is the right place. Let's find a way in."

"He likes techno?" Snow chuckled at Jamie.

"It's worse than that. The man listens to trance music." He rolled his eyes. "It's all *oont-oont-oont-oont* when he's home vegging out. He plays it so loud, I swear to God you can feel it inside your chest. He was a total club kid, you can tell."

I found that information incredibly appealing.

"If that's his only flaw, we'll take it."

"Yeah." Jamie chuckled. "It's not."

Snow laughed, and it helped the tension.

"Here," I said, finding a window into the basement. "We'll get in through here."

It took some doing, but I kicked out the glass, and then we all crawled through the small space. Raza wouldn't have made it. We were all small and thin, none of us heavy with muscle. Lucky. Once we were inside, on the concrete floor, Jamie used the flashlight app on his phone, and Snow called 911.

"God, we don't even know if he's still here." I whimpered, getting more and more worried by the second. "Maybe we're calling the police for no reason."

"But we know he was here, and we know he probably didn't just drop his phone because he's clumsy," Jamie sighed, trying to stay strong. "So even if he's gone and the bad guys with him, this is a good place for the police to start."

"So we need to be careful that we don't mess up any evidence while we're crawling around in here, plus," Snow whispered, "if Raza's still here along with lots of guys with guns... then we need to be quiet and we need some damn backup."

She was right; one way or another, calling the police was a good idea. This was either where Raza was being currently held or a crime scene. I was hoping he was there.

Everything was damp and musty, and I understood why the place had been chosen. It was out of the way and possibly either in foreclosure or in the process of trading hands. I could not imagine anyone had been in the basement for months.

"Do you hear that?" Jamie asked suddenly.

"Don't start with that again. What—"

We all heard the yell at the same time.

"Shit, C'mon, let's go."

The stairs were old and creaky, but once we opened the door that led from underground to the first floor, we understood why no one had heard us.

Raza was screaming as a man cut into his left shoulder.

It hurt my heart.

"Are the police coming?" I whispered to Snow as Jamie lifted his phone and hit record.

"They're coming," she assured me, nodding.

Looking back, I saw that Raza was handcuffed to a statue of Anubis. His wrists were caught around one of the god's legs, and he was bleeding. His shirt was off, he was mottled with cuts, and his left eye was completely swollen shut. The coughing he was doing sounded wet, and his breath was labored. The man who had just sliced into him took a step back.

I saw another man bend to punch him.

Raza squirmed sideways, and the fist connected firmly with Anubis's thigh. I suspected, from the yell, that the statue had to be made of some kind of stone.

"What the fuck is going on?" another man asked as he came striding into the room. "I told you assholes, I'm fucked! Everyone who was at that meeting tonight is going to jail! I want this fucker dead, and I want his body torched."

"Oh shit," Jamie breathed from beside me. "That's Abel Reyes."

So the deal must have already gone down.

"Fucking Feds are looking for him and me! I don't want them finding him. I don't want him cutting any deals! Fuckin' shoot him!"

Another man lifted his arm.

You never know what you're capable of until you're faced with a choice.

I looked at Raza and saw his head back, eyes closed, dead in my arms. I made up my mind that it was never going to happen.

All I thought was that I needed my own gun. It was the only thing in my head. So I rushed the guy standing maybe ten feet in front of me, putting my shoulder into it and sending him sprawling forward onto the ground. Jamie was right there with me, kicking at the guy as other people yelled, but Snow was the one who reached underneath him and pulled out the prize.

I heard the shot even as the gun was shoved into my hands, and we all ran toward Raza. But no one was shooting at him anymore. They were shooting at us.

"What the hell are you guys doing here?" Raza shouted, his roar much louder than I would have thought possible with his injuries.

"We came to save you!" Jamie yelled back indignantly, even as we all fell down around him.

I scrambled close, shielding him with my body, ending up in his lap.

"You're going to get yourselves killed!" He was furious and his eyes were blazing and hot. But I was so happy to be close to him and even happier with my vision....

Raza, pacing and yelling, bandaged, hurting, but in one piece.

I heard the scream of sirens at the same moment jolting me into the present.

"Cassidy!"

Abel had his gun raised, pointed at Snow, and I saw his eyes....

She was on the ground and her curls were washed scarlet.

No!

I swiveled around, but my foot got caught under me, and I ended up falling backward into the statue. My fist clenched around the gun and it fired.

There was yelling then, and feet pounding across the floor.

"Drop the weapon!"

"Put down the gun!"

"Holy shit," Raza gasped.

"That was amazing," Jamie whispered.

And Snow was suddenly in my arms.

"Drop the gun!"

"I'm FBI!" Raza was screaming. "These people are with me! I'm FBI!"

I dropped it and lost my balance, going down under Snow to the floor as she began to sob.

What the hell had happened?

THE FBI took our clothes, our phones, and our statements. Then they questioned us separately and finally put us all together in a conference room and brought us bottled water. I wanted alcohol.

When Agent Kevin Pearlman came in another hour after that to talk to us, Jamie explained to him that we all needed vodka.

"Make mine a double," Snow simpered.

He glowered at her before turning back to me. There was only one question he needed to have answered... why did we go looking for Special Agent Bashandi? I had been informed that because Raza was in field work, the "Special" got added. It was very cool.

I stared at him, into the blue of his eyes. "I had a vision."

His eyebrows lifted. "You're a psychic?"

"Yes," I lied. "I knew he needed help, and since Jamie always makes sure the GPS on Raza's phone is turned on, we tracked him to that gallery."

"Alone."

"As we said, yes," I said, trying not to sound bitchy. "When can we see Special Agent Bashandi?"

"Soon."

"Why not now?" Snow asked.

"Well, we still have—"

"Do you know," she began haltingly. "I mean, did Special Agent Bashandi happen to mention to you who Mr. Jane is to him?"

The question was worded very cautiously.

I held my breath.

"Yes, ma'am, he did."

He did. He told him. I took a breath.

"Special Agent Bashandi has informed us that Mr. Jane is his partner."

Partner.

I was the one he loved.

It was in my chest then, the bloom of uncontrollable happiness. That's what he had meant when he said I was going to complicate his life. Because he had to be honest; he had to claim me and say I was his. It was his way, the honorable way, the right way. I wanted to see him so desperately.

"That was a hell of a lucky shot, Mr. Jane."

I turned to look at him. Shot? "I'm sorry?"

He glared at me. "When you fired up at the statue, it ricocheted off the dog's snout and hit Abel Reyes in the hand. That's why he dropped the gun."

I was lost. What dog?

"That was Anubis standing over us," Snow corrected him. "Show some respect, Agent."

He scowled at her. One of her perfectly formed brown brows rose. I saw him change his mind—not out of respect for the Egyptian protector of the dead, but for the woman in front of him.

"Yes, ma'am, Anubis."

She gave him a nod.

"I guess he was looking out for you." Jamie sighed.

"I guess so."

"Or your man."

My man. It sounded good.

I looked back at the federal agent, who was still gazing at Snow. "Can we see him now?"

"Unfortunately, he's going to be debriefing for the rest of the evening. You should expect him in the morning."

"So he's okay?"

"Yes, Mr. Jane, as I said before... as I've said many, many times at this point, Special Agent Bashandi sustained bruised ribs, a mild concussion, various scrapes, and one large laceration to his shoulder requiring forty-seven stitches to close."

"But he's okay?"

His left eye twitched. "He is in far better shape than any of you."

"We're fine," Jamie assured him, chin up.

"You threw up seven times, Mr. Kidd."

Snow giggled.

"Well, crap."

I took a breath. "So for sure in the morning?"

"Yes, Mr. Jane, in the morning."

"But he's fine?"

The twitch had moved to his jaw.

"Right?"

"He just wants to make sure," Snow assured the man.

"Since he's his partner and all." Jamie beamed.

Agent Pearlman just nodded.

CHAPTER SEVEN

JAMIE decided to sleep at Snow's apartment, which was fine with me. The solitude was nice, especially since I would have them both with me constantly once we made the move to Phoenix.

At home I turned on my laptop before I poured myself some granola, and by the time I got back, my e-mail was up. I sent my mother a message, then Wyatt, and finally Kyle, thanking him for what he did earlier in the day. Rosalie had been thrilled with the idea of me taking Nostalgia on the road and opening a new office in Phoenix. She would be out to shop for property with me at the end of November. She wanted to give me time to settle in before she put me back to work.

After getting up, I left my dirty bowl in the sink, which I normally never did, and staggered to the bathroom. I took a long, hot shower, shaved my head, changed into sweats and a T-shirt, and was on my way to check the burners on the stove before I went to bed—gas stove, never could be too careful—when my doorbell rang.

I didn't check before I opened the door.

"You're supposed to check the goddamn peephole," Raza growled. "That's what it's for!"

"Oh God." I shivered as I reached for him. His left shoulder was wrapped in a bandage, his arm in a sling. He was wearing a T-shirt and jeans, not what he'd had on earlier. "Oh baby, come here."

"No." Raza scowled at me with the one eye he could see out of, his left. "You need to—will you stop that? Listen to me. Get your hands off of—"

"Who else would it be this late at night besides you?"

"You could have been killed right there!"

"Ass!" I yelled, pulling him into my apartment, locking the door behind us, making sure I turned the deadbolt. "Come here!"

"Quit shoving me," he growled, turning to face me.

I grabbed his hand with both of mine and yanked.

"What are you doing?"

"I want you in my bed, but I don't want to hurt your ribs."

"You think yanking on my arm isn't hurting my ribs?"

"Go get in the bed!"

"Come here!"

"I don't want to hurt—"

"Now!"

I leaped at him and he laughed with the impact instead of crying out. Anchoring me with one arm, he carried me to the bedroom.

"Oh God, this is all I wanted—just to hold you." He sounded so happy, so content.

"Jamie's with Snow," I said as I kissed every bit of skin I could reach: forehead, cheeks, gentle over the hurt right eye, his nose, the lashes on his left eye, his eyebrows.

"I don't care."

"He's your ward." I chuckled. "You have to care."

"He's with Snow, Snow's with him, neither one of them are here... I'm glad."

"I—"

"Kiss me."

He lifted his chin and I slanted my mouth down over his, sealing our lips together. I savored his taste, and even more, knowing that he was mine. We tumbled down onto my bed together, and only then did he groan.

"Oh God, I'm so—"

"No," he said, arching over me, closing his left eye when my hands gently cupped his face. "You didn't hurt... I'm... just touch me some more." He was trembling.

"Come lie down with me," I soothed, moving up toward the headboard, grabbing a pillow for him.

Raza was much bigger than me—stronger, heavier, and more muscular. That did not stop him from collapsing beside me. His head was on my chest, holding me tight with his good arm, his right leg sliding between my two.

I sank my fingers into his thick hair and massaged his scalp. The whimper he gave was so sweet.

"Feels like months, years," he mumbled.

"Yes, it does," I agreed, because it did. I had known him not quite a full forty-eight hours, but it felt like we had been together for ages, since back to the time of the pharaohs. We just fit like nothing I had ever imagined or hoped for. "You read about stuff like this, but you never think it could happen."

"No."

"Thank you for coming tonight instead of in the morning."

"Tried to get here earlier," he managed to say as he yawned. "Best I could do."

"You told them," I said into his hair.

"Of course." He exhaled, and I could tell from the way his body got heavy that we were done talking after this. "You belong to me. Gonna get you a ring. I love you."

"I love you too," I said, kissing his forehead and continuing to stroke his hair. In the morning, I would tell him about my plans for Phoenix, about the kind of partner I was going to be. I would tell him that I would follow him anywhere, any time. He could count on me. I was ready for my adventure. I was ready to live.

MARY CALMES currently lives in Honolulu, Hawaii, with her husband and two children and hopes to eventually move off the rock to a place where her children can experience fall and even winter. She graduated from the University of the Pacific (ironic) in Stockton, California, with a bachelor's degree in English literature. Due to the fact that it is English lit and not English grammar, do not ask her to point out a clause for you, as it will *so* not happen. She loves writing, becoming immersed in the process, and falling into the work. She can even tell you what her characters smell like. She also buys way too many books on Amazon.

BELIEVED YOU WERE LUCKY

AMY LANE

I wish you believed in life, believed in fate,
Believed you were lucky and worth the wait…

"(Believed You Were) Lucky" by Aimee Mann

PROLOGUE

VERDANDI woke up and stretched, her fingertips reaching for Yggdrasil, the tree of life, and the blue firmament beyond, her toes digging into the verdant green fundament below it.

Goddess! Didn't everyone need a good fuck once in a while?

Her full, perky breasts still tingled, and all points south? She shuddered deliciously. Oh, yes. Loki could definitely… well, fuck like a god, right?

"Oh, sister!" Urdh must have been wearing her mother form today—because her voice was too.

Verdandi groaned. Really? They were doing the mother thing? She refused. She was young and hot and well used—she was *not* going to go all matronly just because Urdh said so.

"Sister!" Urdh called again, and this time, her voice had become saccharine and irritating—like Verdandi was going to fall for *that* trick again.

"*Sister!*" Oh crap. Dandi had to get out there or Urdh would bitch at her for all of her weaving time. More than one man's fate had been screwed and tangled, because while Urdh's spinning wheel practically had a mind of its own, Verdandi's loom needed her *full* attention.

"*What!*" Dandi snapped. "*What!*" She threw a shift of clouds over her head that fell into an attractive summer dress, and then she stomped from her rank, sexed bed of lush grasses to what amounted to her office on the other side of the tree.

Urdh was standing there wearing a cloud version of polyester slacks and a twinset, complete with fake pearls, her hair up in a sprayed helmet of forced brown curls. Not all of motherhood's guises were attractive.

"Did somebody have a good night?" Urdh asked patiently. "Hook up with a god, maybe? Maybe, I don't know, Puck, perhaps?"

Without meaning to, Verdandi grimaced. No amount of frolicking in a nearby stream made Puck smell like anything but goat. And he fucked like one too.

"Maybe not," Urdh said, speculation written all over the beginning lines of her face. "Maybe someone a little flashier—a little less… woodsy. Hermes, perhaps?"

Ugh! Hermes? Too much tongue.

"Hermes gives face like a slobbering Saint Bernard," Skuld said from her squat near Dandi's loom. She was wearing old crone today, and Dandi looked at her curiously, because Skuld didn't usually speak and she very rarely ventured near anyone else's equipment. Usually she was sorting fiber from the well of possibilities to card. Most thought Skuld's primary job was to cut the thread of life when Verdandi's work at the loom had ended, but really? The materials Skuld chose were incredibly important in deciding when that moment would come. Skuld took her job seriously—and no, she did not venture into anyone else's territory.

Dandi nodded sympathetically, taking Skuld's gambit and running with it. "Really does," she said, looking at Urdh in apology. "If he were human, I'd say he had some sort of spit syndrome."

Uh-oh. Urdh had her famous "Odin give me strength!" look. That didn't bode well for *anyone.*

"So not Hermes," she said slowly, and Dandi raised her eyebrows a couple of times, because given whatever had happened, that only left a few options, and, yes, Verdandi *was* that good.

"Not Coyote, either," she said smugly. Although Coyote was also a wild man in bed, he was not *nearly* as hot as the god who'd left only moments before.

"So, you hooked up with a warrior trickster god, did you?" Urdh asked, her voice cold and long-suffering. "Someone hot, and urbane, and oh so smooth, did you?"

"And good in bed." Verdandi preened. Skuld cast her a droll glance, and Verdandi winked. Whatever the problem was, it didn't change the fact that last night had been so very good. Loki, with his dark looks and piercing eyes and that way he had of burning icy inside your skin.... She shuddered and then remembered that she *did* have responsibilities. "Why?" she asked, suddenly all business. "What'd he steal?"

Urdh told her, eyes smoldering with I-told-you-so, and Verdandi was so surprised she made her sister repeat herself.

"What?" she asked for the fifth time. "He did *what*?" She strode over to the loom, her dress going from floaty and gauzy to woman's power suit with pencil skirt and blazer in one step. Her hair, which had been loose and curling yellow around her hips, pulled up in a tight bun, and she adjusted her cheaters when she examined her precious, precious work.

"*Loki, you limped-dick ass fucker!*" she screamed, and the harpies clattered their feathers in the top of the tree.

"Would you keep it *down*!" Urdh hissed, grabbing her arm. "If Thor finds out about this, he's going to go apeshit! You know how he feels about Loki stepping out—it'll be *Ragnarok!*"

For a moment Verdandi was all hurt maiden. "Sif's in Asgard. Loki told me they'd broken up!"

"They never break up, Dandi," Urdh said, her voice dry. "They fuck around so they can make up. But if Thor finds out that Loki *stole* something, kept something from one of his little side dishes, that'll be different."

"But why?" Verdandi wailed. "Why would he do that? From now on, all those in the line of that tapestry will be shorted. Some part of their line will be deficient, without—their *wyrd*, their *moira*, their—"

"Luck," Skuld said thoughtfully. "But that's not why he stole it. Look here."

"Aw...," Verdandi said, and Urdh and Skuld echoed her. There was nothing sweeter than seeing a man with a baby—even *they* had to admit that.

"Is that his?" Verdandi murmured, and then Urdh, her voice at its most maternal, spoke up.

"No—look at him. The golden hair, the blue eyes."

"Oh shit," Verdandi muttered. "Dammit, fuck, *Scheiße*, shit, fuck, bloody buggering hell."

All three women looked at the baby again, a sort of pained recognition on their faces. This... this, they could not demand be fixed. This thread Loki had stolen was a gift—a gift at a dear cost for both of the gods, the dark and the light, whose passions ruled Jotunheim.

"It's not his, child," Urdh said, because she was the one who organized things. "It's Thor's."

"But what shall we do?" Verdandi said, looking unhappily at the loom. "That ancestry from whence the thread came—they shall be forever doomed...."

"No, no," Skuld said, pulling random sparkling fibers out of her pile of carding. She went to the broken thread sticking out of the loom and took the end coming from the bobbin, then licked her palms and rolled the fibers together along with the two ends of yarn.

"You're *spit-splicing* their destinies?" Urdh demanded, her sense of propriety obviously offended, and Skuld nodded, continuing to roll the fibers between her heated palms until the friction and moisture caused them to meld and felt together.

"But if there's enough fiber to spit-splice...," Urdh wailed, looking back into the tapestry, where they saw the baby take the pretty gold thread into its chubby fist. The thread glowed brightly and then disappeared, but its imprint was still bright on the tapestry itself.

"Yes, I know, sister," Verdandi said thoughtfully, examining the fibers her sister had used. "Neither end of the thread was complete. The one the infant has—it's imperfect as well." She looked up at Urdh and smiled. "It should work. It really should. The family with the thread, they shall be lucky, long-lived, and blessed—mostly. And the family without? They shall be unlucky and doomed—but optimistic and intelligent and resourceful. It's not luck," she said sadly, "but it will last until the real solution arrives. Thank you, sister," she said to Skuld. "That was kind of you, to help that family in the wake of my foolishness."

Skuld shrugged, and for a moment, she was a sly and sloe-eyed girl. "Loki fucks like a god," she said. "Sometimes that's worth the risk."

Verdandi smiled at Urdh in vindication, but she was still wearing her power suit, all-business guise, and she knew the lines around her eyes were deeper and her expression older than the girl who'd awakened that morning, and she was relieved. "Sometimes," she conceded regretfully. "I hope it was this time."

Urdh let out a disgusted chuff of air. "I think both families are going to be buggered," she said, but beyond that, she let the matter drop. The sun had already risen, and the three of them had duties, always duties: the carding, the spinning, the weaving, the cutting, the business of the Fates in the world.

LEIF TORVAL
"DESCENDANT OF THOR"

LEIF TORVAL woke up in the morning because his cat crapped so pungently in its cat box that Leif's eyes watered as he took his first breath of 6:00 a.m. Anyone else would have said this was a shitty way to start the day, but Leif knew different. His alarm clock had died in the middle of the night, and if the cat hadn't had the bowel movement of the apocalypse, Leif would have been late, and his boss would have yelled, and *that* would have been a shitty way to start the day.

Leif hated it when anyone yelled, so he thanked Loki the cat for taking a giant dump, cleaned the cat box, sprayed some air freshener, and hopped in the shower.

He'd been a happy, chubby, cheerful baby, and he was a happy, bubbly, cheerful adult—a life of luck might have made him that way naturally, but his life hadn't been *all* lucky, so maybe most of it was just Leif.

His mother had been a beautiful, golden-haired, tall Norwegian woman who had—counter to all family tradition—died early in a car accident. Leif was supposed to be *in* the car, but his grandmother, Leni, had suddenly decreed that he needed to stay with her one more day and that Ingrid and her new boyfriend could come back for her son in the morning. When Leni got the news that Ingrid had died, her face had slammed shut like a granite vault, and she'd said, "I would have told her, I would, but that one would never believe."

Leif had heard her say those words, and so he'd very carefully believed every word his grandmother had told him about the old gods. He wasn't actually certain they existed, or if maybe they meant something else in this day and age, but he kept his mind and his heart open to things—and, of course, he had the string.

And now, as he stooped in the tiny shower cubicle in his apartment in San Francisco, he closed his eyes and saw the string.

The string was bright gold, and Leif had noticed it the morning after his mother had died. He woke up and closed his eyes, and there it was, snaking from one idea to the next, from one thing to do to the next, until there was his day, too, mapped out by a yellow piece of string.

Grandma, don't go to that place for fish today. The string says to get bagels instead.

The next day, people would be sick from the fish, and Leif and his grandmother would be just fine, living on the bagels from the nearby bakery.

Hey, Leni—you having trouble paying the rent? Here, give me five dollars. I'll be right back.

And sure enough, the string took him to a $25,000 lottery ticket in his first year of college. Leni paid her raised rent, and Leif got his first year paid off in one blow.

The string was not perfect, and it was not invincible. It told Leif not to leave one morning when his grandmother was tired, and Leif didn't save her life that day, but he was able to be there as she passed away, and that was special. The string didn't tell him not to fall in love with Tom Chen in his third year of college, which was unfortunate, because after a two-year relationship, Tom got married to a nice Chinese girl his mother approved of and Leif was left heartbroken and alone. The string didn't tell him which classes to take in college, and when Leif took all the ones in literature and humanities, he was surprised to find himself with a humanities degree and no job skills whatsoever.

But that was okay, because the day after he'd walked the stage—alone, with no one in the audience to cheer him on—and taken his diploma in the humanities, he'd walked by a bicycle messenger service. He *loved* riding his bike in the city. The golden string stretched before him, told him when to go down Polk, when to avoid the Embarcadero, which streets would be clearest when he needed to run parallel to the wharf.

He took the job, and while he had to take another delivering flowers on the side, he didn't mind. He had his tiny apartment (since Leni's house was too much for him to pay rent on) and his bicycle and his city. If the string sometimes told him to turn one way, giving a little warm glow that said he'd find happiness that direction, and if Leif ignored it, well, maybe he didn't want happiness. Maybe happiness got you alone after two years of rooming together in off-campus housing. Maybe happiness left after the one-night stand, and there was no emptier feeling in the world than patting that empty bed. Maybe happiness was just not in the cards for someone who was blessed with luck but not with love, and Leif knew enough about how hard life could be for people with neither that he didn't hold a grudge against the string or the gods or anyone. He got to get on his bicycle and ride down streets with a thirty-degree gradient at Mach 6 with his shaggy red hair on fire, or give people flowers when they were sad, and go home and read Seamus Heaney. Leif may very well have been the luckiest man in San Francisco, and he liked it that way!

So Leif got out of the shower; dried off his hair (needed cutting, because it fell in ragged copper layers around his face, but there never seemed enough time); and put on his thick, warm biking shorts (not the old glossy spandex kind of the eighties, no—but still, just as sleek against his skin) and his long-sleeved wicking T-shirt under a leather jacket, his helmet (decorated in complicated Nordic knotwork using glow-in-the-dark duct tape), and his goggles—the special kind that adjusted to the sunlight. His bike took up half his living room behind the couch, and after making sure Loki was fed and his litter box was clean, Leif hefted his bike over his shoulder and ventured down the stairs.

He lived on the third floor in a walk-up apartment. Inconvenient, really, but there was a super, and even though the apartments were little tiny, they let him keep his cat, and when his toilet had blown up (or, actually, fountained shit all over his bathroom) a couple of months ago, there had been a repairman there immediately, as well as a service to clean up the bathroom and pay for the damage. Again, Leif thought—lucky! One of the guys who came to clean up the bathroom had stayed the night. Leif had given the buzzing gold thread in his head a stern glare, but it had sat innocently and directed him to at least deliver the guy flowers. Leif had, but the affair had still ended there.

He got to the ground floor and stepped out onto Olive Street, which was an alley, really, behind Geary, but it was Leif's alley, and he loved it. There were murals done over one of the doorways—something Aztec and bold, with different lines and different gods than he was used to, but still. There would be a trickster there, like Loki, and a world tree, like Yggdrasil, and a beautiful man with a fearful temper and a wish to do good, like Thor. Having been raised on stories himself, Leif *adored* other people's stories. It was what the other half of his living room—the half not taken over by the modified bicycle with the titanium alloy frame and the specialized concrete traction tires—was devoted to. *The Poetic Edda, Gilgamesh, Gawain and the Green Knight, The Exeter Book, The Odyssey, The Iliad, The Canterbury Tales, Metamorphosis*—you name an epic work of old poetry and Leif had an annotated, explicated tome of it somewhere in the stacks of them that were—more than his double bed and his tiny bathroom—his home. The only thing that was more home to Leif was Loki that cat, but if the animal chose to take an apocalyptic dump before six in the morning again, that might be up for debate.

As much as Leif loved his job riding, at twenty-seven, he was aware he was depending for his living on what his body—young, strong, and hale—could do for him. Somewhere in the back of his mind, he yearned for a job that would allow him to share all of the wonderful secrets he'd discovered in his academic explorations. Wouldn't that be wonderful? But luck had brought Leif a lot in life. He had faith that it would eventually bring him this.

He hopped on his bicycle and ventured from Olive, his little back alley, onto the much more metropolitan Geary, and turned toward Hyde. He rode tight to the side of the road, in the thin layer of air between the parked cars and the traffic, dodging side mirrors as neatly as he dodged pedestrians and spotting holes in the broken lines of cars that allowed him to swoop into the left-hand turn lanes when he needed. Of course, he didn't need any on the way to work—that was nearly a straight shot, give or take a few hills, but his brain, somehow, could not stop working all the angles. That golden thread was always busy, always looking for the quickest cut and the shortest snip through the fabric of the city, and Leif enjoyed it. It was an eely, zooming thing behind his vision, and it felt like an old friend.

He checked the large unbreakable watch on his wrist, one of those things with the hard plastic shell on the outside and the soft rubber layer between the watch and the shell. It could probably outlive Leif in an airplane crash and hopefully wouldn't die if Leif flipped his bike. Three minutes. Excellent. He was a god!

He rounded the corner where the storefront for Hermes, his bike messenger company, resided, then went halfway down the block to the alley behind it, where the bike messengers were given their packages by dispatch.

He barely avoided a collision with Talitha Lincoln, the teeny little student Leif had taken under his wing when she'd first applied. She was fearless in traffic to the point of being frightening, and always on time, but on her own two little feet she was perhaps the most timid person Leif had ever met.

"I'm sorry!" she cried as they slid to a halt. She kicked her stand down and started jumping up and down, maybe because at five foot nothin' she was hoping to get into Leif's line of vision. "I'm sorry, I'm sorry! Dammit, Thundergod, you big goober, I almost took you out!"

Leif stood up and grinned at her, holding out his large hand from his considerable height and putting it on top of her head to hold her down.

"Took me out? No, Lethal, you did no such thing. We avoided each other, right? See? Luck!"

Talitha scowled. "Not luck, skill, Superman—if you couldn't turn and I couldn't stop, we'd be tomato soup."

Leif shrugged. "Then it was lucky we learned those skills, right?"

Her tiny face, as black as mahogany, split into the world's biggest, whitest grin. Talitha adored him, he knew it. He loved her too. "Lucky you taught it to me," she said, and he took his hand off her helmet.

"Are we jumping anymore? You made me dizzy."

She giggled, and had it not been a gray, sort of foggy day in June, Leif might have been able to spot her blush. Yes, she knew he wasn't on the roster, but he'd learned a long time ago that there was no shame in making a pretty girl smile. Pretty girls were just that—pretty, and pleasant, and very often enjoyable company. And the fact that he didn't want to sleep with them was, also very often, more of a plus than a minus in keeping company.

"Okay, I'll buy it. *You* are lucky. *I* am skilled."

Leif laughed, from his stomach, thinking she was adorable and he wanted to tuck her in his pocket like a kitten—but that she'd probably scratch him if he tried.

Together they walked their bikes to the dispatch window, and Hammond (no first name) checked his clipboard. "Torval?"

"Ja!" Leif grinned, because his accent was barely noticeable and he really spoke very little in the way of Norwegian, and because seeing a giant red-headed man say "Ja!" was really frickin' funny.

Unless you were Hammond.

"Fisherman's Wharf, at the bottom of Nob Hill." The long, jowled, fiftyish face didn't move, not even to smirk.

"Careful, Hammond," Leif said, faking seriousness. "If you don't watch it, I'll see a smile."

"Here's the address," Hammond muttered, "and here's the package."

It was a small, unassuming package that fit neatly into Leif's leather messenger bag. Some of the other riders liked the really fancy ones, with the hard shell and the soft rubber insides, and while Leif liked that for his watch, he was not so excited about using one for his messenger bag. His personal bag was leather, worn soft but still tougher than any nylon Leif had ever seen. It was lined with fleece, which made it plenty padded for anything Leif was given, especially since the client was responsible for packaging anything fragile.

Leif looked at the wharf address and felt his face glow. "At the bottom? With the trolleys? Excellent!"

Lethal looked at him uneasily. "There's been road construction up there, Leif. You'd better watch it. There's gonna be tourists getting out for that picture, and potholes and shit. Go down to the wharf first—don't go up the hill."

She was so adorable, warning him like that! He touched a fingertip to her nose, seeing the route in his head, glowing with gold. "I will be fine, Lethal. You worry too much!"

A little furrow marred her perfectly and naturally shaped black brows. "You need worrying about," she told him seriously. She had six little brothers and sisters and a grandmother, all living in nearby Oakland, whom she helped support with her earnings on the bicycle, as well as the college tuition she was trying to pay off. She had perfected the art of worrying, and Leif sighed as he pushed her up to get her assignment. (She didn't like Hammond. At all. Ever.)

She dealt with Hammond meekly, and he dealt with her by not really looking at her. She walked away, giving the piece of paper in her hand a glum, cursory glance, and put the parcel in her bag, sighing. "The Haight? Really?"

"It's a nice little neighborhood," Leif told her, surprised.

"Yeah, but I know this address. They don't tip for shit."

Leif looked mournfully at the address in his hand. "You can have mine," he said, thinking about the glorious adventure of careening down that hill.

Lethal's look was all pity. "No, that's okay, Superman. You go ahead and fly. I can make this one fast enough to get an extra couple of runs in, you feel me?"

"Impossible," Leif said with a straight face. She looked at him and he grinned again. "You are too short. I can't even see you, much less feel you!"

Lethal groaned, and Leif laughed until she joined him. Then they swung their legs up—almost in tandem—and hopped on their bikes and went zoom. The golden thread spooled out in its blazing track, from corner to shortcut to impossible turn, and Leif was, as always, eager to follow.

HACON HALDOR
"SON OF THOR'S ROCK"

HAKE didn't usually take the trolley—hated it, in fact, because he was not overly fond of tourists, and the trolleys were riddled with them. He'd been on the Muni, because that was the most efficient form of travel from his posh residence on Pilot Hill to the Wharf, where the office for his family's shipping business dwelt, but the Muni had broken down, and the trolley had only been a block away. He had a car—and a place to park it, because his little house had a garage and everything—but you did not drive a car a mile and a half in a place already so congested with traffic. It was rude.

But then, so were tourists, and after two blocks of being crammed on a trolley like a head of lettuce, threatening to roll off at any minute, Hake decided to get off at the top of Nob Hill and simply walk down. Yeah, sure, it was some bizarre gradient number, but you could see the bay from the top of the hill, and the pier with his small but successful family business office was only a block west.

Hake glared at the sky as he started walking—slowly, because he was wearing dress shoes and the gradient was terrifying. He was dying to see some damned sun, but it was typically high overcast after early morning fog. Would it kill anyone for a little bit of bay glitter from this view? Hake didn't get to walk often, and he *liked* the sun!

He looked farther, to where some workmen were trying to use a winch and a pulley to get a safe into an upstairs window, and for a moment, he was surprised and interested. Really? He hadn't known they actually *did* that anywhere outside of cartoons. Then he realized he'd have to move off the sidewalk to make room for the workmen, and his good feeling disappeared. He looked cagily at the orange tape the workmen had laid and made sure he was nowhere *near* underneath the safe. Given his family history, no Haldor should *ever* walk under safes, pianos, cranes, or wrecking balls of any sort, and—

"What in the fuck!"

The shout—and the bicycle—zoomed out of nowhere, giving Hake an impression of a red-headed giant riding a whirring fireball. Then the giant shoved Hake violently into a car before the front wheel of his bike sank into an open manhole and the bike flipped, sending the giant who'd been riding it *smack!* into the pavement.

Hacon sat, stunned, looking at the bike that was flipped upside down with the wheel bent and wedged in the manhole so solidly it didn't even tip sideways. In front of it, the giant gave a groan and then started to move gingerly to lean up against the car parked at the curb so he wasn't in the middle of the road.

"Oh, fuck!" Giant put some weight on his arm and then let out a sound like a wounded wolf. "Fuck. Fucking collarbone. Fuck, fuck, fuck." His voice was deep and resonant, and every time he said "Fuck!" it practically reverberated the concrete under Hacon's ass. Hacon struggled to his feet and took one step forward toward the giant to launch into a tirade about riding like a maniac when the giant looked through the blood dripping from a cut on his forehead and grinned.

"You're okay, right?"

Hake took stock: he was bruised a little, and his best suit was torn and his pride was definitely bent, and he was about to list all his grievances when the giant nodded, then winced.

"You look fine. Good. Because you almost fell down that hole, and that wouldn't have been lucky at all!"

And Hacon stopped midrant. *Oh my God and holy shit!* "You just saved my life?"

"No!" the giant protested, cradling his arm as he struggled up using his other one. "No one dies falling down manholes, do they?"

"In my family they do," Hacon muttered and moved to the man's side. "Here, let me get that," he offered, undoing the man's helmet and pulling it off. Oh my God. Would you *look* at all that hair? Copper like apples and blood, it spilled halfway to the giant's shoulders from what started out as a normal layered cut around his face. Hacon pushed it back from the man's freckled, bloodied forehead as an excuse just to touch it, and it was just as soft as it promised.

"I've got a first aid kit on my bike," the giant said with a grunt. "If we can wash the blood off and put a bandage on that, I think I can carry my bike."

"Why would you want to carry your bike?" Hacon was appalled. His palms stung and his knees smarted and he wanted to look and see if maybe his scrape was bleeding, but he'd feel like an idiot next to this guy, who had blood pouring down his face and was grinning like he'd just accomplished something huge.

"I have to deliver my package, hey?"

"How about, I don't know. A trip to the hospital first?" Hake found the first aid kit and grimaced when he realized the soft-sided red bag wasn't just for Band-Aids and disinfectant. There were steri gloves and big gauze pads and, yes, adjustable braces for knees, ankles, wrists, and elbows—and a C-collar for a broken collarbone. There was some sort of symbol on the side—a caduceus, but not the standard one. This one had a picture of Hermes himself on it, holding the staff while on a bicycle. There was a logo on the side, *Hermes Messenger Service*, and Hacon finally caught a clue. The bike messenger had been zooming down the hill, had seen Hacon heading for disaster, and had run his bike into the manhole before Hacon could fall.

He looked down at the messenger and saw all of that gorgeous goodwill shining through the blood and the shock and the copper hair, and squatted down to dress his wounds. It was the least he could do.

"No, no," the giant protested, reaching out with his good arm. "Here. There's a mirror. Let me—"

"Don't worry about it." Hake grimaced. "I can do it. It's the least I can do for the guy who saved my life."

"Happy to be of service." The man grinned. "Leif Torval, saver of handsome strangers."

Hacon blinked and looked at him. His eyes were bright blue— God, the *brightest* blue, the color the bay below them would be if the sun had been out that day—and his grin, still disconcerting with all of the blood, was both enthusiastic and guilelessly appreciative. He wasn't really coming on to Hake—he was just expressing approval.

If Hake had been straight, he could have laughed the comment off and ignored it. But Hake wasn't straight, and holy jebus on a

Norwegian cracker, that man-god had just given him a compliment. He blushed to the roots of his fine black hair as he put on the gloves and tried very hard to keep his hands from sweating and shaking as he wiped Leif's face with a steri-wipe.

After the pause had gone on a little too long, he said, "Hacon Walter Haldor, in your debt."

"Scandinavian!" Leif said delightedly, not even wincing as Hake pulled the edges of his cut together with a butterfly bandage, and Hake raised his eyebrows in affirmation.

"Ja, ja," he said dryly, but Leif's returning grin held no irony.

"I still have an accent," he admitted. "We came here when I was very little—and I spent a lot of time with my grandmother."

Hake shrugged. "I'm fifth generation," he said, scrubbing at Leif's left eyebrow to get rid of some of the blood. His eyebrows had a wicked arch; they set the tone for his whole face, inviting the world to laugh at the joke. "About the only thing I know about Norway is the family curse."

"You have a family curse?" Leif blinked rapidly in excitement. His lashes were as long as a woman's and as red as his hair. "What is it? A sixth toe? An extra testicle? You must tell!" That mouth—wide and mobile with lips that were just full enough, surrounded by red-blond stubble because why shave when the hair was almost transparent, right?—was smiling even now. Leif had blood running down his face and was obviously in pain, but his smile was winsome and inviting and happy, and Hacon found himself staring.

He blushed then, feeling silly for a moment, like he was getting credit for picking his nose in public or something. "Here, let's get your bag off first," he said, carefully taking it from around Leif's neck and down his arm. The man was big and smelled like leather and sweat, and Hacon was forcibly reminded that the last time he'd had sex had been a mildly drunken one-off with someone whose name was still sort of hazy, and it had happened right after his breakup with Andre. Two years ago.

"Could you put that out of the way?" Leif asked anxiously. "It should still be sound, and I don't want it to get hit or anything. I'm already going to be late delivering."

After speaking, Leif closed his eyes for a moment, then opened them. For the first time since he'd come to, flat on his back, his grin disappeared. He muttered something like "That's so strange...," but Hake didn't hear the rest of it because he was propping the package up on the other side of the car Leif was sitting behind.

The leather bag was warm and soft and battered and smelled a little like Leif's sweat too—he probably didn't always travel in the leather jacket he was wearing now. The package inside must have been electronics—it had that strangely weighted feeling, like it was concentrated in some way, inside the box and inside the bag. Hacon dropped it by the car's tire and walked around to Leif, then squatted to help him off with his jacket.

"Christ," Leif swore, his cheerfulness undimmed even though his breathing had grown shallow with pain. "Next time I'll remember to pack Motrin or something. That's going to suck, right?"

"Yeah, big guy, it's going to suck. No worries, I've got some Motrin in my pocket, okay?"

"This *is* my lucky day!" Leif said amicably, right before the explosion rocked the car he was leaning against.

Hacon was knocked flat on his ass, and Leif was thrown on top of him from the force of the small blast knocking the car sideways, and he must have hurt his head again, because as he was sprawled on top of Hacon, he said, "Why do you make the thread go?" before his eyes swooped back into his head and he passed out. Hacon's ears were ringing and his head was too, and he must have hit it as well, because when he came to, paramedics were there, and police cars with sirens, and all sorts of people who were making Hake's ears ring as well.

"This is the *strangest* day," he said as the paramedics rolled Leif off him, and he apparently said it out loud, because he heard a chuckle from one of the helping hands.

"Yeah, Hake, this isn't where I ever expected to find you!"

"Andre?" Hacon looked at his ex-boyfriend, all decked out in his detective's suit with his worn shoes and everything. The man looked good—dark hair, dark eyes, skin a Latino bronze. Normally, that was what Hacon went for in a big way, but he still remembered Leif's guileless, laughing blue eyes looking into his, and suddenly all he saw in Andre was a helpful cop. "God, Andre, what in the hell…?"

Andre shook his head and helped him sit up. There had been two cars—Leif had sat against one of them, and now Hake was sitting against the other, looking to the side where Leif was lying, being attended by paramedics. The first car sat sideways in the middle of the road.

"Yeah," Andre said quietly. "Leif—I hope he's okay."

"You know him?" Hacon was suddenly swamped by a surge of irrational jealousy—and not for Andre, which, considering they'd broken up over two years ago, was just as well.

"You can't walk the city without knowing Leif," Andre said with a snort. "He's one of the best bike messengers in the city. Besides," he added, looking with concern to where the giant was fluttering his eyes and groaning, "he's damned good-looking."

"God, yes," Hake said fervently, and he and Andre shared a look that agreed on more in two seconds than they had probably agreed on during their entire relationship. "And you know," Hake said, wanting to go hover as he had never wanted to go hover, "he saved my life."

"Yeah—was that before or after the bomb went off?"

Hacon grimaced and felt the ringing in his head all over again. "Was that a bomb? That sucked!" A paramedic hovered at his side then, taking his vitals and giving him a bag of ice to hold to his head. "All things considered, he should have let me fall into the manhole."

Andre wasn't stupid. He looked around, saw Leif's bike in the hole, bent in half from the blast. The first aid kit had been scattered, and Leif was still sporting the butterfly bandage and half a C-collar as he muttered and groaned on the ground.

"So," he said speculatively, "Leif saved your damned fool neck but hurt himself in the process. You two were sitting between the cars, and what happened?"

"I moved his messenger bag," Hacon said, then blinked. "To the other side of the car." Oh God. "Luck," he murmured. "Pure luck. If he hadn't crashed, we wouldn't have taken the bag off and—" And no more bike messenger with the big smile and good smell. The potential tragedy of that made Hacon's breath speed up and his skin grow cold just thinking about it.

"He's going into shock," one of the paramedics said at his side, and Hacon wanted to say, "No, just forming an inappropriate crush on a stranger," but he was suddenly shivering so hard his teeth were chattering, and he couldn't quite get it out.

Suddenly the whole world seemed very faraway, and Hake wanted to call it back, call it back, because for a second there, when he realized that he *would* have a chance to know Leif Torval, he saw a faint gold glow around the man who was struggling to sit up even as Hacon himself passed out.

WHEN Hake woke up, he was in a hospital bed in the ER, receiving fluids through a tube in his arm.

"You're awake!"

Hacon turned his head and thought, *You are so beautiful!* But that's not what he said.

"You're alive!"

Someone had done a more thorough job of cleaning off Leif's blood, and he was stripped down to a hospital gown, but the big man still looked both battered and exultant.

"Of course I am alive! I'm lucky!"

Hacon closed his eyes, and he would have shaken his head, but it felt like the bomb was still going off in there, so he didn't. "You're so lucky someone tried to kill you," he said in disbelief. At that moment he heard footsteps coming in and then Andre's voice responding to what he just said.

"Not him, Hake—you."

Hacon's eyes flew open, and Andre was standing there looking handsome and grim, much like he had during the three years they'd dated. Handsome, grim, and unavailable—just the way Hake liked 'em. By the end of the relationship, they'd been roommates in a one-bedroom apartment and not much else.

"Me?" His voice pitched, and he grimaced. Ouch! Could his head possibly hurt any more?

"Yes, you. We called Leif's company—that package he was set to deliver was addressed to you. The bomb squad said it was supposed to go off when you opened it, but the trigger was fucked up when Leif here flipped his bike."

Hacon looked at Leif, who grinned back. "So you are lucky too!" Leif said, and then his grin faded, and he looked troubled for a moment, like a man who was trying to analyze a puzzle he'd thought he'd solved.

"Lucky?" Hacon muttered. "Can you believe this guy? He thinks we're lucky!"

"Well, *you* are definitely a lucky asshole," Andre said dryly. "You got your bell rung, but no concussion. They're going to keep you overnight, give you fluids, make sure nothing inside is bubbling, and you're going to go home." He sent a sympathetic glance to Leif. "I'm afraid our big Scandinavian bastard here has a double concussion—he gets to be woken up every hour for the next twenty-four, and hopefully he won't decide to just keep sleeping. You hear me, Leif? You need to wake up, right?"

Leif smiled at Andre. "I hear you, Detective. It's kind of you to worry, but I'll wake up. There are too many good stories in the world not to wake up and hear them."

"Do you have anyone to call?" Andre asked, and Hake glanced at him sharply. He'd never heard his ex-boyfriend's voice that gentle.

"No," Leif said, smile never faltering. "But that is okay, the hospital staff will take good care of me."

Andre nodded. "Well, since you're up now—both of you—I can ask you some questions, okay?"

So Andre went over it again, and the chill in Hake's bones got more and more severe. "Someone sent me a *bomb*?" he asked and knew his look at Andre was both pathetic and tortured. Of all people, Andre knew his silliest, most off-the-wall fear.

Andre shrugged. "What can I tell you, Hake—it looks like you were right. You really *were* supposed to die young and stupid."

"Is this your curse?" Leif asked, and Hacon looked at him nervously. He'd stood up to the round of questions about getting the package and the address pretty well, but he was starting to droop a little at the edges.

"Shouldn't you rest a little now, before the nurse comes in?" Hacon asked.

Leif shrugged uncomfortably—both of his shoulders were held in place by the C-collar and he could barely move. "She's coming back in ten minutes, and I will sleep then. Now tell me about your curse!"

"You believe in that shit, messenger boy?" Andre asked playfully, and Leif's blue eyes were large and very serious in his long, angular face when he nodded. His face was growing paler by the moment, and the ridge of reddish-brown freckles under his eyes was starting to stand out in greater relief.

"Oh yes," Leif said in sober response to Andre's question. "I believe that very much. Curses are places where the gods have meddled, Detective. You need to take the gods seriously, or they will fuck with you in a big way!"

Hacon didn't scoff at him—although he didn't believe him, either. Instead he got lost a little in the way the man swore. There was something seriously resonant and echoing in the way he said the word "fuck." It needed to be said deeper, and louder, and with passion, when Leif was heaving that long, muscular body inside Hake's in the middle of…. "I'm sorry, did you say something?" Hacon blushed, not sure if the silence was because he said something or hadn't.

"He asked you what your curse was, Hake. Look—I need to talk to you some more about this, but let me talk to Galliano first, okay?" Melissa Galliano was his partner, and Hacon was relieved to know Andre still relied on her. He'd always known they kept each other safe. "You go ahead and tell Thor here about your curse. I'll be back when he falls asleep." Andre looked over to Leif, who looked cheerfully back. "Good night, big man. You take care of yourself, you hear me?"

"Good night, Detective. Thank you for your concern."

Andre turned to Hake for a moment before he left. "Look, you sanctimonious prick—I know we've barely spoken for two years, but I would have been fucking crushed if we'd had to scrape you off the pavement. We're going to have a long talk, you and me, about why someone would be trying to kill you, do you understand?"

Hacon nodded meekly. "Thanks, Andre," he said quietly, and Andre rolled his eyes and whirled—impressive trench coat and spiffy suit and all—to stride out into the taupe corridor. He'd moved out of their apartment without so much as a Post-it note, but in his day-to-day life, he tended toward the drama. Hacon had always liked that about him—he'd just hoped it would have translated more into their everyday living. Hacon knew who he was. He was dour and irritable and incredibly passive-aggressive. He'd thought that Andre, with his drama and his blunt speech, would be his perfect opposite, but it hadn't worked. Andre's job had taught him how to be uncommunicative and manipulative. When the two of them were fighting, they often didn't say a word for days—but the windows would damn near ice over, and Andre had *sworn* the room temperature dropped. He'd had three tanks of dead tropical fish to prove it! Hacon had always said that was because the heater had broken, but still—it had felt cold in their apartment.

"You and he were friends?" Leif asked, and Hacon turned his attention toward the man who had apparently been his guardian angel for the day.

"We lived together for three years," Hacon said dryly. "I'm not sure if that qualifies us as friends."

Most of the people Hake knew would nod and accept that answer as a bit of urbane banter, but Leif looked puzzled. "Why would you not be friends?"

Hake *could* shrug. "Because we didn't talk for six days, and he moved out on the seventh, and for the most part, after that, we haven't spoken until he scraped me off the street. Are you friends with *your* exes?"

Leif's smile held more than a little pathos. "You have to know each other for more than one night to be friends."

Uh-oh. Promising and yet frightening. Hake decided to dig a little harder. "Do you have any serious exes?"

"One. I went to his wedding," Leif said wistfully. "I stood up as best man, and complimented the bride's dress, and bought them a punch bowl, because it was something he and I had never owned. He sends me presents on my birthday."

Hacon swallowed, absurdly moved and a little angry at the same time. "He married a woman?"

"His parents were very traditional. Sometimes, love is not enough to break family things like that." Leif's mouth had closed into a soft line, but his eyes were still clear and open, so when he smiled, it was not much of a shock at all. "So tell me about *your* family thing."

Hacon shivered. "It's not comfortable."

"Neither am I," Leif said, as though broken bones and a concussion and the various cuts and bruises amounted to no more than a little discomfort. "But I still exist."

Hake laughed. "Okay, it's stupid, really, but, well." He looked around the hospital room and shivered again. "Let's just say that today it seems a little more real."

Leif nodded seriously. "Yes—a day like this would make any story of the gods seem real."

"I guess. Anyway, in every generation in my family, *someone* dies a totally unexpected and bizarre death. It's... it's *uncanny* how strange these deaths get. It's... it's *epic*. Poetry has been written for these people. Darwin Awards are given out."

Leif frowned. "Death is death. How strange can it get?"

"You only *think* death is death, but I almost died falling down an open manhole today. I'm thinking anything's possible. So anyway, my father's cousin, Balder—"

"Scandi?"

"You bet. Anyway, he died in some tiny backwater. He was working on a bridge, and he stopped to take a piss, hit a transformer by accident, and—"

"Oh my gods!"

"Right? *Right?* I'm saying! Anyway, so that's one generation back. My grandfather's brother, Ang, *he* got caught in Costa Rica during a hurricane. He got hit by a flying *banana*."

"Get out!" Leif's eyes were wide, and he looked... well, entranced was the only word Hake could use. Hake found himself growing more animated, just to keep that look of fascination on that lean and lovely face.

"No, I'm serious. Apparently they're simply amazing projectiles. My *great*-grandfather died when my grandpa and his two brothers were still babies. Apparently someone shot a bullet into the air, and it hit Great-grandpa Agmar in the head—while he was on a *train*!"

"No!" Leif clapped his hand to his mouth and then winced, because his mouth was a pattern of small cuts and he'd probably jarred his sore collarbone and as well as what Hake could see was a stitched-up elbow as well. "That is too fantastic! Are there more?"

So Hake tried to remember all of them: the great-great-someone who was touring a Scottish castle and got caught under a falling battleaxe, the great-great-great-whositz who was crushed to death by a boa constrictor in a science classroom—the list of strange deaths went all the way back to the Middle Ages, and Hake had spent his life trying not to be haunted by *all* of them.

When he was done with all the ones he could remember, Leif had shadows under his eyes and even *his* smile had dimmed somewhat.

"So that's my family curse," Hake finished, feeling a twinge of anticlimax. "Until you broke it, I guess."

Leif opened his eyes abruptly. "I did not break it, Hake. I just had some luck to spare is all. You still need to be careful. I would listen to what your detective friend said, yes? Be careful. If someone *is* trying to kill you, today was a great disappointment to them."

Hacon grimaced. "Well, it hasn't been a picnic for you, either."

"Nonsense," Leif said, and it even sounded like he meant it. "It was a small price to pay for such a lovely story of the gods."

"That's not a story about the gods," Hacon contradicted, but at that moment the nurse came bustling in. She checked Leif's vitals and his fluids, and then asked him about the pain.

"Nothing to speak of," he said, the corners of his mouth tightening.

"We *can* give you an analgesic, if you like," the nurse said softly. "Mr. Torval, I know they didn't want to give you a narcotic because of the double concussion, but that doesn't mean you have to go it alone."

Leif breathed out in what sounded like relief. "Really?" he asked, his voice gruff and almost pleading. "Because, I must tell you, I'm about to get cranky with it. An analgesic would be fine." He finished it off with a brilliant if weary smile, and the nurse smiled back. Well, of course she did. A *rock* would have smiled back.

"Okay, then. I'll get something and put it in the IV."

Leif's smile became dreamier. "That would be great," he slurred, and Hacon realized that now that their conversation was over, the big man was probably exhausted. The nurse bustled out, and Leif smiled over at Hacon with eyes half-closed.

"I'll be up in an hour," he said eagerly. "Will you be here?"

Hacon nodded. "I will be, but—" He yawned. "I might be asleep too."

Leif's smile was completely accepting. "That's fine," he said. "Sometimes there is companionship in sleep too."

Hacon watched as he fell fast asleep, and then he decided to rest as well. Why not? Who knew when his ex-boyfriend was going to come in and discuss new and horrible ways to die?

INTERLUDE
TAPESTRY DANCING
WITH AN AUDIENCE

URDH noticed the changed thread first.

"Sister?" she said abruptly, looking at Skuld, and Skuld seemed—surprised—at what had mixed with what she'd pulled from the well of possibilities.

"Oh my."

"What?" Verdandi asked, looking from her loom to her sisters.

"You'll see in a moment," Urdh said. "It feels… odd. Like a blend of fibers we've had before."

Verdandi turned her attention to the pattern in the loom she was weaving and then blinked. "Oh no."

"Oh no what?" Urdh asked, alarmed.

"Look. Look at the two of them."

"Oh gods," Urdh muttered, looking at the two men sleeping in side-by-side hospital beds. "I should have noticed. Can you trace their threads, sister?"

"Do I really need to, sister? There's only one god who ever stole from us, and you see right there? The threads. One with the gold and one with the lack, both of them, ready to be spit-spliced whole."

Skuld sucked at her teeth. "They're not… comfortable fibers."

"Oh, I wouldn't say that," said a male voice that seemed to come from a branch of Yggdrasil above them. "One of them is *very* comfortable."

"Loki?" Verdandi murmured. He hadn't visited since last time—but then, he and Thor had been tight of late. Of course, there had been a terrible row for a while after Loki slept with Thor's wife, Sif, and then bragged of it to the gods. Thor had been righteously angry about that. He'd punished Loki with time living as a cow and giving birth and being milked, deep in the bowels of the earth, and that had seemed to be enough. Sif had apologized, and the two of them had lived in harmony for a while, until Thor had released Loki from his time as a cow. For the past few centuries, Thor's wife had been off visiting her sister in the underworld, and Jotunheim had rung loudly with their warrior sex-wrestling.

"Yes, Dandi," Loki said now, standing tall on his branch of the one-tree. "I'm here."

She met his eyes—ice blue, like those of the dark-haired man below them—and saw some regret there.

"I'd say you have a lot of nerve coming here," she sighed, "but I think… we can only weave the thread we're given. Why are you back?"

"I wanted to see," he murmured softly. "I felt them, that first bump of their flesh together." He shuddered almost ecstatically. "Violent. But I wanted to see if they could tangle. Could merge." His pointed features—chin, nose, face—fell a little, grew softer. "And look at him. Doesn't he look like—?"

"Yes," Verdandi said gently. "They both do."

Loki looked speculative. "It could be. Generations come and go—not even you can see the threads merge and split."

"True," Verdandi replied. Her hands never stopped their ceaseless task, and neither did her sisters'. Once the day under Jotunheim began, the tapestry under the world tree was all. But her voice was gentle, and she did not always need to be able to see what she was weaving—on occasion her fingers knew the way. So she didn't break eye contact with her former lover, and to his credit, he gazed at her with contrition—but no remorse.

"Would you like to stay and watch it play out?" Urdh asked after a long silence, not entirely uncomfortable.

"I would," Loki replied, bowing a little from his perch in the tree. He was dressed in black wool, soft and tight to his lean and muscular form. "Thank you for offering."

Verdandi raised her eyebrows. "I didn't. But if you are going to watch over our shoulders, you may as well get comfortable. The world tree will give you a chair."

Loki swung down and reached into the trunk of Yggdrasil, through the wood, until his hand grasped something. He came back with a finely formed chair, polished and grand and fit for a god. He bowed to the tree in thanks and then set up shop behind Verdandi.

"Too close," she snapped, and he pulled back a little until she could breathe. "Good," she told him when he was far enough away. And then, grateful for his compliance: "Can you see from there?"

"Mm, yes. But I cannot smell the fragrance of your hair."

She cast him a droll look over her shoulder. "That, too, is good," she said dryly. "Now hush, they're about to wake up."

LEIF
CLOUDS AND SILVER

ONCE an hour, on the hour, the nurse came in and woke him up. She seemed like a nice girl, really, but he was glad when she changed shift so he didn't have to hate her. Sometime in there, he'd heard the murmured voices of Hacon and his handsome detective ex-boyfriend talking, and Andre came to stand over Leif's bed to say goodbye.

"Goodbye, Detective," Leif had murmured groggily. "Next time, perhaps we can simply say hi, and there doesn't need to be any bombs involved."

Andre had laughed quietly and gently touched his shoulder before leaving. Leif remembered to turn toward Hacon and say, "He's a nice man, your ex-boyfriend," as he was falling back asleep.

"I think you bring it out of him," Hacon said, his voice sour, but Leif didn't have a chance to investigate that, as very tempting as it was.

His next nurse was male, gay, and surly as an awakened bear. His touch was rough and impersonal, and he didn't mind bumping the IV line in Leif's arm, did he! But Leif smiled at him winningly, hoping he could flirt the man's bad mood away, and sure enough, he gentled his movements and even gave the needle in the back of Leif's hand a gentle little caress to make sure it wasn't too pulled upon.

"Thank you," Leif said gratefully, and the man—in his late forties, with graying blond hair and a handsome face when his mouth wasn't compressed like that—smiled a little, blushed, and turned around to check on Hacon's vitals.

The nurse bustled out, and Hacon raised an ironic eyebrow at Leif. "Must be nice," he said dryly, and Leif smiled back.

"You can flirt with him, too, if you like," he said, meaning it. "You are very pretty!" Leif's new companion had straight, dark hair, parted on the side but just long enough for the front to flop over into his eyes. He also had a narrow face with a sharp point of a chin and nose, and slightly tilted ice-blue eyes.

And now he had a nonplussed expression.

"Riiiight," he said, like Leif would lie about something like that. "Are you really feeling okay, like you told the nurse, or are you feeding him a line of bullshit like you fed the other nurse?"

Leif had to work hard to keep the smile on his face. "I am alive, it is all good," he said mildly, and then, suddenly, it was.

"Hey, Thundergod!" came a distinctive little voice, and Leif turned toward his favorite little person who matched the voice.

"Lethal!" he said joyously. "I'm so happy to see you!"

Talitha rushed over to his bedside and dropped the rail so she could hug him tight enough to make things creak. He did not complain. The problem with nurses touching you was that they started up a hunger for a real touch, and here was Lethal, whom he could hug with impunity. It was nice, and downright therapeutic.

Leif raised his uninjured arm—his right—up to hug her back, grateful that one didn't have the IV tube in it.

"God, Leif! Hammond told us you'd gotten hurt—what in the hell?"

Leif looked at her seriously. "It was so lucky, Lethal! You should have seen it. If Hacon here hadn't almost fallen in a manhole, I would have given him the package that would have blown him up!"

Talitha clapped her hands over her mouth, and behind her, a taller young woman, roundly built and also black, came running into the room. Talitha's slightly younger sister, Verdacia, carried a big brown bag of something that smelled fragrant and spicy even from the other end of the room.

"Litha!" Verdacia complained, and Lethal turned around, full of contrition.

"Sorry, Verdi. I just had to make sure he's okay. Here, Leif. My grandma's from the South, you know, so when someone's sick, she cooks for them. She sent me this huge thing of chili and cornbread for y'all, so you don't have to eat hospital food."

Leif looked at her, absurdly touched. "Your grandmother has only met me once!"

Christmas Eve, Talitha had dragged him to the tiny little house in Oakland. It hadn't been the best neighborhood, and the heat had been on absurdly high, but Leif had enjoyed the noisy bunch of children and teenagers who made up her family.

"Yeah, big man, but you make an impression. You brought everybody a gift—and it was all books. She thinks you walk on water. Now here. I have two bowls, you want to share some with your friend who almost got blown up?"

Leif looked over at Hacon, who was eyeing the two young women with surprise. "You want some?" Talitha dished some of the chili from one of two butter tubs and gave Leif a bite. "It's good!"

"Yeah, wait till you have some of my grandma's cornbread," Talitha said practically, crumbling a piece of it up on Leif's chili. Leif smiled at her and reached out with his one good hand and touched her nose. She swallowed and nodded, looking upset for a moment.

"He worth almost getting your big gay ass blown all over Nob Hill?" she asked unhappily, and Leif winked at Hacon, who was getting a bowl of chili whether he wanted it or not.

"He seems very important. The detective thought he was worth it."

Hacon took a giant bite of chili then and started to cough, and Leif looked over at him in concern. "You are okay, Hacon? You want some water? Verdi—"

"Got it, Thor. No worries." Verdi trotted off to fill the small pitcher of water and brought it back for Hacon, and Leif smiled at him as he sucked water through the straw and looked back at him through watery eyes.

"Is good, right?" Leif said excitedly. "It's certainly better than what they brought you for lunch."

Talitha pulled back the spoonful of chili she was in the middle of feeding him. "They didn't bring you food for lunch? Now what kind of service is this?"

"He's not supposed to eat," Hacon said sourly from the next bed. "If he decides to throw up, they don't want him to breathe it back in."

"Now that's just gross," Lethal said, pulling up her upper lip so Leif could see the slight gap between her front teeth. "You gonna blow your chunks, Leif? Tell me truly. I don't want to see my granny's chili go to waste."

Leif shook his head gently. No, his head was spinning, but true to form, his stomach was as solid as an anchor, even if his ship was being tossed in a storm. "No, Lethal. I've told you before, that's the last thing that's going to go. I'm lucky that way."

Hacon was looking at him and shaking his head. "Lucky?" he asked, and Leif smiled.

"I'm lucky for you, at the very least!" he said and allowed Lethal to feed him the rest of the chili. He politely declined a second bowl but told her to leave the leftovers in the small drug refrigerator—there was plenty of room.

"You can't do that!" Hacon protested, but Leif waved him off.

"It's a cold space. Nothing will strike our food dead in there!" he laughed, and Lethal and her sister laughed with him. Now that he was done eating, he wanted the nurse to come, because he wanted his hour's sleep. But he worried about Hacon—whether he'd been expecting them or not, Leif had people come to worry about him. Whom did Hake have?

Lethal came over to his bed then and gave him a kiss on the cheek and an awkward hug around the C-collar. "You going to be okay off the streets for a few days, Thundergod?"

Leif grimaced. "It will be tight," he said truthfully. It wasn't in him to lie or prevaricate, even in the name of pride. "But it is always tight. I work my other job in two days. Once they okay me to drive, I'll be back on the street raising hell. How is that?"

Lethal nodded. "I'll have my granny send some more food," she said seriously, and then Leif groaned.

"Loki! Talitha, I need you to feed my cat! He'll be furious and...." Oh geez. "And clean the cat box. God, I'm sorry. I so hate to ask."

Lethal smiled and said, "Here's your leather jacket. Are the keys inside?" It was scuffed, but untorn, and Leif was grateful.

Leif nodded, although the pain in his neck and head was making it harder to do that. "Yeah. Be careful about Loki, though," he warned, thinking mournfully of his companion, who usually slept on Leif's chest as he sprawled out on his queen-size bed. "He's a trickster. He can escape very easily, you know."

Lethal rolled her eyes. "It's the only time you've ever been late. How could I forget that damned cat? I'll take good care of him, Thundergod. Now give me a kiss on the cheek and let me dream—"

Verdacia huffed. "You dream about him, they'll take you out of the little black girls club!"

Talitha sent a playful smack her way, and her sister danced out of her reach. "All little black girls need to have a dream!" she protested and then laughed at her own joke. She turned back to Leif, who was laughing with her—because she was *his* little black girl, and she knew it—and offered her cheek for him to kiss, which he did.

"Thank you, Lethal. It would have been a long, sad night without your visit."

She shrugged. "You take care, Thundergod. I'll leave the key with your creepy-assed super, okay? Let me know if you need me to take you home. Verdi has the car tomorrow so she can take our auntie to the doctors, but if you give me a timeline, I can work on that."

"I can take a cab," he said, and she shrugged.

"Them things is too expensive—"

"Yes, but so is missing school. I will call you when I'm home."

"That's a deal, then." She turned around and walked out, her sister bickering at her heels, and Leif watched them go with affection.

"I thought you said you didn't have people," Hacon said, and Leif, who had been dozing off, blinked hard so he could stay awake. Hacon hadn't offered a lot in the way of conversation, and Leif wanted to take him up on what he was offering.

"Lethal? She's a friend," he said sleepily. "How about you? You have family—your detective said he'd told them."

Hacon shrugged. "He also told them I was fine. No reason for them to come to the hospital if they're just going to get me out in the morning?"

"No reason except to make you feel better," Leif pointed out, concerned.

"Do you feel better?" Hacon asked, like he truly cared about the answer, and Leif shrugged.

"I do. I feel *much* better knowing that if my thread is cut as I sleep, someone would mourn my passing."

Hacon made a little gasp, and Leif looked at him, an unsatisfying look from the side, since he couldn't really raise his head and he was unable to keep his eyes open much longer. "You will have people," Leif said reassuringly. "Your people will come."

The nurse came then, and he had to sleep. The next nurse visited—"Mr. Torval, can you hear me? Look at the light, Mr. Torval. Look left. Look right. How many fingers am I holding up?" It was like to drive him mad!—and he slept again. He woke up, then closed his eyes, looking for his bright little companion, the gold thread. He gave an unsatisfied grunt. The gold thread was... tangled. It had happened when Hacon touched him that first time. It had been good, that touch, and Leif thought it was almost worth the cut on his forehead to have such a pretty man touch him, show him concern. And then he'd closed his eyes for a moment and his thread—it was there, but it was tangled. He hadn't liked that. Since his mother's death, the thread had been many things: somnolent, busy, convoluted, insistent—but it had never been tangled. It obviously had something to do with Hacon, but that was not Hacon's fault, and Leif wouldn't hold it against him. In fact, Leif wanted to get to know his companion better. But perhaps, given what happened to the thread when they touched, it was better if all they did was talk.

He woke up a little more and looked at Hacon in the next bed. He was fidgeting with his smart something or other on his lap.

"So," he said, looking around. It was nearly nine o'clock at night, and the foggy dark was penetrating the room's one institutional window. "Did you have people?"

Hacon looked at him a little sadly. "No," he said. "My mother's going to come tomorrow to take me home, but Andre told them all I was fine. I'm fine, no reason to come."

Leif was surprised. "It sucks in here," he said baldly. "There's plenty of reason to come."

Hacon let out a rather grim laugh, but he didn't elaborate, and Leif sighed. Hacon was a pretty man, and he'd seemed compassionate when Leif had been injured on the side of the road, but he wasn't an easy man to get to know.

"So, did the detective tell you anything of use while I was asleep?" Leif wished his shoulder didn't throb quite so much, or his neck. He imagined the next nurse would be offering him more pain medication, but he was a big man. What they'd given him had likely worn off, and he hurt too much to turn and even look at the pretty man next to him. If Hacon wasn't going to talk, that was a shame.

"Yeah, he told me that my...." Hake trailed off. "You don't want to hear this."

"Well, I don't want to hear the television! Is that the news?"

"Yeah," Hake said. "The remote's broken. I can't get anything *but* the news."

"Well, turn that shit off. Those stories have no context. I *hate* the news. And I *do* want to hear what the detective said. I wandered into a *very* interesting story. Don't I have the right to hear what it might be?"

Leif saw enough of Hake to know he smiled faintly and turned off the television. Leif relaxed before he turned his head back to a position that hurt less. "You do have that right," Hake agreed. "Are you in pain? You—you don't seem as happy as usual."

"You have known me on a very odd day. Normally I am *much* happier than this!" Leif said with a weary smile, and again, that odd half laugh from Hacon's side of the room. This was not a man much used to laughing, and Leif was driven to know why.

"Well, I guess the least I can do is tell you a story," Hake said, and Leif nodded.

"I don't mind if it is sad or if there is violence or pain. As long as the hero is redeemed at the end."

"Redeemed? Doesn't that mean he does something bad?"

"Or maybe doesn't live to be the person he was supposed to, yes. But that is the point of a hero, right? They are human, but they fix what is wrong, so they can be the best of us?"

There was a surprised sound from the other side of the room. "Never thought of it that way," Hacon said. "Always thought of a hero as someone who could do no wrong."

Leif chuckled. "*That* is because you do not have a degree in humanities, which is wonderful when it comes to thinking about heroes, but not so wonderful when it comes to finding a job that does not get you blown up."

"Now see," Hacon said dryly, "it was my job that almost got me blown up, and I've got a degree in business! I'm thinking that maybe it's not the degree. It's the blowing up we have to watch out for."

Leif felt laughter bubbling up from his stomach—his favorite place from which to laugh. "I'm thinking you're right! Now tell me, why is it we almost got blown up?"

Hacon sighed. "I guess you deserve to know," he said softly. "See, we almost got blown up because I'm a complete and total prick."

Leif wanted to look at him, but everything was hurting worse than it had that morning. "Really? You've been nothing but a gentleman to me."

"Yeah, that's probably because I don't know you. Ask Andre. I can be a real cold bastard when I feel like it. Especially...." Leif waited delicately, wondering if Hake'd follow it up without prompting. "Especially when it's someone I love, I guess," he said after a moment.

"Yeah?"

"Yeah."

"Who did you love until they wanted to kill you?"

"My little brother," Hacon said softly. "Andre told me... shit."

His voice was broken, and Leif offered him the only comfort he'd ever had. "That is a very old story," Leif said softly. "Cain and Abel—they told that story, yes?"

"Yeah," Hacon replied. "I've heard of them."

"Thor and Loki. They had that story too."

"I haven't heard of that."

Leif smiled. Here it was, his one gift, and it was needed. How was that for luck? "There are many stories of the Norse gods—there is *The Poetic Edda*, and *The Prose Edda*, *The Heimskringla*—the list goes on. But you see, scholars, they discuss these stories as though one version and one version alone must be true. They do not understand the nature of stories."

"No?" Hacon asked, and his voice changed. Leif spared a glance and a twinge of pain and saw that he'd turned over on his side and was looking at Leif with avid eyes. Nice. It was nice to be heard.

"No. The nature of stories like these is that they are about gods, and that men try to be like gods every day. So when they tell the story about Loki being Thor's foster brother and going into the mead hall and bragging about his prowess and calling the other gods cowards, some scholars quibble over whether the things Loki says were true or not. That is not the point."

"What is the point?" Hacon asked, his voice throbbing in the quiet.

The last nurse had turned the lights down, and Leif wished his collarbone was better, because he would have loved to curl on his side and face Hacon and tell his story like boys at a campout. "The point," Leif said, closing his eyes in the darkness, "is that Loki wanted to belong. He insulted the gods, and he threatened them, and he claimed to have slept with the goddesses—and all, all, because he wanted Thor to come home and stop him."

Hacon was silent for a moment. "Thor was his brother?"

"Sometimes. Sometimes, Thor was his nemesis. Sometimes, they were fosterlings. Loki was the jealous one, the clever one, and he caused much trouble up in Valhalla and Jotunheim. But Thor never killed him." Leif laughed a little. "Whether they were brothers or lovers—what matters is that Thor saw a bid for attention, and he answered it with threats but did not carry them out."

"Yeah," Hacon said softly. "My little brother, Sven—he's got cell phone records with drug dealers and mobsters."

Leif sucked air through his teeth. "Did you know this?"

Hacon made a grunt into the darkness. "I should have," he admitted. "He... my father died a few years ago. He tried to make us close, you know? But I got the business, and I'd always been going to get the business, and Skali—he was okay. He was going to be a teacher, and that was okay too. But Sven—he... he didn't know what he wanted. I mean, I guess he was young when dad died. He was sixteen, but he was in school and he had his own friends. And he would get in trouble, small trouble, and Skali and I would talk to him, and we would think, 'Hey, he's young. He'll grow. It's no big deal. He'll learn.' He's been coming into the office to help, you know, because we thought, 'Hey, he doesn't seem to have a direction, that's as good a one as any!' But his heart's not in it. This May, he asked to go on a trip to

Europe—we let him go because we thought he might find himself. I think that maybe…."

"Maybe he was trying to lose himself?" Leif said gently, because it was an old story. A sad one, one of misunderstanding and loneliness, but still, a story he could read the lines from.

"So see? We're here because I'm cold as ice, and a prick," Hacon said, his voice ineffably sad in the quiet. "I did not show my brother the love he needed, and now he hates me."

"Do you know he sent the package?" Leif asked, and Hacon grunted.

"No. But they're pretty sure the people on his cell phone records sent it."

"Well, then, maybe he doesn't hate you. Maybe he was desperate, and *they* were mean. You don't know for sure. Thor could have laid waste to Loki at any moment, you understand, but he didn't. He punished him, his little foster brother, and the next poem in *The Edda*, Loki was very helpful. You will see."

"A degree in humanities, is that what you said?" Hacon asked after a weighted silence.

"Yeah. I loved it. If I had money and time, I'd go back and get my master's and my PhD."

"You'd teach," Hacon murmured, and he sounded very tired, just like Leif. "Because I think you're really good at being human."

"And you're not so good at being a prick." Leif smiled. Hacon's wry grunt in reply had the resonance of sleep to it, so Leif finished up with, "Good night, businessman."

"G'night, Leif. Make sure you wake up, okay?"

"Was planning on it. 'Night."

"'Night."

It wasn't a good night, of course. There was the pain, and the nurse coming in once an hour, and the fact that he couldn't turn over on his side. The thread remained a sad, tangled mess behind his eyes. But still—he was alive, and really, he got to spend the night with a pretty man. It was as close as Leif had come to actual sex in almost a year.

HACON
CLOUDS AND STORM

HACON'S mother came and got him the next day, sweet and solicitous, with a leisure suit in a Macy's bag for him to wear home, as well as some high-priced trainers. His mother was an elegant woman, one who enjoyed the life the family's business gave her but who cared for her children in a reserved way. She was of middle height with silvery blonde hair, and she had worn a suit with women's low-heeled dress shoes for pretty much every day that he could remember her. She had never hand-fed him anything—even when Sven had been a baby. That had been the maid's job. Her driver walked her into the hospital this day, and he carried the Macy's bag for her.

Hacon was absurdly happy to see her and then almost embarrassed to introduce her to Leif. This wasn't someone who came bounding in with chili and cornbread just because she was worried. This wasn't someone who would offer to feed Hacon's cat (Hake had asked Andre to do it, and Andre had been surprised that he had a cat at all). This wasn't someone who would worry as to whether he had eaten. But as she offered her cheek to be kissed and inquired solicitously over his state of injury (not bad, considering, but he was going to have to wear a splint on his wrist for a few days), he realized that she was very nearly all he had and that he might lose her if she decided it was his fault Sven had tried to kill him. Or something like that.

But no matter how conflicted Hacon felt when his mother walked in, his mother was still his mother. She waited for a moment while her driver fetched her a chair, then settled herself primly on it.

"So, Hacon," she said, her voice measured. "The police came to my home yesterday and questioned me about Sven. Is there something you didn't tell me?"

Hacon winced. "Mother, have you met Leif? He saved my life yesterday—twice, really. It would be nice if you said hello."

Across the bed, he caught Leif's wry look. The gentle giant had shadows under his eyes and lines etched in the corners of his mouth from a night Hacon would wager had been uncomfortable at the very least, but he offered Mariana Haldor a smile that was no less brilliant for all of that.

"Hello, Mrs. Haldor, it's a pleasure to meet you. Your son has been very patient with me, I must tell you. He let me ramble long into the night."

God, he looked pale. "It wasn't an imposition at all," Hacon said through a tight throat. Leif's voice, gentle, scholarly, had actually helped keep Hake's demons at bay—he'd soothed the terrible guilt, and the even worse sense of betrayal, and generally gave Hacon the sense of being a small craft in a great soothing, crashing ocean. His problems were important, yes, but they were also a part of a larger pattern, one that Hacon could no more control than he could control the wind or the tides or the moon and stars that drove them.

Hake looked at his mother and nodded seriously. "He was kind, Mother. You don't find a lot of kindness or bravery these days."

Mrs. Haldor looked at Leif measuringly, maybe taking in the three days of stubble or the unruly red hair, or maybe taking in the battered coat and bag hanging by his bed. "Well, since he saved your life, perhaps we can pay him—"

"*No!*" Both Hake and Leif shouted the word and then met eyes across the room.

"He didn't return my wallet, Mother," Hacon said, his gaze still meshed with Leif's. "He saved my life. And he's been very kind." *He let his friend feed me chili. He told me stories when I was frightened. He didn't judge me when I judged myself. And he's done it all when he's been in pain and hasn't complained.*

"We will find a way," Hacon said softly, like his mother wasn't in the room. "We'll find a way to show our gratitude." Hacon looked at his mother, who was rolling her eyes at his sentiment. "Mother, what did the police tell you about Sven?"

His mother's mouth tightened. "They said he was into gangsters for money, and they tried to kill you to get the company. I don't believe it."

Hacon swallowed. God, that would be simple, wouldn't it? Just to not believe the bad stuff? Wouldn't it be wonderful to say, *I don't believe this, and so it is not true*?

"Have they talked to Sven?"

His mother's face grew... crafty. "No," she said with composure. "And they won't, either. I called Mr. Winsley. I don't expect anybody to be able to reach Sven until this madness is over." And then, in that abrupt, imperious way that said that Hacon's mother had finished any part of the conversation that interested her, she added, "I'm going to go find your doctor now, Hacon, so I can sign your papers and take you home."

"My home, Mother," Hacon said evenly, "not yours."

His mother gave a disgusted little sniff. "If you prefer," she said and then stood and clicked down the hospital hallway, her driver behind her.

Hacon sighed and looked over at Leif, who had one eyebrow raised in amusement.

"She's formidable," he said.

Hacon snorted. "That's charitable," he shot back. "And I'm sorry she tried to give you money. For someone who thinks she's so damned above it all, that was pretty crass."

Leif shrugged. "And practical," he said with that good-natured smile, "but unnecessary. What are you going to do about your brother?"

Hacon thought carefully. "Well, if she's got him hidden in a vault somewhere, we'll never find out who he got money from, or even if they're the ones behind it. And the police are going to search his home, but I don't think he did any of his business there." Hacon snorted. He'd been there twice—both times it had been overflowing with young people listening to music and ordering pizza and doing things they shouldn't have been doing but Hacon pretended he didn't see. "I don't think even Sven was that foolish."

"Where *would* he do his business?" Leif asked curiously, and Hacon shrugged.

"Well, he doesn't have an office down at the wharf where I do, but he *does* help my assistant sometimes in our little office off of Brannan. I guess he visits once or twice a week."

"Do the police know this?" Leif asked.

Hacon shrugged again and shook his head. "Not if my mother didn't tell them. All of the buildings are listed under the company name. The office is for hard copies of invoices, and it's where we do our master shipping schedules on the big corkboard and keep our archives...." Hacon trailed off and looked at Leif curiously. "Why are you smiling like that?"

Leif shrugged, even though it still made him cringe, and still his smile stayed that same pretty, manic, anticipatory grin. "Well, you wanted to find out if it was Sven. And maybe, if you want to find out first, so you can confront your family, you could perhaps...."

Hacon looked at him in flat disbelief. "I am *not* a detective."

Leif shrugged again. "You're not a mouse!"

Hacon's mouth was opening and closing and opening and closing and nothing at all was coming out. "I have no answer to that," he said after a few moments. Leif's expression was gleeful, and Hacon had to laugh.

"Okay, so I am a detective. Want to come with me?" It was so completely unexpected, for Hacon Haldor. Snooping around his brother's desk was completely unlike him (even with his assistant there to help and witness), and planning an adventure with a stranger was *completely* unlike him. Hell, even as a child, he'd had assigned play dates with specified activities: *We shall spend one hour playing with the trains and one hour playing with the blocks. Would you like to negotiate?* Thinking about it now, he decided it was small wonder he'd had few friends in high school. But this man had saved his life, and somehow, giving in to his playful dare was the only thing that seemed good enough to show gratitude.

"Yes!" Leif said, so enthusiastically that Hacon laughed. Then Leif's face fell. "But I will be here until tomorrow morning, and then I work tomorrow night. You will have to come and tell me how it goes tonight."

Hacon let out a sigh. "Well, I don't want to go without you," he said, disappointed. "You're the only reason the whole adventure sounds any fun at all." Oh God—how third grade of him!

But Leif didn't seem to think any less of him for that child's whine. "Really?" He struggled to sit up and masked a wince. "I could go AMA—I don't want to leave you hanging!"

"You can't do that!" Hacon protested. "A concussion—twice! Your brains are scrambled. Hell, I don't know what your second job is, but I don't think you should be doing it as often as you got your skull rattled. You could pass out or drive your car into a ditch and your head could explode or—"

Leif shrugged. "Or a wrecking ball could come smashing into my crappy apartment and kill me as I lie in bed. No one knows when his string will be cut—it will simply be cut. Some people have warning: they grow sick, and then they can say good-byes, but really, why would you not live your life as though the scissors are out and Skuld is at the ready?"

Hacon wrinkled his nose, pursed his lips, and wrinkled his nose again. "I can't figure out if that's really pessimistic or really well adjusted." He shook his head. "Look, I'll tell you what. When does your job start?"

"Three in the afternoon. Off of Hyde, by Geary."

"Isn't that where your other job is?"

Leif smiled. "Yes—good of you to remember. How do you think I found the job delivering flowers? It was perfect! Except they asked me to drive the van. I had to get a license, and I hated the stress. But it's delivering flowers! How wonderful is that!"

"I don't know. Do you ever deliver to funerals?"

"No, actually. I mean, I take the arrangements in, but you give them to the funeral people, and they're usually very nice. Quiet, you know, because that's the job, but friendly. They like to feed you, and that's always a plus."

Oh hells. This man could find the toy surprise in the shit pile of a pig factory. Hacon looked at those bright bay-blue eyes that felt close and personal from across the room. God, he was pretty. Not stupid, either, just... just pretty. Joyous. Hacon thought he'd do maybe anything to get those blue eyes on him, and only him, and that open smile personal and tender. Twenty-four hours in the man's presence and suddenly Hacon was almost angry at him for risking his life, for almost yanking that big-sky heart of joy out of the world for Hacon, who hadn't seen the manhole because he was looking at the safe.

"I'll come get you in the morning—"

"But it might not be there in the morning!"

"Look—Sven is MIA, and Emma's the only other person besides me who ever goes to that office. Whatever is there isn't going anywhere, okay?"

Leif smiled. "And I can come? Excellent!" He looked embarrassed. "Can you take me home first so I can change my clothes and say hello to my cat?"

Hacon nodded in sympathy. "When Vanir gets mad, he pees in random places that I never find until I get the carpets cleaned. Fucking cat."

Leif laughed, a hearty sound that came from his belly, and Hacon practically glowed from his approval. "And the reason you called him Vanir is because…."

Hacon sat up entirely so they could finish the sentence together.

"Because he thinks he's a god!"

He found he was chuckling from his stomach like he couldn't remember laughing *ever*. He finished laughing and said, "Wait right here. With any luck I can be dressed before my mother gets back."

He disappeared into the bathroom and stripped off the hospital gown. He was lean—almost to the point of being skinny—and you could see the muscles in his stomach without him being accused of having a six-pack. Just not enough fat to obscure them, was all. His chest was a little hairy, but his stomach wasn't, and, well, Leif had called him pretty. He looked in the mirror, saw the narrow chin and nose and face and thought that maybe, coming from a man-god, he'd believe it.

He moved quickly, took a GI shower with a washcloth as he went, appreciating the clean underwear, and was done, dressed, with shoes on and feeling like he could meet his day before his mother could arrive, and he was grateful. He emerged from the bathroom after stuffing his hospital gown into the hamper nearby and approached Leif's bed.

It was the first time he'd seen the man up close without blood streaming down his face. He still had some blood crusted in his hair—

and he smelled like he was on day two of a marathon, there was no getting beyond that—but it was an honest smell. He smiled at Hacon almost shyly, as though he was also aware of the sudden intimacy. There wasn't any hurt between them, or shock. Just two men who liked men in the quiet of an otherwise empty room.

Hacon smiled back and found he was taking advantage of standing up and looming over Leif by raising a tentative finger and tracing the faint pattern on the bridge of Leif's nose. "You have freckles," he said softly. "It must be the red hair."

Under his finger, he felt the heat of Leif's skin. "Just like Thor himself," Leif confessed, obviously embarrassed. "And you are still a very pretty man."

Now Hacon blushed. "I'm looking forward to breaking and entering with you," he said, trying to be funny, and he was embarrassed and disconcerted when Leif laughed like a third grader.

"You did not mean it that way?" Leif asked, looking at his expression with gentle amusement.

"What way? No!" Oh gods! Like he was really that—

"Well then, that is too bad," Leif chuckled, cutting off that thought. Leif's voice dropped, making Hacon bend closer to hear it. "Because I would love to... do some entering with you," he murmured, and suddenly Hacon was too turned on to blush or laugh or do more than turn his head and look breathlessly into Leif's eyes.

"I, uhm, usually do the entering," Hacon muttered, because he did, but Leif was not put off in the least.

"Well, you should probably plan on changing that, pretty man," he said softly, and because Hacon was bending over the bed, Leif was able to reach behind his head with his right hand and pull Hacon to him so quickly, with such firm efficiency, that Hacon had no choice but to kiss him back.

Okay, that was a lie. Hacon was standing up, he was whole and sound—he could have pulled away and said, *I'm sorry, but I'm a prick who has to have my own way all the time and I always top so this will never work*, but then... oh God, then he would have missed out on that kiss.

Later, he was unsure why it was so wonderful. Leif had been drinking lots of water, but he hadn't brushed his teeth that morning, so his breath was not pristine, and his body odor was pretty strong, but still. That hand on the back of his head knew exactly what it was doing—there was just enough pressure to make Hacon stay still and not enough to make him feel threatened, and when he opened his mouth, and Leif entered.... *Wow. Damn. Holy fuck-all and gods-help-us!* It was like an invading army overwhelmed Hacon, all of his worries, all of his proprieties, all of the little hang-ups that had caused him and Andre weeks of frozen silence.... All of those things Hake liked least about himself were destroyed, overrun, trampled under Leif's generosity, his joy, his good nature that was as epic as a cosmic force. Hacon groaned a little and Leif took the kiss deeper, until Hacon was bracing his hands on either side of Leif's body and pulled into Leif's space, plundering *Leif's* mouth and demanding more and more and....

"Hacon?"

Hacon stood up so fast he almost fell on his ass. "Mother?" he said weakly, and Leif's gentle chuckle was not lost on him. Hacon put a finger across Leif's mouth to signal that he would handle his mother, but as he turned to face her, Leif pulled the finger into his mouth and started suckling. Hacon snatched it back and crossed his arms in front of him.

"I was just making plans to see Mr. Torval tomorrow," he said. He knew she wasn't stupid and that she knew he was gay, and he knew it was none of her business, but that didn't stop him from feeling like a little kid caught masturbating in the bathroom.

Behind him, Leif had raised his *injured* arm and was resting it lightly on the small of Hacon's back. Hacon wanted to wiggle his ass— yes, *Hacon Haldor* wanted to wiggle his ass to get that hand closer, to have it all over him.

"I saw what you were just doing, and I'm afraid you must do it later. We need to leave. Good-bye, Mr. Torval. Thank you for your service."

"Good-bye, Mrs. Haldor," Leif said pleasantly. "Hacon?"

Hake turned around, and suddenly Leif's expression wasn't joyful or good-natured. Suddenly Leif's expression was very, very serious.

"What?" Hake asked, his throat dry.

"I think there will be a time when you need to decide whose opinion you value more. Your lover's or your mother's. Not now, but I think that time is coming. I'll see you tomorrow."

Hacon opened his mouth and shut it, then opened his mouth again, then turned around and glared at his mother and turned back and bent down. Once there, he planted a big one on Leif's unresisting (and surprisingly full and pillowy and really kissable) mouth. He scowled at Leif's mocking grin, turned on his heel, grabbed his damaged clothes in their little plastic bag, and was going to stalk out of his room.

Except there was an orderly with a wheelchair behind his mother, and apparently he had to ride that thing out or the hospital insurance wouldn't cover his skinny ass walking through the halls. He turned around and faced Leif in order to sit down, scowling at the big man and sighing.

Leif's booming laugh rang unapologetically through the room, and Hacon gave up on trying to be irritated and just smiled sheepishly. "I'll see you tomorrow, Leif."

"Looking forward to it, pretty man. It will be my pleasure."

HACON got to his home in Pilot Hill and looked around anxiously for his cat. Sure enough, Vanir, a big fluffy orange cat with paws the size of a wide-mouthed bottle lid, came padding out of Hake's bedroom looking smug and self-satisfied.

"Okay, Vanir," Hacon said sternly. "Which one of my shoes did you piss on? I'll give you a freebie today since I didn't bring you home takeout, but it would make a real gentleman of you if you at least give me warning so I can take it to the cobbler and let him clean it."

Vanir sat at his feet and meowed imperiously, and Hacon bent down and allowed the big cat—eighteen pounds big, actually—to jump into his arms. He held Vanir tight, feeling that reassuring rumbling purr coming from his belly, and touched noses with him. Vanir was a social cat who was not truly happy unless someone (Hacon) spent a good half an hour a day appreciating his awesomeness. Hacon had found him as a stray kitten one night, sitting regally on his doorstep and asking where the fuck dinner was and why the service was so shitty in this part of town. It was about two months after Andre left, and Hake had moved across town to a house so he would have *something* and wouldn't feel like such a complete and total loser with no boyfriend and no home and nothing but his job to sustain him, and he often felt like Vanir had kept him from being a bitter old man at the age of thirty-three.

"I missed you too," Hacon said softly, rubbing cheeks with his cat-god. "And I met a man, a giant of a man, who kissed me until my eyes crossed. I have no idea why he did that, but I would really like him to do it again."

Vanir kept purring, and Hacon felt marginally better. He was still a little stiff and a little tired, but he figured he could do some work from his desktop tonight and be all caught up for his day of adventure and snooping in the morning.

Of course, when he sat down, he didn't count on being able to ferret out some answers on the computer that made his next day with Leif that much more exciting. All he knew was that suddenly even his apartment with the dark hardwood and white throw rug looked as blue and as open as the sparkling bay, and that instead of the next day being a gray and foggy repetition of the day that came before it, it was suddenly an exciting adventure, and he wanted to run toward it for maybe the first time in his life.

LEIF
PAWNS OF THE GODS

LEIF was sorry to see Hacon go, but still excited, and not just because of the kiss, either.

Of course, the kiss had been nice. Hacon's breath had been better than Leif's, and Leif swore he'd at least be presentable before they went off on their little sneaking adventure, but beyond that, Hake had been... pliant. Pliant and hungry. Almost desperate for Leif's hand on the back of his head and the feel of his mouth. After Hacon and his mother had disappeared down the corridor, Leif closed his eyes and shivered greedily, and he savored that mutinous pout, how it had felt in the middle of that irritated kiss and how soft it had felt at the end. Nice. Nice. A good kisser, *and* he had a cat, *and* he knew better than to offer Leif money for simply being Leif.

Things were looking up.

Except....

Leif's eyes shot open, and he closed them again. What in the furry hells? The gold thread had been sorting itself out as Leif had snatched naps from the nimble fingers of his able nurses. He would wake up, talk to Hacon or listen to the ceaseless whirr of the hospital around him, the alien echo of tiled corridors and busy people, and then he would close his eyes, and every time he closed his eyes, the thread would stretch, unsnarl, lay itself out like a string on a map.

It had been the string that suggested looking at Hacon's brother's office, and the string that had drooped, dispirited and fading, when Hacon had been planning to go there alone. When Hacon had offered to take Leif home, the string had vibrated, shiny and crisp against the black of his thoughts, and it had zigged and zagged and pointed to something good.

Then he'd kissed Hacon, enjoyed him, thought hazily about maybe having sex that wasn't over in a night, but now that Hacon was gone and he could close his eyes and savor the moment, the string was in a tangle again. Leif was sincerely troubled.

He could not figure out what it meant. The string told him to go blazing down Nob Hill, and so Leif did, and good fortune had come of it. (Not even Hacon could argue with that, although Leif suspected he would try. Leif had never met a man more perversely determined to argue his way out of happiness.) But after their encounter, the string had disappeared, had… had tangled and woven behind his eyes in ways he could not decipher. It had been that, more than the ache in his head, that had convinced him to stay in the hospital an extra night. Normally he would have just checked himself out (and he had, on several occasions, after incurring road rash and broken bones), but the string? That was *important*. That was *necessary*. If the string was tangled and knotted and rewoven in his head, something up there was apparently very wrong.

Except the string had been resetting itself—right up until that final kiss. Leif closed his eyes after the next nurse visit and the string was still tangled. Righting itself, as it had been after the *last* time he'd touched Hacon, but….

But touching Hacon? Was apparently not good for his luck.

Leif felt an acute, painful twinge of disappointment. Well, that wasn't good at *all*. Because if anybody needed some time spent with good nature and luck, it was Hacon, who had worried and fussed and fretted through most of the night until Leif had told him stories just to settle the man down.

But the way the man responded to stories… ah! It was beautiful, hearing Hacon set his world right in the stories of the old gods. It was like being really good at putting together puzzles and then meeting someone who felt the same pleasure in the snap and fit of the puzzle pieces as you did. Except better, because puzzles were finite, precut things, and stories, those were infinite and mutating, changing for the needs of the teller and the listener—stories were the jigsaw puzzles of the gods.

Leif sighed, looking at the poor frazzle of gold in his brain. Well, if touching Hacon made that gold frazzle appear, maybe not touching him would make it go away. But when it was there, the things it told him to do made sure that he *would* touch Hacon and, worse than that, *want* to touch the man. It was a puzzle, that was for certain, and one likely of the gods' making.

He'd already noticed that Hacon enjoyed the puzzles of the gods.

So it was decided. He would help Hacon investigate a bomb and a brother, and whether he knew it or not, Hacon would help him investigate the tangle of his luck and his flesh—because they both seemed to be going in completely opposite directions, and that was not lucky at all.

THE next day Hacon arrived to pick him up, and Leif was embarrassed. Lethal had not been able to bring his books or his clothes, leaving him in hospital scrubs and his biking shoes. That was after having begged a nurse for a toothbrush and some bodywash and shampoo to risk life and limb trying to wash off in one of the cubicle showers. Yes, yes, he'd been planning to take a shower when he got home, but his smell had been rank and irritating, even to his own nose. His exact words to the nurse had been "Please. I have not had an actual date since my last boyfriend was married—I attended the wedding, you understand? Please, is there any possible way this man can come pick me up and take me to my apartment without needing to pull over and douse me with bleach on the way home?"

Pathetic, yes? Effective, but pathetic, and it did not change the fact that he and Hacon were uncertain of what to say to each other when Hake came to collect him. It *certainly* didn't change the fact that Leif was wearing what amounted to pajamas as he allowed the orderly to push him to the automatic doors of the entrance. He limped to the car Hacon had fetched while Leif was signing release forms, and Leif felt gauche and awkward as he climbed into Hacon's nicely appointed black Mercedes with the lovely silver interior. He sat for a moment with his knees up to his chest, and then Hacon said, "Oh, wait—here, let me get the latch," because Leif could barely bend over. Hacon leaned sideways and reached between Leif's legs and fumbled for the release, and Leif went sliding back blissfully with Hake's head on his leg. There was a frozen moment when the thread tangled and Leif didn't care because Hacon was resting on his thigh, and Leif gently lowered his hand to Hake's head as it lay there.

"Generous of you," Leif said, keeping his voice dry with an effort, "but hardly convenient or comfortable in the car."

Hacon sat up and flushed and looked at him slant-ways. "It's been a while since I've done it," he said, his voice gravelly. "Perhaps I've forgotten."

Oh no! Was that a *joke*? How wonderful! Leif put his hand on Hacon's head and ruffled his hair, which was fine and straight, so when he looked at Leif in bemusement, it was scattered all over his head like tossed twigs.

"Then let us hope one of us remembers," Leif said, letting his eyes crinkle in the corners. "It would be a shame to let the art die out."

Hacon blushed, the color sweeping from the roots of his hair and down his neck, and said, "We should get you home so we can go on our adventure," but his voice was pitching a little and strangled.

Leif laughed and rolled down the window, closed his eyes, and let the air of the city wash over him. It wasn't always pleasant—there was plenty of car exhaust and diesel and trash in dumpsters to keep it from being the fresh bay breezes you read about—but he hated being trapped inside of anything for any length of time, and the air reminded him he was free.

There was some heavy traffic on Mission but very little on Geary, and Leif was relieved to see there were a few spaces behind his building on Olive so Hacon could park his car. Leif didn't own a car; parking was something he rarely paid attention to.

Leif took Hacon around the building, trying hard not to let his limp show. He'd torn up his knee in the original fall from the bike, and they'd stitched it up and iced it, but still, it wasn't a picnic. Hacon was a worrier, and Leif didn't want to give him any excuses. First he went to the super, who gave him the key, and the tiny Chinese man eyed him suspiciously and asked him to make sure he checked his belongings. "That girl was there. Your things might not be safe!"

"What things?" Leif asked. "Everything I have is books—I bought them for nothing and she's welcome to steal them for less!"

Mr. Cho was unamused, and Hacon glowered at Leif from under heavy eyebrows.

"What?" Leif asked as they went through the white-painted hallway and up the stairs.

"You're awfully cavalier about your possessions," Hacon said, as though trying to get a handle on that idea.

Leif gave in and grabbed the railing on the third flight, giving himself a good solid haul for some momentum before he arrived at his apartment. He stood at the doorway and fiddled with the lock—it tended to stick—and smiled, a little embarrassed. "You can be generous to the world when you have much to give," he said, and then, to show that he was being ironic, he opened his door with the graciousness and grandeur of a sultan.

And pretended not to notice that Hacon was careful of getting dust on his brand new jeans and summer-weight pale blue windbreaker as he walked in.

Ah, well, that was Leif's apartment. Two rooms with a tiny kitchenette attached to the living room, marked by a six-by-six piece of vinyl flooring instead of the gray-and-brown carpet that marked the rest of the cramped space. (Including the bathroom, much to Leif's discomfort. His aim had gotten very good since he'd moved here, and he was also good at cleaning the plastic mat underneath.)

"My God," Hacon breathed, looking around him. The books were everywhere, and Leif realized that there was no place to sit.

"Here, let me." Leif trailed off as he used his good arm to scoop and heft a stack of books off the couch to the floor, and then another one off the couch to a different, shorter stack of books under the window. The stack wavered precariously, so he took some of the books off until it stabilized and turned around in the two-foot space in the middle of all of the other book stacks, which were hemmed in by bookshelves on all sides, and sighed. "I'll be right back," he said and walked into his bedroom, where he added the books to the three stacks in the corner. He came back to the living room for the final stack from the couch (brown, corduroy, and his only piece of furniture besides the bed) and then ran that back to the bedroom too. His knee and back all hurt, and he felt a little dizzy, and even though he hadn't used the arm with the broken collarbone—it was, in fact, immobilized—well, that hurt too. It was a good thing Hacon was driving them everywhere today, because he was obviously not up to riding his....

"Oh shit," he groaned, thinking that the living room had seemed a little empty.

"What?" Hacon asked, coming into the bedroom behind him.

Leif whirled around, and then his knee gave out and he crashed, ass-first, on his unmade bed.

"My bike," Leif said, dispirited. "I'm scheduled to ride tomorrow, and I don't even know where my bike is." He sighed and then looked up as a familiar growl sounded.

"Loki?" he asked and was rewarded when the bull-necked, melon-headed black-and-white cat stalked from the slightly open bathroom to jump up on the bed. The cat glared at Leif and dared him to scratch behind the ears and under the chin, and Leif called his bluff and scratched him just there. Loki growled, pulled all four feet underneath him, and sat, sphinx-stiff, and growled some more while Leif continued to fondle his ears.

"*That* is a *cat?*" Hacon asked, as though Loki was the most unusual thing about the apartment. "*That* looks like it escaped from the zoo!"

Leif looked at Loki affectionately and reached down to touch noses to him. Loki must have missed him while he was gone, because he didn't rip Leif's nose open with an irritated claw.

"That is Loki," Leif said happily. "Ill-tempered, irascible, and destructive—but you must love him."

"You must?" Incredulity dripped from Hacon's voice, and Leif smiled at him, feeling like the loss of his bike might be bearable.

"Yes. Because every bit of affection he gives you is important. Loki doesn't love lightly." Leif chucked Loki under the chin and looked around his apartment again. No bicycle—that *was* bad luck.

"Was the frame intact?" he asked plaintively, and Hacon looked pained.

"I'm sorry," he said sadly. "It survived the trip into the manhole, but the car crushed it after the explosion.

Suddenly Leif brightened. "Which I survived. And that is a good thing. A bicycle will come my way—that is simply what must happen!" In an unprecedented move, Loki inched closer and rubbed his cheeks on Leif's thigh. "And of course, I still have you, you crotchety prick," Leif said fondly, and Loki grumbled some more and gently clawed Leif's hand for fun.

"I must change," Leif said, feeling his aches but also filled with that need to go with Hacon just the same. "Make yourself at home—" He grinned. "—such as it is."

Hacon nodded, and Leif stood up, disconcerted when Hacon didn't go into the other room. But then, Leif had been the one to initiate the kiss. Hacon stood there and looked at him mildly, and Leif blushed.

"I am bruised," he said, uncomfortable with the admission but thinking it needed to be said. "Not pretty. Not today."

Hacon reached out then, an awkward gesture from a man who seemed so self-contained, but he brushed Leif's shoulder with the C-collar under his scrubs, and said, "I can't believe you're not pretty," very, very softly, and Leif looked away.

"Then you are welcome to stay and see," he said, making his voice light. He still couldn't meet Hake's eyes as he turned toward his dresser and rummaged until he found a fresh pair of underwear (since he was wearing none at the moment), a pair of cargo shorts (although it was seventy degrees outside), a T-shirt, and a hooded sweatshirt. Without turning around (mostly because he'd almost forgotten he had an audience), he toed off his shoes and dropped his scrub bottoms and pulled on the overwashed, thin, and holey blue cotton briefs. It wasn't until he was reaching for his cargo shorts that he realized Hacon had made a sound. He turned back around and brazened it out, trying to lighten the moment.

"Bruised, yes?"

"Oh God," Hacon said softly, moving into his space even as Leif pulled up the shorts with one hand. Suddenly Hacon was tugging the shorts up his hips, reaching around and fastening them, and then ghosting a touch under Leif's scrubs and across his hips and his back and his shoulders, which had been scraped by the car's bumper as it had been blown into the air. "Here. I'm an idiot. There you were, moving furniture, when you look like this."

Leif stood still and allowed himself to be touched, closing his eyes because it had been such a long time—especially with this sort of tenderness. "It was only books. You may think this is the first time I've fallen off my bike, but it's not," he said softly. "We're tough. You've seen us. We don't do that because the pay is good, because it's not."

"Why do you do it?" Hacon asked, taking the hem of the scrubs and pulling the shirt gently up.

Leif raised one arm and allowed the shirt to be dragged over his head and then down the injured arm, although he had to help himself out of the sling for the thing to get taken completely off. "Because I am free," Leif said, acutely aware of the man behind him. Hacon touched him tentatively as he stood there, a finger down the unbruised flesh of his arm, a palm across the small of his back. Leif stayed put, a little like he did when Loki decided to seek affection, and allowed Hake to go get his T-shirt and pull it over his head.

"You're going to have to duck," Hacon said softly. "You're taller than I am."

Leif did so and grinned. "I'm taller than everybody," he said, happy because this had always made him happy. "My grandmother always said it was so my head could be closer to the clouds."

"You like to dream?" Hacon asked, pulling the shirt down and smoothing it over Leif's back.

Leif closed his eyes again and shivered with the touch. God, simple human touch, with that humming tension of sex but not the greed of a one-night stand—when had been the last time…? Leif didn't want to contemplate it, because he knew. "Stories," Leif said simply. "If I am not thinking about them, I am writing them." He gestured to the pile of books, some of which were hand-typed. He had no computer, just his grandmother's old electric typewriter, which he cared for meticulously and ordered ribbon for over the Internet at a local Internet café. "Mostly, it is criticism, although I tell legends of my own sometimes." Leif smiled dreamily. "Someday," he said, "I will go back to school."

There was a touch then, Hacon's lips between his shoulder blades, just under his neck. "That's a good dream," he said softly. Then, with incredible sadness: "I wish my brother had such dreams."

His warmth and his touch disappeared, and Leif turned his head a little to the left and saw Hacon was reaching for his sweatshirt.

"Did you go to San Francisco State?" Hacon asked, and Leif responded automatically with "Yes," before asking, "What did you mean, about your brother?"

Hacon said, "Duck," and Leif did, ducking his head and struggling into it, wincing again when he had to thrust his arm through before pulling the sling out again.

Suddenly Hacon grabbed his hips and turned him around. "Here, let me do that"—and Leif stood docilely and let Hacon tend to him. Finally, he was settled. He stood there for a moment, embarrassed and hating what an ordeal it had to be when you were hurt, but still, Hacon did not move.

"Who is this?" Hacon asked, reaching behind Leif to the picture on Leif's dresser. Leif let him, because he was obviously avoiding the question about his brother.

"My old boyfriend and his wife. It's their wedding."

"You went to their *wedding?*" Hacon looked up at him, horrified, and Leif shrugged with one shoulder, which was something he'd gotten used to in the hospital.

"He told his parents we were roommates for two years—I was his best friend and his best man. Yes, I went to his wedding. It was a way to say good-bye."

"That's awful!"

"Not the best day of my life, no," Leif admitted, taking the picture from him and putting it up on his dresser again. "Were you going to tell me about—"

"Who is this?" Hacon asked, pulling down an old picture—a *very* old picture.

"That is my grandmother and my mother and me," Leif said, sighing as he looked at it. It had been taken perhaps a month before his mother had been killed.

"They are both very beautiful," Hacon said, and Leif had to agree—Scandinavian, blonde, classically featured with wide blue eyes, yes. They were both gorgeous, even his grandmother, who must have been in her fifties at the time the picture was taken. Hake heard Leif's little grunt of assent and looked up at him. "Like you."

Leif rolled his eyes. "That is sweet. Unlike me, though, their thread has been cut."

"How old were you?"

"Eight when my mother died. Twenty when my grandmother went."

Hacon frowned. "No one else?"

It was not something Leif allowed himself to dwell on much until now, and he shifted uncomfortably under the sharp blue eyes of this man who had been surprisingly tender to him. "There's Loki," he said with dignity, "and Lethal. I think she left more chili in the refrigerator. Your brother?"

Hacon turned away then. "Is a drug addict," he said softly, sticking his hands in the pockets of his windbreaker and wandering over to the window that looked out at Olive Street. "Oxycodone. It wasn't too hard to put together. I'm sure Andre knows already, he just hasn't told me yet, for whatever cop reason he has."

"How did you 'put this together,' as you said?" Leif asked, feeling the pain behind his casualness. "Maybe you put those pieces together wrong."

Hake shook his head. "There are some stories you recognize. See, about a year ago, he hurt his back in a snowboarding accident; I remember that. Before then, his grades were okay. He came into the office twice a week, we gave him an allowance for school, he asked questions about the business—but then he hurt himself. I remember that, because we all rushed to the hospital to make sure he was okay, and he was. In fact, he was as high as a kite. We had to scrape him off the ceiling to even talk to him, right?"

"How I was, most of last night," Leif agreed, and Hacon laughed humorlessly.

"Probably not," he said simply. "You barely accepted what they offered. Anyway, I remembered that, after Andre told me, and I went back into the shipping records, and once I decided what the pieces looked like, there it was."

"Smuggling?"

"I told you it was an old story. We ship novelty goods—tourist things. That T-shirt you have on; the one with the seal on it that says 'San Francisco' probably came over on one of our cargo ships and was decaled here. And yeah, we shipped the decals too. So Sven's usual day to come in to the office now—and there's only one—is yesterday.

Tuesday. And there is one company that arrives every Tuesday, and on no other day."

"This proves nothing," Leif said. "Do you have him losing money to drug dealers? Do you have him shoving pills inside of ugly porcelain curios? So far, all you have is a day he comes in and the arrival of a ship. If you can put these things together with drugs, then you can say he's smuggling them—or something—into the country. If you cannot, maybe you can see if your little brother can be saved."

"After he almost killed you?" Hacon asked, whirling around. "I don't think so!"

Leif snorted. "Me? You've known me for two days. He is your family. Drugs are a terrible thing," he added earnestly. "I see people on the streets, and with every fix, they know their soul is a little more in danger, and yet they cannot help it." Leif shook his head. "You do not know if your brother was desperate or what sort of terrible deal he struck. If he'd meant to kill you, Hacon, it would have been more personal."

"You don't know my family," Hacon grumbled. "We couldn't be *less* personal."

"You could be right," Leif conceded, "but I do know that when your mother arrived at your hospital room, she brought nice clothes in your size, and she did not lose her mind when she saw you kissing another man. Perhaps she is not warm—"

Hacon snorted, and Leif pinned him under a stern glare. "It's so wonderful that you are feeling three today. Do you need a snack and a trip to the bathroom before we start preschool?"

"Shut up," Hacon grumbled, but Leif saw the smile he was pushing back at the corners of his mouth and didn't take offense.

"You have a family. You have a history that I cannot even guess at. Don't be so excited to throw it all away when you don't know the whole story."

"What if I do?" Hacon demanded. "What if that *is* the whole story?"

Leif sighed and fought the urge to sit down, because he was already tired. "Even if you *think* that's the whole story, it's never the whole story, *especially* with drugs involved. If he's addicted to prescription medicines, that's pretty hard to kick—and a very desperate habit. If he had no real friends and your family was estranged, then he must have felt incredibly lonely. He probably still feels incredibly lonely, like there is no way to go home. Wouldn't it be wonderful if he had a brother who would let him feel like home was possible?"

Hacon shrugged and resumed his stare out the window. "You are the most naïve man I've ever met," he said, almost to himself, and Leif tried to tell himself that didn't hurt just a little, that his chest didn't feel a little more hollow at Hacon's bad opinion.

"Perhaps," Leif said, thinking he was braver than this. "But then, I have no family, and these two rooms are my home. Perhaps I see more clearly those things you have which are valuable. You know, it is like diamonds. Close up, in the dark, they're rocks. Back away a little, and they blind you with the shine."

Hacon turned back around toward him. "So, this investigation— are we going to be able to see the diamonds? Or see that they've been turned into coal?"

Leif shrugged, feeling bad for him. He sounded so disillusioned. "Coal is valuable too," he said, keeping his equanimity. "Here, let me put my shoes on and we can go. You don't need to help," he said hurriedly when Hacon moved from his place by the window.

"You didn't like my help?" Hacon sounded hurt.

"I liked it very much," Leif told him, sliding his foot into the bike shoe and then tightening the wide Velcro strap. "I liked it *very* much, but...." Leif flashed a smile, very self-conscious. "It's been a while since I've gotten that kind of help from anyone. I wouldn't want to jump on the help and start humping like a rabbit when we have things to do."

Hacon laughed helplessly and moved into Leif's space just as Leif was straightening up. "Bend down," he said, his helpless smile making his eyes crinkle wickedly in the corners.

"Why?" Leif teased, knowing very well why.

"Because I need you to kiss me before we leave, and yes, it's far more important than anything else, before you ask!"

Leif held Hacon's shoulder with his good arm and lowered his mouth, happy to be in charge. Hacon tasted warm and male, and there was a tincture of laughter in the kiss, enough to temper the bitterness of the moment. The taste grew stronger, more addictive, and Leif closed his eyes tight and devoured it, pulling Hacon up against him in spite of bruises, in spite of pain, in spite of the loneliness he knew he'd revealed with such nakedness. Hacon wrapped his arms around Leif's waist and squeezed, sucking on Leif's lip and pulling him down more, and again, until Leif had to pull back or pin the man to the bed. Hacon buried his face in Leif's neck and caught his breath, still nestled underneath Leif's good arm.

"See," Hake panted, hiding his eyes. "That *was* an important kiss."

"Yes, of course," Leif replied, dropping a kiss on that fine, dark hair. "You were right. I should always listen." Hake *felt* important, there in Leif's arms, and Leif had no practice in holding riches to his heart. He worried about letting go.

INTERLUDE
POPCORN FOR THE GODS

VERDANDI'S shoulders twitched as she worked, keeping an eye on the subtle threads of Hacon and Leif as she did so. "Odin's prick, Loki, could you not sit so close?" she muttered. "I can feel your breath on my neck!"

"If you promise not to swear by my father's manhood, my lovely Fate, I promise to move back."

Dandi gasped. "Thor!" She looked over her shoulder, her hands never ceasing, and tried not to let the cocky, boyish grin make her thighs flood. And then gave it up and just appreciated the surf.

"It wasn't a comfortable oath for me, either," Loki protested, and Thor eyed him with a sort of grim drollery that didn't silence Loki at all. It had *never* silenced Loki, which was, Dandi thought shrewdly, probably why Thor used it.

"Look at them," Thor said, his eyes soft. "Which one is—"

"Don't you have a wife somewhere?" Loki asked, his narrow face alight with contempt.

"Yes," said Thor amicably. "It's been centuries since I've taken her to bed—would you like a front row seat as I chase her down to the center of the earth and fuck her in the roots of Yggdrasil?"

Loki turned red, and the contempt drained out of him like blood. "Wouldn't be my choice of amusements, no," he said, swallowing hard.

"Then stop dragging Sif into things when you want to change the subject. Which one is mine?"

Dandi thought it was telling that Thor did not assume the one who looked like him was his bloodline. Thor, perhaps more than anyone, knew that blood was not the only tracer of history.

"We don't know yet," Verdandi said after she realized both gods were looking to her for an answer. "Skuld spit-spliced the broken thread with some chance fibers, and both men are made of those." She paused just long enough to stroke one of the threads she was working with a callused forefinger. "See? Tough and soft, crafty and open—both men. One is simply the darkness and the other is the light."

Thor's slantwise look at a sulking Loki spoke volumes. "May we watch?" he asked, the question sincere.

"Of course," Urdh spoke up, because Odin forbid she be left out of the honor of a visit from Thor. When Loki visited Verdandi's bed, Loki was a dog and Verdandi his tramp, but when it was Thor? Well, Thor could bed whomever he wanted, and Loki was not the only one who prayed for attention when Sif was away. He was the only one who received it, mostly, but not the only one who prayed.

Verdandi rolled her eyes at her sister but was not so far gone that she didn't remember her manners. "Be pleased to pull a chair from the world tree, my lord," she said politely. "But shh... their pattern is becoming busy!"

HACON
THE BITTER TASTE OF
RIGHTEOUSNESS

HAKE was pleased with himself as he drove to Nob Hill and then down to the wharf. He still remembered the regal way in which Leif accepted his touches—much like Vanir, in which, at the first, a firm touch would have only frightened him, but a gentle one pleased him very much.

But then, when Leif had the chance to touch *Hacon*, well, that was a different story. Hacon's entire body tingled from that kiss, from the mastery and power, the certainty that Leif's big, graceful body could contain Hake's narrower, quicker one, could protect it and gentle it too. Hacon, who had not had a lover since Andre (unless you counted that half-remembered encounter immediately after, and Hacon couldn't really, so he didn't count it), could not even fathom that much touch. It would be like living in a different world, being consumed by a whirlpool as warm as blood, with bones and muscles and sinew pulling you into the vortex and not just water.

For a moment though, he feared. That much power—it surely could not have been waiting for Hake Haldor, could it? Hake, who lived in his little house with his cat, playing the family's patriarch because that was what his father (who had been a quiet, kind man, which was why the business was successful but not huge) had wordlessly expected for all of Hake's life. Hacon was a small man with a small life—that was what he'd told Andre, in their final fight. *How can you expect me to share you with the world, dammit! No, I do not understand your hours or your drive or your belief that you will make the world a better place! All I know is that you are gone, and you would rather* be *gone than be here with me!*

Andre had stalked off. *Of course, Hacon, you make being at home so much more attractive, don't you!*

He had been right, and Hacon had not known how to apologize.

Leif wouldn't have stalked off, would he? Hacon didn't know. So far, they had never fought. But maybe it would behoove Hake to find out how big Leif's life really was.

"So," he said as they waited at a light.

Leif was looking eagerly out the open window as if he didn't know this city more intimately on the back of a bicycle than he did from the front seat of Hacon's car. "Yes?" Leif answered him while keeping his eyes half-closed and sniffing the air.

"Your boyfriend got married...."

"Four years ago," Leif supplied. "Right after we graduated from college."

"And since then...." He let the sentence trail off because he wanted desperately to pry but didn't want to make Leif feel trapped.

"Since then I have... lucked into a few nights that were not lonely," Leif said, his jaw tight.

"A few?"

Leif grunted like he was trying to remember. "Five? Six? Men you bed the night you meet them do not want breakfast, Hacon, even if you could find it in the mess."

"I'm sorry," Hacon murmured, feeling slightly awful. "I... I haven't felt this happy to see someone since Andre left. I wanted to make sure—"

"I feel the same?"

Hake stopped at another light and glanced sideways to see Leif looking at him with uncharacteristic somberness.

"Perhaps you should ask me, instead of asking me how many lovers I've had. I'm more likely to know how I feel now than to remember lost touches in the dark."

Hacon blushed. "You sound like old poems," he murmured, mostly for something to say that wouldn't hurt.

"Well, they speak to me more often than Loki," Leif said, and when Hacon looked again, he saw that Leif's habitual half smile was back, and he was closing his eyes to the wind in order to taste the sunshine on his face.

Hacon found an odd feeling in his chest, a new one for him. A letting go. "Well then, I guess old poems are an improvement," he said. "I don't know if I would enjoy you so much if you sounded like a cat."

Leif's laugh boomed through the car, and Hacon smiled and laughed with him. The fog had burned off when Leif had been changing, and it really was a beautiful day.

Hake's real business—the warehouses, the place where the big ships docked and were unloaded by the great cranes and forklifts—was actually in the Port of Oakland. Back in Hake's father's day, the Port of San Francisco had become more of a tourist attraction than a place of business, and when in 2002 the Port of Oakland had adopted the intermodal transportation system for their containers as opposed to the railroad, that pretty much sealed the deal. But Hake's family kept a business front on Pier 41, which was where Hake usually worked and where he met with clients or potential clients. Keeping an office on the pier kept up the idea (illusion?) that the company—actually fairly modernized since Hake's father's day—was still the old-world operation that Hake's great-grandfather had established.

But even that was a front, because although Hake could access much of the family business from his laptop computer, many of the receipts and invoices were kept in a hard copy form in Sven's office on Brannan, which gave them a reason to have Sven go in there. Hake's assistant, Emma Liu, kept that office and kept it pristinely, and Sven's job was ostensibly to go in and oversee what Emma was doing. Emma was doing fine—she was doing all the work, actually. Sven was supposed to be learning the business by watching her work, but since Sven hadn't even graduated from college, the whole family had been content to let the charade stand.

It was time to go get some honest answers from Emma about what Hacon's little brother was doing, and maybe get her help searching for proof (or lack thereof) of Sven's submersion in the criminal underworld.

Hacon parked in a small parking structure, one of the ones where you lived in fear of having to park next to one of the big concrete support poles, because they seemed to take up more room than the parking spot. Leif's shoulders were bunching as they got out of the car, and for perhaps the first time since he'd known him, Hacon saw the big man look really uncomfortable.

"Your apartment is smaller than this," Hacon said gently, and Leif rolled his eyes.

"My apartment doesn't smell like oil and exhaust. I can't explain it. I'm sure there's a word for it, but I hate these places. I pull the flower delivery truck out of the parking lot three days a week and sweat the entire time."

He smiled as he said this, and Hacon smiled back, but Leif was obviously not kidding. Hacon looked at him, thought of all the comfort Leif had tried to offer, all of the reassurances that Hake's life would be okay, and of the bruises on Leif's back and the bandage on his leg and the pain he'd been in the entire time Hacon had known him. In a gesture that would have astounded Andre, Hake reached out and very casually took Leif's sweating hand and held it as they made their way down the stairs and out the door to the street. He went to pull it away casually when they were on the street, thinking that the comfort was not needed now, but Leif tugged back. Without taking his eyes from the street—which was busy with pedestrians and needed watching—Leif said, "It is San Francisco. It's almost expected."

Hacon nodded and kept looking forward so they could continue dodging around people—who walked damned close in this city—but he kept his hand tightly locked around Leif's.

He let go to get them into the office building, and they took the elevator up to the eighth floor, which was practically the attic of the suite. Emma was there, working industriously at her computer, and she actually gave a genuine smile when they walked in.

"Mr. Haldor!" she said. "I didn't expect to see you today!"

And then she launched herself at him and gave him a hug. Hacon was so surprised, he hugged her back. "I'm fine," he said quietly. They stepped back, and her usual mask of quiet efficiency slid back on, but he still felt like he needed to reassure her. "Honestly—I got the wind knocked out of me. Leif was the one who got the hell beat out of him. He needs the hug!"

Emma turned and gave Leif a small smile too, and Leif returned it engagingly. "You are Hacon's assistant?"

"You're Leif?"

The two of them assessed each other. She was a small woman in her late twenties with a square build and a square face and narrow almond eyes. She wore black pants suits and zip-up half boots with *spectacularly* colored shirts underneath her jackets, and her hair was cropped short and (Hacon hoped!) uneven on purpose, sticking up around her ears and her collar in some way that was probably supposed to be punk and cutting edge. She had a social life—Hacon had gotten half-told stories about parties and get-togethers and makeups and breakups to his solicitous questions about her weekends—but she was also very conscious of Hacon's boundaries. Until he'd walked in today, he had no idea if she esteemed him as much as he valued her.

And now, as she finished her almost suspicious study of Leif, standing loose limbed (except for his sling) and wearing his good nature on his skin like an extra shirt, Emma tilted her head thoughtfully. "You're a bike messenger?" she said, as though trying to place him, and Leif's face lit up.

"Yes! I knew I had been here before. I've delivered several times! But surely I'm not the only bike messenger you see?"

Emma shook her head. "No, no. We get a messenger here about once a day—they usually deliver to Sven, and I sign for them."

Hacon and Leif looked at each other. "Really? Emma, where do you put those packages?"

"On his desk. See?" She gestured with her tiny pointed chin, and sure enough, the packages were stacked neatly, all of them six-by-six boxes wrapped in brown paper. "He usually picks them up on his day to work, but he didn't come in yesterday."

"Emma," Hacon said, his voice agonized, "have the police come to talk to you?"

Emma wasn't stupid. "No, Mr. Haldor," she said softly, and then she looked at that pile of boxes, and then at Leif. "Do you know where Sven is?"

Hacon shook his head. "I think our mother does," he confessed, "but… Emma, you see him once a week—I don't. Is there anything you can tell me? What does he do when he comes in? Does he ever open the computer and work? I usually send him some assignments, some things he's supposed to help you with, and they always get done. Does he ever do them, or is it all you?"

Emma flushed. "He's sort of… inexperienced…," she said, trying for tact.

Hake sighed. Not really her strong suit. "He was so completely helpless at everything that you felt like you had to jump in and do it or he'd get in trouble," Hacon said dryly. His heart did a strange, slow dance and drop, and he tried to shrug. "He used to do that as a little kid to get out of his homework."

"Hacon," Leif said quietly, "he's still the same boy you knew. Do you want to see what he was doing when he should have been doing his homework?"

It was not what they thought. They opened one box after another, and instead of discovering bottles of pills or even curios stuffed with heroin (which Hacon had to admit was what he'd thought of), all they found was… knickknacks. Snow globes, ceramic mermaids, stuffed bears with the city logo and the Golden Gate Bridge on their sweatshirts. Knickknacks. On every knickknack was a little sheet of paper with a set of numbers written on it.

"Okay," Hacon muttered, "can we assume this is some sort of code?"

"Absolutely," Leif said, his face alight with excitement. "Emma?" Leif smiled charmingly at Hake's assistant, and Hacon felt a little churning of jealousy chewing in his stomach.

"Yeah?" Emma looked up from the clever statue of a mermaid and a merman, intertwined and about to have what looked like mer-sex, sans genitalia, and smiled at him. As they'd opened the packages, Leif had played with them—shaken the snow globe, spoken to the bear, told the mermaid she looked divine and that her scales were translucent, and he had managed to disarm Emma as well. Now Hacon felt the absurd urge to stalk out and leave them alone.

"These numbers—do they have anything to do with the shipping manifests or container numbers or shipment vouchers or anything?"

Emma looked at them. There were always a couple of letters (teasing letters, like StM or MaGen) followed by a number, a letter, and one to three numbers.

"Well, yeah," she said, her mouth quirking up. "It's so easy—it's like a little kid wrote a code. See that one?" She pointed to a slip on a giant stuffed bird puppet Leif kept flying through the air. The slip of paper read *StM 1-C-205*.

"Yes. You know what that means?"

"It's totally in the shipping manifest. I mean, I don't know what the stuffed animals were for—"

"To make it look like packages and not like information," Leif said smoothly, and Hacon looked at him, realizing he was right. Leif shrugged. "I deliver packages. Do you think I never wonder at their stories?"

"Well, let's look up the story behind these numbers," Emma said, and Leif grimaced, probably because the segue was clumsy. Emma laughed at him and trotted off while Hacon eyed her sourly.

"She doesn't get that happy around me," he said, and Leif turned that sunny smile up at him from his position cross-legged on the floor. Hacon blushed and shifted uncomfortably. "But then, I'm not that happy a person," he added lamely. Leif's smile softened, and his eyes grew hooded, and Hacon suddenly wished very much that they were alone.

Emma came back with the shipping manifests, and they saw rows upon rows of such numbers.

"It's a location," Hacon said unnecessarily. "It's where the container unit is in the dockyard."

"So whatever they were smuggling, it's in that exact unit in that exact place," Leif added, reaching up and taking a manifest from Emma.

Hacon sucked his teeth. It was an unattractive habit, he knew, but he did it when he was concentrating on something and wasn't thinking about people watching him. "But... but Sven *never* goes on the docks. Ever." Hacon gestured vaguely to the nice, serviceable little office space around them. "This? See this? This is as industrial as Sven *got*, and it was almost too pedestrian for him!"

Emma made a little sound of agreement and set three shipping manifests down in front of him. "Your brother really is afraid of hard work," she said, and Leif smiled at her.

"And you are fearless," he told her.

Hacon had the distinctly uncomfortable sensation of watching her preen as she ran back to the file cabinet for more. He didn't even think that was *possible.*

"What?" Leif asked. He had the shipping manifests in front of him on the floor and was highlighting the container information. Hacon was sitting at the desk, consolidating all of those little incriminating pieces of paper to one document.

"You… do you flirt with everybody?" Hacon demanded irritably, and Leif grinned at him.

"Yes. But I don't kiss everybody, so that is something." And then he went back to his task, leaving Hacon at a loss.

Bitterly, he relived his last argument with Andre, and for a moment, he imagined Andre's voice saying, *Yes, I spend more time with my job, but I don't sleep with anyone there, so just relax!* If Andre had said that—even once—they would still be together.

Hacon looked at Leif again, sitting cheerfully at his side, and he reached out and gently stroked that shaggy fall of copper hair back from his face. Leif's smile up at him was sweet, and very, very much only for Hake.

THEY ran out of time in the end—they had a list of shipping containers to search and no idea what was in them, and Leif needed to be dropped off at his delivery job.

Hacon hated to do it. Leif was exhausted, he was in pain, and although his humor was indefatigable, his eyes were shadowed and the lines of tension at his mouth were unmistakable.

"You can't take a sick day?"

Leif's smile was a pale imitation of his usual one, but it was still stronger than most men's. "Not if I want to pay the rent," he said seriously. "Especially if I need to find a new bicycle. I will be fine. I have some painkillers in my pocket—I'll take them as soon as I'm done driving."

"But… but…," Hacon floundered as he pulled the car up to the delivery store and parked it, leaving it to idle. He turned to Leif, put a gentle hand against Leif's cheek, and found his voice. "Don't you have anyone to care for you?" he asked painfully.

"The gods care for me, Hacon," Leif responded, but he turned his face into Hacon's palm and kissed it anyway.

"How will you get home?" Hake asked, his whole body on high alert from that kiss.

"I will walk."

"I will pick you up," Hake said, and when Leif would have argued—Hake saw it coming, and he didn't think he could stomach it—he said, "I will be here when you get off. You might as well get into the car with me, you stubborn bastard."

With Andre, this would have elicited a sullen silence. With Leif, it got him a gentle laugh and an acquiescence to wait for him if he was late.

And then it got him a kiss, with lips that dominated and an unapologetic groan as Leif took his pleasure, pinning Hacon to the back of the seat until he whimpered, wanting to mash himself up against Leif, without clothes or propriety or anything in the way. He was thrusting his tongue into Leif's mouth and groping the man's chest when Leif pulled away, chuckling softly, and went wandering into the tiny florist's storefront, leaving Hacon to his afternoon.

He went home and had lunch (and thought guiltily that he hadn't fed Leif, they'd been in such a hurry to get him back to his job) and then sat at his laptop and did some of the work he'd missed again. He had appointments the next day that he couldn't get out of—he'd told Leif they would go searching on the docks in the late afternoon, but in the meantime it was him and his home full of vanity and his cat. Vanir perched on his desk and purred as he worked, which was nice because it made him feel like a superhero just for breathing, but... but the rest of his house?

He looked around again, at the dark furniture, the kind with the long, graceful legs and the elegant curves. Even his couch was aesthetic and neat, simple blue fabric with little white dots. His throw rug was white and plush, but it was... well, white. His walls were white with pictures of dark flowers on them, and his guest room was a bed—made up, of course—with a plain white comforter and an end table.

Unbidden, a vision of bookshelves crept in behind Hacon's eyes. He would have to move the bed out, wouldn't he? But he could put in six or eight of them and have a nice little overstuffed chair and a computer desk there for Leif. He could go back to school and do his work and ride his bike whenever he needed, and Hacon could....

Could just be with him.

Hacon groaned and leaned his chin on his stacked fists. "Oh, Vanir. He's so pretty. I could live with him—I could. A couple of kisses, some smiles, and I'm gone. What am I to do?"

Vanir batted his nose with a closed paw and amped up his purr, and Hacon swallowed.

"I think that maybe I should bring him dinner," he said after a moment. "And I should stop by the pharmacy. And that I should give you extra kibble and close my closet. The last time I had a business trip for a night, you threw up in my shoes."

Hacon could swear that cat let out a chuckle. He packed a small overnight bag and put his suit and shoes in the garment bag, and that self-satisfied rumble followed him. It was following him still, as he ventured out the door.

But as he was backing out of his garage, he saw someone venturing past his driveway to his doorway and screeched to a halt.

"Sven?" he asked, getting out of his car. His baby brother—the one he'd fed and dressed when the nanny had been too busy and whom he'd taught his letters to before school started and had even warned bullies to leave alone—looked at him with something like joy and anguish and then turned around and started to run toward the red sports car parked at the curb.

"Sven!" Hacon called and went running after him, grateful that he jogged regularly so he could at least not look foolish. "Sven, dammit! Stop!"

Sven could have gotten into his car and driven away then—he could have, but he didn't. He stalled, dressed in fashionable jeans and a sweatshirt with some sort of logo across it fitted tight to his thin body, and hair like Hacon's but cut layered all around his face.

They stood for a moment, Hacon on his lawn, Sven looking at him, half-angry, half-anguished, in a silence that thundered in their ears.

"I'm glad that you're okay," Sven said, his throat working. "I... I didn't think... I didn't know...." He shook his head. "God, Hake—it all got so fucked up so quickly."

"Have you talked to Mother? She's got a lawyer—" Hacon started almost desperately, and the look Sven shot him was betrayed.

"I don't need a lawyer!" Sven shouted. He wiped under his eyes angrily, and Hacon felt his own throat grow tight.

"You could have come to us," he said, thinking about the money from Sven's bank accounts and what had appeared to be a steadily escalating habit. "Drugs... Sven—we would have helped you."

"Yeah," Sven said, his hand clicking on the door latch. "Like you had Emma help me in the office, right? By doing it so I wouldn't have to? I'm glad you're okay, Hake. Don't worry. They won't try that again."

And he jumped into the car and roared away.

Hacon watched him go and decided not to call his mother or the police. Whatever Sven had planned, Hacon wanted to help him stop it, and Leif was right. This was a matter for family.

LEIF
LUCK AND PRIDE

HE FOUND a bicycle in a dumpster on his delivery rounds and was so grateful when the little gold thread behind his eyes brought him to it that he almost broke down in tears. Yes, part of that might have been the pain, and *gods* was he tired, but it was a *bicycle*, and the frame and chain were intact, even if he'd have to modify the rest severely to work. And he wasn't sure it would have hand brakes or gears, but he thought he might still have a kick-back brake assembly under his bed with his tools, so that would work too. He had two spare tires and rims, as well. It was an entire frame—and all for him! If he worked late into the night, he might very well be ready to deliver the next morning.

And then he saw Hacon's car waiting for him in the same space (and how lucky was that!) when his shift ended at seven, and he thought he might have to revise his plans and work early in the morning. It seemed he had plans for the night, which made his luck complete.

"Hey!" he called, hefting the bike frame over his shoulder. "I have some twine in my pocket; can we put this in the trunk?"

Hacon's eyes bulged. "Where under heaven did that come from?"

"Under heaven!" Leif replied, looking at it in admiration. It was beautiful—almost new, titanium alloy, with a nice wide seat. It was 26", too—which was perfect, and very rare. Usually 24" was the biggest you could get, but Leif was over six six, and 26" was about perfect. It was as if the gods had seen his waiting hands and dropped this thing of beauty into them!

"No, seriously?" Hacon asked, popping the trunk, and Leif was too busy gloating over his find to see Hake's reaction when he responded.

"A dumpster over on Haight Street. It was just lying there, on top." Leif looked up from laying the frame down and then testing to see if the trunk could close over it, since it had no wheels. "Isn't that lucky?"

There was something indefinable in Hake's voice when he responded. "Absolutely. Luck at its finest. Who's going to fix it for you?"

Leif was not aware of how weary his smile was until he couldn't make it reach his eyes. "I will, but later. In the morning." He plonked the trunk down and went to go sit in the front of the car. He tilted his head against the rest luxuriously and closed his eyes, feeling the pounding in his temples acutely when he'd been blocking it out by force of will all day. Hacon's door slammed shut and a cool hand reached to gently knead the muscles in his neck, and Leif all but melted into the upholstery.

"That's nice," he said, feeling pathetic and grateful. "I smell something wonderful—did you get dinner?"

"Takeout," Hacon answered. "Italian."

Leif smiled, although he kept his eyes closed. "That's amazing. Thank you—how kind."

Hacon's hand disappeared and the car started to move, but Leif's head hurt too badly for him to even open his eyes. He fumbled in his pocket for a moment and found the little prescription bottle they'd given him (along with advice not to drive or work for a good four days, which he was obviously ignoring) and went to pop a painkiller in his mouth when Hacon said, "There's a bottle of water in the drink holder if you want."

Leif's gratitude knew no bounds. He couldn't bring himself to talk for most of the trip, but as the car came to a stop behind his apartment, he felt the shredded synapses that had been making his head a misery of black and red throbbing detach from his nerve endings and float away, and he felt the tension in his face and shoulders relax a little and float away as well. He smiled at Hacon, refreshed, and said, "If you pop the trunk, I can grab the bike frame."

While he was doing that, he looked up and saw that Hacon was getting a plastic bag of takeout along with what looked to be luggage out of the back. His mouth was halfway open to ask why the luggage, and then he realized *exactly* why, and his face heated.

"You think ahead," he murmured and hefted the frame over his good shoulder.

"I'm a worrier," Hake admitted, and Leif trotted in front of him to lead the way up the stairs. He was feeling much better after his rest, and the idea that Hake was going to spend the night made him feel even better than that.

They got up to the apartment, and Leif suddenly experienced the complete lack of anything he had to offer. "No television," he said quietly. "There's dishes in the cupboard—how about you dish up the food and I'll set up the bike. We'll eat, and then you can talk to me while I start repairs." He grimaced as he reached the landing and unlocked the door while balancing the bike on this shoulder. "It's not the greatest way to start snuggling," he admitted freely, "but we can talk until the moment comes."

"You think there's going to be a moment that will come?" Hacon asked, but there was nothing in his voice but amusement.

Leif stopped and let Hacon pass him, luggage and all. He half closed his eyes at the brush of their bodies and savored the warmth of another human body, the faint smell of aftershave and male skin that came from Hake's neck as he walked by.

"I think it's a certainty," he murmured and then walked in.

He couldn't find his coffee table—it was buried somewhere in his books—so he used two stacks of books to help balance the frame upside down; it rested on the seat and the handlebars while he trotted to his bed to pull out the extra wheels and tool set he kept under it. Leif got to the living room to see Hacon had excavated his coffee table and set their food on it. It was a twist on what he'd expected—and that suited him too.

"I'm sorry," Leif said, washing his hands in the kitchen sink. He dried them off on a towel (or, it was one now—he was pretty sure it used to be a T-shirt) and came to sit down next to Hake on the couch, picking up his plate and sighing appreciatively. He hoped Hacon didn't expect dinner conversation—he was really too hungry to oblige.

When he was done (and Hake had slid a couple of pieces of his own garlic bread onto Leif's plate and those were gone too), he set his plate down for Loki to lick off and pushed back against the couch. He stretched out his good arm behind Hake's shoulders in the oldest maneuver in the book and murmured, "So, are you going to tell me about your day?"

Hake sighed against him. "I saw my brother today." He laughed without humor. "He told me he was very glad I was still alive."

"How did he look?"

"Young. Desperate. In tears. I said the wrong thing. I always say the wrong thing. I told him we could get Mother's lawyer, go straight to the police. I was stupid."

Leif kissed his temple. "No. Not stupid. Rules, Hacon. I think you enjoy them very much."

"Yeah?" Hake looked at him sideways. "What makes you think that?"

"You should have seen your face when I told you that I got the bicycle frame from the trash. Or when you saw my apartment, filled with books and no furniture."

Hake blushed. "I'm not particularly good with anarchy, no."

Leif grunted. "There are big rules and there are small rules. True heroes obey their own code and no one else's."

Hacon looked at him sideways again. "Your code says to rescue strangers from their own stupidity and make them laugh if at all possible."

Leif tipped his head back, the better to look into those clear, pale blue eyes. "Do you object?"

Hacon scooted back further against Leif's chest. "No," he said and then turned his shoulder and captured Leif's mouth in a hungry, aggressive kiss.

Leif returned it and then pushed his advantage, because he had been honest: Leif topped. Leif took over; Leif was the leader, the aggressor, and he tasted and licked, suckled and teased, pushed Hacon back into the couch and overwhelmed him, taking that solid, sturdy kernel of the man and making it his own.

Hacon resisted at first, tried to stay in the lead, tried to hold Leif's face, make him sit still, tried to plunder Leif's mouth as Leif had plundered his. But Leif was tired, and in pain, and he wasn't willing to dance. The warmth, the wet, the haven of Hacon's mouth, that was his reward for this day, that was the pot of gold at the end of the optimist's rainbow, and Leif was going to attack it, plunder it, take it, and revel in his riches, and none of Hacon's attempts to take over was going to dim that shining joy.

The moment Hacon moaned, fell back against the couch, opened his mouth, his entire body to the kiss, was like free-falling through the air to be caught, suspended, and allowed to fly. Leif's good hand was busy pushing under Hake's soft, long-sleeved shirt and rubbing along the ridges of skin and muscle underneath. He pulled his head back for a moment and smiled.

Hacon opened his hooded eyes and managed a "Wha?"

"Hair!" Leif grinned, pleased. "I love hairy chests!" He shoved at the shirt, and Hacon unbuttoned the top button. Leif helped him out of it and then smiled some more. He lowered his mouth to a tiny nipple, absurdly pink, and then stopped after touching it with his tongue to savor Hacon's shudder.

"You're stopping?" Hacon whined, and Leif was practically giggling with glee.

"They're like little hidden treasures," he whispered, then suckled one into his mouth and groaned deeply when Hacon went quietly bananas beneath him. Hacon brought his outside knee up and pressed his foot into the back of Leif's thigh, urging them closer while he frotted his groin urgently against Leif's stomach, and Leif chuckled against his skin. He wasn't hurrying this, oh *gods*, no. How long had it been since he'd been able to linger over a man, taste him, laugh with him?

He didn't want to think about Tom—*couldn't* think about Tom, because Tom was the past, a complicated layer of hurt and joy built up around his heart, making Leif who he was. Hacon was *now*, and he was *real*, and he was simple and honest and guarded and complicated, and Leif was *not* going to let him disappear in the morning or go off and marry his childhood betrothal or even let him lead. Leif wanted him. He wanted him to keep. When Leif touched him, the gold thread went away, and there was no *way* Leif would stop touching him, so he had to believe Hacon was his luck, his thread, his gift from the gods. Leif was going to love him so thoroughly and so well that Hacon could not help but stay.

Leif bit softly and then nuzzled his way through that fantastic dark hair to the other nipple, his free hand fumbling with Hacon's jeans. Hacon reached down and helped him with those, too, and Leif pulled back and pulled off his shoes, one at a time, while Hake shoved his pants and briefs down past his feet (with their white socks still on) and dropped them on the floor next to the couch.

Leif sat up over him and grinned. He was lean, and, yes, hairy, but concentrated, stringy, tough. "You run," he said in admiration, running his hand along a knotted calf muscle, and Hacon shifted, clenched his butt cheeks and his abdomen, and nodded.

"Not as much as I should," he demurred, and Leif chuckled and lowered his head to nibble on a soft-skinned, tight-muscled belly. Hake grunted and bucked, and his erection grew against Leif's throat. Leif sat up again and grasped it, enjoying Hacon out before him, an offering, the best, most lovely thing the gods could offer in exchange for the thread that had lurked behind his eyes for his entire life but had disappeared and snarled with this man's touch.

His cock was lovely, straight and long and a little thin, but perfect, circumcised and symmetrical, with a head that was wider than the shaft. Leif shuddered and bent down some more, scooting back to make it easier to take the thing in his mouth. He groaned as he tasted the saltiness at the tip, the faint musk at the root of it, in the nest of black hair. He enjoyed the quiver of it in the back of his throat as he pumped his head up and down, swallowing, stretching his muscles to accommodate it back there.

Hacon knotted his hands in Leif's hair, massaging at first and then holding, and moans transformed into begging words, pleading words, shocking and filthy and hot. "Oh... oh God... Leif... just keep sucking... hard... grasp my shaft... gods... harder... oh please... oh yes... just like... oh, *Leif!*"

Leif caught the little spurt in his mouth and held still. He swallowed, liking the taste on his tongue, unapologetically bitter, and then let some spit slide down into Hacon's crease. He balanced that wonderful cock against his cheek while he spoke and used his fingers in the slickness of his spit to rub firmly on Hacon's rim, loosening it. Hacon writhed and panted and thrust fruitlessly, just enough for his prick to abrade softly against Leif's stubble.

"Do you really want to come just yet?" he asked, very serious even when he paused to stick out his tongue and lap up a small, clear bead of precome. "If you come, your asshole will be tender… sore and puckered and tight." He slid one finger in, just the tip, and Hacon cried out and arched his hips. "See?" Leif asked sincerely. "It's already very sensitive. I want to fuck you, Hacon, hard, slap our flesh together, strong, like men. Do you really want to come yet?" He slid his finger in then, opening the softened entrance, and Hacon let out a low growl, bucking some more on the couch.

"Auuuughhhhh… *Leif!*"

Leif chuckled and stood, dropped his cargo shorts and his briefs, and toed off his shoes.

"Condoms?" Hacon murmured. "There's some in my… oh my *God!*"

Leif grinned down at his erection, which was bobbing as he stood there. It *was* god-sized, like the rest of him, uncircumcised and long and thick and beautiful. He was not a vain man, but his cock was a thing of beauty, and he would not apologize for it.

"I have some in my pocket," Leif murmured, because he'd gotten them from his end table when he'd been fetching his bicycle tools. He bent down and pulled one out, then grimaced as he brought it near his chest so he could use his other hand to rip the package because the arm was still in the sling.

"Here," Hacon offered, and Leif handed him the little foil, trying not to wither in embarrassment. "It's good," Hake continued, pulling out the sheath and stroking Leif with his hand. "It gives me a reason to touch you."

Leif couldn't argue with him, because his strokes were long and sure. Leif tilted his head back and closed his eyes, quivering with the build of tension in his belly. When Hake's mouth closed over him, hot and wet, Leif had to grab him by the hair or he would have come, poured himself right there into Hacon's mouth, because it was so glorious.

Hacon, who had said he always topped, simply tilted his head back, Leif's fingers still knotted in his hair, and said, "What do you want?"

Leif closed his eyes and wished his shoulder was not still weak. "I *want* you face to face," Leif muttered, "or on my back, slamming you down. I think what I must have is you, bent over the couch. It is very submissive. Can you do that?"

"Unnhhhh...." Hacon was bent over the couch almost before Leif could release that fine, scattered hair, and his ass, marble pale, sculpted by the running and even the walking the city demanded, was offering himself before Leif, softened, dilated little pucker and all.

Leif cupped a narrow hip bone with one great hand and held him there while Leif bent over him and kissed along his neck and down his backbone, stopping to drizzle lubricant from the little bottle he'd gotten from his pocket. Hacon shuddered, because the lubricant was cool, and Leif worked it in gently, using his thumb to stretch the rim some more, make it slack and ready, while Hacon groaned into the couch cushions, begging.

"Oh, yes," Leif breathed as he positioned himself. "You want this, yes?"

"*Yes!*" Hacon screamed into the couch, and Leif gentled the man's flanks and backside, penetrating very slowly, very carefully, feeling the fine tremble in Hake's body as the head of Leif's cock popped in to be swallowed by Hacon's sweet, welcoming ass. Hacon arched his back and tilted his head and groaned, "*Yes, God yes!*" into the air, and Leif took that as his cue and slid all the way in. Hake groaned again and Leif bent over, splaying his hand across Hake's throat and leaning in close so Hake could turn his head and kiss the corner of his mouth. *Ahh....* His mouth tasted so good... so perfect. The tension building, the fierce, unbridled joy in the pit of Leif's gut could not be contained anymore, and he pulled back and slammed forward again, thrusting hard enough that Hacon had to brace his arms against the couch. Hake howled and begged for more, and Leif's skin rippled in excitement, every nerve from his balls to the nape of his neck cold and tingling from the arousal and the need and the *oh my God desire* to pound himself into this man, to make this man his!

Leif thrust some more, and again and again and again, and Hacon gibbered nonsense words, all of them begging for more and harder and right *there* on the sweet spot, and Leif felt his climax approaching with the great mass of a wave, and he was powerless to stop it.

"Grab yourself," he ordered, and Hake did, taking himself in hand and stroking hard and fast. His entire body clenched and spasmed around Leif's cock when he came, spurting across Leif's old couch, and Leif didn't care. Instead, he threw his head back and roared, losing control of his thrusts as he pounded Hake until he collapsed against the back of the couch, then pulling the man flush against his body as he came.

They stayed like that, shaking, Leif's good arm wrapped around Hacon's upper chest as Leif buried his face in Hake's neck and tried to get hold of himself for the trembling that wracked them both.

"God," Hacon breathed, turning his head to nuzzle against Leif's cheek. "You are amazing, Leif Torval, do you know that?"

Leif shuddered hard around him. "I could say the same about you, Hacon Haldor," he panted, liking the man's very Scandinavian name on his tongue. "You're my luck, you know. My miracle. Let me hold you one more moment before we gather our stuff and go to bed."

"Are we going to do that again?" Hacon asked, and Leif nodded, kissed the side of his neck, and then licked the sweat from his skin. Hacon tilted his head and allowed it, and Leif kept licking and nibbling right up to the shell of Hake's ear.

"If the gods love us, we will," he murmured, feeling himself hardening—unbelievable since he was still buried in Hacon's flesh.

Hacon murmured that he hoped so, and it turned out to be truth. The gods *did* love them. The gods loved them two more times.

BUT still, that did not mean Leif could simply sleep, in spite of his body's pleas to the contrary. He'd set his alarm, and *this* time it went off. He woke up and gave Hacon's unconscious body a gentle squeeze with his good arm before sliding out of bed and putting on his briefs and cargo shorts. It was cold, but he didn't want to bother with a shirt (which had been a pain to take off in the night), so he didn't.

He popped a pain pill, took a deep breath, and went to work on his bicycle, untangling his arm from the sling and using that hand when he needed it. Hacon found him there in the morning, sitting cross-legged in front of a working bicycle, leaning back against the wall and fast asleep.

INTERLUDE
MORTAL PRIDE,
IMMORTAL REGRET

"COULD they have *been* any more awkward in bed?" Loki asked with disdain, and Verdandi looked at him, appalled.

"They were very sweet, Loki! They're mortals. Mortals have flesh and limits—their first couplings are all about learning limits, being gentle with flesh. Be kind!"

"We can't all crack the spires of Valhalla," Thor said, his eyes half-hooded and his voice husky.

Loki looked away and blushed. "That was an accident," he mumbled. Then, with some irritation: "Your father was appalled."

Thor nodded, accepting culpability. "Sif wasn't pleased either," he admitted, and his face darkened at the memory. The gods were both promiscuous and madly jealous—Thor's relationship with Sif was no more tranquil than his relationship with Loki, and Valhalla had been destroyed and remade in his battles with his wife *and* his lover—and his subsequent reconciliations.

"It was your pride," Loki snapped. "If you'd only submitted—"

"It was not my place to submit," Thor overrode him. His voice became absolute, and Loki's jaw clenched and his throat worked convulsively. Verdandi risked a look down and saw that through his tight black pants, an impressive erection was showing.

"Yes, my lord Thor," Loki said, and his tone was his customary dry derision—but his eyes were wide and limpid.

Thor leaned over and tapped Loki's cheek with a long, elegant, and yet callused finger. "In due time," he purred. "Let us see how they resolve their fight first."

Loki blinked. "They're going to fight?"

"They fuck like mortals, beloved. They will fight like men."

"How do you know?" Urdh asked, as though this conversation had anything to do with her.

Thor ignored her, and it was Skuld who spoke up. "Oh, sister—these are men. Do you not see the tragic convergence of pride?"

Urdh sniffed. "Well *that's* stupid!"—and then quailed as Thor and Loki pinned her with tortured glares. Of course, this would be the one moment when Verdandi actually *agreed* with her sister. But unlike Urdh, Verdandi had the wisdom to stay silent.

"They're speaking," she murmured, her voice neutral, and the sexual tension under the one tree backed down from a boil to a simmer. Somewhere off in the branches, someone cried out in climax, and they all took a deep breath and acknowledged that the collective of Asgard was now rutting like goats. One look from Thor and Loki and the world did that, fucked like fury.

But not where they were. Now they were all watching the two mortals whose lives were still hopelessly tangled now that the fucking was done.

HACON
SCISSORS AND CHOICES

HACON woke up in a cold and unfamiliar bed with someone's heavy metal music coming from an old clock radio. He grunted, reached around and smacked until the noise stopped, and rolled over, trying to place his surroundings.

God, was his ass sore. And he was covered in come.

The thought was unfamiliar and unaccustomed—and also luxurious and decadent. His *ass* was sore. He'd been caught in the arms of a giant the night before and pummeled and suckled and *fucked* until he'd screamed. Yes, screamed. His throat was the teeniest bit raw too. He'd screamed and gibbered and come and come and come. They'd showered after the second time, but he'd come again, in Leif's hand, while Leif was thrusting between his ass cheeks, and Hacon was so exhausted he could barely summon the energy to twitch and to spurt, one more time, over his stomach and the bed.

And when they were done, Leif had folded Hake's slender body into his one-armed embrace and kissed the back of his neck. "'Night, Hacon," he'd mumbled. "Love you."

It was too early for love in a relationship, wasn't it? For a moment—only one—Hacon contemplated panicking. Contemplated ruining this moment by pointing out that they'd known each other for three days. It wasn't love. Couldn't possibly be love.

Not yet.

It was the "yet" that stopped him short. It wasn't yet. But it would be. One more night like this—hell, one more moment like this one, falling asleep with Leif at his back, stirring the hairs on the nape of Hacon's neck with soft breathing, and Hacon would officially be in love. So which moment would it be, he wondered as he closed his eyes and drifted off to sleep. Which moment would be the one where he fell in love? Would it be this one? Or this one? Or the next one? Or....

But not the moment he woke up in bed alone and covered in come, wondering why Leif's side was so very cold.

He put on Leif's shirt, the long-sleeved knit one that smelled like his sweat and lay crumpled on the floor, then padded into the living room and found Leif asleep in front of the finished bike. Something in his chest twisted. Oh God. Hacon had taken him out of his life, taken his time and his kindness and his... his *sex*, and he'd given nothing back!

"Leif," he muttered, feeling an unreasoning irritation in his chest. "Leif—wake up. Your alarm went off. You're going to have to call in." Leif wasn't moving, so he crouched down, heedless of his lack of underwear, and shook Leif's shoulder.

Leif blinked blearily. "Call in where?" he asked, squeezing his eyes shut and opening them again. He brought one hand up to wipe away the sleep in the corners and then winced. "Oh God. What time is it?"

"Seven." Hacon stood and stretched, saw Leif's appreciative look as the shirt lifted over his thighs. His face heated. "Come on," he said, offering his hand. He was hurt—but unsurprised—when Leif pushed off the wall instead. "We can go back to bed."

Leif shook his head. "I can't," he yawned. "I have to work. You go back, though." He wrapped his good arm around Hacon's waist and kissed his temple, closing his eyes for a moment while his feet faltered on the bare floor. "It will make me happy to think of you here, in my bed."

Hacon pulled back, his heart suddenly sore for no good reason he could think of. "You're going to work? Leif—you're... you're exhausted. You just got out of the hospital! God—I know... I mean... I can see you don't have money. I could—just until you're well... you could pay me back! Just...." *Just don't leave me here alone after last night!* "Just, do you have to go when you're so tired?"

Leif's mouth tightened, and his good nature was obviously pulled up from his toes when he spoke. "It's my way through the world, Hacon. Luck doesn't come to people who can't go out and grab it!" He smiled then, inviting Hake in on the glory of it, and all Hacon could think of was that he was so happy, so sure that he was lucky, and all Hacon could see in any direction was a crumble of departed loved ones and unrealized dreams.

"You think you're lucky? Look around you, Leif—you're lonely! You need someone to care for you—and I want to do that, but you have to let me!"

In just that moment, Hacon looked at his lover's face and didn't see the happy young man with the contagious smile anymore. In that moment, Hacon saw an angry god.

"I *am* lucky!" Leif shouted, and Hacon backed up against the wall instinctively. He was unused to people shouting. "I *am* lucky—*I* have been loved! I have had warmth in my life, and sunshine, and kindness! I have learned *beautiful* things, and *no one* can take that away from me!"

"I don't want to take that away from you!" Hake found he had pushed himself from the wall, and he was surprised to discover that he could shout back. "I just want to make you happy! You keep saying you're lucky, but I don't see it! All this talk about luck, and it really comes down to just barely being able to scrape by!"

Leif stormed though the doorway to his bedroom and started pulling socks from his drawer. "I see people all the time who live on the streets. You think I'm scraping by? I live like a king, Hacon—I eat every day, I have friends who come to visit when I'm sick. Who did you have?"

Hacon grimaced because it was true and because it hurt. "You know who I had?" he snapped back. "I had you. And you made me feel *wonderful.* And it *kills* me to see you killing yourself when I could help you!"

"I don't need help!" Leif growled as he proceeded to put his socks on one-handed. "I don't need *your* help. You come into my home with your money and your family and you look down at my home and the things I love—all I ever wanted from you was your friendship. I didn't talk to you for your money, I didn't fuck you for your money. I just wanted to be with you, and *this* is how you pay me back?"

Oh God. He had his socks on, he was putting his shoes on—he was going to work. He was going to *leave* in the middle of this terrible, terrible fight. Hake had left things bad like this with Andre for *days.* He couldn't do that again!

"Dammit, Leif!" Hake begged, following him to the bathroom and watching him splash water on his face. He started to smear toothpaste on his toothbrush as it lay on the counter, but his hand was shaking so badly Hacon actually took the brush and put the toothpaste on it himself and handed it to him. Leif looked at the toothbrush indignantly and then shoved it in his mouth and started to scrape it across his teeth as Hacon spoke. "Dammit, this is just your stupid pride! I'm not trying to talk down to you or give you charity or—"

Leif pulled the toothbrush out of his mouth and spat viciously into the sink, then rinsed off the brush while he yelled. "You tell me I have nothing, not even luck, and then you think you're not going to hurt my pride? According to you it's all I have, and you want to take it away!"

Leif stalked to his end table, where he snatched his wallet and keys, and then walked into the living room and hoisted his bike over his good shoulder. Hacon made a helpless sound. Oh, damn the man. How could he be so happy with so little, and forgive the world for taking away so much, and then not understand when Hacon wanted to give him the world?

Leif didn't look at him. "You...." He took a breath. "You may stay as long as you need to," he murmured, giving courtesy even when he was too angry to stand still. "I don't imagine you'll want to come back."

Hacon glared at him. Oh no. This was not ending like that. Andre just moved away after a week of silence—this was not going to end in the middle of a fight. Hacon wasn't just going to disappear out of his life and let this die—not after last night. Not after waking up this morning and needing Leif so badly that finding him in his living room, fighting for his livelihood, hurt.

"You *wish* you could get rid of me," he snapped. "You *wish* this was over. I'll be here. We started an adventure together, and you're going to see it through. And we started a relationship together, and that's not over either. We will have this fight some more, Leif. Don't think I'm just going to leave you alone here to die in obscurity in the name of pride."

"I'm *fine*!" Leif growled. "I was fine with just my luck, and once you leave, I'll have it again!"

"Well, today is the unluckiest day of your whole life," Hacon said, aware of how childish he sounded and unable to fix it. "Because if I have to kick down your door, you *will* finish this argument. But go now. Go ahead. Go kill yourself riding down a hill. Go save someone else's life, someone who won't come home into your little apartment and pet your rabid cat and let you make love to them. But you're coming back and finishing this, Leif, because I'll be damned if you walk out of here thinking you're not cared for, even if I don't do it the way you think I should."

Leif looked like he was on the verge of saying something horrible—something truly crushing, something that would make Hacon wish he'd never woken up. And then he stopped, and closed his shadowed eyes, and swore. "Fuck!"

"What!"

Leif stopped, slid the bike down his shoulder, and stomped past Hake into the bedroom. He rummaged through his closet—a tiny thing for both clothes and whatever else he could cram into this shoebox full of books—and came out with two things that made Hacon both really grateful and really pissed off.

One was a helmet. He must have had an old one as a spare, because this one had the same Nordic knot decoration around the edge, but the tape was worn and frayed and bare in spots, and the style looked older—maybe six or so years ago? The other was a shoulder bag—something brand new, and nylon, and cheap. He shook the plastic off of it as he stalked into the living room, and it fluttered to the floor between them while Leif put the helmet on and fumbled with the strap. Hake's hands shook with fury and worry and all sorts of unaccustomed things as he walked up to Leif and hooked the strap under his chin and tightened it up, and Leif's jaw was set at a sulky angle as he said, "Thank you."

"You're welcome."

"I get off at two."

"I'll be here."

"I doubt it," Leif said shortly and then shouldered his bicycle again and clattered down the hall. Hacon watched him go with an aching heart and a steely resolution. Leif *was* a lucky man. He just didn't know how lucky—but he would.

HAKE fumed for a solid half an hour before he got ready for work. He fumed while he did the dishes and fumed while he restacked some of the books so they wouldn't fall over. He fumed as he sorted Leif's manuscripts—all of them bound by a printer even if they'd been typed out on an old electric typewriter—and he fumed as he fed the damned cat and cleaned his cat box and put a Band-Aid on his new scratch, and fumed as he took the sheets off the bed and put them in the hamper and then searched the little tiny closet for another set. He found the other set, made the bed, and then sat on it and sighed.

He had to have another night with this man. He had to. He had to make Leif see that his pride and his luck were not worth giving up another night together or a morning that could begin sweeter than this one had. It was with this resolve that he went in to shower, realizing that he'd put off showering just so he could keep smelling Leif on his skin.

EMMA was meeting him at the tiny office on Pier 41 today, and she was dressed in her usual efficient black suit with a bright aqua top underneath. He stopped off at Starbucks and got her a large caramel latte, because he and Leif had taken her away from her regular work the day before and he wanted to thank her.

He walked in a little early and gave her the coffee while he sipped his own—also a caramel double latte, although usually it was a small coffee, black—and he smiled absently at Emma's narrow-eyed scrutiny.

"What?" he asked, and she grimaced.

"You smell different," she said. She sipped her coffee suspiciously.

"Smell different?" Perplexed.

"Yeah. Usually you smell like… Mennen. Something that smells like lilacs on you, even though I think it's supposed to smell like men's stuff. It was my first tip-off that you were gay."

Hake choked on his latte and set it down so he could hang up his summer-weight coat and take his briefcase back into the tiny office behind the reception room. (He also made a mental note to change his body wash and his deodorant, because that right there would have been some good information to have when he'd been trying unsuccessfully to pick men up at clubs after his breakup with Andre.)

"And what do I smell like now?" he asked when his office was settled and his computer was booting up. He glanced at the clock—he had fifteen minutes before his client actually showed up. They had time for this.

"Mmm… something hot! Something a straight guy would use. It's like… I don't know. Wood chips and horse sweat and mint and ambergris—whatever it is, you should keep it!"

Hacon blushed—a true blush, he knew it—and Emma looked at him curiously.

"Come on, Mr. Haldor—what is it? What are you wearing? Give?"

Hake mumbled into his coffee, and she insisted on making him speak up.

"What?" she asked one more time, and he blushed some more and said quite clearly, "It's Ivory soap and Leif."

He'd never seen her smile that brightly—as God was his witness, he hadn't.

"Leif?" she asked, purely delighted. "You and him…." She raised her eyebrows meaningfully, and Hacon felt a little slighted.

"Well, yes, me and him! Why would you think he'd spend his morning off investigating my family's problems?"

Emma shrugged. "I don't know, Mr. Haldor, I thought you paid him."

"I don't have to pay him!" Hacon snapped, stung by the reminder of the morning's fight. "God, do you think maybe I have something to offer the man besides my money?"

Emma looked at her coffee and then pasted an insincere smile on her face. "Of course you do," she said, and Hacon felt his eyes bulge.

"He *liked* me!" Hacon defended in outrage, and Emma raised her eyebrows.

"Liked?"

"Yeah." Shit. "Yeah, he liked me," Hacon sighed, deflated and dying to talk to someone about this. "He liked me right up until I offered to help him with money so he didn't have to go into work this morning."

He looked up and saw Emma looking at him funny, and he sighed and put his chin in his cupped fists. "What?" he asked wearily.

"You offered him money? In the morning? After you... I dunno, changed your smell?"

Hacon's blush got worse. "Yeah."

"So, did you tell him to buy himself something pretty?"

And now he sat up straight. "It wasn't *like* that!" he defended. "Holy hell, Emma! You didn't see him! He got up after we'd fallen asleep and fixed his bicycle so he could leave at fuck-all this morning and work his job. He fell asleep *against the wall*—and he... he was exhausted. And still hurt." *And I just wanted to take care of him, that's all.* "And all he could talk about was his luck. He went off about his luck, and how he would be okay because he was lucky. He has no one—no family, two jobs that are killing him, and a room full of brilliant dissertations that he'll never afford to go back to school and publish." Yes, Hacon had read a little while he was straightening up. Leif was every bit as smart as Hacon had suspected: his literary theories were erudite enough that Hake would normally not have been able to follow them, except Leif made them human and real and interesting. "He's got nothing, and he won't take my help."

God, he'd be a good professor. He just needed some help to go back to school.

"So you offered him money," she said again, and he grimaced. "And you told him he wasn't really lucky. Did you do anything else? Throw his cat out the window? Piss in his kitchen sink?"

Hacon grunted, trying to maintain his temper. "Emma, he's a grown man. Even he can see that he needs—"

"Something to offer you besides a good lay," she said, and Hacon was too angry to flush now.

"That's not even your business!"

Emma sat back and set her coffee down and shook her head. Very distinctly, she muttered, "Asshole!" before opening her laptop and getting pointedly to work.

Hacon swallowed. Shit. Shit, shit, shit, shit, shit. He closed his eyes, opened them, looked at the clock, and saw five minutes until their client arrived.

"Could you, uhm...." He took another sip of his coffee and swallowed. He wanted to make this right. "Could you, uhm, explain that?" he asked in his humblest voice. "Please?"

She did that strange thing women do with their upper lips that conveys not only disgust but also irritation and condescension. Then she sighed and looked at him over the laptop. "Mr. Haldor, you seem like an okay guy. You go to work, you take care of your family, you're nice to the help." She indicated the latte with her chin. "But Leif—he's more than an okay guy. He's a *great* guy. He wants to give something to the world. I knew him for, what? Five minutes? If you told me something bad happened to him, I'd weep my heart out. And part of that is that he believes the universe is kind to him. He has luck. I'm Asian, Mr. Haldor. You don't fuck with that when you're Asian. A belief that you're lucky? It's *everything.* It's your confidence, it's your ability to give obeisance to the gods and say 'I'm a person! I'm important!' If he's got nothing, like you say, then taking away his luck? That's taking away the last thing he's got that makes him a man."

Hacon didn't want his coffee anymore. His stomach was too upset. "I just wanted to take care of him," he mumbled, suddenly not caring if she knew that part.

She sighed. "Well, doesn't that make him lucky?" she asked, and he looked up from the desk and gave her a tentative smile.

"Yeah. I hope so," he said, and she smiled back.

"Then maybe tell it to him that way," she said. "Sometimes, it's like a story. All the stories are the same, you know that, right? Sometimes, it's all in the telling."

Hacon swallowed. All the stories are the same. He could make this work with Leif, or he could walk away. He could take care of Leif on Leif's terms, or he could nag Leif until Leif asked him to leave. Leif hadn't asked him to leave or told him not to show up. He'd just assumed Hacon would not. And why wouldn't he make that assumption? Everyone else had left him. Emma was right. All that was left *was* his luck.

It was up to Hake to make sure that luck changed.

HE WAS sitting on the entryway stairs, looking down Geary, when Leif limped up, the bicycle over his shoulder, with Lethal walking her own bike by his side. His "new" used bicycle was looking a little worse for the wear—the back wheel was bent in half, the spokes crushed, and one of the forks bent outward.

Leif was dripping blood down his right shoulder—the one not broken—and his hip, and his thigh, and his knee. His helmet looked like a grapefruit that someone had skinned half of.

His smile of triumph was undimmed until he saw Hacon on his stoop.

Lethal showed no such dampening of the spirit. "You should have seen it, Thundergod's boy! Man, you should have *seen* it!" she chattered as Hacon stood up and looked at Leif with absolute anguish in his eyes. "Oh. My. God. It was fucking *epic*!"

Leif turned toward her and cast Hake a smug look from the side. "You don't doubt me any longer, do you?" he asked Lethal, and Hacon found his hands were shaking and his throat was dry. Leif was *bleeding*. Hacon had let him leave on an angry word and he was *bleeding*.

"Not for a minute, Thundergod!" Lethal was saying. "Man... you should have fucking seen it!" She was looking at Hake for confirmation, so Hake nodded at her to talk before he took the bike from Leif. Leif gave it up without any resistance at all.

Leif was wobbly. Slow, like his body didn't know the way, and Hacon kept wondering if he was going to topple as he stood.

"What is it I should have seen?" he asked, even though he honestly didn't want to know. God, if he had seen the moment this had happened, his heart would have stopped.

"Wait a minute here while I lock up my bike, yo?"

Hacon waited, put his free hand out, gently, to Leif's unbloodied side, and very tentatively, he touched. Leif tilted his head back and shuddered like the touch was too gorgeous to be believed, and Hacon shuddered too.

Lethal, on the other hand, was oblivious to all of that. She started a running narrative as she squatted, doing complicated things to a titanium chain and a big back-tire lock, and she continued it as she straightened and they followed Leif up the stairs.

"So our boy here was zooming down east on Market, right? And taking a left on Van Ness—I was going straight up Van Ness, so I saw the whole thing—and this *douche bag*, I don't even know *what* he was thinking—he bumps the back of Leif's bike while he's going. Now, if it'd been me? I would have gone over and gotten squashed by the fucking garbage truck that was right on his ass, and thereyago, bye-bye, no more little black girl, right? But it's Thundergod here, and he manages to keep control, but his bike is *spun the hell around*, so he's going the wrong fuckin' way—down Market, mind you, right? And he starts doin' this bike bouncin' shit—like he's king motocross or something—and the first thing he does is do some bobbin' and weavin', straight *over* the divide for the Muni, right, and it's the *Muni* that gets his back wheel. It knocks him down, but he's on the sidewalk by then, so he's golden—he's roadkill in front of the fuckin' Honda dealership, but he's golden! And the Muni guy, he felt so fuckin' bad, he like, gave us a ride, because I was there to help scrape Thor's sorry ass off the pavement, right? Anyway, he took us up Van Ness to Castro and drops us off, but he's got a friend waiting on an off-service route from Castro to Geary, and then we got another bus on Geary, and then *his* buddy bus driver dropped us off like, half a block away. I mean, I ain't never seen nothin' like it. It was like the gods were giving him a ride home."

They were up to Leif's apartment by now, and Hake was feeling the weight of the twisted bicycle on his shoulder, and his hands were shaking from the bulk of Lethal's narrative. Oh gods—oh holy, merciful, cruel, capricious gods. They paused while Leif unlocked the door, and Hacon saw his hands shake. Hake reached out and took the key from him and opened it, and allowed Leif to lead the way inside.

Hacon turned to Lethal with genuine affection. "Talitha, my dear, could you do me a favor?" he asked, and Lethal smiled like she was ready to do anything he asked.

"Could you set his bicycle up to be repaired? I'm going to rinse him off and see if he needs to be bandaged, okay?"

Talitha nodded. "Just some light gauze and some ointment, I think, until it's all pussed out, okay? Nothing too big. He probably has gauze in the medicine cabinet."

"I do," Leif said, and his earlier smugness was gone, and what remained was a man who probably would not have walked another step if he didn't have to.

"Good," Hacon said, before guiding him into the bedroom and sitting him on the bed. He shed his coat and his suit jacket and went into the bathroom for antiseptic and gauze, and then went into the kitchenette for a small glass bowl full of hot water and a washcloth. When he returned, Leif was looking at him, his eyes slightly unfocused and his expression as lost as Hacon had ever seen it.

"See," Leif said, his voice empty. "I do have luck, of sorts."

"I believe it," Hacon rasped, not wanting to talk about it. "I believe it because you're here, alive, and you might not have made it through all that if you didn't, and I don't want to think about that."

He took the cloth and helped Leif gingerly out of his long-sleeved T-shirt, unfastening his helmet first and seeing the place where his cheek had scraped the pavement.

"I am lucky," Leif insisted, his voice gaining a little passion, and Hacon agreed with him, cleaning the blood off his cheek and deciding not to put the gauze there because the adhesive would probably drive Leif mad.

"You are," Hacon murmured. "You are."

"Tom didn't think it was enough," Leif continued earnestly, and Hacon's hand started to shake, so he brought it down to the hot antiseptic water and carefully wrung out the cloth.

"No?" Hacon asked, his voice so thin he wasn't sure if Leif could hear him.

"I told him," Leif continued, his voice wandering a little. It was like this thought was the one clear one left wandering around, when pain and shock and a couple of severely fucked-up days had blasted all of the other ones clean away.

"Told him what?" Hake resumed work, this time on Leif's bleeding shoulder, which *would* need gauze.

"Told him that he could stay with me, and we would find jobs and a way to live, and my luck alone would mean we could be together. He said it wasn't." Leif looked at Hacon, his face so bare and vulnerable, Hake almost wanted to look away to respect his privacy. But he didn't.

"What did he say?" Hacon asked, still lost in those bright bay-blue eyes.

"He said luck didn't make up for family, or fortune. He said he didn't think it would be enough for him to stay with me if we would be poor. So he married the girl his parents chose, and asked me to stand up with him instead." Leif blew out a breath and closed his eyes, giving Hacon the ability to breathe. He finished washing the wound the size of an index card across the front muscle of Leif's shoulder.

"He was a fool," Hacon whispered as he held the gauze and taped it. He stood up a little and kissed Leif's forehead. There was still a butterfly bandage there from four days ago, but Hacon didn't think Leif would care.

"Not if I am not lucky."

Hacon nodded and felt it deep in the pit of his stomach, what luck would mean to such a man. "Well, then, you must be lucky," he said, moving on to Leif's ribs. "Because I am not a fool." Three years, living with Andre, suspecting him of cheating, never being able to prove it, and suddenly Hacon felt that weight drop from his shoulders. He was not a fool, because here he was, tending for a good man, one with inarguably extraordinary luck.

Leif
The Assorted Properties
of Twined Fibers

It was actually pretty wonderful to have Hacon's touch on his body again. The truth was, Leif was about done. He was so tired after the adrenaline faded he could have slept for a week and so sore he didn't want to lie down. Hacon washed the gravel out of his shoulder and his ribs and the front of his hip and then changed the water and washed him all over, like a shower but better, because it was Hacon's touch. Leif found himself nodding off, even when the washcloth touched his inner thigh, and Hacon told him to go ahead and sleep. He'd finish the sponge bath and leave Leif for a little while—but he'd be back.

Leif hadn't even had a chance to tell him how just seeing him there, still on his stoop, had given him the strength to walk up the stairs. He'd come back. Leif had been wrathful and angry, and Hacon had still come back. Tom had always feared his temper, although Leif had never hurt a soul, but apparently Hacon knew temper, and he knew what it could do and knew what it didn't when its master was in charge.

So Hacon had not been frightened off—had, in fact, come back to visit and had almost saved Leif's life just by being there. It was like the gold thread—which had saved his life during that exhilarating moment in traffic—was tired now, and Hacon had come to take over.

He dozed for a moment and was awakened when Hacon came back and pulled the covers up to his chin in defense against the chilly San Francisco afternoon.

"I am going home for a moment," Hacon said softly. "I need to get clothes and feed Vanir and clean up whatever he destroyed. I need to call my mother and check on Sven. I called while I was waiting for you, and I think she lost track of him—she had her lawyer babysitting him. I think he got away. I need to call Andre."

Leif grunted and tried to form real words. "Why Andre?"

"Because I think I can help get the people smuggling stuff through my company and leave my brother out of it. I need to. Sven is young and stupid, but he's not evil. I have to believe it."

Leif reached out of the covers and clasped Hacon's hand. "Okay," he said, fighting the swampy feeling of exhaustion. "Do that. Just come back. Promise."

Hacon leaned over him again and kissed his cheek. "I have to," he said. "You're here. I have to come back to you."

And on that, Leif fell asleep, dreaming of Hake's lips on his skin.

Loki, contrary to all previous experience, actually parked his ass on Leif's head and purred, which was somnolent and soothing. The cat stayed on the bed in spite of the fact that Lethal came in to wake him up three times after that. The first time she said it was to ask where the cat food was, and the second time it was to ask for the phone. He didn't have a house phone; he told her to use his cell, then remembered she had her own, *then* fell asleep. The third time she came in, with some tinned soup in a bowl, it occurred to him that she was checking up on him.

He blinked against the ache in about every part of his body and sat up. "You are doing this on purpose," he accused, letting the sheet slide down his bare chest.

"Yes, yes I am," she said, pursing her full lips without remorse. "You bonked your noggin too goddamned many times to just go home and go to sleep. Me'n your boy are taking turns."

Leif smiled faintly. "I think 'my boy' is a few years older than me."

Lethal sniffed and set a cloth on his lap with some pieces of buttered bread to dip in the soup. "I think that boy's been older'n you since he was born. Doesn't make him any less your boy."

Leif took a sip of the soup—cream of mushroom—and sighed with appreciation. Simple things, sometimes. Mushroom soup and buttered bread. Lethal, who had no compunction about invading personal space, sat her tiny bottom right next to his hips and picked up a piece of the bread, which was fine, since she'd probably buttered half a loaf.

"We had a fight this morning," he confessed, and she looked at him in surprise as she dipped the bread in his bowl.

"Yeah, what about?"

"He tried to offer me money to stay home, and then said I had no luck."

Lethal took a bite of the bread and contemplated as she chewed. "Now, that first one's not so bad, you know. My sister Verdacia, she's been trying to get some man to pay for her to stay home since she turned fifteen. It ain't worked for her, but you ain't Verdacia."

Leif grinned and looked at her with raised eyebrows, and she smirked.

"Yeah, I know, obviously you ain't Verdacia, but just sayin'. Men've asked for worse things after a night in the sack."

God love her. "This is true," he conceded, "but the—"

Her mouth was crammed with bread and butter, but that didn't mean she couldn't talk with it full. "The luck? You know, Leif—I gotta say, if I'd had my coffee this morning, you would have made me wet my pants. Whatever that freaky shiz you pulled off on Market and Van Ness, that was just... that was the gods reachin' down to save you, that's what it was. The fact that he tried to get you to stay home? That was just proof. It's not that the boy doesn't believe in your luck. I think he wants to *be* your luck. He wants to be your mojo. That's not such a bad thing." She dipped the bread in the soup again and this time fed it to him, because he'd stopped eating. He took a bite dutifully, and so did she, and this time she swallowed before she spoke. "I mean, he's got to take care of you if he wants to be your luck."

Leif took another bite of soup and was too weary and too sore not to say this next thing. "People leave, though," he said thoughtfully. "The luck never has."

Lethal chewed, considering, and Leif waited for her opinion. She didn't know her father, and her mother had simply walked away from her and her siblings one day. This would mean something to her. "Yeah," she said after a minute, "but I always thought my grandma was my luck. You know she's the best person. I love her to death. So some people walked away, but that one didn't. It only needs one person to make you really lucky, you know?"

Leif nodded. "Something to think about," he said, feeling tired all over again. He set his bread down in the soup and gestured to Lethal to have the rest.

"I'll finish this," she told him, before holding the bowl up to her mouth and used the bread to scoop the soup in. She took a bite, swallowed, spoke around the next one. "And you settle down to sleep. You may want to get up next time so you can pee, and then go to bed at twelve and maybe not get your days and nights so fucked up."

Leif made an "uhm-hm" sound and settled down in the covers, pulling them snugly over his shoulders. Usually he was a sprawler, but not tonight.

Lethal left and turned out the light, and Leif had one last thought.

Lethal said Hacon was his luck. Maybe it was true. Maybe that was why he didn't see the thread when he touched Hacon. Maybe it was simply that with Hacon, Leif didn't need luck. Could Leif live with that? Hacon was warmer, sweeter on his skin, than luck had ever been, it was true. And he was real, and he was kind, and….

Leif's last thought was that he wished Hacon was *there*, before he fell asleep, dreaming of searching for the man but having no luck at all.

WHEN he woke up again, it was maybe six thirty at night, and because it was late June, the sunlight was streaming slantwise and orange through the bay window next to his bed. (The window was probably the apartment's only redeeming feature.) There were voices in his front room. One of them was Hacon, and that was comforting, and the other one was Lethal, and that was nice, too, but the third he did not know, and that was upsetting. He made to push himself up and *everything* hurt, and it hurt even worse than it had after the explosion, so he made a helpless sound, collapsed back, and swore. Loki batted his head through his hair, and even *that* hurt.

And Hacon was there immediately with a small prescription bottle of painkillers in his hand.

"This is a refill of what you got before," he said. He had a plastic bottle of 7-Up in his hand, and Leif eyed it covetously. "Lethal said you didn't eat much. You need some sugar, I think, and some painkillers, and then maybe something simple to eat."

"Toast and soup would be good again," Leif said. His neck hurt, and that was making his head hurt, but he was secretly relieved not to feel the same bell-ringing sensation of his concussions, like Lethal and Hacon had worried about. So much to worry about—it was good that would not be one more thing. "Thank you."

"I got takeout," Hacon said, leaning against the doorframe. "Salmagundis, soup, and sandwiches. Don't argue with me."

"I won't," Leif said mildly. "Thank you again."

Hacon's mouth twisted, and he sat down next to the bed and put his hand on Leif's forehead, smoothing back his hair. "You will not thank me so much when you find you have another guest. Here."

Leif took the painkillers and then a long drink from the 7-Up. Oh, gods yes… that was wonderful. He tried to look past Hake and into the living room and couldn't. "Who's in there?"

Hake grimaced. "My brother Sven. I think Lethal's giving him a lesson in what the real world is like even as we speak. Sven might beg for prison if he says one more thing about the books or the dust."

Leif rolled his eyes and drank more soda. "He's welcome to make fun of the books and the dust, you know that, right?"

Hacon shook his head with great decision. "No one can make fun of your stories. That is my rule. Nobody. As far as I'm concerned, your stories saved your life today, and two days ago, and maybe for your entire life, just long enough for me to meet you. Lethal can have his head on a plate if she wants."

Leif found his mouth twitching up. "But that would make a dinner pretty unpleasant."

Hacon smiled and cupped his cheek. Leif could feel his stubble rasp against Hacon's palm and wished that maybe, one day, he could put on some good clothes and shave and get his hair trimmed and have this man see him cleaned up and high-class.

But Hake didn't seem to mind. "Then I guess we can leave Sven's head where it is for now," he said and leaned close enough for Leif to smell him, and then touched lips.

Leif grunted, put the soda on the end table, raised his hand, and pulled Hacon closer. Touching lips was not enough. Leif needed to be *fed* on him, he needed to *devour*, because something in his soul had not been fed when he'd left that morning, and he was starving for it now.

Hacon melted into his chest and kissed him back, palming his bare skin with shy, sinuous motions until Leif caught his hand regretfully. "Can we wait until later?" he asked softly.

"Probably best," Hacon admitted. "But... but I'm so afraid." He half laughed and buried his face against Leif's chest.

"Your brother's mobsters?" Leif wrapped a protective arm around Hacon's shoulders, and Hacon shook his head.

"No. I mean, I should be. They pretty much beat him up and left him on my lawn. He looks like hell. I wanted to take him to the hospital, but he threatened to run away, so...." Hacon sighed. "I told him just to come with me. I wanted to find the right words. Apparently the right words were a lie. But they worked."

Leif took his turn to stroke Hake's hair away from his face. "What were the right words?"

"I'll never let anything hurt you."

Leif blew out a breath. "Those are powerful words," he said quietly.

"I want to say them to you," Hacon murmured. "I want to tell you that I'll never let anyone hurt you. That no one will ever leave you. That you'll never be lonely again."

"They're my favorite story ending," Leif confessed, feeling a slow red blossom open up in his chest, something painful and beautiful and lonely and craving. "But you have to be sure the adventure is ending and the happiness is beginning. Then you can say them."

"Then we will wait for then," Hacon said softly. He lifted his head and kissed Leif on the corner of the mouth. "But you need to know I have them ready for when that happens."

"That's awfully quick for a man in a suit," Leif said, knowing it was true. Hacon, with his suit and his pessimism and his responsibilities... men like Hacon didn't say "I love you" after a week. Leif had never expected him to.

"If you knew the man I was with Andre," Hake said slowly, "you'd know that what I feel for you is different. Stronger. I would never have come back after a fight with Andre like that. Andre would have had to apologize to me, even when I was wrong."

Leif frowned. "Were you wrong a lot?"

Hacon shrugged. "Fifty-fifty," he said. "But Andre still insists it was eighty-twenty."

Leif laughed. "You spoke to him?"

Hacon nodded. "Yes." He pulled away reluctantly. "We have a plan of sorts. Would you like to hear it?"

Leif did, very much, but at that moment a young man poked his head in. He was built like Hacon—slight and thin, with pale blue eyes and dark hair, but one of his eyes was blackened, and his nose was swollen. He had a cut on his cheek, and he moved a lot like Leif did—as though every joint, muscle, and bone in his body had been hit by a wrecking ball.

"Hacon," Sven said peevishly, "are we really going to stay in this dump overnight? There's not even a television, and this... this *person* keeps telling me to shut the fuck up!"

Hacon rolled his eyes. "You are safe here," he said, his voice sharp, "and Leif is too hurt to go gallivanting out to some other place, and since you had something to do with that, I think you should follow Lethal's advice."

Sven stopped short and looked up guiltily at Leif. "No one was supposed to get hurt," he said, risking a glance at his brother with an expression of supreme unhappiness. "I had no idea they were sending anything to Hacon, and...." He stopped and shook his head. "Whatever. I'm sorry. I'll go hide in a pile of books now."

"Don't touch the ones that are typed up and bound!" Hacon called as the young man left, and Leif laughed.

"You are hard on him," Leif murmured, and the look Hacon gave him was so lost and full of yearning.

"He hurt you," Hacon whispered. "Whether he meant to or not."

Leif swallowed. "I hurt you too. I am very, very sorry."

Hacon shook his head. "I hurt you first. I...." He smiled wistfully, with a touch of resignation. "I wanted to take care of you. I *always* want to take care of you. And I don't care if it's too early in the story, Leif. I am afraid that I am not enough, and I will share you with your luck, because I will *never* let anything hurt you."

A curious thing happened then, to the thread in Leif's brain, the thread he'd always thought of as his luck.

It bound itself, twirled around Hacon's energy like wool around a drop spindle, circling around and around, binding Hacon as securely in its brightness as it had entwined with Leif all his life. It felted them, joined them, wove their fibers together as tightly as any matron's spit-splice had ever bound worsted, until they were one piece, one skein, one sock, one sweater, one scarf. All of their colors, their textures, the selves of the two of them were twined in one blessed gold thread that knit and wove as the two of them danced.

Hacon gasped and jerked back, looking at Leif with a sort of puzzled wonder. "What was that?"

Leif grinned, finding the energy inside him to make the whole of the grin and not just a small piece. "That was you," he said merrily. He was still sore, and still hurt, and still done with anything physical for the day—including the thing he most wanted to do, actually—but his heart, which had been shrouded in a pall of pain and some doubt, was glimmering and bright as the sun.

"Me what? I didn't do anything!"

"Oh yes you did," Leif said, still not quite believing it, but there it was. He could not believe in the lucky gold thread at all if he didn't believe the thing he just saw happen was true. "You just became my luck, Hacon—*you* became my luck. You believed in it, and now...." Suddenly Leif grew sober. "You had better have meant what you said. If you leave me, you take away *everything*, including my luck. You have it. It's wrapped around you, protecting us both. I *really* hope you're true to your word."

"I am," Hacon said with such quiet assurance that Leif had no choice but to believe. "I meant it. Don't worry, Leif. Your luck—your belief, it's still whole. It's still true."

"Good," Leif said casually, although he was still grinning. "Good. Then, if our luck is true, maybe we should plan how to save your little brother, you think?"

At that moment there was a knock at the apartment door, and Hacon grimaced.

"Ye gods… peace. I want a few days of peace with you, is that too much to ask? When this is over, I'm *making* Sven run the company so I can take you to a timeshare someplace warm and keep you in the hotel room so you can't get tan."

Leif laughed. "Wait until my shoulder heals, would you? I have plans for that."

Hacon shook his head and stalked off, grumbling, and Leif called, "You may as well bring everybody in here. The bed is the only place in the apartment everybody can sit down!"

Which was only the truth, but it was also how he came to have Lethal practically sitting in his lap while Hake leaned on him from the side and Sven sat resentfully at the foot of the bed, leaning his weight on his knees. Andre stalked like a lion in front of the bed in the small space left by the books stacked up against the wall, and that made Leif nervous. He was used to being the lion in the room, and he was not thrilled to have Hacon's ex-lion there when that was Leif's job.

"So, did you brief everyone?" Andre asked, his voice brusque, and Hacon's feathers ruffled.

"No, I did not brief everyone. Do I look like a police officer or military personnel?"

"Well, what were you doing here?" Andre asked, annoyed, and Hacon raised the corner of his lip in a way that was haughty—and enchanting.

"I was falling in love. Do you have any objections?"

Andre rolled his eyes and then checked Leif out appreciatively. "Only that he seems to have questionable judgment, but that's his problem."

Leif grinned back. The open statement about *everything* seemed to give the lion more room. "Well, I *have* been hit on the head several times this week," he said, and it was Lethal who turned to him in disgust.

"Now that's not funny. Just don't even joke about that, because I will beat you dead."

Leif kept grinning at her, and she turned her back on him and shook her head at Hake. "Don't let him look at you like that. That man will smile you stupid. It's embarrassing."

"I know," Hacon confessed to her, smiling with his own actual embarrassment. "It's a gift."

Andre shook his head at them. "Can we get on with this now?" he asked dryly. "Or do we have our next conversation in a morgue?"

Sven grimaced and looked at his brother. "This one's a prize. I can't believe you let him go."

Andre snarled. "Hacon, so help me, I'm doing this for—"

"I know, I know!" Hake stood up and looked at them all. "Okay, so let's start this again. Andre, I appreciate you being here. I appreciate your willingness to treat Sven as a source and not a suspect. Sven, I would really like to see you neither hospitalized or jailed, so if there's any way you could not antagonize the nice policeman, that would be a plus. Lethal—"

"What?" She had one eyebrow raised mutinously, and her mouth was pushed to the side in a way that signified danger.

"Could you give Leif another pillow, please, sweetheart? He's sort of sliding down the bed."

"No problem."

"Thank you," Leif said dryly, very much amused. "Anything I should do?"

Hacon shook his head and smiled winsomely. "No, Leif, I think you're fine."

"He's more than fine, you lucky bastard," Andre sighed. "I have no idea how you pulled that off."

Hacon preened, and Leif enjoyed watching that very much. "That is for me to know. Now, are we ready? Do you need me to go bring the principal, Mr. Guest Speaker, or can you do your job?"

"No idea at *all*," Andre muttered. Then he took Hacon's place at the foot of the bed again, apparently sure that all of the unruly elements in the room had been subdued. The handsome detective ran a hand through his criminally short hair and unbuttoned the jacket of his very nice suit, and Leif couldn't help thinking that, for all that Hacon had worn a suit in this apartment before, Andre's looked much more out of place.

"Okay," Andre started again. "Here's what we know. Sven here made a deal with a shady friend of a friend for more oxycodone—"

"Wait," Hacon said abruptly. "Sven?"

His brother looked at him, but Leif could tell it was an effort.

"Sven, could you tell me more about that? I know"—Hake held up a hand to forestall Andre's objection—"it's not necessary for tomorrow, but I would like to know."

Sven blushed but nodded. "I... well, I was stupid and hurt my back. You know that. And you all rushed to the hospital, and you were so... so nice. So sweet. It was like I was young again, and the family was all there. And when you left...." He sighed. "It was like I wanted that feeling again. It was easy to tell myself it was the pain pills that gave it."

Hacon sighed. "Did you think of talking to us?"

Sven shrugged. "Did you think of talking to me?"

Hacon shook his head and Andre grunted. "Kid," Andre said, "you were born into the wrong goddamned family for that."

Hacon looked stung. "I can change," he said, but his eyes sought out Leif's, and Leif nodded encouragingly.

"Of course you can," Leif said, thinking that he already had.

"Right." Andre snorted. "Your deep freeze actually killed off our fish."

"I know, right?" Sven interjected. "He used to kill off mom's flowers all the time. He'd get pissed and just walk by them and they'd wither. He's like walking permafrost!"

Leif chuckled. "I beg to differ," he said mildly. "Would everybody here like to know how I know?"

He was suddenly the center of three horrified gazes.

"*No!*" Everybody cried—everybody except Hacon, who was blushing warmly and looking at him like he hung the moon.

"So back to your drug use," Leif said gently. "Did you get help, Sven, even if it wasn't your family?"

Sven nodded. "See, I had the friend of the friend—his name is Bill Winters, but everyone calls him Monkey Man, I have no idea why—anyway, he'd write me false prescriptions. I started out paying him, and that was... well, it was dirty, but it was fine. Then...." Sven looked down at his hands. "They didn't want the money, and... I was fucked up. I was fucked up all the time. The only time I was even functional was when I went in for those days at the office." Sven looked at Hacon with honest remorse. "It was stupid, Hacon. I'd go in and I'd look at that list you'd left me—and you always had something there about 'Please let me know if you need help!' or 'I'd like to come in and go over this with you. Let me know when.' I'd read those and think I wish you really meant it—"

"I *did*!" Hake exploded. "Of *course* I meant it! I didn't know what you were doing, but I missed you! You came to my home three times a week when you were in high school. You asked me about everything—even girls, which was the saddest conversation I've ever had! And you get to college and suddenly I wasn't good enough to talk to?"

Sven blushed and looked down at his hands. "I wanted to do the work," he said roughly. "I'd try one or two things, because you asked me, and I'd be hopeless... I couldn't think through the drugs, and I was usually trying not to take them those days, and I could think even less...." Sven looked at his hands some more. "And then they asked me to start accepting packages. And I had an address I was supposed to send the numbers to. It was so easy. And I didn't have to worry about the money or anything."

"So you did that?" Hacon asked. "Why did things change?"

Sven shrugged. "I... remember—I took a trip in May?"

Hacon nodded. "Europe? Yeah, I remember. You just got back a week ago."

"Yeah—I didn't go to Europe. I went to rehab. I took all that money and went to rehab, and I got clean."

The look on Hacon's face hurt Leif's heart. "Alone? Nobody visited?"

Sven looked up then and blinked back tears. "Would you have visited?" he asked, and Hacon nodded.

"Yes. Yes, little brother, I would have visited you. I'm so angry at you for thinking I wouldn't have!"

Sven wiped his eyes with the back of his hand. "Well, you're going to love this part. It almost got you killed. So, I came back from rehab and told them that I wouldn't do it anymore."

Leif blinked. "A week ago?"

Sven nodded deliberately. "And I went and told Monkey Man that I wasn't going to be accepting packages anymore. And he asked why, and I said I didn't want to betray my family anymore and that I was going to go tell you everything."

Hacon closed his eyes like that hurt, and Leif could see why. "And two days later, they tried to kill me."

Sven sighed. "And... I hadn't gotten my courage, Hake. I... I swear—it was part of my plan. You're supposed to make up for things you've done when you're high, and this was a doozy. But... I wanted to be straight first. I wanted you to know I meant it when I said I was sorry. I didn't think they'd try to kill you, I just wanted to stop lying—"

Hacon still stood by Andre, looking at his little brother in horrified sympathy. Leif glared at him until he looked up and met Leif's eyes, and then Leif pointed to Sven and mouthed "Hug. Him." His mouth moved unmistakably, and Hacon opened his eyes a little wider—and then did as Leif demanded. He sat next to his little brother and wrapped his arms around the boy's shoulders as Sven fell completely apart.

"Now tell him it's all right," Lethal ordered, without Leif's subtlety.

Hacon tempered the glare he shot her and then melted against Sven. "It's all right," he murmured. "I told you, I'm not going to let anything hurt you." He sighed and shook his head. "Not even me."

Andre grunted and waited, arms crossed in front of him, for the theatrics to end, but Leif was happy. Lethal was curled up on his lap like Loki (who had disappeared into the stacks of books the minute everyone invaded), and Hacon was being the hero Leif had always dreamed of. What could they not accomplish with such a man in their midst?

INTERLUDE
NIMBLE FINGERS

THOR'S face was inscrutable, and so was Loki's, and Verdandi breathed a sigh of relief. Good. Because she was going to have to do some fancy twining if the tapestry was going to weave like she thought it would. The Fates weren't supposed to play favorites… but then, who wanted to be there in the room when the true favorites of the gods bit the big one?

Suddenly Loki spoke up. "What in the hell was that?"

"What?" Verdandi asked, although she knew.

"The spinning of the gold," Thor asked. "I know you saw it, little sister. How did that happen?"

Skuld cackled behind them, which was an unlikely sound, since she was wearing her maiden form in front of the gods. "Spit-splicing," she crowed. "Spit-splicing of the gods."

Loki grimaced and looked at Verdandi to explain, but Verdandi's fingers were working cleverly, making the most of that mortally wound gold thread. "Ask her," Dandi said tersely. "It's her work."

"*She* gives me the creeps," Loki confessed, and Verdandi sighed.

"Urdh, could you show this one what we had to do so that we didn't annihilate an entire family when he messed with our craft?"

Loki grunted, but Verdandi couldn't risk a glance sideways.

"Go," Thor said to Loki. "Go watch her. She will show you." Then he leaned over and spoke softly to Verdandi. "I see what you're doing, little sister. All I can offer is my gratitude."

"Thank me if it works," she muttered and began to weave the elements of sea and sky, of iron and concrete, until the pattern came up. Four men—all bound in some way, whether it was by love or by blood. They were walking quietly in the shadows, looking at packing crate numbers and opening the big metal doors of the giant shipping containers that ventured across the ocean.

"Look," Loki said, glancing over his shoulder. "They are at the meeting place. Shall we look and see what happens?"

Oh, lovely. Now she had an audience. Verdandi didn't waste energy on swearing, she just kept weaving and shuttling and working that subtle magic with the loose fibers that all raw material left when it was being worked, trying hard, so hard, to leave threads of safety for her heroes to cling to.

Gods... so many ways a thread could be cut in such a place. She was not ready for that to happen. Like Thor and Loki, she loved these men too.

HACON
SPIT-SPLICING AWAY

HACON didn't do a lot of work out at the docks. He thought that Leif might want to, at some point, when their relationship had progressed to where Leif didn't think it was charity, because the docks were very visceral and very exciting and muscular. There was also a need for intelligence and finesse when directing all of that heavy machinery, and Leif could manage both elements very well. But the night they went to the docks—the night after the meeting in Leif's bedroom—Hacon wasn't planning on how to get Leif to work for him. All he was really thinking about was how the cargo containers were organized, and he knew the letters on the front of the little code referred to cargo from a specific ship and row number and column number and layer.

They were fortunate, he would think later, that the layer number for the cargo from the ship they were going to check out this night was on the ground floor, because otherwise things might not have fallen about so well. It was, as Leif would say, the most extraordinary luck.

They went in the still-light evening the day after Leif was hurt, and Leif seemed to have recovered almost completely. The night before had been… quiet. Andre kindly took Lethal home to her family when they were done discussing the plan, but Sven had slept on the couch in a pair of Leif's sleep shorts, knotted at the waist, and an old sweatshirt that went halfway down to his thighs. He could have worn a 1950s smoking jacket and fur-covered slippers for all Hake gave a damn—Sven was on the couch, and neither he nor Leif were public men, and there would be no sex on the couch again, and certainly no sweating, screaming, noisy fornication in that teeny tiny bedroom with the paper walls, which was a shame.

But that didn't stop them from talking quietly after Andre left. After Sven's meltdown, Hacon and Sven eventually separated long enough to hear Andre's plan about going to investigate the cargo with police backup on the alert and Andre's partner, Galliano, watching things from afar in case any bad guys showed up. Hacon managed to refrain from asking how badly Sven had to have been fucked up in order to align himself with anyone named Monkey Man, and everyone speculated as to the nature of the contraband the ships were smuggling. Most of the ships that were marked had come from South America, so the general perception was drugs, but since Sven's addiction had been to prescription drugs—ones not generally processed in South America—their imaginations ran the gamut. It was Lethal's suggestion that maybe it was ancient Aztec archeological pieces of extreme historical significance, as well as some crystal skulls, that had basically broken up their little powwow. Obviously, if they had gone there, they had gone too far, and it was time for everyone to get some sleep and some perspective, and that was the end of the matter.

Andre squeezed Hacon's shoulder as he left and shook his head at Leif. "Are you sure?" he asked Leif, a sort of pained wonder on his face. "Because I swear, I was going to ask for your number."

Leif shook his head. "Two pretty men at the same day? That's an embarrassment of riches right there," he said, smiling, and Hake remembered what he'd said. He flirted with everyone—but he only kissed a few. One. Hacon. "I wouldn't know what to do with such an offer. Perhaps you'd be better off giving that attention to someone who is more in need."

Andre rolled his eyes. "I'll remember that." He scowled at Hacon a little and then relented. "Look, I won't lie. The guy you're hooking up with really can freeze the 'nads off a guppy in a heated tank—but he won't ever hurt you on purpose. He won't ever lie to you. He won't ever betray you. That's a lot of good, if the right man has him."

Leif practically glowed. "See," he said to Hacon. "I *am* the right man."

Hacon gave him a kiss on the cheek and went to follow Andre out.

"I don't understand," he said, standing on the stair landing while Lethal went down to the street to unlock her bike. "Why can't we just have you tell everybody you're following a tip, and then the police can do this thing tomorrow evening?"

Andre blew out a breath. "Because if the police get there and start opening crates, they're going to track the contraband back to your brother as a suspect. If we get there and open the crates and come to them with the complete theory, we can cite your brother as an informant. I'm not thrilled about it, either, Hacon. Given when that bomb went off, and given the timetable of the other ships that have come in with contraband, I'm thinking if the bad guys haven't gone in and gotten their shit by now, tomorrow's the night. I'm sort of expecting them to appear, to be honest, but like I said—if we get there first and Sven points the way, we can talk to the DA and keep his name off the list of indictments. If we're just there with information, he can get put on the list of the bad guys, and since he's the one who squealed…."

Hacon nodded and shivered. "Andre, how widespread is this 'Monkey Man'? He obviously has contacts in South America, but if we sent Sven, say, back to the old country to discover his roots or something, would there be scary men with guns waiting for him?"

Andre looked compassionate then, and for the first time, Hacon respected what he did in his job. "Probably not, Hake. But if we do our jobs here, there might not be any scary men with guns waiting for him here, either."

"What about witness protection?" The thought bothered him. He didn't want his little brother to have to go away without his family quite so soon. He *certainly* didn't want to explain to Mother how it happened that her youngest son, the one who could do no wrong, was living in Albuquerque under an assumed name.

Andre shrugged. "We'll see, Hake, okay? Don't borrow trouble. Right now, we want to go after the big fish and catch him so your fishy little brother doesn't get fried, okay?"

Hacon grunted. "Very poetic. Maybe you *should* give Leif your number."

Andre raised his eyebrows and just looked at him, and Hacon blushed.

"Scratch that," he said sourly. "Then I'd have to gut you like another fish, and I was just starting to like you."

Andre smiled then, the charming one with the dimples that used to send Hacon into a frenzy of lust and jealousy. Now it just made him glad he had a friend. "I'm glad for you, Hacon," he said softly. "You're a good man—and I left things really badly. Hang on to this one, okay? Don't kill any fish with him. Talk to him first."

Hacon shook his head and rolled his eyes. "I swear," he muttered, "*you* were the one who killed the fish."

Andre laughed, and Lethal stuck her head in the doorway down the stairs and called up, the sound echoing off the stairwell. "Anyone going to come down and take me home? It is time for good little black girls to get the hell off the street, yo!"

Andre laughed some more, stuck a piece of gum in his mouth, and trotted down the stairs to take Lethal home, and Hake went back inside.

Sven was there, sitting on the couch, playing with his phone, which was plugged into the charger. He'd had to move a couple of stacks of books to get the charger in. It was, in fact, Leif's charger, because Leif's phone was perhaps the one bow to technology in the entire apartment, and Hacon blessed it because it meant Sven could watch a movie on the tiny screen.

"What'd he say?" Sven asked anxiously. He was already wearing Leif's borrowed clothes, and he looked like a little boy in them. Hake remembered when Sven had been *his* little boy, his little responsibility, and Hacon wondered when he'd carelessly abandoned that. How could he be angry at the gods for deserting Leif when he was young, when it seemed like Hacon's family had abandoned Sven without the excuse of death as a mitigating factor?

"He said that it will be dangerous tomorrow, but he wants you to lead us to the crates so he can present you as an informant and keep you out of prison."

Sven grimaced. "What if they don't get everyone?"

Hacon sighed. "Then we shall all go undercover in Albuquerque. You can call me Bjorn, and Leif can be Thor, and you can be Loki—"

"Me?" Sven grimaced, wrapping his arms around his knees. "Why can't you be Loki?"

"Because Loki is the name of Leif's cat. That would be wrong in ways I cannot explain."

Sven chuckled and looked at Hacon sideways. "You're funny," he said, almost in wonder. "I'd forgotten that." He grimaced. "I forgot so much. Don't hate me, Hacon. Please. I'd forgotten that you were funny, and that Skali offered to have me come stay the summer with him and his wife, and that mother always knows our sizes and the stores we shop in for Christmas. We're not warm people—but that doesn't mean I wasn't cared for."

Hacon nodded and then ruffled his little brother's hair. "You are young, Sven. All sorts of bizarre behaviors can be explained away by insufficient age."

"What about hoarding books? How's that get explained away?" Sven looked around the apartment like all of the books were strictly imaginary and would melt away to reveal a fully functional entertainment center.

"He's brilliant," Hacon said quietly and with great pride. "Not everybody gets the same breaks you do, Sven. Your family wasn't warm, no—but you had one. You have brothers to go to and a mother who tried to protect you. All Leif has is a dream of someday being able to go to school and put all this knowledge to good use."

"And you," Sven pointed out.

Hacon looked down at his nice office shoes and then looked up, smiling. "Yes. Now he has me. But before then, all he had was his brains and his luck. Don't crap all over either thing—they've served him well."

"Is he coming tomorrow?" Sven asked, and Hacon couldn't tell if he wanted it to happen or not.

"Yes," Hake said, feeling the answer carefully. "I think Leif will want to know how the story ends."

"Good," Sven murmured, curling into the corner of the couch and even further under the hand-crocheted blanket. "I think we're going to need some extraordinary luck. Bill Winters—Monkey Man—he's the only one I really met. My friend, the one who turned me on to him, is back east doing his own rehab, but Bill was bad enough. He's...." Sven paused distastefully. "Oily. Like the ocean in Oakland." He shuddered, and Hacon nodded, understanding. He made sure to pass close enough to his little brother to ruffle his hair again and squeeze his shoulder. Sven grabbed his hand and squeezed back. Hacon had made his promise, and even if Sven knew he might not be able to keep it, apparently the fact that Hake made it meant a great deal to his little brother, and that was an improvement.

So Hacon closed the door connecting the bedroom and the living room and at last was alone with the man he'd bound his luck to in a matter of days. Leif was dozing, his eyes shadowed in the lamplight, his chest—which had a small mat of curling red hair between his lean pectoral muscles—bare. He still had yellowing bruises from the day they'd met, and tiny cuts around his mouth and his cheek, and Hake had to stop categorizing his injuries or he wouldn't be able to climb in bed, he'd just start shaking in the corner, afraid.

"What are you worrying about now?" Leif murmured without opening his eyes.

"That I think you are going to come with us tomorrow, and I worry that you'll get hurt."

Leif grinned and opened one sleepy eye at him. "Really? I would have thought you'd be worrying about yourself. You do have the family history, remember?"

Hacon grimaced and started laughing. He unbuttoned his slacks— he'd been so busy with Sven that he'd neglected to change out of his work clothes—and his shirt and toed off his shoes while he spoke. "I'd almost forgotten about that, but thank you. I think you're right—having Sven or I die in a hail of bullets while busting a smuggling ring would certainly keep up the family legend, you think?"

Leif's mouth pursed seriously. "We must keep a sharp eye out on your little brother, then," he said. "The luck isn't telling me not to go tomorrow night, which must mean you're safe."

Hacon stood there in his white boxers and undershirt and stripped off his black socks, thinking that was both reassuring and a really odd thing to say.

"The luck tells you what to do?" he asked, and Leif nodded before saying, "The undershirt too."

"What?"

"Take the undershirt off before coming to bed."

Hacon blushed. "Yeah?"

"Skin to skin, Hacon."

"But we're not going to—"

"Skin to skin. Don't make me cranky—look at me. I'm at death's door." Leif's eyes were crinkled in the corners and his lips were compressed, probably so his habitual grin wouldn't peek out. Hacon stripped off his undershirt and quit objecting. This big beautiful god-man was going to *touch* him. Why object?

He slid under the covers and was immediately mauled. Leif's big hand was all over him. (The other one was *still* in the sling. Oh gods, what could this man do to him when he had the full use of both arms? It was boggling!) His ribs, his stomach, his flanks—all of them were smoothed, gentled, *touched*, and for a few minutes Hacon relaxed into it, allowed himself to be handled and stroked and *touched.* He did not get aroused, but for a moment, his entire body quivered—and then went limp. It was like a climax of the skin alone, and Hacon wanted to cheer. His breathing evened out, and Leif's big hand was still in his hair.

"Here," Hacon said, turning toward him. "My turn." Leif was on his back still, tilted a little toward his side, but not entirely, so he didn't put any weight on the shoulder with the broken collarbone.

"That would be nice," Leif said, rolling so he was completely on his back again.

"So what did you mean?" Hacon asked, rubbing Leif's chest and smiling because, hey! Who wouldn't smile when touching that chest? Defined muscle but not bulky, smooth skin, just that little bit of ginger hair.... Mmmm....

"What did I mean when?" Leif asked. His voice sounded drowsy, and why shouldn't it? The man might have already had a nap, but he'd also had one hell of a week.

"When you said you followed your luck?" Hake was not quite solicitous enough over one of Leif's bruises, and Leif's entire body jerked at his touch. Hacon continued the caress, though, but gentler, always gentle, as he stroked the taut stomach and the thick bicycle rider's thighs.

"Mm...." It was a thoughtful sound and not the nummy *Mmm, that feels good* sound, so Hacon kept rubbing gently and waited, all senses on alert, for the reply.

"Mm?"

Leif sighed. "You really did kill those fish, you know."

"I *what*?" Hacon jerked back, stung, but Leif kept his eyes closed, grasped Hacon's hand, and put it on his cock—where it most definitely *hadn't* been when Hake had moved it.

"I'm not insulting you," Leif growled. "And I'd really like you to do—yeah. That."

Hacon tightened his grip and stroked slowly, and Leif's hips shifted in response.

"We can't make a lot of noise," Hacon whispered, and Leif half opened his eyes and grinned.

"I can be quiet," he said. "When I'm not fucking you into the couch, I can be almost human."

Hacon tightened his grip, Leif grunted and thrust a little, and Hacon *made* himself relax his hand so they could have this conversation at the same time. "Start with my fish," he demanded, and as cranky as the conversation was making him, he was also getting hard. Exasperating man!

"You will not believe me," Leif said and then hummed low in his throat as Hacon rubbed his broad, flat cockhead with his thumb.

"Do you want me to quit?" Hake asked ill-temperedly, although he'd die before he quit. He hadn't tasted Leif the night before—not really. He wanted Leif to spurt down his throat this night, wanted Leif's spend to spill down his mouth.

"God forbid," Leif grumbled, shifting his hips again. "But it is simple. You were touched by the gods too. Your family, like me. Like my luck."

"Your luck just happens," Hacon muttered. The man's chest rippled as he undulated his hips, and now Hake was hard against Leif's thigh and wanting to just grab him and frot against him madly. He didn't, because he didn't want to grab any of his preexisting bruises, but that didn't mean that the urge wasn't almost overwhelming.

"No," Leif said, surprising him badly. Not bad enough to relax his grip on Leif's cock, which was now drooling precome pretty steadily, but badly.

"No?"

Leif grunted and thrust his hips. "My luck tells me where to go—how to turn the bicycle, which dumpster to look behind, and we're done with this right now!" He never raised his voice, but he thrust hard into Hacon's hand, and Hacon ducked under the covers and took his erection—massive and thick and literally hot and throbbing—into his mouth and suckled hard until he was halfway down the thing and swallowing desperately to take more.

Leif's hand held his head—not hard, just firmly—and he panted, thrusting his hips gently as Hake let that wonderful cock slide in and out of his tightly gripping mouth.

"Uhng... a... ahhhhhhh...." The sound, quiet and suppressed as it was, seemed to vibrate from Leif's stomach, and just the softness of it was sexy as Leif convulsed around Hacon's head and shoulders and filled Hake's mouth with come.

Hake swallowed most of it, salty and bitter, and let the rest slide down his chin while he groaned, grinding his erection against the mattress. Leif reached down and pulled him up by the arm, and Hacon fitted himself against Leif's body and frotted as Leif took his mouth, dribbling come and all. Leif thrust his tongue in and Hacon let him, opened his mouth for possession, relished the feeling of his cock against the coarse hairs and tight muscles of Leif's thigh. Leif reached down between them and grasped him, squeezing and stroking, and Hacon grunted, keeping his noises small, and then groaned again, a little louder than last time, and thrust *hard*, spilling all over Leif's hand and thigh and his own stomach. He panted a little and laughed into Leif's mouth and then closed his eyes as Leif very deliberately, very sensually, proceeded to lick his chin and cheeks clean. By the time Leif was done and taking his mouth in another kiss, Hacon was honest-to-gods giggling, and Leif's smile could be felt as he kissed.

Leif pulled back, and Hacon rested his damp cheek on Leif's chest, lower than his shoulders because both of them were sore. "I love you, Leif Torval," he said, so relaxed, so very happy, that the words came without self-consciousness and without worry. This moment, here, with this man? It was the best of moments, and he would not doubt it and wouldn't worry about it. He would say this thing in his heart for *this* moment, and trust that either there would be more moments like this one or that their lives would end tomorrow, and it would be worth it to have the words around them, settling into their skin.

"I love you too," Leif said, and this time, Hacon knew he said it on purpose.

"Are you going to tell me some more about your amazing luck?"

Leif chuckled. "Only that it's an active sort of thing. It told me where to look for the bicycle, it showed me a map for how to dodge traffic after I got tagged by that car. The day I met you, it had been *shoving* me up Nob Hill. I almost offered your package to Lethal, and it felt like a part of me had died. If she had taken me up on it, I don't know what I would have done—the sensation would have driven me mad."

Hacon blinked at him seriously. "That's almost like a premonition," he said and found that it must have been in his blood somewhere, because he could believe that. Now that he believed in Leif's luck, believing in a premonition and its truth was almost easier.

"Yeah," Leif agreed, closing his eyes a little.

"So, what does your luck say about tomorrow?"

Leif blew out a breath. "Nothing. It says nothing."

Hacon looked at him curiously. "That's good, right?"

Leif shrugged. "It means what I told you, Hacon. You are my luck. If we are there together, then our fates are bound. Good or bad, I would think."

Hacon shivered, thinking that he alone would be the one to protect Leif. "I would prefer you had a magic intuition taking over your fate," he said, never quite feeling so inadequate in his life. But Leif simply put that big hand on Hacon's head and pressed him into that magnificent chest.

"And I am happy knowing our fates are bound together. Quit worrying, Hacon. Our threads will be cut when the time calls for it. Otherwise they're twined together. Simply believe and it will be so."

Leif was half-asleep, but his hand was moving down Hacon's neck and back, and Hacon did something he rarely did: he let go of his worries and put himself in the hands of the Fates.

LEIF rested most of the next day, and Hacon, without fuss, paid the bills on the tiny kitchenette counter while Leif was napping. There were quite a few of them, and some were overdue, but Leif had said their fates were intertwined now, so Hacon felt no compunction about taking over his finances without asking. Leif had his luck, Hacon had his money—it was a poor substitute for luck, but Hacon would use it as he saw fit. If they survived this night, his next task would be to buy Leif a new bicycle. Ta-da! Hacon really was his luck now, so there!

And then that night, Andre came to collect them. They took Andre's car, and the ride over was strained. Leif sat in the front seat because his knees threatened to shoot through the back of any seat he scrunched up against. Hacon and Sven sat in the back, looking at each other moodily.

"I'm sorry," Sven said as they crossed the bridge and took the exit. "I couldn't stay with Mother's lawyer." A look of purely age-appropriate irritation crossed his face. "That man had no sense of humor. And he refused to let me order takeout—it was like peanut butter and jelly was penance."

Hacon grimaced. He and Sven—they'd both hated peanut butter and jelly as kids. "I'm sure they'd feed you better than that in prison," he said, and he was wholly serious, and Sven nodded appreciatively.

"You understand," he said with just the right touch of melodrama, and the awkwardness was broken.

Andre drove up to the security station and flashed his super policeman's ID, and then they were in, driving the service road to the pier on the far end of the gigantic endeavor of man, soft earth, and ocean. The cranes loomed above them like the still, giant bodies of ancient evils, and the stacks of shipping containers were high enough over their heads to make Hacon feel as though they were in an alien forest.

Oddly enough, Leif seemed to think it was an outing.

"Would you look at those cranes!" he crowed. "They are amazing! You must take me here sometime, Hacon. I want to see them work!"

Hacon, Andre, and Sven were all hunting dutifully for the appropriate column of the single-wide-sized packing containers while Leif wandered to the end of the dock and looked down into the blackening water.

"Oh, this is interesting," Hacon heard him say. "I guess the dock wasn't finished. See—there's two concrete pylons in here—gods, they're enormous! Yuck—the water between them looks foul."

Sven elbowed Hacon in the side, and Hacon grimaced, sneaking a look at his usually stern ex. Andre, however, simply shook his head, enchanted.

"I love that guy," he said, letting that killer smile loose. "God, he should have been Special Forces or something."

Hacon found himself laughing softly. "Stay here," he said. "The one we're looking for should be down this aisle."

He trotted down the dock to find Leif standing on the yellow warning board and looking down. "What is that for?" Leif asked, and Hacon looked down in the fading light. Sure enough, about five feet from the end of the dock, two sunken concrete pylons were mostly under the water. They were maybe six feet apart from each other, and the parts that protruded from the water were crusted over with iron rebar and sharp corroded metal. Whatever they'd been before, they were long defunct now, and Hacon was relatively sure that ships didn't come this far down the dock. Leif was right about the water too—the concrete was overgrown with algae and oil, and even though seawater lapped gently at the pier, there didn't seem to be any movement between the concrete pillars at all.

"I don't know," he answered and then blushed. "Honestly, whenever I come here, I sort of stay out of the way. I'm a suit. Emma knows more about the dock work than I do."

Leif looked indulgently at him. "You're such a bureaucrat," he said, but he put his good arm around Hacon's shoulders and squeezed. He was wearing jeans and a hooded sweatshirt this evening—Hacon had needed to help him into the sweatshirt again. Hacon had no idea what they must look like, with Hacon in his very conservative khaki slacks and windbreaker and Leif still dressed like a college student, but he *felt* so very right.

"Well, not everybody has your curiosity," Hacon said, admiring him tremendously.

"But how do you know your stories if you do not know your setting?" Leif asked, and Hacon was going to answer, but then they heard a curious sort of sound. It was a loud, short *pop*. It didn't sound like the thunder of the gods, and it didn't sound like anything you would hear in the movies, but Leif must have recognized it, because he grabbed Hacon's arm, looked briefly around, and then hauled ass for the side of the packing containers nearest them and pressed flat against it.

In the corridor created by the metal containers, the metal popping sound was louder, and they heard shouting and Andre screaming, "Shoot at us all you want, assholes, I've got fucking backup coming!"

Leif took a deep breath. "Stay here," he murmured down near Hacon's ear. Then he leaned carefully around the corner, paused for a second, and came back.

"Your brother has been hit—the shoulder, it does not look bad," Leif said calmly, and Hacon thought he might vomit ice.

"And Andre?"

"Has them back between the two rows of crates. They have cover, but the men are coming closer. If Andre runs out of bullets before the men get there...." Leif shivered. He looked behind Hacon and gave Hake's arm a jerk. Hacon took a step forward and literally peeled his jacket away from the metal crate.

"What in the hell?" he asked, trying to keep his teeth from chattering.

"I told you," Leif said smugly. "I have my luck. You too have been touched by the gods." His face grew grim again. "I have a plan," he said. "But you need to trust me—and our luck."

Hacon blinked. "Of course I trust you," he said, and he didn't hesitate. But inside he was thinking *My luck? Our luck? Hacon's luck?* Leif's luck he had come to believe in. But his own? He'd lived too long looking for falling pianos not to believe that one wasn't coming for him.

Leif seemed to read his mind. "You trust me, right?"

"Yes," Hacon said, and the chill around his bowels seemed to thaw slightly.

"Then trust that you're lucky because you found me."

Hacon nodded and swallowed. "I can trust that," he said softly, and Leif grinned.

"Good. Now think cold thoughts. If you can frost the wooden pier, that would help us too."

And then Hacon's big Viking did something that frightened Hacon so badly he really did frost the wood beneath their feet.

"Hello! Gangsters?" he called, jumping into the opening and waving his hand. "We've seen you! If you don't kill us before the backup gets here, you're royally fucked!"

Hacon's jaw dropped and his head swiveled through thick water as he stared at his insane lover.

Leif grinned at him. "Hacon?"

"Yeah?"

"Run like hell!" He grabbed Hacon by his upper arm and steered him from the back of the packing crate to the end of the pier.

And Hacon knew just where they were going.

"We're never going to make it!" he cried. His foot skidded as a crisp, slick layer of frost formed beneath his feet.

"Of course we will!" Leif called joyously. He didn't even seem to be running. It was more like loping, like a giraffe with cement on his shoes.

"We're not going to make it!" Hacon moaned as they neared the end of the pier.

Leif didn't stop running. He didn't even slow down. Instead, he grabbed Hacon's hand and shouted, "*Jump!*"

And Hacon did, and Leif clutched him to his chest as they fell toward that tiny slice of ocean between the two concrete pylons. Even as their feet hit the water, Hake could hear Leif's furious chant of "Believe, believe, believe…."

INTERLUDE
FIRE AND FROST

"OH," SAID Loki curiously as they watched the two men leaping to what very well could have been their deaths. "The small one is gifted too. How did that happen?"

Skuld shrugged. "Some fibers are sweeter on the skin than others. Does it matter?"

Verdandi rolled her eyes. "It was the spit-splice," she said, irritated. "We had to gift the children you'd robbed with *something.* The only problem was, the men who usually inherited that fiber—"

"Died young," Loki said, reading the pattern fairly adeptly for one who was usually so self-absorbed.

"Yes," Verdandi said, her fingers continuing their weave. The three bad men with guns came sprinting across the boards of the pier, and one of them slid on Hacon's frost footprint and went down with his gun facing up. The gods didn't even blink as his brains, bones, and blood sprayed across the pier. The man slightly ahead of him turned around and slipped. As he was finding his feet, the gang's leader, who was bringing up the rear, let off a shot toward their two intended targets, who had just leaped off the pier. The shot went wild, and the stumbling man in the middle went down.

The gods and Fates were all holding their breath as Leif and Hacon disappeared off the end of the pier, but a shout from behind the bad guys pulled their attention for a moment. Andre was there, having seized advantage of bad guys with their backs toward him, and was running toward the last man with a gun. The man with the gun looked behind him and then followed his targets off the end of the pier....

And onto the rust-encrusted concrete, where junior coroner's assistants would scrape off his remains for days.

And the gods ignored his corpse too, and stared, entranced, at the dark water, holding their breath, and waiting, waiting, waiting....

Leif
Warp and Weft
and Wellness

THE water was foul. Leif could feel it clinging to his skin as he and Hacon dropped like big river rocks neatly between the concrete pylons into the algae-clogged wastewater in the middle. Hacon froze in his arms, and Leif kicked hard as soon as the water closed over their heads. He didn't want to let go of Hacon, so he used his bad arm to hold onto him and his good arm to stroke them both strongly to the surface. After a few strokes, Hacon started kicking too, and Leif let go as they both sputtered to the surface.

Their first breath was reeky with the stench of the fetid saltwater, and Leif wanted to scream with the urge to climb out of his own skin, but they were alive.

"Pfaw!" Hacon spat, and Leif nodded.

"Don't get that shit in your mouth!" he advised, kicking hard to keep his head above water.

"Are we alive?"

"Looks like." Leif's hand hit the algae as he sculled the water, and he shuddered. "Oh God," he said, "I may die of the ick on my skin!"

Hacon turned to him quickly and grinned through the filthy water streaming down his face. "We'll live, Leif. We're lucky, aren't we?"

And Leif grinned hugely. "Very!" he said, laughing. And they were!

OF COURSE, later, after they'd been bailed out of the ocean by a rescue helicopter and taken to the hospital for emergency baths and heavy doses of antibiotics and steroids for their skin to combat whatever bad things had been lurking in the stagnant water, they found out exactly how lucky they were.

"All dead?" Leif asked, sitting next to Hacon on the hospital bed. Yes, they were both in the hospital again, but this time, they wouldn't be spending the night across the room from each other. Sven was actually lying on the bed across from them, the wound in his shoulder bandaged and fluids being pumped into his arm. He'd been tended to while Hacon and Leif had been given scrub brushes in impertinent areas, and Leif had been given a new C-collar and topical anesthetic so they could scrub his open wounds until they bled.

"Really?" Hacon asked now. "All of them?"

And Andre explained the bizarre set of circumstances that had led to the deaths of all three of the main players in Monkey Man's smuggling racket.

"Angel Guerrero slid on the pier and shot himself. John Daniels skid on the same patch of something—wasn't there when we went to look, by the way—right into Bill Winters's line of fire. By that time, backup had actually arrived, so I went to chase Bill, and he jumped off the pier. Except"—and Hacon's ex-boyfriend glared at them—"unlike you two, who were apparently just plucked from the jaws of death by the frickin' *gods*, Winters landed on all of that sharp metal and gutted himself. Unbelievable. Seriously fucking unbelievable. You two...."

"Lucky," Sven half laughed across from them. "They're lucky. Leif, Hacon, you're really lucky. And now, so am I."

Hacon was looking at Andre beseechingly. "He is, isn't he? He's out of it, right?"

Andre shrugged. "Hacon, we've got nothing. Nothing on him. I mean"—he dropped his voice—"you and I know about the packages, but they were all bike messenger. One word from me and Thundergod's boss here loses all his receipts. It's not FedEx there—no one will know."

Hacon looked at Leif, who nodded. "Please, Andre?" he asked. "We can just say this end of the smuggling ring has been put paid, right?"

Andre nodded. "He'll be safe, Hacon. If he's learned—"

"I have!" Sven spoke up. "Please, Andre...."

Andre looked over his shoulder and grimaced. "God, kid. You'd better take this chance and run with it, you hear me?"

Sven smiled at him, the expression tempered by a little bit of hero worship. "I hear you, Andre. I promise."

Leif thought that his expression was particularly limpid, and he watched as Andre swallowed and grimaced.

"Yeah," he said. "Sure." Then he looked at the two of them. "You two going to be okay?"

Leif saw Hacon shrug. "Well, we could use a ride to Leif's home. We'll come back tomorrow and get Sven, but I'd *love* a shower that didn't smell of antiseptic."

Leif blew out a breath and then thought of something. "So, all of the guns and the beating up of Sven and all that—what were they smuggling?"

Andre blushed, and it must have been hot, because a blush should have been hard to see on his bronze complexion. "Remember your friend Lethal?"

Leif nodded and then started to laugh. He looked at Hacon to share the joke, but Hacon was still stuck in disbelief. "Crystal skulls?" he asked incredulously, and Andre rolled his eyes.

"No—but smuggled Aztec artifacts, you betcha. It seems that Monkey Man was called Monkey Man because he liked to smuggle artwork of actual monkeys. He was getting South American golden artifacts—probably one important piece per shipment. That's where he got his medical connections—he sold to high-end clients. One of them probably wrote Sven's prescription." Andre sighed. "We won't go that far into the ring," he said regretfully and looked at Sven. "You really *do* have some of your brother's luck. Remember that, kid."

Sven nodded, and for a moment their eyes locked across the room.

Leif looked at Hacon, but he was looking at his little brother in surprise and speculation. Well, apparently it was a surprise to Hacon too.

Hacon caught Leif's look and leaned his head on Leif's shoulder. "That is their story," he said softly. "Our story is waiting for us. I would really like to sleep in my own bed."

Leif was hurt for a moment, and then Hacon straightened up and rolled his eyes. "Any bed with you in it is mine," he said and then sighed. "But I'd really like you to see my little house and my cat. You would like Vanir very much."

"Tomorrow," Leif promised against his temple. "Tomorrow I will spend the day at your house and get to know your cat. It seems that I am temporarily out of work."

Hacon smiled at him and then looked sad.

"What?"

Hake shook his head. "I'm thinking about the future," he said. "And I'm thinking that we may have more arguing to do, and that I will have to be lucky enough to win. But not right now." Hacon looked up and hopped off the bed. "Andre? You *can* take us back to Leif's apartment, can't you? Leif, did you get your keys?"

Leif did not hop so lightly off the bed, because all of his hurts from the day before had been opened and scrubbed and regauzed, and because everything hurt all over again from the fall, but he was game enough as he slid off the bed.

"Bye, Sven," he called softly, and Hacon went over to his little brother's bed and dropped a kiss on his hair. "We'll be back tomorrow."

"I won't be released for two more days," Sven said with a smile, and Hacon met Leif's eyes.

"We'll be back tomorrow anyway." His lean mouth tilted up at the corners. "It sucks in here. Who wants to spend it all alone?"

"Besides," Leif said cheerfully, "I'm pretty sure Lethal will want to talk to someone who's had a gunshot wound!"

He caught Hacon's and Andre's incredulous looks but ignored them and fished his keys out of the clothes in the plastic bag the hospital had given him. It was more than time to go home.

LATER—much later, after he and Hacon had showered and used soap that didn't smell sick like the hospital and he'd put their clothes on the landing outside the door because Hacon promised to have them dry-cleaned in the morning—they lay side by side in Leif's bed and Hacon spoke haltingly of the things he'd like to see in their future.

"I'd like you to move in with me," he said shyly. "And Loki too. And I have a room for your books. And... and I could help put you through school. I think you would be a wonderful professor—"

"Because you're afraid of being seen with a bike messenger?" Leif asked, trying very hard not to be hurt, and Hacon's response was gratifying.

"Because you're too smart to hide all of that lovely gift in this crappy apartment. You should share it. You believe in luck, you believe in the gods, you believe in sharing your gifts with the world. Is it so bad that I want to help you do that?"

Leif grunted, his head aching and his body reminding him that this week had been extraordinary. "I'll think about it," he promised, and then he yawned, and Hacon yawned, and this night they really did just spend sleeping in each other's arms while Loki the cat camped out in the space between Leif's shoulders.

And that was how they were until the wrecking ball crashed through Leif's living room in the morning, taking out part of the roof and some of the books and leaving the bedroom covered in debris, but the men inside unhurt.

INTERLUDE
GODS AND MACHINES

VERDANDI almost stopped weaving, she was so angry. "You *fucker*!" she shouted, glaring at Loki, and Loki raised one shoulder, ignoring everybody's outrage.

"I don't know why you're so surprised. It's not like I didn't see you working like a madwoman when they were at the pier."

Verdandi didn't even blush. "That was *subtle*, Loki! You put a wrecking ball in their living room! What in the world was your purpose?"

Thor grunted like he knew, and the look Loki cast him was both passionate and pained. "You heard them. They were just going to get into a big, nasty, bitching weepfest about the big one's pride and the little one's money and what worth is a man and—who fucking needs it? They're meant for each other." He swallowed and glared at Thor. "They're meant for each other, and I, for one, didn't want to watch them suffer in ignorance when all it would take was a little…." He waved his long, elegant hands gracefully.

"Deus ex machina?" Thor suggested in a voice that would have sucked the water out of oceans of ice.

"Deus ex fucking machina," Loki snarled. "They're mortals, Thor. They don't have hundreds of years to sneak around their wife's back because the weight and peace of Valhalla rests upon their shoulders. They have heartbeats to get their shit together and decide to be happy. I gave them a few heartbeats more!"

"You could have killed them!" Urdh snapped, and Loki rolled his eyes as though bored already.

"They're fine," he snapped. "I even saved the cat."

Thor nodded and moved into Loki's breath. "You did," he said gently and caught Loki's pointed chin between his thumb and forefinger. "You saved their cat, and you saved them from considerable grief. Would you like to be rewarded?"

Verdandi risked a glance behind her and then wished she hadn't. The look on Loki's proud face was hauntingly needy, terribly beseeching. It was humble and defiant and so hurt that Verdandi thought her own chest would bleed.

"Yes, my lord Thor," Loki whispered, and Thor barely brushed Loki's lean lips with his own full ones.

"Excellent," Thor murmured, and then the two gods were abruptly elsewhere. The Fates worked in silence for a moment, and then the sound and scent of sex began to fall out from Valhalla, through the leaves and branches of Yggdrasil, and upon the heads of the Fates.

"Oh shit," Skuld swore succinctly. She still had her scissors in her pocket from when she'd taken them out to snip the threads of the gangsters who were the tiny aberrations in the pattern. "Where am I going to find a man at this short notice?"

Urdh groaned, spinning away. "I shall have to go to the Greek gods," she said after a moment. "After watching those two for so long, I don't want anything to do with a Scandinavian man. The best and the worst of them, oh yes they were."

"Leif and Hacon or Thor and Loki?" Verdandi asked, and Urdh and Skuld both snapped, "Leif and Hacon!" before she could finish.

"Really," Skuld sniffed. "Can you believe the ego on Loki? Seriously?"

"Well," Verdandi said, smiling gently, remembering his touch, tender and haunted, in her bed so long ago. "He did save the cat."

"Of course he saved the cat," Skuld muttered. "It was named after him."

Verdandi laughed and looked back at her tapestry, where the two mortals were gathering themselves in the dust. The cat skittered from a pile of books in the living room to under the bed, and even through the time and the distance of the world tree to the mortal world, she could hear Leif's exhilarated laugh and Hacon's surprised agreement. Yes, yes, they were indeed lucky, there was no argument from Hacon at all.

Well, maybe Loki had a point.

Above them, there was a groan and a pleading that was unmistakably the trickster god, and Verdandi quivered in want. Well,

Loki was busy this evening—but maybe Hermes was available? At least he gave face. It was a comforting thought as the gods continued to wreak sexual havoc in Valhalla, and it steadied her hands as she continued her work.

AMY LANE is a mother of four and a compulsive knitter who writes because she can't silence the voices in her head. She adores cats, knitting socks, and hawt menz, and she dislikes moths, cat boxes, and knuckle-headed macspazzmatrons. She is rarely found cooking, cleaning, or doing domestic chores, but she has been known to knit up an emergency hat/blanket/pair of socks for any occasion whatsoever or sometimes for no reason at all. She writes in the shower, while commuting, while taxiing children to soccer/dance/karate/oh my! and has learned from necessity to type like the wind. She lives in a spider-infested, crumbling house in a shoddy suburb and counts on her beloved Mate, Mack, to keep her tethered to reality—which he does while keeping her cell phone charged as a bonus. She's been married for twenty-plus years and still believes in Twu Wuv, with a capital Twu and a capital Wuv, and she doesn't see any reason at all for that to change.

Visit Amy's website at http://www.greenshill.com. You can e-mail her at amylane@greenshill.com.

Romance from ANDREW GREY

Novels by
ANDREW GREY

Accompanied by a Waltz
Dutch Treat
Three Fates (anthology)
Work Me Out (anthology)

ART SERIES
Legal Artistry • Artistic Appeal • Artistic Pursuits • Legal Tender

BOTTLED UP STORIES
Bottled Up • Uncorked • The Best Revenge • An Unexpected Vintage

CHILDREN OF BACCHUS STORIES
Children of Bacchus • Thursday's Child • Child of Joy

LOVE MEANS… SERIES
Love Means… No Shame • Love Means… Courage • Love Means… No Boundaries
Love Means… Freedom • Love Means … No Fear • Love Means… Healing
Love Means… Family • Love Means… Renewal

SEVEN DAYS STORIES
Seven Days • Unconditional Love

STORIES FROM THE RANGE
A Shared Range • A Troubled Range • An Unsettled Range • A Foreign Range

TASTE OF LOVE STORIES
A Taste of Love • A Serving of Love • A Helping of Love

Novellas by
ANDREW GREY

A Present in Swaddling Clothes

BY FIRE SERIES
Redemption by Fire

CHILDREN OF BACCHUS STORIES
Spring Reassurance • Winter Love

LOVE MEANS… SERIES
Love Means… Healing • Love Means… Renewal

WORK OUT SERIES
Spot Me • Pump Me Up • Core Training • Crunch Time
Positive Resistance • Personal Training

All published by
DREAMSPINNER PRESS

Romance from MARY CALMES

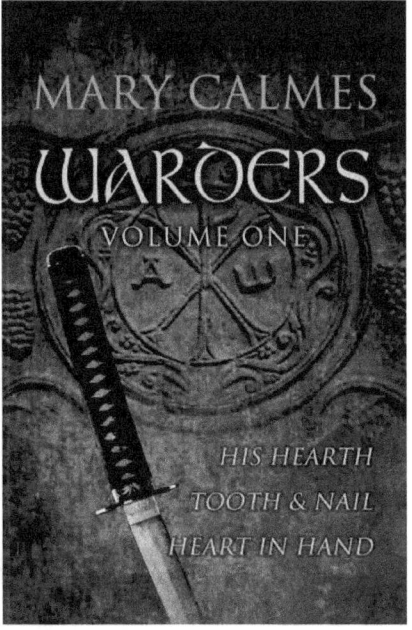

http://www.dreamspinnerpress.com

By MARY CALMES

NOVELS
Change of Heart
Honored Vow
Trusted Bond

A Matter of Time Vol. 1 & 2
Bulletproof

Acrobat
The Guardian
Mine
Three Fates (anthology)
Timing
The Warder Collection Vol. 1 & 2

NOVELLAS
After the Sunset
Again
Any Closer
Frog
Romanus
The Servant
What Can Be

THE WARDER SERIES
His Hearth
Tooth & Nail
Heart in Hand
Sinnerman
Nexus
Cherish Your Name

Published by DREAMSPINNER PRESS
http://www.dreamspinnerpress.com

Romance from AMY LANE

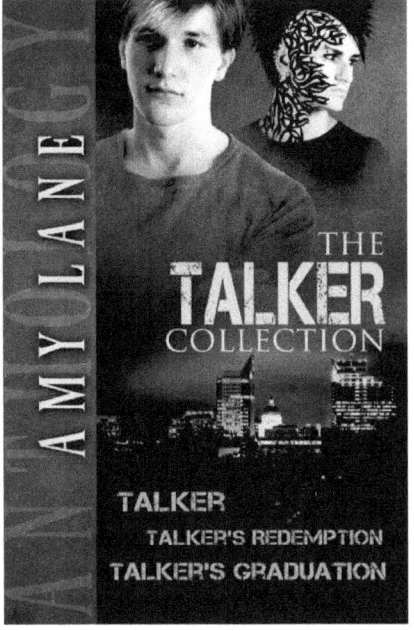

By AMY LANE

NOVELS
Chase in Shadow
Clear Water
Gambling Men: The Novel
The Locker Room
Sidecar
A Solid Core of Alpha
The Talker Collection (anthology)
Three Fates (anthology)

THE KEEPING PROMISE ROCK SERIES
Keeping Promise Rock
Making Promises
Living Promises

NOVELLAS
Bewitched by Bella's Brother
Christmas with Danny Fit
Hammer and Air
If I Must
It's Not Shakespeare
Puppy, Car, and Snow
Super Sock Man
Truth in the Dark
The Winter Courtship Rituals of Fur-Bearing Critters

GREEN'S HILL
Guarding the Vampire's Ghost
I love you, asshole!
Litha's Constant Whim

TALKER SERIES
Talker
Talker's Redemption
Talker's Graduation

Published by DREAMSPINNER PRESS
http://www.dreamspinnerpress.com

www.ingramcontent.com/pod-product-compliance
Lightning Source LLC
Chambersburg PA
CBHW070048030726
47506CB00002B/398